FEDERAL PROTECTION AGENCY

BOOKS 1-3

BY EVIE RILEY

FEDERAL PROTECTION AGENCY

BOOKS 1-3

COPYRIGHT © 2022-2023

EVIE RILEY

SECOND EDITION

ISBN: 978-1-77357-700-5

PUBLISHED BY NAUGHTY NIGHTS PRESS LLC

COVER ART BY WILLSIN ROWE

FEDERAL PROTECTION AGENCY: BOOKS 1-3

Mason

There is freedom in acceptance...

Mason Wright works for Homeland Security focusing on crimes against children. Recently diagnosed with PTSD, Mason takes some much needed time off to go visit his brother, but the little vacay unexpectedly turns into yet more work as he's assigned the job of creating a task force.

Rafe

A chance to find real love...

Ex-SEAL, Special Agent Rafe Dallas spent years working for the DOJ after his medical discharge. Now, he's joined a special Task Force fighting crimes against children. After successfully completing his first operation, Rafe is determined to give everything he has to save as many children as he can.

Ryzen

True evil lurks in the darkness…
Recruited at eighteen by the CIA, Ryzen is one of the best snipers in the world. Now, he's working with the Federal Protection Agency to aid them in their fight to track down the vile people who perpetuate crimes against children. Always hidden behind his dark sunglasses, Ry is a mystery to everyone and he prefers it that way.

Trigger Warnings: Murder, Violence, Drugs, Abuse, Kidnapping, Captivity, Crimes against children.

MASON

FEDERAL PROTECTION AGENCY

BOOK ONE

BY EVIE RILEY

MASON

There is freedom in acceptance...

Mason Wright works for Homeland Security focusing on crimes against children. Five year old Koda is his beloved K9 partner, and aside from his brother, Koda is the only family Mason has. Recently diagnosed with PTSD, Mason takes some much needed time off to go visit his brother, but the little vacay unexpectedly turns into yet more work as he's assigned the job of creating a task force to track down Jasper Monroe for his crimes. Monroe leads them on a merry chase but as they head into Mexico, Mason has a plan to take the dirty cop down.

Jarod Lopez is a new detective in the police force. Saddled with a homophobic partner, Jarod remains in the closet and just does as he's told as the rookie of the department. Caring for his drug addict mother and hiding from his father's past, Jarod keeps his head down and doesn't make waves. The situation makes for a lonely life with little chance of his skills as a detective being put to good use. When the coveted chance to join a recently developed task force drops in his lap, Jarod jumps at the opportunity. Paired up with Mason as his new partner, Jarod finds himself experiencing things he never thought possible.

Will the pair find love while they chase down the bad guy and bring him to justice?

CHAPTER ONE

Mason

POSTTRAUMATIC STRESS DISORDER is a psychiatric disorder that may occur in people who have experienced or witnessed a traumatic event such as a natural disaster, a serious accident, a terrorist act, war/combat, or rape, or who have been threatened with death, sexual violence, or serious injury. Symptoms include: intrusive thoughts, nightmares, avoiding reminders of the event, memory loss, negative thoughts about self and the world, self-isolation, feeling distant, anger and irritability, reduced interest in favorite activities, hyper vigilance, difficulty concentrating, insomnia, vivid flashbacks, avoiding people, places and things related to the event, casting blame, difficulty feeling positive emotions, exaggerated startle response, and risky behaviors.

"What a bunch of bullshit," I said, and tossed my phone onto the dash of my rental truck.

The shrink I had hired to help me with my insomnia had just diagnosed me with PTSD and it was a load of shit. Just because I had some of the symptoms, didn't mean that was what was wrong with me.

I was able to function.

I was doing my job.

I just had some problems outside of it.

I was having a hard time sleeping, and when I did, I usually had nightmares. I was a bit on edge, but never in the field. I wasn't angry or lashing out at people. I wasn't having flashbacks or panic attacks. Sure, at times, I had a hard time sitting still. I got anxious sometimes at night but I would just go for a run with Koda and I was fine.

I didn't have PTSD.

Besides, I didn't even know where it

would have come from. I was a federal agent with Homeland security. I specialized in crimes against children and, yes, I saw some horrific things, but nothing that the other Agents hadn't already seen.

Agents that had been on the job for twenty years were fine with the things we see, so how could that give me PTSD when it didn't with others?

The shrink was wrong. It was just that simple. Everyone struggled with sleeping from time to time.

And if I had to have a few drinks in the day to get through the night, then so what?

I never drank while on duty. It was always after work. I wasn't drinking an excessive amount, just enough to help me fall asleep when it had been a few days. I was coping and there was nothing wrong with it.

Koda whined beside me and I glanced over at him. Koda was my K9 partner, a beautiful German shepherd.

I loved this dog.

I didn't know what I would do without him.

I've always loved dogs and when the

opportunity presented itself for me to be a K9 handler five years ago, I jumped at the chance. I've had Koda ever since he was an eight week old puppy, and I couldn't imagine not having him in my life.

My greatest fear is for Koda to be hurt in the field.

"You want to go and see Uncle Ro?" I asked the dog as I started to pet him. I was currently sitting in my rental truck out front of my older brother's house.

Roland, or Ro as I always called him, was a local cop. He was also ex-military and had been a cop in New York City before he moved out here. I was surprised when he decided to move to a smaller town like Gaithersburg, but it was his life and he was free to do with it as he wished.

He knew I was coming by, that I had taken some vacation days. He didn't know about the real troubles I'd been having with my sleep. I wasn't about to tell him and add to his own worries and stress.

Letting out yet another sigh, I removed my seatbelt and got out. I might as well get this over and done with. The second we opened the door and strolled inside, Koda ran right toward the kitchen where I knew Roland would be.

"Hello, my sweet boy," Roland said as he started to pet Koda. "You know he loves me better, right?" he teased as he looked right at me.

I couldn't help but roll my eyes.

"He only likes you because you slip him food from the table when you think I'm not looking."

Roland was terrible at keeping Koda on his proper diet and schedule. He was always slipping him people food, even when he knew he wasn't supposed to be. It wasn't that Koda couldn't have a treat, but he had to earn it. He needed to work for it. That wasn't my rule, it was the rule for all of the working dogs.

"How was the trip?" Roland asked as he reluctantly moved away from Koda and opened his arms to give me a hug.

Roland was massive. It never failed to gain attention. He was twice my size and I wasn't a small guy. I had muscles and was more than capable of holding my own in a fight.

Roland had taught me how to fight. When I decided I wanted to be a federal agent, Roland had made sure I would be able to handle anything that came my way. He trained me in multiple fighting styles and shooting. He made sure I was ready for any fight.

We had a similar look, though, in terms of hair, eye color, and the shape of our face. You could tell by looking at us that we were brothers. We were both good looking and both gay. Though, unlike me, Roland took a long time to come out.

"Not bad. Airplanes are nothing for me. So what's been going on since we last spoke? You seem to be in a better mood than you were a few days ago. I expected to find you on the couch in sweatpants with empty pizza boxes and beer cans all around you."

When we had last talked, Roland was in a dark place. The guy that he liked, Tyler, hadn't spoken to him in a couple of weeks. He had also taken a week off of work.

It was the first time he had truly liked another guy since he had lost Shane. Shane was the man that he was madly in love with when he was younger and still in the Army.

Shane was out and proud, but Roland had been afraid to come out. Don't Ask, Don't Tell, was no longer in effect, but that didn't mean an organization flooded with alpha males would be open-minded about serving next to a gay man.

Roland had stayed in the closet and there was only so long Shane could handle it. One night, after an epic fight, Shane stormed off in the car, only to be hit by a drunk driver. Shane died on impact and the drunk driver got away. Roland then quit the Army and joined the NYPD. He was the one that caught his lover's killer a few years later. Roland hadn't been in a relationship with anyone since.

"Tyler came over last night. We had a great conversation," he said, and flashed a warm smile.

"Oh, just a conversation?" I teased as I grabbed some coffee and headed for the table.

"A bit more than that. It started off with a conversation. He told me that he needed time to get his feelings in order and to process everything that had just happened."

"Makes sense, he thought he was straight his whole life. Having a guy kiss you out of nowhere can be shocking," I said with complete understanding to my voice.

"And that was my fault for doing it that way. It came out of nowhere. Thankfully, though, I didn't scare him off for very long. He told me he had feelings for me, too. That he didn't even sleep with the two women he had been dating in the past two months. He's actually never slept with a woman before, or anyone."

"Damn, you bagged yourself a twenty-two year old virgin. Now I'm jealous."

I was a sucker for a virgin or a spinner. I liked the smaller guys, the ones that you could toss around and overpower. I wasn't a fan of vanilla sex. I liked to have power over my lover. I liked to use toys and restraints. Sex was supposed to be fun and I believed in trying many different flavors of it. I tended to go for smaller guys, because they loved to bottom and I was only a top.

"The point is, we are taking things slow. We watched a movie and made out a bit last night before we went to sleep, in separate rooms. I'm trying to make him feel comfortable and allow him to stay in control of the sexual progress."

"I am happy for you. It's been a very long time since you've allowed yourself to be with another man. I know what happened with Shane was devastating, but you've kinda been putting your whole life on pause, Ro. I don't know what it's like to lose the man you love, and I didn't know him as well as I should have, but he wouldn't want this for you. He wouldn't want you to be alone and heartbroken for the rest of your life."

"I'm trying. What about you? Any new guy in your life?"

"Not right now, no. I've been too busy with work. I'm not really the dating type, anyway. It's easier to keep things to friends with benefits or one-night stands."

I held zero interest in dating someone. With my job, it really wasn't even possible. I worked too many hours and I traveled all over the country at a moment's notice. It wasn't conducive to a healthy relationship.

"Always such a romantic," Roland teased, and once again I rolled my eyes.

Before I could comment, Koda's head snapped up and he looked right at the door. Instantly, I was on edge and ready for an attack. I knew it wasn't a normal reaction, but it was what always happened, now, when there was a knock at the door or the phone rang. I was always ready for an ambush and there was nothing I could do about it.

"You expecting someone?" I asked, doing my best to keep my voice calm and casual. I wasn't sure if I was able to pull it off.

"It's Isaiah, my friend with Social Services. He's coming by so we can talk about the foster home situation," Roland answered as he got up to let him in.

Roland had told me about Tyler, his current love interest, and his old partner, Jasper Monroe's reaction to each other. When he told me that Tyler seemed scared of his old foster father, I could tell it was bothering him.

Tyler had grown up in the foster care system and, for a couple of years, he'd had Monroe as his foster father. Monroe had never told Roland about it, not even after him and Tyler started to hang out. We both found their reactions to each other suspicious and decided that it should be looked into.

It wasn't common for a former foster child to have that much fear toward a foster father. Something had to have happened and I was worried what it was. I didn't want my brother to be caught in a deadly situation if it came back that Monroe was a dirty cop.

"Hey man, come on in," Roland said warmly as he opened the door.

I peeked around the corner so I could see what Isaiah looked like. I don't know what I was expecting for Isaiah, but I wasn't expecting what stood on the other side of the door. The man was a bit chubby and average looking, probably a teddy bear, but he looked like a wreck. Like he hadn't slept in days. I wasn't sure, but something was going on with him.

"Is your brother here?" he asked as he walked in.

"Yeah, in the kitchen. Come on back and grab a coffee. You look like you could use it."

"You wouldn't believe what I found, Roland," he said as they ambled toward the kitchen.

I had no idea what he had found, but by how he was behaving, he found something huge.

My gut said it was something I wasn't going to like.

"Mason, this is Isaiah. He works with Social Services and is who I reached out to about intel on Tyler," Roland said to me.

"It's nice to meet you," I said as I held my hand out for Isaiah to take.

He easily clasped my hand in his before he spoke.

"Nice to meet you. I have a feeling we're going to need your help on this one."

I didn't like the sound of that. It was one thing to need a cop, but to need a federal agent, that meant something huge had happened.

"What did you find?" Roland asked, getting things started.

"I started by looking through Tyler's time with Jasper. As you know, he was there between the ages of twelve and fourteen. He was one of eight foster kids, sometimes a little less over the two years. On the surface, it all seems perfectly normal and there weren't any red flags in Tyler's file for Jasper. Before that, he had been through a lot of rough homes and had been abused. It all stopped for two years before he was sent to another foster home, and then it picked up all over again."

"Okay, but I'm not hearing anything to

imply that something is wrong with Jasper. Sounds like you need to review all of the foster homes in the system, though," I said.

It wasn't uncommon for there to be a few bad apples within the foster home system. However, it sounded like they had more than a couple in this town.

"Tyler was diagnosed with a protein deficiency when he was eight. It makes it hard for him to gain weight. Aside from that, and the asthma, he was perfectly healthy. Broken bones and bruising, but no illnesses. For the two years he was with Jasper, everything was perfect. Too perfect. Bruises were gone, he went to school, everything was normal and without complaint. Then, all of a sudden, he is being transferred, by Jasper's request to another home and the hell started all over again. Only, he was there for two days when he started to get very sick. His social worker saw how sick he was and took him to the hospital. They ran his bloodwork and discovered he was going through cocaine withdrawal."

"Whoa, what?" Roland asked, shocked and outraged.

That wasn't good.

That confirmed that something more was going on within that foster home and it wasn't going to end well.

"There was no way of telling how it got into his system, just that it was there. His social worker asked where he got the drugs, but he clammed up. Jasper was brought in to be questioned, but he was a Detective, even back then, so the worker believed everything he said. He said Tyler must have gotten it from school, that he had no idea. They went with Jasper's story and never looked into his home or any of the other children."

"It's not uncommon for children in their young teenage years to get their hands on cocaine. I find it hard to believe that no one would have noticed. If he was going through physical withdrawals, he had to have been doing it for months and in large doses. Were any of the other children checked out?" I asked.

"That's the thing, the social worker never spoke to any of the current children or looked through his home. So, I did." He placed a rather large brown file on the table as he continued. "That is Jasper's and his wife, Dana's, fostering file. It includes every child they have ever taken in, including the current ones. Currently, he has nine kids all between the ages of nine and fourteen. I've started to go through the process of pulling the previous foster children's files, but there are over a hundred and fifty of them."

"Shit," Roland said, obviously shocked that it was that many.

That *was* a fast turnaround.

I knew that some homes kids came and went at one hell of a pace, however, that was usually in larger cities. The smaller cities, the kids tended to stay with their one foster parent unless something was wrong with them. Kids didn't tend to get passed around like Christmas candy in towns this size, as a general rule. There was no reason for Monroe to have that many previous children.

I was getting a bad feeling about this and it wasn't going to end well. Monroe was Roland's past partner. They were still partners when they needed backup on a case. This wasn't going to go well if Monroe was dirty, and it was starting to look like he was.

"It's going to take some time to pull all of their files and go through them to see if any doctor reports were made after their time with Jasper. Some were also moved to another city and I don't have access to their files," Isaiah continued.

"I can get 'em. I just need their names and I can pull the file, no matter where they were placed in the country. We need to do a sneak and peek at Monroe's house and see what is going on. I'm assuming you are operating under the impression that Monroe is cooking drugs in the house," I stated.

I had come here for a vacation, but I also knew that Roland was worried about Tyler. It was the least I could do after everything my brother had done for me.

"Last night, I looked through twenty files. Twelve of the kids were admitted to the hospital with withdrawal-like symptoms. Not all of them were given blood work. Most were told it was the flu and they would feel better in a few days. It's enough for me to make the hypothesis that cocaine is being either cooked at the house around the children, or the children were weighing and packaging the cocaine."

"That sounds like a reasonable hypothesis. I've never noticed any problems with Jasper being sick, though, in three years," Roland stated.

"Depends. I've gone into a lot of homes where the drugs were made in the basement and the kids were sick but the foster parents weren't. The kids were the ones touching the drugs and breathing it in as they were either cooking or packaging it. The parents were fine, because the ventilation system in the upstairs of the house was solid. It kept the fumes down in the basement and when they needed to go down there, they wore the proper protection. It's completely logical that Monroe isn't breathing it in. Just like it's logical that he is breathing it in, but he's never not been around it. His body could be addicted to it and he gets his fix by being in the house," I pointed out.

"Let's get the files and go through them. See which kids were hospitalized after leaving Jasper's. I'll loop in Captain Perry so he's aware of the situation. Yes, we'll need to do a sneak and peek at his house. Mase, can you get a warrant from a judge? We gotta keep that out of town."

"I'll get it. With those files, we should have enough for a warrant," I said confidently. That was easy enough to do and I agreed that it needed to be out of town. A town this size, everyone knew everyone and no judge was going to give us a sneak and peek warrant with what we had.

"Okay, I have to go to the office and start pulling them. Do you want to join me there, or do you want me to bring them back here?" Isaiah asked.

"It would be better to do it here. We don't know who will talk to who. I want to try and keep this as quiet as possible," Roland answered.

"I'll be back in about an hour or so, then," Isaiah said, before he finished his coffee and headed out.

"I'll grab my bag and get my laptop out of it. I'll get A.S.A Crawford up to speed and he'll grab us a warrant," I said as I stood.

"Not exactly the vacation you were looking for. I'm sorry."

"It's okay. The drug cases are the easiest. Have you thought about just asking Tyler again? Tell him you know that Jasper could be mixed up with drugs."

It would make things easier if he talked to Tyler about it. It was most likely the reason why Tyler didn't want to talk about Monroe. That old fear was still inside of him, but if Roland could get him to open up, it would help a lot.

I might not be able to get a sneak and peek warrant with what we had. We might need Tyler to go on the record about what happened in that house to do something about it.

"No, I want to keep him out of this. I don't know what is going on, but I know that when drug dealers feel threatened, they'll attack the one they feel is responsible. I don't want Tyler getting hurt. It's better to leave him in the dark."

"It's your call. I'll support you in whatever you decide, Ro. I'll go grab my gear," I said with complete understanding to my voice.

I knew how dangerous drug dealers could be, especially with children. If he didn't want to bring Tyler into this just yet, that was his call and I would respect it.

Hopefully, we wouldn't need Tyler and I could secure us a warrant without anyone on record.

One thing was for certain, this wasn't the type of vacation I had been planning.

EVIE RILEY

CHAPTER TWO

Jarod

I WAS BROUGHT out of my lovely dream by the annoying beeping sound coming from my alarm clock. Groaning, I rolled over and pulled the blanket over my head.

I wasn't a morning person. I wasn't even a mid-morning person. I was often up late at night reading something so I went to bed way too late for me to be able to be up at seven in the morning. I would normally hit the snooze until I was almost late, leaving myself only fifteen minutes to get ready and get out the door. The solution was moving my alarm clock to the other side of the room. That way, the only way to make the obnoxious beeping stop would be to get out of bed and physically turn it off. This morning, though, that was the last thing I wanted to do.

At twenty-five, you would think I would be happy and excited to start a new day. And maybe I would be if it weren't for the fact that my day consisted of being trapped in a tin can with a homophobic asshole that I would love to punch right in the mouth. I would never, though, because despite my desires and thoughts, I was still a timid person. I would never have the guts to punch my partner. Hell, I don't even have the guts to tell him to shut up. I don't exactly have the personality one would expect a cop to have, but I wasn't your typical cop, either. I was the smart guy in the room. I was the *smartest* guy in the room, actually. At least book wise speaking.

I didn't ask to be smart. It wasn't like I spent all of my free time studying growing up just to grow my IQ. I was a child prodigy. I didn't have a choice in if I was smart or not.

There were a lot of times where I was

thankful for my IQ. Plenty of cases that I worked where it came in handy. I had a great solve rate and I even helped out with other police stations within the nearby towns. I never told anyone that, though, because I was not looking to make waves. My plan was to keep my head down and try to help as many people as I could without being noticed. It was a fine balance, but I was doing well with it.

There were more times than I would care to admit that I would have been happier to not be smart. I would have loved to be normal and be one of the guys. I would be able to fit in better. I would be able to understand some of their jokes that they all thought were hilarious. I would have loved to be able to just lie down and sleep without my mind going over everything.

It was why I was such a night owl. It was hard to get my mind to shut off at the end of the day. The only way I could make it shut off was by reading. Books had been my sanctuary throughout my life and I had no idea what I would do without them. I always had one with me. Sometimes it was a non-fictional book to help me learn more, and sometimes it was a fictional book. They weren't always in English, either. Some were in Spanish. I loved to read and I would read anything and everything.

I let out another groan as the beeping started to get faster. I vaguely wondered if it would explode one day. Forcing myself to finally get up, I pushed the blanket off my head and sat up. I picked up the book that I had been reading when I fell asleep and placed it on my bedside table. I then rubbed my hands over my face and climbed from the bed.

I smashed the off button on my alarm clock a bit too hard, but I was tired and I didn't care. Not this morning, anyway. Seven in the morning was an ungodly hour and anyone that was a morning person had to be certifiable. That was the only logical explanation.

I hit the bathroom, did my business, brushed my teeth and washed my face. I quickly got dressed in the work clothes that'd I'd laid out the night before, making sure every thing looked neat and tidy. I made my way down to my kitchen and headed straight for my coffee maker.

I didn't have anything fancy in my life.

I didn't care for high-end electronics or fancy clothes. There were only two things I cared about, my books and my coffee maker. It's why I had one that could be programmed to brew my coffee in the morning so it would be ready when I dragged my ass out of bed.

I grabbed my large to-go mug and poured the coffee in before I added about six spoonfuls of sugar. I had been given crap about how I take my coffee for years, but I didn't care. I needed the sugar to help with the bitter taste. I'm not a fan of coffee because I like the taste. I'm a fan of coffee because it wakes me up. It was that simple.

I grabbed an apple from the basket on the table and then headed over to where I'd dropped my gun, badge, and keys on the sideboard when I came home last night. Strapping on the side holster and shoving my phone and badge into my front pants pocket, I was out the door and headed for work.

I didn't live too far from the station. Something I would like to correct once I had more money saved up. I wanted to purchase my own land so I had some space. I wanted peace and quiet, but also privacy.

I liked the idea of having space. I liked the thought of not being able to hear my neighbors. I would like to get a dog or two and enjoy their company. I could have a garden and grow my own fruit and vegetables. Have a couple of different apple trees. It would be peaceful and I couldn't wait until I could make that happen.

At the sight of the station, I felt my stomach drop. I hated being there. It sounded ridiculous because it was my job, but nonetheless, that's how it had become. I was a police detective. A good one, I thought.

It wasn't the job that I hated.

It was my partner.

Detective Baxter was a veteran detective. He had been working as a cop for twenty-five years. He was an old timer with old-fashioned beliefs in and out of the department. He was a hard ass, and he didn't believe in people being able to change. He hated everyone that wasn't a white male, and he held zero patience for anyone who was the least bit different.

He was also one of the biggest homophobic assholes that I had ever met.

MASON

All day long, I got to hear about how much he hated gay people and why they all should be put into a camp or shot. It would be hard for anyone to listen to, yes, but when you were also one of those gay people that he hated, it wasn't easy to listen to and not react.

I wasn't exactly *out* at the station.

I always said I wasn't in the closet, but I wasn't partaking in any pride parades, either. I didn't believe in hiding who you were, but I also didn't believe in standing out. I didn't believe that anyone should have to tell people what their sexuality was and it shouldn't be the first thing that people see.

I wanted people to see that I was a capable detective. I didn't want anyone to assume that because I was gay that I was promoted to try and fill some type of quota. Not to mention I was half-spanish, so I already stood out among the ever-prominent white male crowd that made up the police force.

The only ally that I had in the station was Detective Roland Wright. He was openly gay and he had no idea that he had become my hero. He didn't hide that he was gay. He never allowed it to define him. He stood up for what he believed and he didn't care if someone didn't agree or like it.

The highlight, though, of my career so far, was when I got to witness Detective Wright knocking out Baxter in the break room just a couple weeks ago. It was the greatest moment of my life and a moment that I often replay in my head when I need a pick-me up.

That man was my hero.

I got out of my car and strolled inside with my coffee in hand. The station wasn't very busy. Most of the time the cops that worked here were out on the street either driving around or walking the street. We didn't get a lot of calls or emergencies here. It was mostly civil disputes that we would assist with. We had gangs in town, but unless you could catch them in the act, there wasn't much we could do.

It was hard for me, because I wanted to help. I wanted to be active and make the world a better and safer place, but all I could do was what was in my power to do in this town.

Most would argue that I could move to a bigger town, a place like New York, or even work for a federal agency. That wasn't possible for me. I couldn't go to a big town or become a fed.

Not with my past.

Or rather, my father's past I should say.

All I could do was what was in my power here in town. It would simply have to be good enough.

I made my way over to my desk that was off in the corner. I was the newest rookie detective and the privilege not only came with verbal degrading from everyone that outranked me, but also a tiny desk in the corner. Everyone's paperwork that they didn't want to do themselves always ended up on my desk. I knew I had to work through it and just wait until there was fresh meat for them to enjoy. Even once there was, I doubted I would stop being their punching bag.

I didn't fit in.

I was too smart and too shy and quiet.

They were all loud and not the brightest bulbs in the pack.

I slid into my chair and started to grab the first file that was placed on top of the pile and got to work. It was about ten minutes later when I was being interrupted by Baxter's voice, along with

Jasper Monroe's.

I couldn't stand Jasper anymore than I could Baxter. There was just something off with Monroe. I didn't know what it was, but I'd never liked him. He'd always felt off to me. If one could feel evil and darkness, that is what Monroe felt like to me. I didn't like being around him, not when I could help it.

The problem was, Baxter and Monroe were best friends.

Not that they would call each other that, because according to them they were not thirteen year old girls.

"I'm telling you, Jas, you would not believe the set of tits on this woman," Baxter started, and it took everything in me not to roll my eyes.

"I can't believe you went to the strip club without me," Monroe complained.

"I thought your wife didn't like it when you went to the club."

"I can do whatever I want."

Idiots.

They were both sexist idiots and I didn't know how long I could sit there and listen to them. I flinched when I felt a ball of paper hit the side of my head. I looked up to see both of them smirking at me.

"What about you, Rookie? What's the biggest pair of tits that you've seen?" Monroe asked with a smirk.

Too many times I'd had to deal with them asking me about my sexual conquests. It didn't matter how many times I'd told them it wasn't any of their business, they kept asking me.

"I don't kiss and tell." I had lost count how many times I'd told them the exact same sentence.

"I'm starting to think you've never been kissed so you have nothing to tell, Rookie," Monroe teased.

"Or maybe he has kissed, but he's been kissing fags like Wright," Baxter said with a disgusted look on his face.

"Naw, he don't look like a fudge eater. We should take him to the club, let him get a ride on a stripper. Get his willy wet and maybe he won't be so damn boring," Monroe said before he gave a chuckle.

The last thing I would be doing was going to a strip club with them. Thankfully, I was saved from further conversation when Monroe got a call on his cell phone.

I couldn't help but notice that he had a different cell phone. He normally had a black shiny one, but this one was black with a matte finish. It was also a tiny bit bigger. He obviously got a new cell phone within the past couple of days. I shrugged it off as just one more thing that was none of my business.

Monroe didn't answer the call right there, though. He got up and walked off before he even hit the button. That was strange, but it could have been his wife.

I pushed it off to the back of my mind and turned my attention back to the stack of paperwork. If I wanted to get out of here today, I needed to make a serious dent in the pile.

CHAPTER THREE

Mason

"ALL RIGHT, I got the no knock warrant," I said as I walked into the tactical room at the station.

I had been there for two weeks since I had arrived in town for my time off. Two weeks of me helping Roland and Isaiah try and figure out what was going on with the foster system. This wasn't what I was supposed to be doing and yet, I was here helping. At the end of the day, Roland needed help and I needed the distraction.

I had been staying with Roland for the past two weeks and, so far, he hadn't noticed that anything was different about me. It helped that he almost never slept, so for me to be up with him, it didn't raise any red flags. I had been trying to get a sneak and peek warrant, but we didn't have enough intel. No matter what circumstantial evidence we had, it wasn't good enough. Not when we were looking to get a judge to approve of a sneak and peek warrant for a decorated police detective.

All of that changed when Roland had spoken with his boyfriend, Tyler, last night and got him to tell his story on the record. I couldn't believe what I heard when he played it this morning at the station for me and his Captain.

Captain Perry.

Monroe not only had his foster children cooking the cocaine, he had also killed the ones that became too sick or were looking to talk. On top of that, he had sold other children into the sex trade when it suited his needs or when he needed to get rid of a child.

This sick fuck was making hundreds of thousands off of these children and it needed to end.

Thankfully, that recording was all I

needed to get a judge to sign off on the warrant. Tonight, we were going to be raiding Monroe's home that he shared with his wife, Dana.

We had to be careful with the children being in the home, though. The last thing we needed was Monroe feeling threatened and hurting one of the children.

We called every detective in the police force to come in to help with the arrests. We also had Isaiah sticking around so he could handle the children. The problem was, the other cops in the police force had no idea that anyone had been looking into Monroe.

He was a decorated and well loved detective. He had been there for a very long time and he was highly respected. We were about to reveal to them that he was a monster and he needed to be taken out. It wasn't going to go over well and it would be a shock.

I just hoped it wouldn't blow back on Roland.

"We brief everyone in ten," Captain Perry said in a tense voice, before he headed out of the room.

I couldn't blame the man. This was his station and he'd had a dirty cop working underneath him since day one and he never suspected anything. I couldn't hold it against him. This was a small town, things like this weren't supposed to happen.

I knew it could, though. I had seen it plenty of times while being on the job. It wasn't always major towns that had the worst monsters. Sometimes, the smaller the town the worse the monsters were. They took comfort in the fact that the town was so small. They could fool everyone and be free to hurt anyone they wanted because no one ever looked at one of their own as a monster when something went wrong.

I started to grab the tactical gear I would need, as I hadn't brought any with me.

"What about Koda?" Isaiah asked. He seemed uncomfortable being around this many guns. He was a man that cared about peace more than the violence that it takes to bring peace.

"I'll bring him with me so he can help with the children. We have no idea what the kids are going to be like. Do you have transport for the children?" I responded as I started to get ready.

"I have a fellow social worker on standby with a van to transport the children to the hospital. I haven't found new placements yet, though. I wanted to see what their condition was and if they have any cocaine in their system first. Chances are they will, and they'll need to stay in the hospital for at least a week. What about the other children, though? The ones that were sold. We can't just forget about them."

That was going to be harder. Selling a child wasn't like buying a piece of fruit from the store. They didn't get a receipt for their purchase and the seller didn't have to claim it on their taxes. Children were traded for cash, diamonds, drugs... hell, even bitcoin, now. It made it extremely difficult to track and even if we did find who the original buyer was, that kid could have been sold twelve additional times before we even found the first one. It was a nightmare, and that was before we factored in that a child could be out of the country.

"I've already contacted my boss about the situation down here. He's going to talk to the Governor about what can be done," I answered.

I wasn't sure what was going to happen. Chances were everything would be passed off to a federal agency to try and work the case. At the end of the day, it would be one more case file to the ever-growing pile. Unless those kids were found in a raid, we were never going to find them.

"Let's go get this bastard," I said as I snapped the clip into my gun.

We all moved out and walked into the small briefing room that also worked as the roll call room. It was a small police station, but I had been in smaller.

It was a perk to be a federal agent that traveled all over the country. I could find a spot to work anywhere, no matter how big or small the police station was.

Captain Perry was already in the room, ready and waiting for us. We moved over to the side of the room to give Captain Perry our full attention.

"Before we begin, I want to make one thing very clear, this is not a training exercise. You are the more experienced detectives that I have. Some of you have never done a raid before outside of a training exercise. The majority of you have only ever done one or two raids when a nearby town needs more bodies. Due to the type of raid that we are about to go on, I am going to rely on experience to lead us. Detective Wright and his brother, Special Agent Mason Wright, they will be taking point on this raid. I expect everyone to follow their orders and do as they tell you, myself included. What matters most is that we all come home alive and no one gets killed tonight. Do I make myself clear?"

Several heads nodded amid a shuffling of feet. Everyone in the room had a serious look on their face, but I could tell that some didn't think much of this. They were expecting this to be a simple little raid.

They had no idea what was coming their way.

"Keep an eye on Baxter, tonight. I don't know if he'll be a team player," Roland whispered to me.

Roland had told me about Baxter. He had punched him a while back when Baxter wouldn't shut up about gay police officers. Roland had become sick and tired of hearing Baxter's homophobic bullshit and finally knocked his ass out.

I didn't really need Roland to tell me

why he felt I needed to keep an eye on the man. If Baxter was that old fashioned that he didn't believe in gay cops or even female cops, then he might not want to believe a fellow detective was doing this to children.

The old timers were always the hardest to convince, because they were brought up on the blue wall. You never betray or rat out a fellow brother in blue, no matter what it was. We were about to arrest one. It could get ugly if the old timers wanted to make it that way.

"We have secured a no knock warrant for the home of one of our own, Jasper Monroe. He has been under investigation for the past few weeks for suspected drug trafficking. We secured the warrant based on an eyewitness account of drugs being produced in his house in the basement. We also have evidence of him killing foster children or selling them to pedophiles for close to two decades. We have an arrest warrant for Jasper and his wife, Dana," Captain Perry continued.

"You expect us to believe that one of our own, a cop who has almost thirty years on the job, is not only a drug dealer, but a child killer? Who is this eyewitness,

Santa Claus?" Baxter asked, clearly not believing anything Captain Perry had to say.

I expected as much from Baxter. But what was interesting was the kid next to him, the unsurprised look on his face. I knew Jarod was Baxter's partner. I had seen him around the station over the past two weeks, but we had never spoken. Hell, I'd never heard him speak to anyone. He seemed to always be on his own.

"Why doesn't the kid seem surprised?" I whispered to Roland.

"He's only been a detective for a year, but he joined the police force at eighteen. He's only twenty-five and has a shit load of potential. I don't know anything else about him other than he keeps everything personal under wraps. He's smart, though. Smarter than he wants people to know. He could have easily seen something," Roland whispered back.

That was interesting. I love smart people. They had a way of seeing the world that everyone else couldn't. Smart people, they could see through the world and that was a huge asset to have in an investigation.

"The witness' identity is being kept a

secret for obvious reasons. We have more than enough evidence to back up the claims. Once we get into the house, we'll find the lab in his basement. He currently has nine foster children that we will need to ensure are safe before they are transported to the hospital for evaluations. Due to the nature of this investigation, all cell phones will be left here in the station. I don't want anyone reaching out to either Jasper or Dana. Agent Wright, you wished to say something," Captain Perry said with a pointed look at me.

I didn't have anything to say.

I didn't *want* to say anything, but apparently Captain Perry felt otherwise. I moved to the front of the room and gave the typical speech.

"Due to the connection Jasper has to this police department, his charges will be placed by Homeland Security, making them federal charges. He will be eligible for the death penalty, which means anyone that tries to contact him or help him in any way will be charged with aiding and abetting a wanted criminal, as well as an accessory after the fact. You will be facing hard time in a federal prison and I will personally ensure you are placed in gen pop and not solitary." I paused to allow the seriousness of the situation to sink in before I continued.

"We are going to hit his home in two teams. Roland's team will hit the front door and my team will hit the back and hold down the perimeter. Once the arrests have been made, Isaiah will then handle the children. If you cannot do your job, then speak up now, because once we leave, you will have no choice but to do your job and ensure that Jasper does not evade arrest."

"You heard him, does anyone want to be kept here?" Captain Perry asked.

I was waiting to see someone raise their hand, but surprisingly no one did. They weren't happy, but they were riding with us. I knew there would be hard feelings, though, and this would be talked about once they were allowed. It was going to be the talk of this whole fucking town for months to come.

With nothing else to say, we all started to get ready. Phones were placed in a basket before we made our way to the cars and headed off.

I rode in the vehicle with Roland and a

few other detectives. The atmosphere in the car was tense, to say the least. No one talked, not that I expected anyone to. They all just had a bomb dropped on them so, right then, something like small talk wasn't important. That was perfectly fine with me. I wasn't in the mood to talk any more than they were.

This was a lot for me to be taking in. I was wearing tactical gear that was not mine. I was using a gun that was not mine. I hated this and the slight feel of anxiety started to creep up my spine.

I was supposed to be getting a break from all of this. I had taken a month off from work to escape and relax. To take the time and get my head on straight. I wasn't down here to work a case. To go on a raid with a bunch of cops that would have loved for me to not be here. This was the farthest thing from stress free and relaxing that you could get.

Pulling up to the house, we all got out of our vehicles and instantly made our way into position with our respective teams. While Roland ran with his team to the front of the house, I went to the back of the house. In my team, I had Jarod and his asshole partner, Baxter, with me.

Yup.

I was just that lucky.

I looked at my team and I could see that most of them looked about ready to throw up. They were not prepared for this mentally, whatsoever. They most likely had only done this in a training exercise and I knew that was far from the real thing, especially if bullets started to fly. Real bullets that could kill you and not the dummy rounds that just burned.

"Remember, there are kids in the house and in the basement there will be chemicals that can explode if hit with a bullet. When we breach, I will stay out here with Lopez in case anyone runs out the back. The rest of you go in and start clearing the house. Based on the blueprints, the access to the basement is closer to us, so go down first and secure the children."

They all gave a nod in unison and then I heard the Captain's voice over the coms giving the all clear to breach. The others went in and I stood at the ready, facing the backdoor with Jarod to my right.

I knew it would have made more sense for me to be going in, but I wasn't certain the person I left out here wouldn't let

Monroe leave. I had to make sure if he ran out the back, that we would get him.

I could feel the tension radiating off of Jarod. I had no idea why he was so tense and nervous. He should feel the safest, really. He was outside and he had me with him. Even if he doubted his own skills, I was a federal agent and that generally made local police feel better in the field.

"You all right?" I asked, without taking my eyes off of the door.

"I'm fine, Sir," Jarod said in a tight voice.

"No offense, but you aren't radiating fine." I should have let it go. It wasn't any of my business what his problem was. He said he was fine, and I should drop it. For some reason, though, I didn't want to.

"I have no problem arresting Monroe, Sir. I'm upset about the children. They shouldn't have to go through this. Children are supposed to believe in superheroes and magic. They are supposed to believe monsters are mythical creatures that don't exist. They aren't supposed to know the truth yet, Sir."

I couldn't agree more. Children were

supposed to be innocent, but millions all over the world were living in hell and no one was coming to save them. I had been working hard to try and save as many as I could, but always felt like the more I saved, the more who got thrown into hell. It was an endless war and it would never end.

It was why so many agents on my unit burned out so quickly. It was a tough life to live. It was hard to see the worst that humanity had to offer, but stepping away from that, to me, it felt like I was turning my back on all of those children and that wasn't something I could live with.

"You can drop the *Sir.* And you're right. They aren't supposed to know about this yet, but they do, and it's our job as adults to save them and try to get them help. That's all we can do."

It was a moment later when the children started to file out of the house, guided by some of the officers on my team. They all looked sick and I knew they were in for a long recovery after all of this.

"Monroe isn't here," a detective informed me as he moved on with the children.

"Fuck." I grabbed the radio. "House is cleared, Monroe isn't here."

Monroe was on the run, most likely.

It was late at night.

He should have been here.

I couldn't help but wonder if someone had said something. If someone had gotten wind of what we were trying to do, tipped him off, and Monroe took a runner.

I made my way to the front of the house and went over to where Captain Perry was standing. I saw Roland making his way over as well, after putting Dana into the squad car.

"She give anything up?" I asked, once he was close enough.

"Apparently, he's away on a surprise boys weekend," Roland answered.

"Bullshit," I instantly said.

"He's up to something. You think he caught wind of the investigation?" Captain Perry asked.

"Someone who has almost thirty years of experience on the job holds a lot of connections. There's no telling who he could have heard something from. Could have been someone within Social Services. It would make sense that he had a mole on the inside. Someone that could feed him the children that no one would think twice about going missing. Someone to help cover it all up. He could have been made aware of the investigation once files started getting pulled," I stated.

"Shit. And now he's in the wind," Roland said as he shook his head.

"Detective Wright, Sir," Jarod said with an uncertain voice as he made his way over to us. He was clearly nervous about walking in on our conversation, but he seemed determined to do it. He was holding a folded up piece of paper in his hand and he spoke as he held it out to me.

"One of the children said he was told to give this to you."

"What is it?" Captain Perry asked as Roland grabbed the paper.

The second he opened the note, I could see all of the color drain from his face. Something was on that piece of paper that none of us were going to like.

"Roland, what is it?" I asked, now on edge.

"Tyler," he said, before he took off for his car.

I grabbed the note and gave it a quick read. I knew exactly what made Roland's blood run ice cold. I passed the note off to Captain Perry as Koda and I took off to join Roland in his car before he had a chance to run off.

There was no way I was going to allow my brother to potentially go into a trap. I was going to have his back, no matter what. The note itself was simple, but the words were already circling around my head, haunting me as every second passed that we spent in the car.

It's your fault for him breaking the rules. Dead men tell no tales, Wright.

CHAPTER FOUR

Mason

WE ARRIVED AT the bar that Tyler worked at to find it engulfed in flames.

I could feel the fear radiating off of Roland and I hated that I couldn't make it better.

The second we were out of the car, though, my fear escalated when Koda instantly started to run toward the building. He was trained to help, to save, and when he saw the fire and smelled a person inside, he ran like he was trained to do. It was why he, normally, had to be kept on a leash that was attached to my hip unless I released him. I hadn't done that, though, because he typically stayed with me unless ordered to do otherwise, even in a firefight. Both Roland and I ran after Koda and into the bar.

The whole place was covered in flames and smoke. A bar was the worst place to have a fire because of all the alcohol. It only fueled the flames and made them eat everything in their path. We could barely see anything and the smoke was so thick it was hard to breathe.

"Koda!" I yelled out to try and find him.

A set of sharp barks hit our ears and I instantly ran in his direction. I found him on the other side of the bar, along with Tyler. Tyler had one of the shelves that fell from the back of the bar trapping him on the floor and, not wasting any time or thought to my own safety, I was quickly removing it, just as Roland arrived.

"Get him up," I said as I moved the heavy shelf.

Koda had latched on to Tyler's wrist and he and Roland pulled Tyler from under the shelf as I lifted. Once he was free, I dropped the shelf as Roland scooped up Tyler into his arms. I snatched Koda up in my arms and carried him as we all ran out.

I could feel the heat from the fire on the bottom of my feet and I was wearing boots. The floor was way too hot for Koda's paws to handle for long. The second we made it outside we all started to cough and Koda whined in my arms.

An ambulance was already here and I watched as Roland placed Tyler down on the stretcher. Something was wrong, though, because Tyler kept coughing and he wasn't able to open his eyes. I stood back and watched as the paramedic had to intubate him.

I could see the fear and worry in Roland's eyes and I hated that I couldn't make it better for him. The man that he was in love with was struggling to breathe. There was nothing I could say that would make it better for him.

He looked back at me as they loaded the stretcher into the ambulance. I gave him a nod to assure him it was okay and that I would be fine. That was all he needed before he climbed into the ambulance and it drove away.

"It'll be okay, boy," I said to Koda as I carried him over to the squad car. The dog gave a weak whine once more that tugged at my heart. I needed to look at his paws and make sure he didn't have any burns that I needed to tend to.

Just as I placed him down in the back seat of the car, my phone beeped with a text message. I pulled it out and saw that it was my boss. He was in town and wanted to meet. It seemed like my night was just getting better and better.

CHAPTER FIVE

Jarod

THIS WAS UNREAL.

I knew it was true, but it was all so unreal to me. I had no idea when I was called into help with a raid that it would be an actual raid. I had done a few training drills and it was all the same. They came in at random times and days to help make it more authentic. To help you be ready for when that call could come in. I enjoyed doing the training exercises, though. It always made me feel like I was being a real cop. Only, this wasn't a drill, it was an actual raid for not only a criminal, but one of our own.

I had always suspected that Monroe was dirty. I never had any proof and even if I did, I doubted that anyone would listen or believe me.

The raid wasn't what I thought it would be. I don't really know what I expected, exactly, but that wasn't it. It annoyed me that I was kept outside instead of going in.

If anyone shouldn't have gone in, it should have been Baxter.

There was no way he would believe that Monroe had done anything wrong. I knew that even seeing the children and the drug lab, Baxter would have blown it off as a coincidence. Tried to make it seem like it was all Dana and Monroe was completely innocent in it all. As if a detective with close to thirty years of experience would miss the cocaine lab in his basement.

I shouldn't have been kept outside. I felt like they were babying me, putting the rookie in the corner so he couldn't be hurt. I was a good detective and I was trained just like the rest of them. I took extra courses in tactical advantages, hand-to-hand, and shooting. I made sure

I would be ready, no matter what came my way. It wasn't just that, I loved to learn and I didn't really care what I learned as long as I could put it into play to help others.

Finally allowed to go in the house, I pulled out a pair of black latex gloves and made my way back to the door and slipped inside. Dana had been taken to the station and the Wright brothers headed out of here in a panic once I handed them that note. I had read it and I knew they would be going to find Tyler.

I had overheard Detective Wright talking about him quietly to his brother. Everyone seemed to always forget I was around, that I could hear. It was a fact that I had been using to my advantage to collect intel from everyone I worked with. Monroe was on the run and I was willing to bet there had to be a clue in this house somewhere that could lead us to where he was.

"Find anything?" I asked Baxter as I made my way into the basement after putting on a mask.

Even with the mask, I could smell the fumes from the chemicals down there. I couldn't believe the children had been down there working without a mask. It was too intense for me and I was a grown ass adult. There was no telling what would be wrong with the children.

"Just chemicals. It doesn't mean anything," Baxter said, and I could tell he was in denial.

"They're not making breath mints down here," I commented before I could stop the words from coming out of my mouth. It was the wrong thing to say, I knew that, but it just slipped out.

Baxter instantly turned around, and before I could even register what was happening, a hard right cross hit my jaw and I stumbled into the wall.

That was going to bruise.

It wasn't the first time I had taken a hit, but it was the first time my partner had hit me. At least, someone that was supposed to be my partner.

"Jasper is a good man. He isn't involved in this and there is nothing in this place or what someone could say that would make me believe it," he said with an edge to his voice before he stormed off.

Yeah, he's a real good man.

That was why he had nine children around dangerous chemicals.

Why there's testimony from a witness that saw him kill and sell children.

It was all a coincidence or some type of ploy to take down a good man.

I rolled my eyes and let out a sigh.

It was bullshit and, eventually, Baxter was going to have to wake up and face the facts. The trick was, if Monroe knew Baxter would be willing to help him flee, Baxter might be going down as well by the end of this investigation. Letting out another sigh, I turned my full attention to the room. There had to be something in this house that could help and I was determined to find it.

CHAPTER SIX

Jarod

IT HAD BEEN less than twenty-four hours since we had done the raid on Monroe's house.

I had stayed there for a good six hours combing through everything, but there wasn't anything that would indicate where Monroe would have run to.

Everything I found only linked back to Dana.

I suspected that was Monroe's whole plan. He wanted to make sure his wife was left holding the bag. It only further proved what type of man he was. He wasn't even brave enough to face the consequences of his own actions. Instead, he made sure it all connected back to his wife so she would have to take the full ride. With all of the evidence connecting back to her, it would be harder for the prosecutor to pin the crimes on Monroe.

Any defense attorney could argue that Dana was the culprit and ringleader. That Monroe had no idea anything sinister was happening within the house. It wouldn't get him off entirely, but it could drastically reduce his charges and he could actually end up on probation instead of spending the rest of his life in jail.

It was a mess.

That was the only way to describe it.

I made my way through the hospital to go up to the pediatric floor so I could check in on the children. I was hoping they might be able to tell me something that we could use to not only find Monroe, but charge him with everything. These children were witnesses and they needed to be protected until we got Monroe in custody.

I made my way to the playroom where some of the children were set to be. I had reached out to Isaiah, their social worker, to let him know I was looking to speak with some of the children. I knew Isaiah had to be there during the questioning with them not having any parents.

I walked into the playroom and saw that there were only two children there. They didn't look too healthy, either. I knew they were from Monroe's house because we were using one of the playrooms strictly for the children that we saved last night.

The hospital had been good about closing this room off to the other children so we could do interviews in a more friendly environment. These two looked to be the older children out of the nine that we saved. I knew who they were. I made a point of knowing everything that I could about the children we rescued. I didn't want them to feel like I didn't care enough about them to even learn their names. I had no idea what they were feeling, though. I had never gone through the foster system. I was lucky in that sense.

My parents weren't amazing. Hell, I grew up being ignored and treated as an inconvenience, but I didn't have to grow up not knowing who I would be living with or where I would be sleeping at night. I didn't have to go through the horrors that so many children experience within the foster system. I didn't have a picture perfect childhood, not even close to it, but I didn't have to be afraid all day and night long. I had never been touched sexually or abused physically. I wasn't wanted or loved, but I came out of my childhood without any major scars.

Isaiah came over to me and I held my hand out for him as I spoke.

"Afternoon."

"Hey, any news yet?" Isaiah asked as he shook my hand.

"Not yet, no. I'm hoping to get something out of these guys."

"You can try, but others have already asked. No one is giving anything up. They all keep saying it was Dana."

"Okay," I said, giving him a nod before I made my way over to the kids.

I sat down on the rug with them. I wanted them to feel like I was on their side and not on a different level than them. I didn't want to intimidate or scare them, either.

"Hey guys, my name is Detective Lopez, but you can call me Jarod. I was hoping I could talk to you both about what has been going on," I started calmly.

"Dana had us working on the drugs. Mr. Monroe is a good man and he didn't know about anything going on in the house," Jeff said in a dead tone. He was twelve and one of the oldest out of the nine kids.

"Isaiah has told me that everyone seems to be saying that. But let me ask you guys this, how is it possible that Mr. Monroe didn't know about the drugs or about the abuse?" I asked next.

"He works a lot and when he is home we keep to ourselves and stay away from him so he doesn't know about it," Chris answered this time. He was thirteen, and the oldest amongst the nine kids. I suspected he was the group's protector, given that he had more injuries than the others. Both Chris and Jeff weren't going through withdrawals yet, so they had a lot of cocaine in their system built up. It also meant once the withdrawals started to hit, it would be hard on the both of them.

"But he's a detective, why didn't anyone tell him about what was going on?" I asked next.

"Dana made sure we never talked. It

was safer for the other kids if we stayed quiet," Jeff answered.

"I don't know what you want us to say, but Mr. Monroe had nothing to do with anything that went on in the house. He didn't know. He's a good man and would never do anything to harm a child. You won't get us to say otherwise," Chris said with conviction to his voice.

They did everything they could to protect the younger children and they still were. I had a feeling they were scared that Monroe would do something to them. They were most likely threatened with death if they ever talked and Monroe found out about it. Even after he was out of the picture, they were still too scared to cross that line and say anything against him. None of the kids would and pressing them to tell us the truth would only make them worse.

"Okay, I appreciate you guys speaking with me. Do you think it's okay if I hang out for a little bit with you guys?"

I didn't want to just leave and make them feel like they weren't important. I wanted them to know that we were on their side, even if they couldn't tell us the truth. And maybe, spending time with them would help to build up some trust and they just might talk or let something slip. They both gave a nod before they went back to building with the smaller Lego pieces.

I looked over at Isaiah and gave him a nod to let him know I wouldn't be questioning them anymore. He gave a nod and headed out.

I spent the next fifteen minutes hanging out with Jeff and Chris. I was casually building something with the Lego to try and build some type of a connection with the boys when the door opened.

The sound of the door opening had caused them both to flinch and I knew it was ingrained into them.

"It's okay, he's a cop," I assured them when I saw Agent Wright.

He was technically a federal agent, but I didn't want to scare them anymore than they already were. I also noticed that Agent Wright's dog was here with him as well. His dog had some gauze wrapped around his paws, presumably from the fire last night. I had heard about what happened to Tyler at the bar. Everyone in the station was talking about it.

We all suspected that Tyler was the

eyewitness to Monroe's crimes and he was looking to take him out. Tyler was the one adult that could put Monroe in an active role of what happened at the house. It only made sense for Monroe to want to eliminate Tyler and better his odds. It didn't work, though, as the Wright brothers were able to get to the bar and save Tyler before it was too late.

"Hey guys, how are you feeling?" Agent Wright asked, as his dog walked over to us and, to my surprise, lay down next to me.

I loved dogs, but I knew that working dogs always stayed by their partner. I didn't expect for the dog to come to me and just lay down right next to me. I reached over and gave him pets as Chris spoke on behalf of him and Jeff.

"We're fine."

"We were just seeing what we could build out of these Legos," I said, but I shook my head slightly so Wright would know that they didn't want to talk.

I was hoping he would understand and not press them for answers they were never going to give. He gave me a small nod in return and I knew he understood me.

"I just wanted to check in on you guys. Koda was also really worried about you."

"That your dog?" Jeff asked.

"He is. He's my partner. He goes everywhere with me to help me protect children, like yourselves. He rescued someone from a fire last night, so his paws are a bit sore."

"Will he be okay?" Chris asked, with a hint of worry for Koda's welfare lacing his voice.

"He'll be okay in a couple of days. We'll leave you to your building. Come, Koda."

Koda tilted his head up and looked over at Agent Wright for a brief moment before he placed his head back down on his paws. He held zero interest in moving and I could tell, based on the slight look of shock that went through Agent Wright's eyes, this was a first for him. He was used to Koda always listening to his commands. For some reason, though, Koda didn't want to leave.

I suspected it had to do with the children.

Dogs were very attuned to children and their emotions. He would be able to pick up on them being hurt and scared.

"Looks like he wants to hang out with

us. We can keep an eye on him, right boys?" I asked them, flashing a warm smile.

"I'm very good with animals. I don't mind watching him," Jeff easily agreed.

"All right, if you're sure. I'll come by shortly to pick him up," Agent Wright said.

I could tell he felt uneasy about it. He liked having Koda by his side and I suspected he felt like a piece of him was missing when he wasn't. K9s and their partners were supposed to share a very strong and special bond. A bond that was deep and unwavering. It made sense that he would prefer to have Koda around him.

If I hadn't known it before, I knew then that Agent Wright was a good man and I had more respect for him than ever. He was going to push himself through the discomfort just so he could help provide some comfort to the boys. I gave him a warm smile, hoping that would help ease some of his discomfort, and he returned the smile before he strolled out.

With Koda here, I hoped that maybe the boys would open up more and I could get something out of them that I could use to find Monroe. I was determined to find him and I would not rest until I did.

CHAPTER SEVEN

Mason

THIS WAS A shit show.

That was the only way I could think to describe the situation. I was supposed to be coming down here on vacation. This was supposed to be my time off. My time to get my head back on straight and try to fix myself. This was not the time for me to be going after an evil man that enjoyed using children to cook drugs and killing the ones that became too troublesome. This wasn't what I was supposed to be doing. I was trying to get a break. A break I desperately needed and, now, I was roped into this. I'd committed myself despite the fact that I really did know better. It was too late to turn around and ignore it all. I *had* to help, it was who I was, what I did. That didn't change that I wasn't mentally prepared for it.

I pulled up to the rest stop just thirty minutes outside of town. My boss, Special Agent in Charge, Derek Keyes, wanted to talk with me. I knew he wasn't happy about losing Jasper Monroe. Monroe was a serious offender and he was also a cop, or, well, ex-cop, now. That made him a huge offender that needed to be brought to justice. Now that everyone at the station knew that Monroe was a dirty cop and on the run, Roland was safe in the sense that his fellow cops knew the truth. But he and Tyler wouldn't truly be safe until Monroe was in custody or dead.

Koda whined and I reached over to give him a quick pat on the head before I got out of my truck and made my way over to Keyes, who perched on top of a picnic table at the edge of the rest stop, a good way from the doors to the small coffee shop there. It was getting dark out, but it was quiet and we were alone. I went and hopped up next to him as I spoke.

"Boss."

"How are you doing, Wright?"

"We lost Monroe. We recovered the children, but there are more buried somewhere that we'll need to find. His wife is going to jail, though. The piece of shit did a runner and left her holding the bag."

"He needs to be found. But there is also a problem with the foster care system in that town. It's not normally our jurisdiction, however, the Governor has decided to make it our jurisdiction. His order is that I assemble a task force that will operate in Gaithersburg to ensure the foster system in that town is corrected."

"Their own police and social workers can do that. Why would the Governor want a special task force?"

It seemed ridiculous to have a task force organized just to handle something that could be done through town. They didn't need federal agents, especially for something like that.

"The task force will be made up of federal agents and local police, but also social workers. The primary objective is to help to correct the foster care system in town, but the team will be going after the most violent offenders for crimes against children. The local boys don't have enough experience on their own to handle this. They need someone experienced in the field to lead the team. The social workers will help to place the children recovered from the takedowns in secure foster homes or back with their family. It's going to be a major undertaking, but will lead to saving a great deal of children. The task force is being given special privileges by the Governor. The Governor cares about results and not necessarily the means to get there. He is offering complete immunity to everyone working in the new task force. Now, that is, within reason. Obviously, if one of the members commits murder, sexual assault, or a crime against a minor there wouldn't be any immunity and they'd be prosecuted. Everything else will be at the discretion of the task force leader."

I wasn't expecting that. I knew the Governor was looking to lower the crime rates against children. Almost every politician gives the same speech about reducing crime rates, but very few of them try to do something about it. Apparently, the Governor was sick of waiting around for others to jump on the cause. If the task force was successful enough, he could easily rise in the political race. It was a smart call for him to make career wise. It might sound cold, but if it meant that more children would be saved from horrific crimes, that was all that mattered.

"A lot of responsibility for one person. Is that why you're here? You moving?"

"Hell no. I like New York. The Governor has allowed me to choose who will run the task force. I'm choosing you."

"What?"

How many ways could I say *hell no*?

I speak three languages in addition to English, so I could really say it a lot of different ways. I was not going to be running any task force. I didn't care what he had to say.

That was way too much responsibility.

I wasn't ready for it.

There were plenty of guys older than me, more experienced than me, who could run it. I was only seven years in. I wasn't ready to run something of this magnitude. I wouldn't even know where to start.

"You are the perfect agent to run this task force, Wright. I am promoting you to

Supervisory Special Agent. You will select your team from any active federal agent. You will also get to decide on who joins you from the local police and the social workers that you want to bring into the task force. Your first objective is to find Jasper Monroe and bring him to justice."

"You are making it sound like I don't have a choice."

"Because you don't. It's a direct order. This task force is yours to run. If you succeed, you save a lot of innocent children. If you fail, your career will be over and you will have failed a lot of innocent children," he said, his tone firm and brooking no argument. He sat back with a shrug.

The fact that he could dictate the order as easily as if we were talking about the weather told me how serious this was. Keyes always got like this when everything was on the line. He tried to downplay it by talking nonchalantly about it. As if that would somehow ease the gut punch he sent your way.

I didn't like this.

I didn't like that I wasn't getting a say in my own career.

I didn't like that I was being thrown

into the deep end with this task force. I had no idea what I was going to do or how to run a task force. And now, I was going to have to figure it out whether I wanted to or not, regardless if I felt out of my depth.

"How do I select the people for the task force?"

"You have access to the federal agent database, look them over and see who pops out for you. I would recommend choosing people who have a great reputation, and that you think bring something to the task force. You will want to focus on different areas. At minimum, you're going to want a tech specialist, a sniper, someone who is well rounded all across the board, a hand-to-hand specialist, a smart guy. You know, figure out who would help make the task force better. Focus on people that bring something unique to the table that will help you catch more criminals. It's a specialized unit that you are building, Wright. You got this."

At least he was confident, because I wasn't. This was too much responsibility for me to be taking on, especially right now. I was supposed to be on leave. I was supposed to be able to have a break and now, I was being thrown back into action when I wasn't certain I was ready. I couldn't tell Keyes that, though, because then I could kiss my career goodbye. I had to endure and hope I didn't screw this up.

"Any other bombs you'd like to drop on me?"

"No, that was it. I gotta head back. You got this, Wright," Keyes said again as he slid off the picnic table and casually strolled away toward his car.

I didn't have this.

There was no way in hell I was going to be able to pull this off.

Could I find Monroe, sure, that was simple, that wasn't anything I hadn't done a hundred times before.

But could I run a team?

Could I chase down leads and do whatever it took to bring down different criminal organizations as the lead agent?

I doubted it. I was only seven years in. Sure, there had been a lot that I had learned, but there were still a great number of things that I didn't know.

Things that only experience and time could teach.

In the field, you rely on someone that

has the experience. It's why Agents in Charge are older, in their forties or fifties. They have that experience. They know what to expect, what to look out for, how to respond when a situation is presented to them. I didn't have that experience and that lack of experience could get someone killed in the field.

"Fuck," I said, and let out a sigh, running my fingers through my hair.

I climbed off the picnic table and jogged back over to my truck. Koda was instantly poking me with his nose and I reached over to give him some love as I slid into my seat.

"What am I gonna do, Boy?"

Koda whined and pressed his nose into my neck. I wrapped my arms around him and took comfort in his soft fur. Koda always knew when I needed a hug or some love. He was very attuned to my emotions and that was something I relied on more and more, lately. After a moment I pulled back and spoke.

"We gotta go see Roland. He's not going to be happy about this."

I already knew that Roland wasn't going to like that I would be going after Monroe. Even more so, that he couldn't help.

He had to keep an eye on Tyler. He needed to make sure Tyler was safe and I knew he was the best man for the job. He was in love with Tyler and that meant there was no one better to protect him.

I wasn't certain if Monroe would go after Tyler again or not. It would be smarter for him to get the hell out of the country, but I also knew that wasn't going to be simple for him. Chances were, he was on the run and getting as far away from the State as possible. It wasn't going to be a simple and easy find.

He was a cop.

Had been a cop for a long time.

He had an escape plan and he was days ahead of us.

I put my truck in gear and headed back to town. I needed to update Roland and let him know what was going on. Then, I would need to find a motel room to stay in until I could find my own place. I knew I could stay with Roland and Tyler, but I needed my own space. I needed a spot where I could be alone and not have to put on a show for anyone. My life was changing once again, and I wasn't sure how I felt about any of it.

CHAPTER EIGHT

Mason

"ANY UPDATES?" I asked Roland as I handed him a coffee.

Tyler was still being kept in the hospital to help him heal from all of the smoke he inhaled. I knew from personal experience it wasn't good to breathe in that much smoke, and for a person with asthma like Tyler had, it'd be far worse.

I still couldn't believe when we had arrived at the bar that it was up in flames that badly. My heart went straight to my throat when Koda ran right into the blazing inferno. His paws were going to be a bit sore from the heat of the fire, and the scare had taken years off of my life, but thankfully, he was okay.

"The doc isn't going to give him any more sedation. He thinks it'll be okay for him to wake up today and then he'll pull the tube out."

"Good. That's good, Roland."

"Is Koda okay?" he asked, concern lacing his features.

Leave it to my brother to be concerned for my dog. I smiled, touched at his troubled state. He loved Koda, too, and it showed.

"He's good. A doctor checked him over for me and put some cream on the bottom of his paws. First degree burns, but in a few days he'll be okay. I've got his paws wrapped to keep him from getting any dirt in and aggravating his burns. He's hanging out in the kid's playroom, right now, on the floor."

"You left him there?" he asked, clearly confused. Not that I could blame him, Koda went everywhere with me.

When I'd arrived at the hospital, I'd immediately headed to where the children from yesterday were being held. They were all being kept to ensure they didn't have any problems from the drugs they'd been breathing in. When I got there, that cop, Jarod, was there with Isaiah, a social worker. They were making sure the kids were okay and well taken care of. I knew Isaiah would have his hands full with trying to get the kids placed in safe foster homes. It was just another reminder that I would have to help them overhaul the foster system in town. It was going to be a lot of work.

"Jarod was there with the kids as Isaiah worked with one of the doctors. I called Koda to come when I was ready to leave, but he didn't want to follow. Apparently, he's happy to lay next to Jarod."

"Maybe Koda finally sniffed out your soulmate." Roland couldn't help but chuckle at that.

I rolled my eyes at him and made sure he knew it. I didn't believe in soulmates. That was just some bullshit that Hallmark put out into the world to make people keep chasing after people.

To seek out romance so they could try and find their soulmate.

Deep and meaningful connections were pointless.

Dating was pointless.

Everyone was either fake and hiding their true self, or they cheated. It was better to stick with having a one-night stand. No emotions were involved and both parties got what they wanted.

It was just that simple.

Besides, Jarod wasn't my type. I liked the spinners, the ones that were small and easy to toss around a room. I didn't bottom and I was not interested in some top trying to convince me I should.

Who says Jarod is even gay?

He didn't come across as gay. I knew I didn't, either, but people knew I was gay. It wasn't something that I was interested in hiding. I saw what happened with Roland when he tried to hide it. He lost the love of his life to a drunk driver all from a fight about him coming out. It wasn't worth all of that heartache to hide who you were.

"What do we know?" Roland asked, moving our attention back to what mattered the most.

"Well, the tests have started to come back and it's looking like all the kids are addicted to cocaine. The doc is going to keep them for at least a week, possibly two, depending on how bad the withdrawals are. Dana has lawyered up. Apparently, she expected Jasper to come back and rescue her. Once she figured out he left her holding the bag, she clammed right up and yelled lawyer. I'm trying to get her denied bail, but I don't know if it'll stick. We have all of the electronics from the house and more than enough evidence of the drugs. But we still can't find him. None of the kids are talking about it. The few that have talked, all said it was Dana, that Jasper didn't even know about the drugs."

I had managed to get an update on everything that had been going on with the case. It was a lot to try and manage, because we had to make sure Dana also went down for the crimes that happened in the house.

"Bullshit. It was in his basement. Of course he knew about the drugs. He's trained them to put all of the blame on his wife. Like a fucking coward."

Of course he did. That is exactly what a coward does. He had it all figured out. He knew how to make it appear like it was all Dana and not the dedicated and highly decorated cop. He was smart and it was going to take a good amount of work to try and find him. We would, but I didn't know how long it would take.

"I got a BOLO out on his ID and his photo is being sent to every federal agency all across the country. I'll find him, but it might take some time. I've been put in charge of the task force that is going to be dedicated to finding Jasper."

There was more to it than that, but we didn't need to get into everything, right now. Roland had enough on his plate to worry about. He didn't need this to go with it.

"Once Ty is set back home, I can help you with finding Jasper."

"You're not on the task force, Roland."

He wasn't going to like that fact, and I knew he was going to snap at me over it. I couldn't blame him. If I ever loved someone like he loved Tyler, I would have been pissed and looking for blood. He wasn't going to like it, but there was nothing he could say to change my mind. He was too close to it and he needed to stay with Tyler to help him recover and to make sure he was safe.

"What the fuck are you talking about?" Roland snapped, as expected.

"You can't be out there looking for Jasper. I know you want to, I get it, but if you are out there with me, who the hell is going to be protecting Tyler? The only way to make a case against Jasper for multiple counts of murder and child trafficking is Tyler's testimony. Jasper knows that and he won't stop until Tyler is dead. You need to be with him, protecting him."

I could tell he wasn't happy about it, but he could also understand where I was coming from. He let out a sigh and gave a small nod in defeat. I went and put a comforting hand on his shoulder as I spoke.

"I'll get him, I promise you."

"I know."

Roland's faith in me was unwavering and that only added to the pressure I was already feeling. The last thing I wanted to do was to let him down. I was afraid, though, that I already had before this thing even started.

"I'm going to grab my stuff from your place and grab a motel room, for now."

"No, Mase, you can stay with me," Roland instantly said.

"I know, but it'll be easier for me to

stay at a motel. I'll be working late and you will be busy keeping Tyler safe. The Government pays for it, anyway, so it's not like I'm out money. I'm gonna get going. I have a lot of work to prep."

I needed to start to figure out who I was going to bring onto the task force and who would be able to pick up everything and move to a new town. I wasn't just asking them to come down for a case. This was a permanent move. That wasn't easy. I would need to find people that were skilled and would be willing to relocate. It was going to be a lot of work and I wasn't sure if I was truly ready for it, but I hadn't been given any choice. I would run this task force the best that I could. I just hoped it would be good enough.

CHAPTER NINE

Jarod

WALKING INTO THE station today felt different than it had yesterday.

I didn't feel different, though. Well, I felt sore from the punch I took. I woke up this morning to one very nasty looking bruise along the right side of my jaw line. I had taken some over the counter meds and I was hoping they would kick in soon.

The atmosphere was what felt different in the station.

Normally, when I walked in, you could hear chatter or someone laughing. Things were kept pretty light and carefree. We didn't catch darker cases. There were no homicides or sexual assaults that sucked the life out of you. Today, though, there was no talking, no soft chuckles. There was nothing but silence. The energy in the room was tense and filled with unease. It was as if everyone was afraid to say the wrong thing so they were all opting for this awkward silence.

It was uncomfortable.

I made my way over to my desk as quietly as humanly possible. I didn't want to attract any attention, because I knew the tension would be taken out on me.

It normally was.

The second I sat down, Baxter was instantly on me. He was not in a good mood. I could clearly see it all over his face. He was still pissed off at me for my comment yesterday about Monroe. I shouldn't have said it, but the words were out before I could even stop them.

It didn't happen often, but when it did I always regretted it. I was, normally, pretty good at not saying things out loud. I had a great inside voice, but every now and then, I used my outside voice and typically it resulted in a punch.

"You are late on Rasp's paperwork.

You were supposed to have that in yesterday," Baxter said with a tough edge to his voice.

Typically, I had to do everyone's paperwork. That was a rookie's job, according to over half of the police force. The only ones that didn't have me doing their paperwork were Detective Hollingsworth and Detective Wright. It didn't matter how many months I had on the job. It didn't matter how many cases I'd closed. All that mattered to them was that I was the newest detective, so I would always be the rookie. Even if another officer was promoted to detective, I would still be the punching bag because I was the opposite of everyone here.

"I'm sorry, I was pulled in for the raid and then, I was working the crime scene and talking to the victims."

"That's not your job. You don't get to work crime scenes or talk to any victims or suspects. Your job is to do paperwork until you have proven that you are not a useless idiot. And until you can manage to get paperwork in on time, you will never be out in the field again. You're the most worthless and useless rookie I have ever had to put up with. The day you get kicked out of here, the better this town will be." Baxter headed off and I could see that everyone was staring at us.

I could see the disgust in their eyes. Baxter obviously had told them what I had said in the basement and the blue wall was in full effect. I was going to be going through hell, now more than ever, because I dared to say something about a highly decorated detective.

These next few months were going to be brutal.

I grabbed Rasp's folder that contained the paperwork that was now past due and got to work on it. I was going to have to stay late tonight if I wanted to get all of this done.

CHAPTER TEN

Jarod

I WAS ONLY an hour into my work when Captain Perry came out into the bullpen. We all gave him our attention as we heard him coming our way.

Captain Perry had a heavy walk. You could hear him coming and there was no mistaking it. I was hoping he had an update on the case.

"I need you all to work on clearing out the small conference room. Agent Wright has been cleared to put together a task force with federal agents and local police to go after Monroe. The task force needs a place to work. I would appreciate it cleared out quickly. They should be here shortly."

A task force?

This was a huge opportunity. An opportunity I had been waiting for. I had been offering my skills to other police departments in nearby towns, but a task force that had the ability to hunt down Monroe, no matter where in the country he was located, it was a huge opportunity. It wasn't just an opportunity for me, but any detective here that had wanted to move up in rank. A task force opened so many doors. It could be a career changer for anyone that got to be on it.

"Will any of us get to be on it?" Detective Hollingsworth asked.

"That is up to Agent Wright. It's his task force and his call. I will supply him with files for detectives that I think would be helpful to him. It's up to him, in the end."

I had to talk to Captain Perry to see if I could be one of those detectives he handed over to Agent Wright. I knew I was on the low end for experience, and I literally had no seniority, but I had a great solve rate.

I would have an even higher one if the other detectives who I'd helped to solve their cases allowed me to put my name on the case. Even the detectives that I helped in other stations—they'd let me work the case, but they always took credit for the arrests.

It had never bothered me before. I wasn't in it for the spotlight in the newspaper or the "atta boy" that followed. I wanted to help people, to protect them. Solving a case was all that mattered to me. Getting the bad guy was all that mattered to me.

Now, though, I was hoping it wouldn't hurt my chances of getting onto this task force. I couldn't be a federal agent or go to a major city, so working on this task force might be my only chance at experiencing true police work. I couldn't let this opportunity pass me by.

We all got moving and I approached Captain Perry. I needed to speak with him for a quick moment before he started to go through the files he wanted to hand over.

"Captain Perry, could I speak with you for a moment?"

"Of course. What would you like to

discuss?" he asked as he guided me over to a more quiet area in the bullpen.

"I wanted to talk to you about my file being an option for the task force."

Captain Perry gave me a small nod and I could tell by the blank look on his face that I wasn't going to like this. He always got that look when he was about to give someone news they didn't necessarily want to hear.

"I appreciate your enthusiasm, Lopez. However, I'm only handing over files for veteran detectives with extensive field experience and a high solve rate. You don't have the type of experience that the task force is in need of to catch Monroe. They need guys that can hit the ground running without having to train or explain things. You're a good detective, Lopez, but you aren't ready for something as serious as the task force."

The only thing that hurt more than not being selected, was being told by your Captain that you weren't good enough to even be considered.

That stung, and it stung hard.

It took everything in me to school my features and not let that pain show through. I was good at my job. At least, I thought I was, but now, I was starting to doubt it. I knew that my name was often kept off of the arrest reports. But I thought that *he* at least saw me. I thought that my own Captain noticed the hard work that I put in. That he noticed the long hours I worked. That he noticed me volunteering my time at other police stations. I thought he saw me. I thought he saw my potential and my hard work, but apparently I was completely unnoticeable.

Maybe Baxter was right.

Maybe I was useless.

"Of course. I understand, Captain," I said, maintaining a neutral voice.

He gave me a warm smile before he headed off.

I sucked in a shaky breath and did my best to make it seem like I was not upset. Being upset in this station, around these men, it wasn't a good idea.

I went to start to help clear out the room, but I didn't even make it outside of the bullpen when Baxter was back, and based on the pleased look on his face, he knew what had just happened between Captain Perry and me.

"You actually thought a little shit like

yourself would be placed on an elite task force?" Baxter said with a chuckle.

"You are nowhere good enough for something like that. You will never be good enough. The only reason you even got promoted to detective was because the force needed to be more diverse and you are one of the few legal Latino's in the country. Give it up, Rookie, you will never be good enough for anything more than filling out paperwork. And you can't even do that right," Baxter said as he walked by me, making a point of hitting his shoulder against mine, pushing me back into the wall slightly.

Today was not going so well.

It was bad enough I already felt like crap after being hit by someone that was supposed to be my partner, but I just got smacked down by my Captain. I discovered that my own Captain didn't think I was capable of doing more on this job.

That I wasn't good enough.

Baxter's words only twisted the knife in further.

I turned and headed outside. I needed some air. I needed time to get my thoughts and emotions back under lock and key. I couldn't be around these guys today until I did.

The second I walked outside, I took a deep breath in to try and get the hurt out of my system. I knew it wasn't that simple. It was going to haunt me for the rest of the day.

Hell, for most of the week, most likely.

Still, I was used to the abusive words. I was used to having to keep all of my emotions and facial expressions in check. I had done this for the majority of my life and I would keep doing it until the day came when I could finally be myself with someone. When I could finally trust someone on a deep level that would allow me to be vulnerable with them. I doubted that person would ever be in my life, though. Even if they liked me, I knew if they knew who my parents were, it would all be over.

I was pulled out of my thoughts when three cars and a truck pulled up. I instantly noticed Koda in the front seat of the truck and Agent Wright in the driver's seat.

I couldn't help but notice how sexy he looked.

He was wearing all black, once again,

and I wanted nothing more than to run my hands all down his chest. I would bet my entire paycheck that he looked remarkable underneath his clothes.

Agent Wright got out of his truck and Koda jumped down from the driver's side. Koda bounded over to me and I bent down so I could give him some love.

"Hey Boy, how are you feeling?"

"Detective Lopez, right?" Wright asked me as he walked over to us.

"Yes, Sir," I answered, before I stood. I went back to petting Koda's head as he insistently nuzzled my thigh.

"You can drop the Sir. And Koda is doing good. His paws are healing great. Did you get any more out of those boys?"

"No, they wouldn't talk. They're too afraid to go against Monroe. I suspect that Monroe threatened the other children if any of them spoke."

"That's normally the case. Even if they did say Monroe was there at the house, and was the ringleader, we could never get them to testify. Even if they agreed, I couldn't in good conscience allow them to. It would be too dangerous for them. We'll find Monroe another way."

He sounded so confident and I couldn't

help but wonder how many times he'd done this before.

How many criminals did he hunt down without any evidence or leads?

He worked for Homeland Security, but I didn't know what exactly he did there.

"Do you hunt down a lot of criminals like Monroe?" I couldn't help but ask.

"I work for the Special Victims Unit. I go after criminals that commit crimes against children. So yeah, I go after guys like Monroe every day." He gave me a small professional smile before he continued.

"I gotta get my guys in there and brief them. I'll see ya around."

"Yeah, of course. Good luck," I said slightly awkwardly.

I desperately wanted to be one of the guys that got to help, but I knew that was never going to happen, unfortunately. I was a paper pusher, and it looked like that was all I would ever be in this station.

CHAPTER ELEVEN

Mason

I WAS DRAGGING my ass this morning.

Today was the day my guys would be coming in and I would need to get them all caught up on Monroe and everything that they were signing on for. I didn't inform them before hand that this could be a permanent placement. I wanted to get guys here to help me find Monroe and then, if they wanted to stick around that would be great.

I knew I was supposed to be building a task force, but I couldn't do that, right now. At least, not fully. I had to focus on getting Monroe.

I had reached out to Isaiah and he had agreed to be on the task force as a social worker. He also recommended his colleague and friend, Travis Manning.

I now had two social workers and three temporary guys. I also knew that Captain Perry was going to be pulling some files of his best and most veteran detectives for me to go through and pick who I wanted to be on the task force.

I knew I had to have a local detective or a couple of them, but my issue with that was the fact that Monroe came from this station. I knew that didn't mean they were all bad. I understood that there were bad apples in every good bunch, but I couldn't help but question how many bad apples there were in this station. I couldn't go off of the files alone. I had to ask Roland about some of them and see what he thought.

Task forces were generally built to catch as many criminals as possible. That didn't always translate to veteran feds or detectives. You had to put a group of people together that all brought something unique to the table, but something that the task force needed to make them more efficient. Having over a hundred years of experience on a task force didn't always work. Having too many people that believed their way was the best didn't work and that was what you typically had when you got a group of veteran detectives in the joint.

It was going to be a fine line I would have to walk, and to try and figure out how to best maneuver with Captain Perry. We would be operating out of his station, at least until we had received some funds to make our own station, but that wouldn't be until we could prove ourselves and that started with this case.

After saying good morning to Jarod, who was sporting a new bruise to the side of his face, I strolled into the precinct. I'd wanted to ask him about it, but it wasn't any of my business, despite how it pissed me off to see it.

Koda was screwing with me, too.

Koda never acted that way to a stranger. He'd never stayed with someone else, especially after I called him to come. I couldn't help but wonder what he was picking up that I was missing. And, of course, now, I couldn't stop thinking about the milk chocolate-skinned man with soulful brown eyes. He wasn't my type.

He was the opposite of my type, in fact, so then why couldn't I get him out of my head?

"Agent Wright, I see you have brought some men with you today," Captain Perry said as we walked in.

"Captain Perry, yes, I have brought some guys from my neck of the woods, specialized federal agents to help find Monroe. Do we have a spot we can work from?"

"I have the small conference room being cleared out for you. Should only take another moment. If you come with me to my office, I'll hand you those files."

I simply gave a nod and followed the Captain down the hallway. I knew the guys would stay there until I came back and I could show them where we would be setting up shop. This was nothing new to them. We had never all worked together before, though, and I was expecting a shitshow until everyone settled in.

I closed the door to Captain Perry's office behind me. He immediately went over to his desk and grabbed what looked like ten files. He spoke as he handed them to me.

"These are the more experienced detectives I have. They have over twenty plus years each and their track records are impressive."

"Thanks, I'll review them. Where's Hollingsworth?"

I didn't know who I could trust within the station, but I did know I could trust Roland. He told me that Hollingsworth would be an asset. He only had five years on the job, he hadn't joined until he was twenty-two, but before that he was in the air force and I had a huge respect for veterans. I knew they could handle themselves out in the field and they saw things differently. They were trained to see small reactions within people, to sense their surroundings. It was a huge asset to have out in the field. Not only that, Roland trusted him and Roland had vouched for him, so I knew I could trust him and that meant more to me and my gut instincts than any experience written on a piece of paper.

"Oh, he's not what you are looking for. He's only been on the job for five years and only a detective for one. He doesn't have the experience that someone would need for this type of work."

"Experience isn't everything, Captain. Right now, it's about who I can trust to follow orders and do what it takes to help me find Monroe. Now, I don't *need* to include anyone in the station, but we are working out of here and we are supposed to be working together on this task force, so I would like to have a couple of detectives. Who I pick, though, is up to me and Ro says I can trust Hollingsworth."

"Ro?" Captain Perry asked with a smirk.

"I couldn't pronounce his name when I was younger so I called Roland *Ro* and it's always stuck. I usually try to remember to use his full name when in company but occasionally it slips. Where's Hollingsworth?" I wasn't in the mood to go down memory lane, right now. I needed to get everyone caught up so we could get going on this manhunt.

"He's here today. He'll be in the bullpen. Will Roland be on the task force?"

"Not for this case. The Governor is looking to make this team permanent if it works out. If that happens, then he will be on the task force. For now, he needs to be close to Tyler in case Monroe goes after him. The other kids aren't talking, which means the only witness that can testify is Tyler. He needs to be protected until we get Monroe in custody."

"Understandable. What type of cases will the task force be working on after this?"

I could tell that Captain Perry was very interested in having the task force here. I couldn't blame him. It would make the station stand out amongst the others in the nearby cities.

"Crimes against children all over the country. It has the potential to be pretty major. Right now, though, we have to focus on finding Monroe before anything else can happen. No one knows that there is a potential for the task force to stick around, not even Roland, so please keep that under wraps. I don't want people to know until it's official."

I was trying to not think about the fact that this task force could be major. I didn't want to get ahead of myself. I didn't want to worry about what could happen after this case. I wasn't ready to lead a task force and I was not telling myself that I was leading a task force. I was running an investigation to find Monroe so the man that Roland loved remained safe and no more children would suffer under that monster's hand.

"That sounds like it will be a huge opportunity, but also has the power to do a lot of good. I hope it gets to continue after this. A lot of children need someone like you looking for them." Captain Perry gave me a small smile before he spoke again.

"Come on, I'll show you where you guys can set up and get Hollingsworth for you."

I gave a nod and we headed out. As we went back to the bullpen, I could see all of the detectives were looking at us and I knew they would be waiting to see if I would be picking them for this task force.

"Hollingsworth, with me," Captain Perry said.

I could see that everyone was surprised that Captain Perry was calling for Hollingsworth. He didn't have anywhere near the experience level as most of the detectives here, but I didn't care about that.

I could also see that others were

assuming that Hollingsworth was going to be the task force bitch and run around doing our grunt work. I wasn't about that, though, not even with my own rookies.

Rookies weren't there to be grunts, they were there to be trained so they could grow and become their own agent that could save more lives. Treating your rookie like a dog didn't help anyone, especially not the innocent people in the world.

Hollingsworth got up and he followed all of us as we were guided to the little conference room that had been cleared out. It was undersized, but we could make it work. We had worked in smaller places. The room had a table big enough to fit six people, and all along the walls were white boards. We would have enough space to get the files up on the walls and keep everything organized in terms of leads.

"Let me know if you need anything," Captain Perry said to me before he strolled out and closed the door behind him.

I tossed the detective files down on the table as my guys all stood around waiting to see what was going on. I had only told them that I needed help finding someone. I didn't want to have the same conversation over and over again, so I figured I would wait to reveal everything at once.

I did see the file boxes that we had for Monroe were already in the room so we could hit the ground running, at least.

"As you all know, I'm getting a task force up and running to find Jasper Monroe. I'll get into who he is in a moment. But first, I am Supervisory Special Agent Mason Wright. I have been with Homeland Security for seven years. I know three languages and I am a K9 handler," I said, before I gave a nod down to Koda as I continued.

"This is Koda. He is five years old and has been my K9 partner since he was eight weeks old. He is trained in attack, scent tracking, bomb detection, and he is good with victims." I then pointed over to Hollingsworth for him to go next.

We needed to get the introductions out of the way so we could focus on finding Monroe. I hated this part, but it was needed so everyone knew something about the person they were standing beside. Trust was huge and you couldn't trust someone that you barely knew.

"Detective Logan Hollingsworth. I'm twenty-seven and have been on the job for five years, one year as a detective. I joined the air force when I was eighteen and was medically discharged when I was twenty-one after a bad plane crash. I can fly any plane or chopper, and I have no idea why I'm here." Hollingsworth said, clearly confused why I would select him. I couldn't blame him. He didn't have the experience that most would assume was needed for this.

"You're here because you have the training from the air force, plus my brother trusts you. He vouched for you and I take that very seriously. It's not always about experience, Hollingsworth, it's about the skills that you bring to the table. I got no problem training. I got a problem not being able to trust someone. That's why you're here."

"I won't break that trust," Hollingsworth promised.

"I'm Cooper Jones, but everyone calls me Coop. I'm twenty-nine and have been a Fed since I was eighteen. I'm a hacker and analyst. I work for Homeland Security for the Counter Terrorism department.

There isn't anything I can't hack. I've been doing it since I was seven years old."

"So, you're a hacker prodigy?" Hollingsworth asked.

"Let's just say, be happy that I work for the good guys," Cooper said with a wink.

"I'm Special Agent Rafe Dallas. I'm thirty-five and have been working for the Department of Justice for five years. Previously, I was a Navy SEAL. I run investigations into dirty feds and get them prosecuted. I specialize in hand to hand combat and tactical."

"I'm Ryzen, people call me Ry. I'm thirty and a sniper."

That was all he was going to give us?

I wasn't sure about Ryzen. Rafe and Coop, I knew I could count on and trust. I knew they would be huge assets to helping me find Monroe. Ryzen though, he was a wild card and, normally, I wouldn't be interested in a wild card, but he came highly recommended. His file didn't have a specific loyalty that set claim to him. He didn't work for anyone, but he did work for everyone. Whenever the FBI needed a sniper, they went to him. Whenever NCIS needed a sniper, they went to him. Whenever Homeland Security needed a sniper, they went to him. It was weird, because, as a rule, people didn't float around. He was a Fed, I knew that for a fact, but I couldn't find the agency that was laying claim to him. He also had no last name, not even in his file. There was nothing on this guy in terms of personal information. I was starting to suspect he was CIA, but he would never tell me if he was. Because he couldn't.

"That's it?" Rafe asked, annoyed and confused.

"You wanna know my favorite color?" Ryzen snarked.

"Now that we all know each other, we can get started," I said, shutting it down before it could go any further. I didn't need a pissing contest.

"Jasper Monroe was a detective in this station for almost thirty years. For close to twenty of them, he has been a foster parent, along with his wife, Dana. My older brother, Roland, his new boyfriend, Tyler, was one of those foster kids that lived with them. A few days ago, Tyler gave his testimony against Monroe. Monroe and Dana have been using their foster kids to cook cocaine, package it and deliver it to their dealers in other towns nearby. Monroe has killed some of the foster kids that were either too sick from the drugs or were bringing too much attention to their operation. He has also sold kids to the sex trade when he felt like it. It had been going on for twenty years and, at this time, we have no idea how many were sold and how many have been killed. We don't know where the bodies are buried, either."

"Jesus, fuck. They both in the wind?" Rafe asked, clearly pissed that someone who was supposed to be keeping children safe was hurting them.

"When we did the raid Dana was there, along with their current foster children. Nine of them. We have the drugs and we have Dana, but Monroe disappeared a couple days ago. Dana won't give anything up. Claims she had no idea it was even in the house. She is sitting in jail and we were able to get bail denied. She believes that Monroe will come back for her. The children, they all say the same thing: that Monroe is a good man and he didn't know what Dana was making them do. We have tried to talk to the kids, but they are too scared to go against Monroe. It's on us to find him."

"Monroe also set fire to the bar that Tyler works at. He tried to kill him before he skipped town. Thankfully, Tyler is fine and going to make a full recovery. But if Monroe gets wind of Tyler surviving, we believe he will try and have him killed again. We don't have very many dangerous criminals in town, but Monroe has been a cop for a long time. He could have any number of connections to the underground that could come and kill Tyler. Without Tyler's testimony, it would be hard, if not impossible to convict him," Hollingsworth added.

"He couldn't have gotten that far if he's only a couple days ahead of us," Cooper stated.

"This the case files?" Ryzen asked as he kicked the box on the floor.

"That's everything we have. Let's get the intel out and set up. We need to find him before he disappears for good. Or worse, he takes another set of kids."

I wasn't certain what Monroe would do. He was used to having all of this money and now, he would be limited to what cash he had been able to take out or store. We had no idea how much money he had, but a man like him wouldn't be happy if he had to save and scrape by. He would want to get his empire back up and running and in order to do that, he would need to have kids. He couldn't be a foster parent any longer, but that didn't mean he couldn't get kids. There were plenty all over the country who were homeless or in foster homes that wouldn't report them missing.

Monroe would likely have endless connections with the men he associated with. It wouldn't take much to get himself back up and running and we needed to catch him before he did.

CHAPTER TWELVE

Jarod

IT HAD BEEN three days since the task force had started working out of the station.

It hurt a great deal when I discovered that Hollingsworth was singled out for the task force. He had less experience than I did, and yet, he was chosen. I didn't know why he was selected over me, but I suspected it had to do with how close he was with Detective Wright. The two of them had been working a lot of cases together and you could tell they were friends.

Detective Wright had taken Hollingsworth under his wing from the moment he came into the station. I knew they were both veterans and I suspected that old veteran connection was still strong within them.

Everyone else, though, they were also pissed off.

They were clearly jealous and they were not afraid to hide it.

They all believed that Hollingsworth was the task force bitch and was doing all of the grunt work, including bringing them coffee. I had never seen Hollingsworth doing that, but I was also keeping my head down and working so I wouldn't have to make eye contact with anyone. If I made eye contact, I was opening myself up to be berated once again. There was only so much one man could take and I was reaching my limit.

It was a dangerous place for me to be in, because I didn't want to lose this job. I just had to grin and bear it and hope that once everything with Monroe was finished it would blow over and I could go back to being out on the street. As it stood, I could barely leave my desk to take a leak.

Today, my morning was going to be

extra special, because I needed to stop in and visit my mother. My mother was a lovely woman. At least, that is what I was told.

Growing up, my parents were all about themselves. They loved each other and they loved spending time together. When my mother got pregnant, it wasn't in their plans, but they had me anyway. They weren't abusive, but they weren't loving, either. Most of the time, they could go all week without saying a single word to me. We would have dinner and I would sit all alone at the table while they were off eating outside on the deck. I was more like a house cat. I could co-exist with them, but I couldn't interact with them. I couldn't destroy their perfect bubble of love they shared for each other.

I had made peace with it a long time ago, that I wasn't important to them. That they didn't want me, but they were going to keep me alive until I was eighteen and could legally leave. It was fair, and I didn't ask for more than I knew they wouldn't be able to give me in terms of love.

I made sure when I was hurt or sick that I took care of myself, unless there was something I needed an adult to do. I was always afraid that if I bugged them too much, they would leave me somewhere and that was the last thing I wanted.

For the first fifteen years of my life, everything was fine. It wasn't what society would dictate was an acceptable environment for a child to grow up in, but I was surviving. I was getting good grades. I had three meals a day. I was never abused or went without basic needs. I was fine. And then, Special Agent Morgan Torres with the FBI showed up at our front door with an arrest warrant for my father.

As it turned out, my father had been killing women for close to twenty years.

He was a serial killer.

We didn't want to believe it, at first, but then they found his trophies in the basement. There had been a hidden room behind a work shelf that held a photo of each of his victims and a lock of their hair. They were all in plastic ziploc bags and dated.

It was earth shattering and it destroyed my mother and her world. She never wanted to believe it. She believed that someone else had done those crimes.

That someone must have broken into the house and planted the evidence.

It was ridiculous and no one believed it.

He was serving five life sentences in a maximum-security federal prison.

It was why I couldn't be a Fed or a cop in a bigger city. If people knew I was the son of a serial killer, one that killed close to a hundred women, they would assume I was a killer, too. I had to stay in a smaller town and do what I could for the people in it.

That was the only way I was going to be able to help people.

After my father had been convicted and sentenced, my mother lost it. It didn't matter that she still had me. I wasn't worth anything to her. She didn't love me, and even if she cared a little, it was definitely nowhere near the amount she loved my father. She started to use drugs, heroin, and before I even knew it, my mother was a full-blown addict.

For the next two years that I was at the house, we made it work. I would clean and cook and make sure she was taken care of. It didn't matter that she was the parent. I knew she couldn't do it. So, I took on the responsibilities. I made sure the bills were paid, I made sure my homework was done, that we had food, and that my mother ate three times a day. I would transfer money from her bank account into my own so I could make sure she didn't spend it all on drugs.

When I left at eighteen to go into the police academy, my mother went downhill and she hasn't stopped. When the mortgage for the house was too high, she sold it and moved into an apartment. When the rent for the apartment was too high, she moved into a rundown piece of shit place. All so she could spend more money on drugs.

For the past seven years, I had been trying to help her without enabling her. When she didn't have any food, I would buy her groceries. When she was behind on rent, I would cover it by paying her landlord directly. I knew it wasn't helping her to get sober, but I was terrified that she would die because she didn't have food in her fridge or a place to sleep at night.

I had paid to put her through three rehab centers for treatment, each one failed to keep her sober for more than thirty days. Two years ago, I had to pay off her debt to her drug dealer after he beat her into a coma for being behind ten grand. Between the rehabs and her debt, I was tapped out in savings.

Ever since being back in town after the Police Academy, I'd been going by every couple of weeks to check in on her. I hated going there, but I felt like I was responsible for her. It was because of my father that she was the way she was, and even though it wasn't my fault, I still felt responsible for her.

Walking into her apartment, I was immediately hit by the smell of old food and drugs. She lived in a rundown apartment building on the Southside of town. The building itself was very old and everyone that lived here were either junkies or prostitutes. My mother currently lived alone, but she was often with other people at the apartment. Almost like a flop house. The rent was cheap and I was fairly certain she was paying some of it on her back to the current landlord.

I knew she was prostituting and I hated it, but I couldn't fix her. I wished I could, but she was the only one that could make that choice. I had tried for years to get her to choose a healthier lifestyle, to decide on getting sober, but she just wouldn't.

"Hi, Mom," I said as I walked over to the small kitchen with the couple of bags of groceries I bought for her.

She was sitting on the couch and high, but I could tell she hadn't just done it so she was more lucid. Sometimes, that was worse than when she was passed out from it. If she was lucid, she was talking and, sometimes, what she said was not something I wanted to hear. Today was already going to be bad enough with having to be at the station and around everyone. I didn't want to add more abuse to my day.

"What are you doing here?" she said with a slight disgust to her voice. Apparently, she was in a mean mood.

"I'm bringing you some food," I simply said, making sure to keep my voice calm.

"I don't need your fucking charity."

"It's not charity, Mom. I just want to make sure you are eating properly," I said as I started to put things away. She wasn't in the mood for company, at least, not my company, so the sooner I got out of there the better.

"You want to do something for me? I could use a couple hundred bucks."

I bet she could. She needed her next fix just like she always did. Ever since she started to use it, she was always looking for her next fix. I had no idea who had introduced her to heroin, but from the moment she first injected it into her vein she was hooked. There was no going back from it and I had to watch her slowly deteriorate in front of me.

"You know I won't give you money for drugs."

"What good are you, then? I got stuck with a worthless son, who can't even give his mother what she needs. You've always been worthless, always crying when you were younger. All you do is take from me. You took everything from me. The least you could do for your mother is make sure she has cash on her."

I don't know why she seemed to think I was always crying growing up, unless she was referring to when I was an infant. She always made it seem like I was annoying and took everything from her when I was younger but that couldn't be further from the truth. I kept to myself. I made sure I didn't ask them for any help unless I had no choice to. I don't know why she felt like I had taken her life from her.

"If you weren't doing drugs it would be a different story. I can't support your decision to get high, Mom."

This had been a conversation we have had before. She knew I wouldn't support her drug addiction. I suppose I was supporting it by bringing her groceries and helping to pay her rent when she couldn't cover it. I had also paid off her previous debt to her dealer when she was almost killed. Some could call me an enabler, but I refused to give her cash. I knew she would only use it to purchase heroin.

I had tried to get her sober many times, but she didn't want it. She wanted this life. I don't know why she wanted it, but she wasn't interested in getting healthy and making something of herself for the rest of the life she had to live.

"Then get the hell out! You're worthless to me. I wished you had been killed when I was pregnant. You ruined everything in my life. I hate you!"

I finished putting the two things away before I headed out. I didn't even bother with saying goodbye. It would only fuel more hatred from her. I had heard it all before. She often told me how I was worthless and should never have been born. That she wished I had died.

It wasn't anything new.

Still, it hurt to hear.

I made my way back downstairs and out to my car. I had to get to the station for my shift. As badly as I would have loved to call in sick, I knew it would only make things worse for me tomorrow. I had to suck it up and focus on the work. That was the only way I was going to make it through.

CHAPTER THIRTEEN

Mason

IT WAS NEARING ten o'clock at night when I finally decided to call it a night. At least, at the station. I would be going back to the motel and doing more work.

It had been a week since the task force was put together and, so far, all we had managed to do was not find Monroe. Cooper had been all over Monroe's computer, but there was nothing on it that could link to a location or a person we could reach out to. He had even searched his cell phone and work computer. We had nothing in that sense.

We needed to find something, a place where we could start. A person that we could talk to that we could try and flip to get Monroe's location.

We had shit and it had been a week.

We were all trying our best, I knew we were, but our best wasn't good enough. Not this time around. Too much was riding on us finding Monroe. Roland had already lost one man that he loved. I couldn't be the reason that he lost another.

I had to find Monroe, no matter what.

I made my way back down the hallway to reach the conference room. I was the only one left in the station. Any calls that would come in, not that there would be any, they were forwarded to whoever was on call for the night. There was no reason to pay to have people sitting around all night doing nothing.

Just before I walked into the conference room, I noticed Jarod standing there looking at the evidence board. I didn't even know he was still there. I hadn't paid much attention to the other detectives in the station this past week, but every time I looked into the bullpen, I saw Jarod at his desk, working. It seemed like he always had work to do when everyone else had none. I couldn't help but wonder if maybe he was being bullied because he was new.

"You're working late," I said as I walked in. Koda lifted his head, but just laid right back down. He was in no hurry to get up.

Jarod turned around, a bit startled to see me, even though Koda was still in the room. I suspected he figured he could slip out before I got back from the bathroom

"I was just finishing up some paperwork. Sorry, I didn't mean to invade your space."

"Sure you did, that's why you're standing in it. I don't mind people being inquisitive, and never apologize for being curious, Jarod. You're a detective, it's part of who you are."

I didn't like how he always seemed so unsure of himself. From what Roland had told me, he was smart. He suspected that Jarod was a genius and I was leaning toward agreeing with him.

When you deal with guys that have a higher IQ, you tend to have to deal with their quirks. They were normally awkward, shy, and a bit weird. They tended to like things done in a certain order, or they always forgot where they put their keys. It was little things, but generally that indicated that they were smarter than the average person.

I like smart people.

I like geniuses, because they don't see the world, they see through the world. It was always an asset to have on a team. I hadn't brought any other detectives onto the task force, yet, because I wasn't sure who I could trust. I didn't know if I could trust Jarod because his partner was Baxter, Monroe's best friend. Jarod could have bad practices or he could believe that the blue wall protects every cop, no matter the crime. He could be a wild card and I already had one with Ryzen. I didn't need another one.

"Yes, Sir. I'll get out of your way," he said, but before he could move I spoke.

"What do you see?"

I moved closer so we could talk normally and for him to not feel like I outranked him. I was a Fed, but I wasn't a cop. We were on the same level, as far as I was concerned. I knew some would think otherwise, but I never got caught up in rank when it came to local police.

"A puzzle. One that is missing a lot of pieces. I see a man that is meticulous, organized. He plans ahead and he has back up plans, should he need them. This man is playing chess when everyone around him thinks they are playing checkers. He has everything linking back to his wife, so he must have an escape plan. He knows police protocols, so he knows he can't fly out of the country, he can't drive across either border. So, he needs a new identity, and I wouldn't be surprised if he already had one stashed away. He probably had a go-bag in the trunk of his car just waiting for when he might have to use it. If it was me, I would have multiple license plates so the car couldn't be tracked on satellites."

I couldn't help the smile.

Fuck, he *was* smart.

He knew more than people were giving him credit for.

I had seen his file. It wasn't that impressive. However, I knew that most rookies didn't get credit for arrests. That they had to earn it, and in a police force this size, there weren't many opportunities for him to earn it.

"Why don't the others like you?"

I could very easily pick up the tension in the bullpen when Jarod was there. They gave him dirty looks, they dropped their files on his desk, they didn't like him, and I needed to know why.

Jarod let out a soft sigh before he spoke.

"I said something to Baxter in Monroe's basement on the night of the raid. He was in denial about everything, even the chemicals being used to make cocaine. I made a comment about them making breath mints instead and he didn't take it too kindly. Even with all of the evidence staring right in their faces, they all want to put their heads in the sand and pretend like it's not happening. When good people do that, the bad people get to keep hurting people and then we become just as bad, if not worse, for standing by and doing nothing to stop it."

"I couldn't agree more. When good people do nothing, the bad people get to keep hurting innocent lives and it's those innocent lives that matter. People need to act when they see something wrong happening. And that is what a cop is supposed to do. No matter who the criminal is. I have to imagine, though, it can't be easy to be the only non-white person in the room."

Jarod was the only person of color in this whole station. For a town that was small and had a problem with gay people, I couldn't imagine they were very friendly with people of color, either.

"I'm Latino, and I don't have an interest in going to bars or strip clubs. It makes it hard to make friends with the white alpha males in the group. Still, I never let it hold me back."

"I don't doubt that."

He didn't come across as someone that took shit lying down. He was strong and he kept showing up to work even when everyone else treated him poorly. He just wanted to help people and it was refreshing. Jarod didn't have an agenda, he wasn't trying to get the highest solve rate so he could be promoted and move on to a bigger city. He was genuinely helping people because he wanted to, because he felt that was his calling.

It was so fucking refreshing.

"You know what I don't see? A cell phone," Jarod said, referring to the case.

"It's right there," I said with a nod to the items on the table in evidence bags.

"Coop, our tech guy, he went through it, but there's nothing we could use."

"I'm not talking about that cell phone. Monroe had another one."

"How do you know that?"

We had spoken to everyone who was friends with Monroe, on and off the force. No one had said anything about another phone. There was nothing in his financials that would indicate he had another phone he was paying for. His finances were perfectly clean. There were no cash deposits at all that didn't line up with him working on the force.

Dana, on the other hand, she was a whole other issue. The money they made went into her account and, considering she was a stay-at-home mom, there was no reason for the large deposits.

If Monroe had another phone, not even his closest friends knew about it, so how did Jarod?

"I saw him with it. A couple of weeks before the raid, he was in the bullpen talking with Baxter. He got a text or a call, I can't be sure which, the phone was on silent, but he pulled it out of his pocket, looked at it, and then headed outside."

"It could have easily been his normal

phone," I started, but Jarod cut me off.

"It wasn't, it was different. His normal phone is black and shiny, but this phone was black and a matte finish. It was also just slightly a different size and there was no power button on the side. It was on the back. The only phones that have the power button on the back are the LG phones. Monroe always used an iPhone for his personal calls. He used to get pissed off at it when it would randomly decide to update. Not to mention when he got a call on his iPhone, he would take it in the bullpen, but whenever someone called him on the LG phone, he wouldn't answer until he was outside. I just assumed he was cheating on his wife."

See, that right there was why I loved smart people.

Holy fuck, he had another phone and we didn't have it, so either he hid it very well at his place, or he had it with him. That phone had to have all of his contacts for the drugs and maybe even the human traffickers that he dealt with. That phone could lead us to a person that might know where he was, right now.

"That's impressive, Jarod. You are very observant. No one else in the station even knew Monroe had another phone. They never cared to pay attention to the little details. Those details can be what breaks a case. Now, we have to try and trace where he bought it so we can try and find a number."

"I already did. I came in here to put it on the table for you," Jarod said as he pulled out a piece of paper from his pocket.

"I suspected the phone was a burner, because I thought he was cheating on his wife. Having another phone statement would raise a red flag, so I went to the shops in town that sell burner phones, but none of them sold one to him. So, I went to nearby towns and, finally, a shop owner that is an hour away from here recognized Monroe's photo. He paid in cash, but the phones all have to be inventoried for the government, including phone numbers."

I took the offered paper and looked down at it to see a phone number. Now that we had the phone's number, Coop could try to trace it. Even if he couldn't, he might be able to pull some numbers off of it from the servers.

Jarod was impressive and we needed

him.

"Nice work. Your skills are definitely wasted here in a small town like this. But I'm lucky you're here. You start tomorrow, eight in the morning."

"Start what?" he asked, confused.

"You're going to be my partner. You're working the task force."

I could tell that he was shocked. He wasn't expecting to be given the opportunity, even after he worked his ass off to get the phone number for us. He was completely prepared to have to go back to doing paperwork tomorrow morning while we went after Monroe.

I didn't believe in screwing people over. He worked hard to track down this number and I believed that hard work should be rewarded.

"But I don't have the experience," he instantly said when the shock wore off.

"Experience isn't everything. You can't teach someone to have good instincts. You can't teach someone to be smart. That's natural to someone, and I would rather train a person who will grow to be a huge asset than to use someone with twenty years of on the job experience that will contribute nothing."

I could tell he was still feeling unsure about himself. I hated that he felt like he wasn't good enough because he didn't have what other people on the force did. Years of experience meant nothing here and I could tell he had gotten shit for it over the time he'd been a detective. I placed my hands on his biceps as I continued.

"You are incredibly smart. I am willing to bet that you are smarter than you have allowed people to see, because then you would stand out and you don't want to. For whatever reason, you don't want to be noticed and that's fine, until it's not. Until that fear keeps you from helping more people. It doesn't matter what everyone else thinks of you. It doesn't matter what everyone else sees in you. What matters is what you think of yourself. What you see when you look in a mirror. At the end of the day, Jarod, you have to be able to see your reflection and not be disgusted or disappointed in it."

I could see the flood of emotions flickering through Jarod's eyes. It was as if he had never had someone tell him something like that before. As if no one had ever said anything nice to him. There was a raw pain behind his eyes and I hated seeing it. I hated knowing that someone or multiple someones had been putting him down to the point where he felt so unsure of himself. I could tell he didn't even know what to say to me and I doubted he would be able to say anything at all without his voice catching. I decided to put him out of his misery and change the subject. I spoke as I moved back.

"Come on, let's call it a night, Partner. Koda."

Koda got up and Jarod snapped himself out of it and got moving. We both headed out and I waited to make sure he grabbed his stuff to go home. I didn't want him to sit down and keep working. I didn't care what paperwork he had for someone else to finish, he was mine now, and I was not going to have him too exhausted to function properly.

Once he was ready, we both strolled out into the night and went our separate ways. I was really hoping that Jarod would be able to loosen up and feel more confident in himself as the task force went on.

I also had to ignore the slight warmth that spread throughout my chest and down to my crotch at the thought of having Jarod around me all day. I didn't care what my body said, he wasn't my type and it was just that simple.

CHAPTER FOURTEEN

Jarod

TODAY WAS THE day that I had been waiting seven years for. Today was the day I was going to be a real cop, a real detective. I was going to work on a case that mattered. A case that would save a lot of innocent lives. Innocent children's lives. I was going to get to help the task force bring Monroe to justice.

I knew when everyone in the station found out, they would make it seem like I was just going to be running errands and fetching coffee, but I didn't care. Even if that was what I ended up doing, even if it was grunt work, it would be worth it, because I was still helping them.

Plus, I had given them a huge lead with the phone number that could lead to even more leads that could lead us to Monroe, and it all would have stemmed from that phone number I found. It might be a small role in the larger picture, but I didn't care because I got to help and that was all I wanted.

I walked into the station just before eight, ready to go. The bullpen already had other detectives there, including Baxter. Seeing him normally killed my good mood, but not today.

"Rookie, where's my paperwork?" Baxter demanded as I walked by.

"It's on my desk. You'll have to finish it."

Baxter gave a chuckle as he turned to look at the others in the room before he spoke. "Oh, I'll have to finish it? Paperwork is a rookie's job. You are our bitch and will do whatever the hell it is that we say. Now, get your Mexican ass in your seat and don't move until it's all done."

"I can't. I'm working with the task force. So, all of you will have to do your own paperwork until Monroe is caught."

"Bullshit you're working the task force. They already have a bitch with Hollingsworth, they don't need someone useless like you," Baxter instantly responded.

I could tell none of them were happy about this new piece of information. A good deal of them were bitter that they hadn't been chosen to be on the task force, but Hollingsworth had. It was a blow to their egos that they had been denied the right to be on an elite task force. Now more salt was being poured into the wound by me being selected over them.

"We got a problem here, gentlemen?" Mason said as he walked over to us with a tray of coffees in his hand.

"Nothing that concerns you, Fed," Baxter said.

Mason spoke as he handed me a coffee.

"It does if you are harassing my partner and keeping him from his work."

It warmed my chest to hear Mason refer to me as his partner. I wasn't sure if he meant it, or if it was just a temporary thing, but it still sounded really good to me.

I had never been called a partner before.

Baxter always called me Rookie or his bitch. Baxter laughed at what Mason said and I knew this wasn't going to end well. There was no way Baxter was going to let me slip away without getting the last word in.

"What part of what I said was funny to you?" Mason asked with an edge to his voice.

"Oh, nothing. I just never figured he worked on his knees. But it does make sense how someone as useless as him got on the task force. I guess liking dick is genetic for you, eh?" Baxter said with a smirk.

Oh, that was going to be bad. I didn't know Agent Wright very well, but I could tell he wasn't impressed by the twitch in his jaw. I knew his brother was gay. I obviously didn't have a problem with it, but I wasn't sure how Mason felt about it. Some guys were cool with their sibling being gay and others were uncomfortable and disgusted by it. I wasn't sure what category Mason would fall under.

"Because I picked an intelligent

detective over you, that must mean he only received the position because he lets me bend him over the table to fuck him? It has absolutely nothing to do with the fact that you were useless and hold no value whatsoever to a task force. I'm sure the fact that you failed to notice that your best friend was a drug dealing, child murdering, child sex trafficking asshole doesn't reflect your detective skills, at all. Why don't you do us all a favor and fill out paperwork, seeing as how you couldn't possibly be played by it. I have a task force to run and I need my partner to be all caught up."

Wow... Just, wow.

That moment right there was the best moment of my life.

He actually said that to Baxter. He said it out loud for everyone to hear and he did it without shrinking back or wavering.

God, he was awesome.

Best day ever.

Mason placed his free hand on my back and started to guide me down the hallway, but before we left the bullpen completely, he stopped and turned back to say one more thing.

"Oh, and for the record... yes, I do love dick," he said with complete confidence and the sexiest smirk I had ever seen in my entire life.

Fuck, this man was not only sex on a stick, but he was gay.

He couldn't have been any more perfect.

I had always been attracted to guys like Mason. I liked them bigger and able to defend themselves in a fight. I liked muscles and someone that had no problem being in control and tossing me around. I didn't like it to be violent, but I did like being a bottom and I didn't mind it being a bit rough. It had to be passionate and sometimes passion didn't mean gentle and sweet.

This man was perfect, but he was my boss, my partner, and that meant we had to keep it professional.

Mason started to move and I had no choice but to move with him. He softly spoke to me as we traveled to the conference room.

"You know, you punch him as hard as you can to his mouth, he'll stop talking shit about you. Or are all of your muscles just for show and you can't fight?" he teased.

"I can fight. I'm just not the type of person to randomly punch someone."

I didn't care for violence and I wasn't one to generally have conflict in my life. My mother was a perfect example of it. It took a lot for me to hit someone without being hit first. Maybe it was my intelligence that made me not see the point in inflicting violence onto someone when you could talk through the conflict. It just wasn't my style.

"I can understand that. But every now and then, assholes need to be punched hard enough to knock some teeth out," he said as we walked into the conference room.

"Who are we punching?" Rafe asked.

"Baxter," Mason answered.

"Oh, fuck, pick me, please," Hollingsworth said as he raised his hand.

I couldn't help the small chuckle at that. Apparently, I wasn't the only one that had been on the wrong end of Baxter. Even Hollingsworth, who was allowed to go out and celebrate with the guys.

"See, he gets it. Every now and then, you gotta just punch the guy to shut him the hell up," Mason said as he placed the coffee down on the table for the guys to grab.

"This is Detective Jarod Lopez. He is our newest member. He was the one who gave us our lead on the cell phone," Mason continued.

"Coop was telling us about it. Nice find," Rafe commented.

"Thanks," I said, slightly awkwardly. I wasn't used to anyone giving me positive reinforcements.

"So as we all figured, the phone was a burner, so I can't put it in Monroe's hands even though we have an eye witness that sold it to him. He could easily say he gave it to someone. I tried to track it, but it's turned off. He most likely bought a new one and dumped this one," Coop started.

"You can't get anything off of it?" Rafe asked.

"I didn't say that," Coop said with a cocky smirk.

"Before, during times of landlines, when you made a call it disappeared the second you hung up. But in the twenty-first century, when you make a call or a text message, it is sent to a satellite that stores the data for forty-eight hours, before it goes to a final server where it remains for thirty days. Now, those servers the general public don't know about. Only computer geeks like myself know they exist, and how to hack into them."

"Legally?" Mason asked.

"Does that matter?" Cooper asked, genuinely confused by the question.

"Not really, just curious," Mason said with a shrug.

Apparently, the need for a warrant to gain access to secure information was not above him. I wasn't too bothered by it. I knew that the Feds did things a bit differently at times. We were hacking for intel on Monroe, not spying on innocent citizens.

"Naw, it's not legal. But no harm, no foul. I was able to pull the phone numbers that went in and out of the burner phone over the past thirty days. Now, they are all burner phones, but I worked all night building an algorithm that allows me to find cell towers and satellites that picked up those numbers for outgoing calls. I was able to trace where the bulk of the calls were originating from. Columbus, New Mexico,"

Coop said with a proud smile.

Why would he be calling someone in Columbus, New Mexico?

That made no sense to me. We were nowhere near it. It was a good thirty hour drive. They were on the other side of the country.

How would they be of any help to him while on the run or even before it?

How was he dealing drugs or connecting with child traffickers from all the way out there?

"Alright, Hollingsworth and Lopez, tell us why," Mason said.

I instantly looked at Hollingsworth because I had no idea. I was hoping that maybe he would know, but he looked just as unsure as I did. The trick was, neither one of us wanted to admit it, because the job hadn't really taught us to admit when we didn't know something.

"That was exactly my point. You can't be afraid to ask a question. If you don't know something, then say it. Ask your questions. Voice your opinions. We're all here to catch a criminal and you have to speak up. Hollingsworth, Lopez, no one here is going to ridicule you for asking a question. No one is going to tell you to shut up or make fun if it sounds like a stupid question. There's no such thing as a stupid question. That is how you learn and I would rather teach someone who wants to learn than to deal with an idiot who wants to slide by. Now, with that said, are there any questions?" Mason reassured in a calm voice.

I had never had someone like him in my life. More often than not, if a rookie had a question, they kept their mouth shut and tried to figure it out for themselves.

Mason, though, he had no problems with people learning and that was refreshing and freeing.

"Why is he communicating with people that are over thirty hours away?" I instantly asked.

"And why would they be communicating with him? If they wanted drugs or children, they could easily get that from the area they are in. Why risk transporting drugs and kidnapped kids across multiple state lines?" Hollingsworth added.

"Look at that, they do know how to ask questions," Rafe said with a smirk.

"Can't answer why, without knowing

who," Ryzen answered cryptically.

I didn't know the men in this room outside of Hollingsworth, obviously, but Ryzen seemed very odd. He barely spoke. In fact, this was the first time he had said anything since I arrived this morning. He had a dark aura about him and I could feel how dangerous he was. I didn't know his story, but I couldn't imagine there was a happy one with him.

"Columbus, New Mexico is right on the Mexico border. It is often used as a pit stop for criminal organizations. The town is very small and it's mostly desert and there's no patrol. It's a spot where traffickers can meet to get drugs out of Mexico, get kids and guns going both ways. It's a hot zone and most live in El Paso, which is about an hour up the road," Mason explained.

"So the guys that Monroe called most likely live in El Paso and traveled to Columbus to make the calls, probably while they were already there doing business," I stated.

"Exactly. One of the owners of those phone numbers could get us Monroe. We gotta get to El Paso and start looking into them. I'll make the call for the plane.

We're wheels up in two hours," Mason said as he pulled out his cell phone.

"Wheels up? We're going there?" I asked, shocked. I would have figured Mason would have reached out to another Fed to keep looking into it.

"Of course we are. We're running this case. Wherever the leads take us, that's where we go. Pack up. We'll meet at the Baltimore airport in two hours. Pack for at least a week. We don't know how long we'll be gone."

Cooper broke his computer down as everyone else started to head out.

I couldn't help but be shocked. I didn't expect that we would be traveling the country. It was exciting, though. We were actually going to be roaming around and actively looking for Monroe. It felt very official and I was going to remember this for the rest of my life.

With a big smile, I headed out of the conference room and made my way to my car. I had to get home to pack.

I was going on a manhunt.

CHAPTER FIFTEEN

Mason

FLYING WAS NOTHING new to me. Just like flying on a federal jet was nothing new to me. I could tell, though, that it was something special for Jarod. He was like a kid in a candy store the moment he arrived at the airstrip. I couldn't hold it against him. I was like that, too, when I first joined the bureau and got to fly on the private jet that Homeland Security had. It was all very exciting and now, it was just another day to me.

I missed that excitement.

I miss being surprised and full of life at

the prospect of a new case. Everything back then was always so new and exciting and now, it was just another day. Another case where I got to experience the horrors this world had in store. That light that I used to see, it was almost too dark to make out now, and I doubted it would ever get bright again.

I mindlessly gave Koda some love, stroking my fingers through his fur as my mind couldn't help but slip back to my conversation with Roland before I headed for Baltimore.

The second Roland opened the door I could tell he had been hoping that I was coming with news for him. I hated that I didn't have anything more actionable for him. Something that would end all of this and he could stop living in fear that one day the man that he loved would be killed. That he would have to lose yet another good man before he had the chance to truly live and love him. I wasn't about to let that happen, but I also knew I couldn't promise that it wouldn't and I hated that. More than anything, I hated that I could be failing my own brother.

"Mase, why are you knocking? You have a key," Roland said, flashing a warm

smile as he moved back to let me in.

"Well, I wasn't sure what you and Tyler would be doing. I didn't want to walk in on anything I can't unsee," I teased as I strolled inside.

"Cute, but Tyler still has to heal up before we have some fun in the bedroom. Or in the kitchen, on the couch, the back deck..." Roland said with a smirk.

"You're an animal, but at least one of us has a chance of getting laid," I retorted as I plopped down on the couch.

"You have plenty of options. Hollingsworth is gay and I also know on the down low that Lopez is, as well. See, he's your soulmate."

"Shut up. I didn't come here for that. Besides, I can't have sex with anyone on my team. That would be unprofessional."

"True, but lots of people do it. Plus, sex is the best way to relieve stress and help people sleep at night. You have not been sleeping. Just because you aren't at the house anymore, doesn't mean I haven't noticed. What's going on with you, Mase?" Roland asked gently, his concern lacing his voice.

I was not about to tell Roland about what I was diagnosed with. The shrink *was a quack, anyway. There was no way I had PTSD. Telling Roland about it would only make him worry and he had enough he needed to worry about with Tyler's safety with Monroe in the wind.*

"Nothing is going on. I'm fine."

"Bullshit. Don't give me that crap. We both know that you are not fine. You've been different since you pulled up to my house before this shit show started. Something is going on. What aren't you telling me, Mase?"

This was not a conversation that I was willing to have right now. Hell, it wasn't a conversation that I wanted to ever have. Now was definitely not the time for it. I had to keep my mind focused on Monroe and this case. Afterward, I would have to figure out what I was going to do with my life and how to cope with everything.

"I've brought Lopez onto the task force. He noticed that Monroe was using a different phone than the one we have in evidence. He went all over the nearby towns and was able to track down the store and got a phone number for it. Coop ran it, but it's turned off. He was able to get some phone numbers that were on the phone for the last thirty days. They all

originate from Columbus, New Mexico. We're flying out to El Paso within the next two hours to track them down. Hopefully, one of them will have intel on Monroe."

"That's good. I'm glad you picked up Lopez. He's a good detective and he should bring a different viewpoint on the case. Though, I did notice you ignoring my question. You have to talk to someone eventually, Mase, before it eats you alive. The job that you do, it's dangerous but it's also soul eating. You can only see the things that you do for so long before it becomes too much. You need to talk to someone. It doesn't have to be me, but talk to someone."

I hated that I was making him worry. He didn't need to worry about me. I could handle myself. I had been doing this job for seven years and I was fine. I hadn't been shot or stabbed. I had been in fights with taking down a suspect, but that was it. I was lucky. I was one of the lucky ones that hadn't been seriously hurt in the line of duty. I had nothing to have PTSD over. It was stupid and I didn't believe in things that were stupid.

"I'm fine. I just wanted to give you an update on the case and see how things

were around here. Did Tyler remember anything more that we could use, maybe?"

The night that the bar was attacked was all a blur to Tyler. It was from his slight concussion. Memory loss was common. I was hoping he might remember something from that night, because the person that torched the place was quite possibly in the bar when it was open. I knew for a fact that Monroe didn't do it. He was already out of town before the raid went down. He had to have someone else torch the bar to try and kill Tyler. If we could find the perp, it would help prove that Monroe ordered a hit on someone.

"Not yet. He wants to help, but he still has no memories of that night yet. At least, not while he was working. If he does remember something, you will be my first call. I promise, little brother."

"All right. I have to get going. I still gotta get out stuff from the motel and head to the airstrip in Baltimore. I'll call you later on and check in," I said, as I stood.

Roland stood as well and he pulled me in for a hug.

I instantly wrapped my arms around him and took in the comfort that his embrace always brought me. Even when we were kids, whenever I was scared I always felt better when my big brother wrapped his arms around me. He had a way of making me feel like everything would be okay, even when the whole world was on fire.

Roland didn't pull away, though. He continued to hold onto me until I was ready to let him go. He knew something was wrong and he was allowing me to have all the comfort that I needed in order to get me through. And it was just another reason why I loved him so damn much.

"Everything okay?"

I was jarred out of my thoughts by Rafe's voice. He had taken a seat across from me. He had obviously moved while I was lost in the memory. I didn't really know Rafe. I knew of his reputation of being good at his job and that was what I needed. We had never needed to cross paths with him working for the DOJ. He seemed like a good man so far, though.

"I'm good, just thinking about the case. What about you?"

"I'm solid. Hell, I'll go anywhere. I don't care. You just seemed lost in thought for a few minutes, there. Just wanted to check in and make sure you were okay,

Boss."

"Naw, I'm fine. You got any family?" I figured I should try and get to know these men a bit better.

"Nope, just myself. This life doesn't really promote stable marriages or relationships. Most people get annoyed when you get called away at a moment's notice. Kinda kills romance and any time off. What about you? You got a boyfriend?"

"How did you know I was gay?" I couldn't help but ask.

"Oh, we all heard you say how you love dick. I figured it wasn't just an expression," he said with a small shrug.

"Nope, I really do."

"Shit, who doesn't?" he said with a smile and I knew right then I wasn't the only one on this plane that preferred men to women.

That was interesting, because according to Roland, both of our detectives were gay as well. Leave it to me to find the few gay men in law enforcement and stick them on a task force. I couldn't help but wonder if Coop would be as well. I doubt Ryzen was, but you never knew. Maybe I would get a clean sweep all across the board.

"Weirdos, mostly. Do you like your position within the DOJ?"

If I was going to make this task force permanent, then I needed to know which of my men would be willing to stick around. If they all wanted to go back to their lives, I would have to start all over again and I wasn't sure how well that would go over. I had chosen each and every single one of these men and I did so with a purpose. If none of them wanted to stick around long term, I wasn't certain I wanted to work with another team. At the same time, I wasn't sure I wanted to be here either, so it wasn't like I could hold it against anyone for wanting to leave after one case.

"It's all right, yeah. Sometimes, I get bored. There's a lot of sitting around and waiting. It's nice being more active again. I miss doing this type of investigation where you have to go from the ground up and build a case. Most of the time, when I get a case file, the legwork is already done for me. I miss getting to do this."

I could understand that. He had been an active Navy SEAL. They didn't do a lot of investigation work, but they did help with the ground level and build up from there. They would focus on the little fish within a terrorist organization and they would work their way up until they got the head of the snake.

"At least you are enjoying the break. Hopefully, we can find Monroe quickly."

"What about the other kids that were killed or sold?"

I had been wondering about that myself. The ones that were killed would be easier to find. There had to be some type of mass grave that Monroe used to hide the bodies. The ones that were sold would be harder. We would have no way of knowing who Monroe sold the children to or where they were taken. They could be dead or they could have been sold and shipped off to another country. We would have no way of tracking them down unless Monroe either admitted to it, which I doubted, or he had some type of ledger that we could use. The harsh reality was, those children would be long gone and we most likely would never find them until it was too late.

"I'm going to see about having someone go looking for the grave. It would have to be close to town, but not in a place that it could be stumbled upon. As for the kids sold, we'll have to see what we can get out of Monroe. Chances are, we'll never be able to find them."

"Yeah, I was afraid of that," Rafe said as he turned to stare out the window.

I knew he was upset.

I couldn't blame him.

This wasn't easy to accept.

He had never had to deal with children in this sense. I was the only one that had to experience the horrors of mankind on a daily basis. The others were used to chasing after criminals that were killers, maybe rapists, but nothing like this. It was hard to handle and I wasn't sure if any of them would be willing to do this for a living.

That wasn't something I had to worry about, right now, though. For now, I had to focus on this case. I was going to find Monroe, no matter what.

CHAPTER SIXTEEN

Mason

WE WENT STRAIGHT to Homeland Security the second we landed.

I had been there before so I easily guided us through the security process and headed up to where visiting agents could work.

We made our way into a conference room that was twice the size of the one at the police station back in Gaithersburg. It would give us all enough room to spread out and work without being on top of each other.

"All right, get set up and start looking

into any of the main players in the area. Coop, start trying to track the phone numbers and see if any of them are on or made calls recently. We need someone that we can interrogate to get to Monroe," I said as I placed my bag down.

They all gave a nod and started to spread out and get set up. There were laptops there that they could use, and I knew Cooper had his own rig with him.

I headed back out of the room and moved over to a quieter spot on the floor. I needed to call Roland and check in with him. He answered after two rings.

"Mase, how was the flight?"

"It was fine. We are just getting set up in the conference room, now. Listen, I need to talk to you about something."

"Anything. You know that."

I knew he was expecting me to talk about something personal and not the case, but I wasn't at that point yet, and I doubted I ever would be.

"The children that Monroe sold, they are going to be almost impossible to trace. However, we can find the children that he killed and buried somewhere. Do you think there's anyone in the station that you could trust to find them?"

I could hear the soft sigh that Roland tried to hide. He was disappointed that I hadn't opened up to him, but he would get over it. We were past the age where he could demand that I tell him what was wrong. And I also knew he understood how important it was to give the kids a proper burial. Not to mention, some of them could have families and they deserved to know what happened to their child.

"I don't know about in the station, but I do know two private investigators that stop at nothing to help children. Damien and Sebastian. They'll find the graves and make sure the kids are identified and taken care of. I'll call Damien right now and get him caught up on the cases and he'll start to look for them."

I wasn't sure how I felt about private investigators doing it, but I trusted Roland's judgment. I knew there were some great private investigators in the world.

Ones that did more than just chase cheating spouses.

There had been plenty of times when I was on a case and a private investigator was helping either the local police or an

Agency. Some of them were ex-cops or ex-feds that wanted to make a difference in the world without having to conform to the constraints of the law.

"All right, do it. If you think they can be trusted, that is good enough for me. If you could have them focusing on those children, then I'll focus on Monroe. If we can get him alive, we might be able to get him to flip on the men that he sold the other children to."

"Monroe won't do it for free. He'll want some type of deal."

I knew that to be true, but I also knew there wasn't much wiggle room we would be able to give. He was already going to go away for life. The only thing we could give him would be to put him in a lesser prison and put him in protective custody with him being an ex-cop. Other than that, there wasn't much I could do. He had too many federal charges up against him and none of them could be overlooked.

No judge would ever allow it.

"We don't have much wiggle room and he knows it. If he wants to live in prison, though, he'll agree to it. Again, though, that is assuming we will be able to take him alive. He might not let us."

"I know. Just be safe, that's all that I care about," Roland said, and I could hear the deep worry in his voice.

"I'll be fine. Don't worry so much. I gotta get going. The sooner we can track down one of these contacts, the sooner we can, hopefully, get Monroe."

"All right, be safe, and I love you."

"I love you, too, Ro," I said as I ended the call.

I took in a slow and deep breath to calm my anxiety down before I turned and headed back inside the conference room. I had a job to do and I was going to do it.

CHAPTER SEVENTEEN

Mason

"ALL RIGHT, WE have three rooms, so we need to double up. Coop and Hollingsworth, Ry and Rafe," I said as I handed them their room keys.

It was nearing nine o'clock at night when I had decided to call it a day. We all needed to get some sleep or we were going to be useless tomorrow.

We had been able to find one of the contacts in Monroe's burner phone. Jose Vilenti was a major trafficker. From guns, drugs, people. Shit, even exotic animals. If you wanted it, he could get it for you. He was known as a Connector. His job was to put people together and get your product from point A to point B. He worked for a lot of cartels and he made millions a year doing it. He was a major player, and if he dealt with Monroe, that meant that Monroe was a supplier for a cartel.

It was not what I had been expecting. I'd thought Monroe was only a little fish selling children to other little fish. As it was turning out, Monroe was more of a supplier than I thought he was. He was supplying the cartels with kids, but also drugs.

Cartels would use a lot of random people, men and women, all over the country, to help them generate more money. They would have small time cooks, dealers, kidnappers to produce drugs, sell them, and then send a cut to the cartel. A driver would show up once a month to pick up the cash they were owed and bring it to a cartel stash house. The system was very intricate and it wasn't as simple as taking out one single player. If you wanted to cripple the cartel, you had to take the whole house down. Something that was virtually impossible because any of the higher ups were heavily protected with soldiers, and more often than not, even local police.

"We'll meet back here tomorrow morning at nine to head out to Columbus for the stake out," I added.

We would be heading to Columbus tomorrow and waiting for the chance to grab Vilenti. With any luck, we'll be able to grab him and I could get intel out of him on Monroe. There were a lot of 'what ifs', but that was what this job was in the beginning of a new investigation.

We all made our way up to our hotel rooms. I was ignoring the fact that I would be sharing a hotel room with Jarod. I didn't like sharing hotel rooms, especially since my issue with sleeping had picked up, but it couldn't be helped this time around. I was hoping that I would be able to sleep without too many problems.

The last thing I needed was the guys questioning if I could do my job or not. As far as they would know, I was completely stable and the picture of perfect health, and that was how I was going to keep it.

CHAPTER EIGHTEEN

Jarod

THE RED NUMBERS on the clock told me it was two in the morning. That clock was mocking me, I swear.

I should be exhausted.

I was tired, but I couldn't get my mind to turn off enough for me to fall asleep. I generally read when I got like this, but when you are sharing a hotel room with your new boss, you couldn't exactly leave the light on so you could read.

Not being able to read meant I couldn't get my mind to shut up.

I couldn't stop going over the case and

what our next moves should be if this turned out to be a bust.

What if we couldn't find Vilenti?

Where would we go from there?

Or what if we did find Vilenti and he didn't talk, or he didn't know where Monroe was. I had all of these questions and I had no answers to any of them. I didn't know what the answers would be. I hadn't been able to truly learn while being a detective, because no one in the station wanted to actually teach me anything.

I knew I could have asked Mason or the guys, but I wasn't too comfortable with voicing my questions, just yet. I knew Mason said to ask questions and voice our opinions, but I was still waiting to be told to shut up. I was still waiting to get the same lecture that I had heard a hundred times since I had been promoted.

That I was useless and unimportant.

It wasn't something I could get over in a day or two. It was going to take time, which all seemed pointless because I was only on the task force for this one case. The task force was put together to find Monroe and once we did, there wouldn't be a point in the task force any longer. All of this stressing would be for nothing.

I let out a soft sigh as I rolled over onto my back once more. I was trying to be as quiet as possible so Mason wouldn't be kept awake as well. He had lain down with Koda around midnight and had been asleep ever since. I envied him for being able to fall asleep so fast.

I wished I could do that.

"Can't sleep, either?" Mason's husky voice broke the silence.

How was it possible this man could be even sexier in the middle of the night?

I rolled over so I was facing his bed and saw that he had done the same, without me noticing, as if he was some type of ninja. Hell, maybe he was before all of this. I didn't even know him. I knew his brother had been in the Army before he was a cop.

"I can't get my mind to stop racing," I admitted.

Mason gave a soft hum before he spoke.

"It's a common problem with smart people like yourself. Your mind is going all day long and that makes it hard to shut it off at the end of the day. There's not exactly an off switch you can flip."

My God, he got it.

He actually understood without me having to tell him what was going on with me.

I didn't think this man could get anymore perfect.

I really didn't.

I had lost count of how many times I had lost a boyfriend because of how I slept at night. They always made it seem like something was wrong with me because I could just lie down and cuddle with them. The ones who wanted to cuddle, anyway.

My romantic life had been a series of bad boyfriends and one-night stands that I picked up in a bar. I had not been lucky in love, but at the same time, I hadn't really been trying.

"Be great if there was," I commented back.

"Yeah, a magical switch that can be flipped, and for a good eight hours you stop thinking about anything. That'd be nice to have."

I couldn't help but wonder if Mason had his own issues with sleeping at night. The way he sounded, it made me feel like something more was going on with him.

Like he was in desperate need of a switch to flip to get his mind to stop, too.

"I would have to imagine with the type of cases you get, you must see some pretty horrible things," I said with complete understanding lacing my voice.

I didn't know what it was like for him. What it was like to see children hurt and chase after criminals to try and save more innocent lives. I would have to imagine, though, that it took a toll on a person.

It couldn't be easy.

Nope, not at all.

"I am not a stranger to all-nighters or having a hard time getting to sleep. I try to relieve stress when I can, but it doesn't always work that way when you travel as much as I do."

"Your stress relief doesn't travel with you?" I asked, slightly confused by that.

"No, the TSA frowned upon me putting random guys into my suitcases," he lightly joked.

"Ah, that kind of stress relief. And here I was foolishly using a book. I should keep a good looking guy tied up in my room," I teased back.

I wasn't hiding being gay, and with Mason gay as well, there was no point in denying it or tiptoeing around it. It wasn't like he was going to care. Besides, it was nice to be able to talk about being gay with someone.

I didn't really have any friends that I could be honest and open with. I didn't have a true partner on the force to share any personal details of my life with. It was just me and my mother, and she was not someone I was about to open up with.

"I find that is the best way to get a good night's sleep. You just gotta let him go when you are done so you don't have to worry about kidnapping charges."

"Is that what you do? Keep someone tied up in your bed and let them go when you have shown them all the pleasure in the world?"

I was willing to bet my life that Mason was amazing in bed. He seemed like the type of guy that could throw you around and make your eyes roll into the back of your head. Sex with him was probably earth shattering, ruining you for other men.

"More often than not, it helps to shut my mind off long enough for me to fall asleep afterward."

"I usually read, but your way sounds

much more fun," I said, flashing a small smile even though I knew he couldn't see it.

I would have loved to know what his hands felt like against my skin, but I knew that he wouldn't be interested in someone like me. I was willing to bet he preferred small guys. Most tops who looked like him liked to have smaller guys. They either didn't like to have a larger guy underneath them, or they assumed the guy was a top. Not that I was very big, but I wasn't a small spinner, either. It could make for a bit of an awkward meet up if the guy I'm hooking up with believes I like to top.

"We should try and get some sleep. Morning is going to come a lot faster than you think," Mason said after a moment.

I let out a short hum in agreement, but I knew the chances of me sleeping were pretty slim. Now, my mind couldn't stop thinking about Mason and what he would be like in bed. My body was reacting to my thoughts and I was grateful for us being in the dark.

The only light was from the small streetlights that were on the other side of the window. We were on the third floor, so the lights were still bright enough to reach us, but just enough for us to be able to see the outline of the room.

I was thankful for the darkness, it was the only thing keeping Mason from seeing my growing hard on. Now, this night was going to be even longer and I would be waking up sexually frustrated come morning.

It was a good twenty minutes of nothing but pure silence when Mason's growly voice broke it once again as he turned the small lamp on that was between us.

"Do you have a boyfriend?"

"No. You?"

I wasn't sure why he was asking me. I guess he couldn't sleep any better than I could.

"I don't. You know, we're both single, we both can't sleep, we could do something to relieve stress together," he said, and I could see the heat in his eyes.

I knew exactly what he was talking about and my dick was instantly rock hard. Every logical excuse as to why this was a bad idea went through my head. He was currently my boss and he had the power to ruin my career, mostly. I had every reason to say *no*. To play it off as if he was joking and act like it never happened come morning. That was the most reasonable and responsible thing to do in this situation. And yet, I wanted to throw caution to the wind and allow this man to pound into me.

I didn't do reckless things.

I made sure to be safe and cautious with every single guy I had laid down with. This would be reckless and could come back to bite me in the ass one day.

"I only bottom."

Mason gave me the sexiest smile I had ever seen as he pushed the covers off of himself and made his way over to me. He pulled the covers off of me and then his body was covering mine. The second his lips touched mine, my whole body was on fire. It wasn't just the kiss, but the weight of him against my body.

I loved being with larger men, muscular men, feeling their weight, their strength on my body, it always brought comfort to me. I opened my legs to allow Mason's hips to touch mine. The second our dicks touched we both moaned. We were both already half-hard and Mason ground his chub down onto mine.

I moaned into his mouth as sparks flew all down my spine.

Mason broke the kiss far too soon for my liking, leaning up to just gaze down at me for a moment.

I could see the heat in his eyes and I knew this was going to be earth shattering.

His hands were instantly going to my clothes and I sat up and started to remove his. We were only wearing t-shirts and sweatpants, so it took no time at all to get naked.

I thought he was glorious with his clothes on, but it was nothing compared to the view of his naked form. He was ripped with muscles all over his body. Even his thighs looked like they could squeeze the life out of someone. Then there was his dick. Just the sight of it was making my mouth water. It was beautiful, big and thick, and it was going to feel amazing inside of me. I couldn't help but lick my lips at the glisten of pre-cum on his tip.

"See something you like?" he asked with a cocky smirk.

"Very much so," I answered honestly.

He threaded his hand through my hair

and kept a grip on it as he spoke. "Go ahead and get a taste."

That was all the permission I needed.

I licked my lips, my mouth watering in anticipation of his taste. He guided my head to his dick and I was instantly licking at his tip, pressing my tongue into the slit before sucking on it. I couldn't help but hum my appreciation at the sweet taste of his precum.

I needed more.

I started to take him further into my mouth and I didn't stop until I got all the way down to his base. He was gloriously big and I had to relax my throat so I would be able to take him all the way in.

Mason let out a groan as he started to lightly rock his hips. I couldn't help but moan and whimper as he took control.

I loved it when a man was in charge. I was a bottom. I couldn't help it. I loved to be dominated and I loved when the man I was with took control. I had always been like that and I stopped trying to understand why a long time ago.

"You like that, eh? You like when I fuck your mouth," Mason panted out as he moved his hips faster.

A begging whine escaped my throat. I

did like it when he fucked my mouth. He felt so good in my mouth and in my throat. I could do it all night long and never get tired of it. All too soon, though, he was pulling my head off of his cock and a small whimper escaped me at the loss of him in my mouth.

He sat back and grabbed his pants, pulling out a crumpled condom wrapper and a packet of lube. I watched as his shoulders suddenly slumped as he unfolded the condom.

"I'm sorry, Jarod, I don't have any condoms. This one is damaged and I didn't stop to pick up any, for logical reasons. I didn't expect to hook up while on a case. In fact, it's been a long time since I've been with anyone so grabbing condoms was kind of the last thought on my mind when I packed for this trip."

The man's sudden explosion of diarrhea of the mouth was truly sexy.

"Me either," I breathed out, and my breath hitched.

I wanted this.

I wanted Mason, and I wanted him now.

Could I forgo using a condom?

Did I trust this man enough to do

that?

"I swear to you, I've always used them before, and I get tested regularly. I'm negative," he said.

"So am I."

"You sure you're okay with that?" He tilted my face up with a finger, cupping my cheek in his palm, and concern filled his eyes where before there was nothing but unbridled desire.

I knew I should be saying *no*.

I had never had sex without a condom on before. I always practiced safe sex, even though it'd been a really long time since I'd been with anyone. Still, there was this uncontrollable need within me to feel Mason's skin inside of me. I wanted to feel the heat of his cum buried deep inside of my ass.

Screw logic, tonight I was just going to feel.

"Yes," I simply said.

"On your knees, I want your ass up," he ordered, relief filling his features, and I was instantly following his command.

I felt him get off the bed as I got onto my hands and knees. I bent down on my elbows so my ass was up and on display to him. A moment later, I felt his hands grip my thighs and then he was yanking me to the edge of the bed. I felt his weight on the bed once again, followed by the sound of the lube packet being ripped open.

Mason placed his hand on my ass and ran it over my cheek before he gave it a light slap, causing me to whimper and involuntarily buck my hips.

"You like that, eh?" he asked in a husky, lust-filled voice.

"Yes," I said breathlessly.

He then slapped my ass even harder and I let out a deep moan.

I loved being spanked. I'm sure there was a Shrink somewhere just dying to get their hands on me.

He did it a few more times, each harder them the next, and it only resulted in my dick dripping with precum onto the bed.

"Such a pretty pink," he said as he ran his hands over the heat on my ass cheeks.

"Spread these cheeks for me," Mason demanded, sliding one digit down my crease.

I easily moved and grabbed my ass, spreading my cheeks so he had a clear view of my hole. A moment later, I felt the tip of his lube covered finger pushing inside of me. I sucked in a breath, reveling in the slight burn as he pushed his finger all the way inside of me.

Some bottoms preferred to only have a dick rather than a finger in them. To me, I didn't care what it was as long as it felt amazing.

Mason worked my ass quickly. I knew he was in need just as badly as I was. He quickly added a second finger and started to scissor me so I would be able to accommodate his large dick. When he added a third finger, he hit my sweet spot dead on and I saw stars as heat sizzled up my spine.

"Mason," I moaned.

"I'm going to pound the hell out of you," Mason promised.

"Fuck, yes, please," I begged.

There was nothing that I wanted more than to feel him inside of me. I needed to have sex, I needed to feel a very large dick inside of me and Mason definitely had that.

He removed his fingers from my ass and he then placed his hand on the back of my neck, possessing me and keeping me in this position. I couldn't contain the moan that escaped from my lips. It was like he just knew exactly what I needed.

I felt the crown of his shaft against my hole and it was only a second later when he was pushing inside of me. My eyes closed at the pleasure that surged through me.

He felt so good.

His rigid steel under velvet skin member pushing outward against the heat of my walls, the feeling of fullness, and the burn of the stretch, everything felt like Heaven and I never wanted to leave.

"You're so tight, Baby. It's been a while since you've had a big cock inside of you, eh?"

"Ooh, yes, way too long. Don't stop," I begged.

I needed to feel all of him.

"I'm not stopping until my cum is leaking out of this tight little hole," he promised and that only made me whimper with need.

Once he bottomed out, his balls pressed up tight against my taint, Mason kept his word.

He didn't go slow.

He pulled out almost all of the way before he slammed back in. His pace was fast and rough, and I loved every single second of it.

I couldn't contain the moans, even if my life depended on it. It felt too good. It felt amazing, beyond amazing, and I never wanted it to end. When his dick hit my glands dead on, I had just managed to turn my head into the bed as I screamed in pleasure.

"That's it, Baby, scream for me. Let everyone in this hotel hear how much you love my dick pounding into your ass," Mason said as he picked up his pace even more, snapping his hips and slamming into my ass.

He made sure each thrust hit my prostate and I couldn't stop screaming out. I had never felt this good, not even by my own hand. Mason was playing my body like an instrument and I loved it. I was craving more and he gave me more than I could ever ask for.

I could feel my legs shaking with my need to come. I wanted to touch myself, but I didn't dare. I wanted to see if Mason could do what no man had ever been able to do before. I wanted to know if Mason could make me come without touching my dick. If he could milk me simply from the pleasure he brought from fucking me.

I had lost track of time. The only thing in the world that existed was me and Mason in the hotel room. Time held zero meaning to me. All that I could feel was overwhelming pleasure and it all boiled over when Mason hit my sweet spot with even more force.

I gave a loud scream as I felt my dick pulse and come. I couldn't stop moaning and writhing, bucking my hips and pushing backward as my dick was milked by Mason's thrusts.

He let out a deep moan as he continued hitting my sweet spot even faster.

"Fuck, that's it, Baby. Come for me."

Every time he knocked my sweet spot, it made me come even more. I couldn't believe how this felt. I'd suspected that Mason would be remarkable in bed, but I had no idea it would be this remarkable. It was earth shattering and he was going to ruin me for other men. From this point forward, I was never going to get this level of pleasure from any other man ever again in my life.

I was officially ruined.

Mason's thrusts were becoming more erratic and I knew he was close. A few thrusts later, when he was snapping his hips forward and back in a rapid beat, I felt a wash of heat hitting my walls.

"Fuck," Mason growled as his dick throbbed inside of me.

Feeling his come inside of me made me feel owned.

Like I now belonged to him.

It should have bothered me, but it only made me even more turned on. I wanted to belong to him. I wanted only him to use my body, and no one else.

Mason spoke as he kissed along my spine.

"You feel so good, Baby. So tight and hot. A perfect little ass."

"You feel so good inside of me," I easily agreed.

"And we're just getting started."

"What?" I asked, even though I felt that he was still half-hard inside of me.

"I told you, you were going to have my cum dripping out of you. That doesn't happen after only one time. We got at least two more rounds to go."

"Oh fuck, yes," I whined.

I didn't want this to end. He could have tied me up and left me here for the rest of my life and I would have died happy. We needed sleep, yes, but fuck it, sleep was overrated. This was a night I was never going to forget and would happily submit to Mason for the rest of it.

CHAPTER NINETEEN

Mason

WORDS COULD NOT describe how last night felt.

I knew suggesting that we have sex so we could try and sleep would be a bad idea, but I had no idea it would be bad for this reason. I figured it would make things awkward between us or Jarod would get the wrong idea. I wasn't looking for a relationship. I never was.

But that didn't happen.

It wasn't awkward. In fact, it felt like a normal night for us. As if we always had sex and then go to work the next day.

Which was odd, because I had never felt like that before with anyone. The bad part, though, I was already craving his body. As a rule, I could have sex with someone and then forget about it the next day, but for some reason my body was not looking to forget about Jarod's body underneath mine.

When he said he only bottomed, I expected what typically happened with guys his size. They like the bottom, but they still like to be in control. I didn't really enjoy sex with men who wanted to top from the bottom. With Jarod, though, he loved to bottom. He loved to be submissive, to let me control everything, and it was that fact that was driving me crazy for more.

I thought it would only be one time, one night, but I couldn't do that. I was going to need to have him again. There was no way I could not feel him underneath me again.

Soon.

For now, though, I had to focus on what was going on for today.

We had arrived in Columbus about four hours ago and, so far, all we had accomplished was my ass going numb from sitting in the car for so long. We were here to find Jose Vilenti. He had been in touch with Monroe quite frequently and I was hoping that meant he knew more about him than the others.

We needed to grab Vilenti so I could get Monroe's information out of him. Vilenti wasn't a major criminal. He had his hands in a few different organizations. He was a labor man; someone that floated around and took work wherever it was needed. It worked in our favor because that meant he didn't hold any loyalty to one organization over another. He went where the money was and right now, there was not going to be any money from Monroe.

"Is this guy ever going to show?" Rafe commented over the coms.

I knew the others were getting restless.

I couldn't blame them.

Stakeouts were the worst, especially when said stake out was in a desert. It was hot and there was nothing to look at to try and keep you entertained. There were no people walking around, nothing. It was just hot and made your body hurt from sitting for so long. Vilenti was set to show, though, so everyone was going to have to suck it up.

"He'll be here, relax," I said.

"Can I ask you something?" Jarod said from his seat next to me.

"I told you, you can ask any question you want."

"If Vilenti works for all of these different criminal organizations, how are you going to get him to roll on Monroe? Wouldn't he be even more worried about talking to the police with all of his connections?"

It was a logical question. Most people refuse to snitch when they are loyal to just one organization. Vilenti had multiple organizations that could try and kill him if word got out he was talking to the police.

"Technically, he has more to worry about with having multiple criminals that could come after him. However, because he floats and has all of these criminal connections, those organizations might not suspect him as being the snitch. He has a lot that could come after him, but he also has the protection that he's so low on the importance list that he can easily be overlooked as the snitch," I explained.

"He's protected by the numbers above him," Jarod said, nodding with complete understanding.

"Do you think he will talk?" he asked.

"I'll get it out of him," I said confidently.

"You sound so confident. I don't even think I would know what to say to someone in an interrogation."

"You've never done one before?"

It wasn't really that surprising. He worked in a small town.

I mean, seriously, what did they have to interrogate someone for?

Cow tipping?

If they did, in fact, buy a hooker?

There wasn't much at stake in a town like Gaithersburg.

"No, I've never seen one being done. I'm not really allowed to get that close to a case. I usually just handle paperwork."

"Because that is all they will allow you to do. I've seen your file and I know that you have helped other stations with cases. You have more closes under your belt than what that file says. You let people push you around, so they will naturally take advantage of that. It's why you have to stand up for yourself, Jarod. Be dominant at work and keep all of your submissiveness for the bedroom," I said that last part with a sexy smirk as heat filled his cheeks.

"I guess I've always been submissive in life. I don't like confrontation. Growing up, I did what I was told and stayed out of the way. I guess I'm just used to being ignored and doing what I'm told," Jarod reluctantly admitted.

I could see how it would be hard for someone like him. He didn't have much confidence in himself. He knew he was skilled, but even that lacked confidence. He was so much better than he gave himself credit for. Again, though, that could be connected to his intelligence.

"Not liking confrontation can be hard when you need to stand up for yourself. You're a genius, Jarod, that can make for a difficult time socially. You don't interact like the other guys at the station do, so you don't know how to connect with them. You just need to find your people and they will protect you from the assholes of the world."

"I don't want protection, though. I should be able to protect and defend myself," he said, and I could hear the self-hatred edging his tone.

"You have to learn how to stand up for

yourself and part of that is feeling safe while doing it. That's where the protection comes in. If you knew without a doubt that whenever Baxter said something homophobic that you could punch him and nothing would happen to you, then you would do it. You would tell him to shut the hell up, because you knew that your people would keep you safe from him. The first step in standing up for yourself, is allowing that protection to come from people."

It wasn't easy to learn if you had never experienced it when you were younger. I could tell by the way Jarod interacted with the guys on the team that he didn't get many social interactions growing up. In high school, and even grade school, kids naturally flocked to their own kind. Jarod would have interacted with the other smart kids in the school. Unfortunately, that would have only added a bigger target on his back from jocks and bullies. And smart kids didn't have the social skills or the physical fitness to stand up for themselves and their friends. There wasn't really a set protector in the group and that resulted in adults who didn't know how to stand up for themselves.

I wasn't sure how long I would have with Jarod, but I was going to make sure he knew that I was there for him. Even if he didn't want to be on the task force after this, I was still going to be in his corner, protecting him. And when I couldn't be in town, I would make sure Roland was watching over him.

"It's a learning process, I guess. I always thought I wasn't too bad at interacting with different people. I'm good with victims, but the other cops at the station, I guess I just go back to my high school days where I kept my head down and did what I was told. The bullies didn't beat you up if you did their homework," he said with a small shrug.

"Here's what your fellow cops won't tell you. They aren't allowed to touch you, otherwise they would lose their job. The cops in your station, Jarod, they're all bark. They lost their teeth a long time ago. They have nothing to bite at you with. All you have to do to get them to shut up is hit them with a rolled up newspaper and show your teeth."

"A dog analogy from a K9 handler, I'm shocked," he lightly teased.

MASON

"Don't make me get the newspaper out," I warned playfully.

"I guess that would depend on where you're going to hit me with it," he said with a cocky grin.

I couldn't contain the groan that escaped my body. My mind was flooded by the sounds of his moans and whimpers from every time I slapped his ass last night. He did like to be spanked, and I loved spanking. It was like he was made for me and that should have scared me, but it didn't.

I had no idea what was happening. I had never felt like this before with anyone I had been with, not even my long-term fuck buddies. There was something special about Jarod and my body wanted an endless supply of him.

"We got movement at your ten o'clock, Boss," Ryzen's voice came over the coms.

I turned to look out of my window and I saw Vilenti walking over and sitting down on a picnic table. The area was deserted, so I knew we wouldn't have to worry about anyone getting the jump on us. He was there to wait for a shipment of drugs and when he wasn't there, the drug runners would wait for further instructions.

"Move in," I said over the coms.

We all got out of our vehicles and made the distance toward Vilenti. I thought he would run when he saw us coming, but apparently the man was too lazy for it. Not that I minded. I wasn't in the mood to chase after him in this heat.

"Jose Vilenti," I started.

"Fed," he said with a nod.

"You're coming with us back to El Paso for questioning," I stated.

"Questioning for what? I haven't done anything. Unless it's illegal to pull over for some fresh air and a smoke?" he said with a smirk.

Technically, we couldn't arrest him. He wouldn't have anything on him that we could use for grounds for an arrest. He also had no outstanding warrants.

Vilenti had been careful in his criminal life. He only had a couple arrests as a juvenile and the records were sealed. Nothing as an adult, and at thirty-eight, that was impressive. He was smart, but I suspected it was more than that.

"I didn't say you were under arrest, I said we're going to question you. I don't need to charge you with anything to do that."

"Get up," Rafe said as he grabbed Vilenti's bicep and lifted him off of the picnic table.

Vilenti was not a big guy and when you were Rafe's size, you could throw a grown ass man around like a rag doll. He slapped some cuffs on him before we all headed off for our vehicles.

We now had Vilenti and I would be getting any intel he had on Monroe out of him. I was not about to let that son of a bitch slip away. Vilenti would talk or I would make sure he didn't live very long once we let him go.

If he was as smart as he thought he was, he would spill and live to see another day.

CHAPTER TWENTY

Jarod

THE DRIVE BACK to the Homeland Security Field Office in El Paso was done in silence. It wasn't an awkward silence, though, so I was happy for it.

I wasn't sure what this morning would be like with Mason after last night. I wasn't sure if it would be awkward or uncomfortable. I hadn't been with someone in a good chunk of time so the whole 'morning after' scenario was pretty new to me.

I didn't expect for it to feel so comfortable, though. Routine, almost. As if that had always been our morning. It made no sense, because we barely knew each other, but I couldn't help but feel like we were kindred spirits, in a sense.

I wasn't expecting the connection, but I also wasn't expecting for him to be so understanding and insightful about who I was.

Most people didn't understand my mind. They didn't understand how my intelligence did make it hard for me during different social situations. I was so used to having to be quiet all the time. Having to take up as little space as possible so my parents wouldn't see me.

It had been the same in school.

Bullies were everywhere, so I stayed hidden. I stayed in the library when I could. I didn't go to social parties. I was the awkward smart kid who was an easy target for everyone in the school.

I thought when I became a cop that it would be different.

I figured that cops wouldn't be bullies. I thought that they would understand and accept that everyone was different and it would be okay. I thought that I would have finally found my place in the world.

My family.

But I had only been proven wrong.

It was like school all over again, and I had fallen into the same patterns that worked for me while I was in school. It never even crossed my mind that I should be standing up for myself. That I could stand up for myself without the fear of being hit.

It was a nice thought, but what Mason didn't know was that it wasn't true.

I had stood up for myself a few times with Baxter, but he had hit me. There had been a good handful of times that I'd had a black eye or a bruise on my cheek that I had to lie about.

I didn't know what I was going to do after the task force was completed. I knew the abuse with Baxter would get worse, because I would have had a hand in arresting his best friend. A man, despite all of the evidence, he still believed was innocent.

That was a problem for another day.

When we arrived, we all headed up to our area. I went with the others to the interrogation viewing room on the other side of a two-way mirror.

Mason took Vilenti into the interrogation room and attached the cuffs to a metal hoop in the center of the table. This was going to be my first interrogation and I was looking forward to seeing Mason's technique. This could very well be the only interrogation that I got to view if Monroe decided not to give himself up. I wanted to learn as much as possible.

"Jose Vilenti, I am Supervisory Special Agent Mason Wright with Homeland Security. You are here today because you have been in contact with a fugitive that we have been tracking, Jasper Monroe," Mason started.

"Never heard of him," Vilenti instantly said and I rolled my eyes. Of course he would say that.

"We have your phone number in his burner phone. We already know that you have spoken with him on numerous occasions. Just like we know he has been using the foster children he had taken in to cook cocaine and sell it. He has also been selling children to a sex trafficking ring and has killed numerous other children who threatened to expose him. We can do this whole dance if you want, but do you really want to protect a child murderer? Do you really want to protect someone that is selling children to be raped and, eventually, killed?"

"Why would he care?" I couldn't help but ask.

Vilenti was a criminal. He was connected to a lot of criminal organizations that did all sorts of things.

So why would he care about Monroe's crimes?

"Believe it or not, but criminals also have a code. It's why in prisons they have to put child molesters and child abusers in solitary confinement to ensure they don't get killed. You could murder a thousand people and no one would care. But if you killed a child, if you molested one, they'll all try to kill you," Rafe started.

"Children are meant to be innocent and protected, even criminals know that. None of them will try and protect someone like Monroe. Mason isn't going to waste time trying to dance around. Sometimes, it's easier to tell someone the truth and let their moral compass do the work. It doesn't work for every crime, but in this situation it does," Cooper added.

That made sense, but I wasn't sure if it would work. We had no idea what Vilenti had done for Monroe. He could have been helping him hide children that were to be sold, for all we knew. Still, it was an interesting piece of knowledge that I would be keeping with me.

"Let's just say that I did know a Monroe, I didn't know he was into any of that," Vilenti started carefully.

"You are a small-time fish, Vilenti. I don't care what you do for the other organizations you work for. I don't care about the shipment of drugs you are supposed to be picking up, right now. I don't care that you were running drugs for Monroe. All I care about, is getting this son of a bitch and finding the kids that he sold like cattle. If you give me what I need, you can walk right out of here. You still got enough time to get back to Columbus and make it look like you were fashionably late," Mason said.

I could see Vilenti was thinking about it, but I knew he would take it. You could tell he wanted to get out of here, and if he had to roll on Monroe, then he would do it. I was hoping he would be able to tell us something that we could use to find Monroe. I didn't want to go on a scavenger hunt for this man.

"I knew about him making drugs, but I

didn't know he was a foster parent or any of that stuff with the kids. If I had known, I would have killed him. I was just picking up the drugs and running the money to where it needed to go. I don't know where he is, but I know he's connected to some big hitters."

"How do you know that?"

"Because when I would run the money, it was always fifty grand and it was given to the same guy. He's a runner for the Sinaloa Cartel down in Mexico. He's the border guy. There's always talk within the grapevine about who the new members are of the cartels. Monroe, though, he's an old guy with them. Everyone who is anyone knew of him. He had been around for decades and all of the runners knew better than to cross him. As far as we all knew, he was a drug leader for the cartel for the East Coast."

If he was connected to a cartel, this was going to be even more complicated. I didn't know much about cartels, but I knew that their reach went very far. They had cartel members all over the country and there was no telling where Monroe could be hiding out.

"Where is he?" Mason asked.

"I don't know. He sent me a text, though, letting me know his new number. I can give you the number."

Mason pushed the pad of paper and a pen over to Vilenti as he spoke.

"If you hear from him before we grab him, you're going to text me. I need him alive so I can try and track down the children he sold."

"I got ya," Vilenti agreed.

Mason handed him his card before he got up. He removed the cuffs and walked him out of the room.

We all headed out of the viewing room and Mason handed Cooper the pad of paper before he walked off with Vilenti to let him go. The rest of us moved to the conference room and Cooper was instantly going to his laptop to try and find Monroe from his new number.

"Could Monroe really be connected to a cartel?" Hollingsworth asked.

"People who make drugs are generally connected to a gang or a cartel. They have the market and it's not like you can open a mom and pop drug making business," Rafe answered.

"How would he have even gotten involved with a cartel, though? He's always lived in Gaithersburg," Hollingsworth asked next.

"You'd be surprised what people can do in their free time. He could have had a friend from growing up that is in a cartel now. You never know where your childhood friends will end up," Rafe answered again.

True, but this seemed really farfetched. He had to have gotten involved with them, somehow. He had to cross paths with someone that got him involved and he must have gone from the ground up. We had no idea how high he went, but if Vilenti was tight, he was supplying drugs to the East Coast. That was no small feat and he had a lot more runners than just the kids he was fostering.

Mason walked into the room roughly five minutes later and I could tell he was itching to move. We were getting closer with each lead we found and this could be what brought us to Monroe finally.

"You got him, Coop?" he asked.

"The phone is on. He's not expecting for us to ever find the new number. I'm tracking it, now."

"Do you think he'll be local?" I asked Mason.

"I doubt it. If he's connected to the Sinaloa Cartel, he could be anywhere," Mason answered.

"Aw, shit," Cooper said from his spot.

"How bad?" Mason asked.

I had no idea how he knew that whatever Cooper found was going to be bad, but apparently, they had already developed a shorthand with each other.

"I can't pinpoint a physical address. That will take a lot more work to get, but I know what town he's in," Cooper started.

"Where?" Mason asked.

"Mexico City."

"As in Mexico?" I asked, shocked.

If Monroe wasn't in the States, did that mean we couldn't go after him?

I had no idea what type of reach the task force had, but I knew as a cop, I could only operate within the United States.

"The one and only. It's going to take me time to find a physical address, Boss," Cooper answered.

"That's fine. Everyone pack up and let's get to the airport. We need to get to Mexico City. When we get there, Coop, start looking for Monroe by his phone. The rest of us will see who he could be connected to in Mexico City. We know he's most likely connected to the Sinaloa Cartel, so let's see what stash houses they have where they could be hiding him," Mason said.

Apparently, we could operate in Mexico.

Holy shit, I was going to Mexico.

I had never been outside of the country and I didn't think a manhunt would be my reasoning for it. This task force was bringing me a lot of firsts and I had no idea how I was ever going to survive going back to being just a detective in Gaithersburg.

I was going to die of boredom after all of this.

We all started to pack up the conference room before we would need to do the same for our hotel rooms. We were going to Mexico and, hopefully, we would be able to bring Monroe to justice.

CHAPTER TWENTY-ONE

Mason

"HOW WAS THE flight?" Roland asked.

We had landed roughly two hours ago and had settled into the hotel for the night. Tomorrow, we would be trying to locate Monroe in Mexico City. I was hoping he was laying low somewhere and not in a Sinaloa Cartel stronghold. That would make everything more complicated and I wasn't certain we would be able to extract him without getting everyone killed. I would have to wait and see where Monroe was hiding out. Maybe we would get lucky and he was sitting in some motel, somewhere.

When we had gotten in the room, I had set up my laptop and video called Roland to see what he had.

"It was fine. Any news?"

I was hoping to get some good news from him. It was sad that good news in this case would be to locate a mass grave of children's remains, but it would at least be something. Depending on how Monroe killed them, there might be evidence still left on their bodies. Evidence we could use to put the final nail into his coffin. It was one thing to try and play dumb about drugs being made in your own basement, it was another to have evidence of you killing a child. He wouldn't be able to talk his way out of that. And no jury in the world would believe he didn't kill and bury all of the kids, if we had evidence that connected him to one single body.

"Damien and Sebastian were able to locate the mass grave for the children. It was approximately forty-five minutes from town, in a clearing in the woods. They went in with ground penetrating sonar to locate the grave. They haven't started to dig yet, though. They wanted to see what you wanted them to do. But Mase,

Damien said it looks like there's close to a hundred remains in the clearing."

"A hundred?" Jarod said as he got up off the bed and joined me at the table.

That was a lot higher than I was expecting. I knew Tyler had said that Monroe had killed a few when they became too much of a risk, but I didn't know it would be anywhere near that number. He had clearly been killing kids a lot longer than we expected.

"Is Damien sure they are children and it's not a Native burial ground?" I asked.

I wasn't sure if the woods that Damien located the bodies in were sacred at some point in history. It wouldn't be the first time I had been looking for a mass grave and stumbled upon a native burial ground.

"Damien isn't an expert at reading skeletons from sonar, but he did say they were small. None of them appeared to be large enough for an adult. There's also no markings in the area to indicate that it is sacred ground. Sebastian also did some research, but nothing has come up that would lead us to believe that Natives are buried there."

"But a hundred? How could he kill

that many kids and no one noticed anything? Gaithersburg isn't exactly a big town, someone had to have noticed the children missing at some point," Jarod commented.

He took the words right out of my mouth.

I knew Monroe had been a foster parent for close to twenty years, but a hundred kids, that was five kids a year. Five kids every year that went missing, all before they were old enough to be a legal adult. It wasn't like Monroe was taking on seventeen year olds that you could kill and say they aged out. He was taking kids under fourteen. You can't kill kids that young and have it go unnoticed. Someone should have noticed that Monroe was losing five kids every year. There was clearly a pattern. No one was that unlucky that they had that many kids go missing every year.

"There's no way he doesn't have someone on the inside in Social Services," I said.

"I ran every name with Social Services, starting with Tyler's social worker at the time. Everyone came back clean. However, Isaiah and I have been going over every file for every child that Monroe took in. It's close to three hundred kids. All have come from towns all around us, all with different social workers. However, the ones that Tyler remembered being killed or sold, they all had the same Social Worker. That Social Worker died of cancer three months ago."

"So what, Monroe made sure to only kill those kids?" Jarod asked, confused.

"Did he cover the other kids up?" I asked, because that was weird to me, as well. Monroe wouldn't have been able to predict which kids would be at risk of talking. Yes, he could pick which kids he was going to sell, but you couldn't control what kid would open their mouth or not.

"We're just starting to really trace everything. It's a big ass paper trail, but from what we can tell, some of the kids that have gone missing were transferred over to that Social Worker. A David Burn. He had been working for Social Services for thirty years. I suspect that Monroe and Burn knew each other and were in on it all together. I'm working on getting Burn's finances and going through them to see if he got any money outside of his paycheck."

"All right, chase it down. We need to know if anyone else within Social Services has been helping Monroe. I don't want to leave any dirty Social Workers behind. We need to do a clean sweep of all Social Services in the surrounding towns, too. I'll let my boss, Keyes, know what is going on and he'll help you if anyone wants to give you trouble handing the files over."

I wasn't about to allow anyone to hurt or exploit a child. If there were more dirty Social Workers, I was going to find them and make sure they paid for their crimes. They were supposed to be there for children in need. They were not supposed to add more pain to their lives.

"I'll handle it. What do you want us to do about the grave? Do you have someone that could handle the recovery, because we sure as hell don't."

"I'll put the call in and have a forensic team and an anthropologist down there to handle the recovery and look over the bodies. Collect all of the files for the children that have disappeared and see about any dental records for them. The anthropologist will need something to identify the bodies with."

"I'll get right on it and try to have what

they need by the time they arrive. Most haven't been reported missing. It looks like Burn just has them relocated to a place that doesn't exist. It's going to take time to figure out just how many have been sold over the past thirty years and if Monroe was the only foster parent doing this. We're going to have to go through all past and present foster parents to make sure none of them are dirty, as well."

That was going to be the issue.

It was a huge undertaking, but it was one we needed to take on. It wouldn't be instant, it was going to be a lot of long hours over months to go over every single file, but it had to be done. I couldn't control what happened outside of Gaithersburg's area, but I was going to be living there, now. That town was going to be my home and I was not about to let any child in my area be in danger.

Not while I could prevent it.

"We'll get everyone we can on it. Damien and Sebastian also have their own guys that can jump in to help go through the files. Isaiah had brought on Travis to help as well. We'll get it done, no matter how long it takes. Every child will be identified and buried properly," Roland said with determination in his voice.

"You're damn right we will. Get everyone you can on it. I'll get the team down there right away. They should arrive tomorrow morning just before noon."

"Everything else going okay where you are?"

"We're gonna track Monroe down tomorrow and, hopefully, we can easily extract him. I'll let you know when we have him. Keep an eye on Tyler. The closer we get, the more heat Monroe will feel."

"I have him in my eyesight at all times. Don't worry about us. you focus on grabbing Monroe. I love you, little brother."

"Love you, too."

"Keep an eye on him, Lopez," Roland said with a nod to Jarod next to me.

"I promise, Sir," Jarod easily said.

If Roland only knew just how much of an eye Jarod had been keeping on me. We said a quick goodbye before I ended the call.

Jarod went back to work on his own research while I made the call to Keyes and got him fully updated. He was going to get us a forensic team down to the mass grave and get us the best anthropologist to help make the identifications.

It was going to take time.

I knew some of the remains we wouldn't have any dental records for. Children who grew up in the foster system didn't often visit a dentist unless the foster parent had no choice. Some of the older remains were going to take a lot more work to try and identify, and the reality was, we might never be able to. That was okay, though, because we would give them names and a proper burial.

We would make sure they were never forgotten again.

It was nearing eleven at night when my eyes could no longer focus to read. It had been a long few weeks and I hadn't been sleeping very well. That was the problem with being dyslexic. If I didn't get enough sleep, after a while the words all blurred together and the letters got mixed up. Reading became impossible.

I let out a sigh and rubbed my eyes to try and get them to wake back up.

"You okay?" Jarod asked from his spot on his bed.

"Yeah, I've just lost the ability to read,"

I said with a sigh.

"Can you read this to me?" I asked, pointing to an email that I was trying to read.

"Um... yeah, sure," Jarod said and I could tell he wasn't certain if I was playing around or not. He came and sat down next to me and I turned my laptop around so he could see it.

"All right, it says that Monroe has not been placed on any watch list. The feds in Mexico had no idea he could be connected to the Sinaloa Cartel. There's no file on him on any federal level."

"I didn't think there would be, but it had to be checked."

I could see the question in his eyes, but he wasn't going to ask. It wasn't something that bothered me nor was it something I had been trying to hide.

"I have dyslexia. When I get too tired, the words and letters get mixed up and I can't read."

"It's impressive that you've been able to become a federal agent with it. I know some learning disabilities can be really hard to overcome. Just goes to show how determined and resilient you are," he said with a warm smile.

MASON

This man was remarkable.

I was never sure how someone was going to react to hearing that I had a learning disability. There had been a point in my life where I couldn't read at all. Roland had been the one to spend hours with me, helping me learn how to rewire my brain so I could read. Most tended to think something was wrong with me, that I had been given special treatment for me to be a Fed. I didn't have a propensity to tell people about being dyslexic, but I suspected that Jarod wouldn't hold it against me.

"I think it's time to call it a night," I said as I closed my laptop.

"But how will we ever fall asleep?" Jarod said with a playful grin.

Having sex with him more than once could very well be dangerous. I knew that. But fuck, it was so good, and I had never slept better in my life.

We were only having fun.

There was no harm in that, right?

I couldn't help but smirk at him as I reached for my handcuffs that were sitting on the table.

"I can think of something," I said as I dangled the handcuffs off my index finger.

Jarod gave a soft whimper at the idea and I knew he was on board.

I stood as I spoke again.

"Strip."

"Yes, Sir," Jarod easily said with a playful smirk.

Hearing the *Sir* coming out of his mouth only made my dick throb and grow hard.

He got up and started to strip for me, keeping his gaze on me as he removed each article of clothing. Once he was naked, I allowed myself to take in how beautiful his body was. How smooth his olive skin was.

I could still vividly remember how amazing his body felt against my own skin last night. How tight his ass was around my dick.

I could never get tired of it.

A dangerous thought, in and of itself, but I pushed that away, for now. The only thing that mattered was the naked body in front of me.

I removed my own clothes before I grabbed some lube and then made my way over to Jarod. I placed my hand on the center of his chest and pushed him back toward the bed.

Tonight, we were going to do things a bit differently.

Once I got him down onto the bed by the headboard, I grabbed each of his wrists and brought them up to the post. I cuffed him so he wouldn't be able to remove his arms from the position I wanted him in. I then went and placed myself before his legs, legs that he eagerly opened for me.

I could see that he was already hard without me even having to touch him. He liked to be dominated and that only made him even sexier. I bent down so my mouth was just above his.

"Don't move," I demanded.

"Yes, Sir," he said in a breathy voice.

"Good boy."

I closed the small gap between us, pressing my lips against Jarod's. He was instantly hungrily kissing me back. I could feel the need in him was growing fast. He had clearly been sexually starving for a long time, now. Maybe he didn't get out much and had one-night stands, or the men he had been with couldn't give him the dominance his body was craving.

I couldn't blame him.

There had been too many times where

I had to settle for something less than what I wanted in the bedroom. Sometimes, the need to have sex was too great to wait around for the right person to come along.

I pulled back and grabbed the lube. I slicked up three of my fingers and watched him as I inserted my index finger.

Jarod gave a throaty moan as I entered him and he wiggled his hips slightly.

"I said don't move," I said with a sharp edge to my voice.

"Sorry, Sir," Jarod easily said, and I could tell he was struggling not to push down and get my finger in further.

He was in a deep need tonight and that only fueled me on. If we hadn't been on a clock, I would have dragged this out for hours. I would have slowly finger fucked him until he was begging me to pound the fuck out of him.

However, sadly, we were on a clock.

We couldn't be awake all night having mind-blowing sex, so I would have to settle for a preview of what was to come.

I quickly added a second finger and Jarod moaned and fought not to move his hips. He was able to keep himself still, though, and I rewarded him by adding my third finger.

"Oh god," he moaned as his pleasure was spiked. And again he stayed still like he had been told.

"That's my good boy. Tell me, what do you want?" I asked in a husky voice as my fingers just missed his sweet spot.

"You. I want you, Sir," he said with a whimper as I continued to move my fingers close to his sweet spot, but purposely never hitting it.

"To do what?"

"Fuck me, Sir."

"You mean like this?" I asked as I playfully circled around his prostate, just skimming it with my fingers.

"Oh, please. I need to feel your dick inside of me, Sir."

The sweet begging coming off his lips was what did me in. I couldn't hold out any longer. I had to feel him, again. Next time, though, next time I was going to be dragging this out.

Once the case was closed, he was going to be all mine for a whole night.

I removed my fingers from his ass and grabbed the back of his thighs, lifting them up to his chest. The position put his ass completely on display and it also almost folded him in half. He was completely at my mercy, and I loved it.

What made it better was I knew he loved it, too.

I easily lined myself up with his hole and slowly pushed my tip in between the tight muscles. We both moaned at the glorious sensation and I knew there would be no holding back tonight.

"It's gonna be hard and fast. You feel too good," I warned.

"Fuck, yes. Fuck me, Sir."

I pistoned my hips forward, slamming every inch of my dick inside of him, relishing in the friction, and hitting his glands dead on.

Jarod gave a loud moan as he was finally getting exactly what he wanted.

He was so tight and hot.

I would never get tired of this.

I kept my pace fast and brutal. I knew this round was going to be quick, but I had no intention of going just one round. I wouldn't keep us up all night, but I was going to enjoy Jarod's body for a couple of hours.

I made sure to aim for his sweet spot each time, bringing him closer and closer to the edge.

"Oh fuck." Jarod moaned deeply as his cock pulsed and released some precum.

I knew he was close, his shaft was straining against its skin, the tip already purple and filled with blood, but he needed some help to get over the edge.

I snaked my hand around his hardness and started to jerk him off in unison with my thrusts.

"Come for me, my little Slut."

A shiver of pleasure shot throughout Jarod's whole body as he moaned at my words.

"Someone likes to be called a slut. Or maybe it's because you're *my* slut," I whispered against his skin as I pressed kisses along Jarod's neck.

"Yes, Sir, only yours," he said breathlessly as his legs trembled with the need to come.

He was so beautiful like this.

I had no idea he would ever be this much of a submissive bottom. He didn't look it, but he did like to be dominated, and his love of it was only driving me crazier.

"You're so close. Come for me, now."

Jarod gave a deep moan and a

whimper as my words pushed him over the edge. Due to our position, though, his cum hit his face. Between the sight of his own cum on his face and the tightness of his walls around my dick, I was falling off the cliff right behind him.

I felt Jarod pulse out more cum as I came hard inside of him.

I was never going to get tired of this sensation. Of feeling how tight and hot he was. His walls hugged my dick like they never wanted to be without it.

We were both breathing heavily, but that never stopped me from continuing before.

"You look so sexy like this. Restrained with your own cum on your face. Most beautiful thing I have ever seen," I said as I bent forward and ran my tongue along his cheek to get some of his cum. I couldn't help but moan at the sweet taste of him. I hadn't tasted him before. Our first time, I wasn't certain how adventurous he was and it was more about just trying to burn off energy so we could sleep. But now, I knew he liked to be dominated. He liked being submissive, and that opened up a whole world of possibilities.

I moved and kissed him roughly and he melted into it. He eagerly opened his mouth when my tongue licked and chewed at his lips. The second my tongue was in his mouth, he let out a breathy moan as the taste of himself hit his tongue.

His tongue was licking at my own, trying to get every trace of taste off of it. At just the knowledge that he liked his own taste, I was rock hard again and ready for the next round.

Tonight was only a preview of what was to come for us, because once this case was closed, I was going to need at least a couple of days alone with him before I would be satisfied.

CHAPTER TWENTY-TWO

Jarod

THE SOUND OF groaning brought me out of a deep sleep.

I squinted my eyes open and saw that it was only three in the morning. I let out my own groan as I realized that I had only been asleep for an hour.

Mason and I had thoroughly enjoyed the other's body for close to two hours before we decided to call it a night. I knew what we were doing was stupid. I shouldn't be having sex with my boss, even a temporary boss, but Mason was too good to resist. His skills in the bedroom were off the wall amazing.

I was never going to regret it.

The groaning sound turned into moans of what sounded like pain.

I pushed myself up and looked over at Mason's bed. We didn't sleep next to each other, that wasn't what we were doing. What we shared was just sex, cuddling was off the table.

I could see Mason's brow creased, even in the darkness of the room. He was having a nightmare. I reached over and turned on the bedside light between us before I got up. I knew better than to shake a highly trained man while he was sleeping. Mason hadn't been in the military, but he was just as deadly. Koda's head had popped up and I figured maybe he would be able to help me.

"Koda, wake Mason up."

I knew Koda didn't have to listen to me, but thankfully, he jumped up from his spot on the bed and instantly went over to Mason. The German Shepherd laid down on Mason's chest, and started to nudge and lick at his face.

"Mason, come on, wake up," I said a bit loudly to try and help Koda get him awake.

MASON

It was a moment later when Mason's eyes snapped open and he shot up into a sitting position. He was breathing heavily and I could see his body trembling. Whatever the nightmare was, it was bad enough to affect his whole body.

"It's okay. You're in Mexico City," I said.

Mason looked over at me and I could see the confusion in his eyes starting to dissipate.

However, it did nothing for the deep pain that I saw there.

I needed to take that pain away.

I wanted to make it better.

I wanted to get rid of that pain from him.

There was this undeniable pull I had toward Mason. I had no idea what was going on between us. The connection I felt for him was so intense and it made no sense. We barely knew each other and yet, everything in me was screaming for him. I felt like I had known him my whole life, which was insane and not something that had ever happened to me before.

Mason looked around the room before his gaze landed on me. I could tell he was embarrassed about waking me up from him having a nightmare, but he had no reason to be. We all get them and I would be willing to bet my life that his nightmares were a direct result from the work that he did.

"Sorry," he said with a shaky voice.

"You have nothing to be sorry for. If I had to see half of the horrors that you have with doing this job, I would be terrified to close my eyes. You're really brave to keep doing this job."

"No, I'm not. I'm weak." Mason looked down as he spoke.

I moved so I was sitting on the bed in front of him before I spoke in a gentle voice.

"No, you're not. Why would you think that?"

I could see the self-hatred flash through his eyes. Something more was going on with him. I couldn't help but be worried that something was wrong with him, that he had been hiding some type of medical condition. Because there was nothing he could tell me that would have me believing that he was weak. He was the bravest man I had ever met and there was nothing he could say that would ever change that.

"I was supposed to be on vacation when this case started. Everyone thinks I'm just taking some time to unwind, but an outside shrink diagnosed me with PTSD."

I could hear the self-hatred and disgust in his voice. He thought that made him weak. He thought it made him less of a man because he was experiencing problems from the horrors he had seen.

It wasn't even just what he had seen. I saw him naked. I had seen the scars. He had been in fights. He had experienced trauma along with the mental abuse he had experienced every day he went to work. The fact that he had been diagnosed with PTSD and he was still here, still fighting to find Monroe and save children, it only showed me how strong and dedicated he was to helping people.

I reached out and placed my hand on the side of his face as I spoke.

"That doesn't make you weak. The fact that you are here, still doing this job with PTSD, that makes you strong. Babe, the very last thing you are is weak."

"I don't want anyone knowing."

"Your secret is safe with me," I easily

promised.

He gave me a small smile and I could tell he needed a distraction. He had just told me something very personal and it was only fair that I did the same for him. I didn't want to tell anyone this, but it only seemed fair to share something this personal with him after what Mason had just shared with me. I was also hoping that he wouldn't judge me or hold it against me. That he would understand what my father did was completely out of my control and it didn't mean that I would be a killer as well.

"My father was the River Walk Killer."

"What?" he asked, confused. I could tell he wasn't confused by the sudden change in topics, but what I had changed it to.

"Deigo Santiago. That was my father. I was fifteen when my mother and I discovered he was murdering people. Agent Morgan Torres from the FBI showed up on our doorstep with his arrest warrant. We thought they were confused, but then, in a secret hidden room in our basement, they found photos and a lock of hair from each of his victims. Ninety-three women were killed by his hands."

"Holy shit. I heard about that case. It was discussed in my training classes in the academy. It was huge. You changed your last name."

"I did, but not to my mother's maiden name. Lopez is actually my middle name. I didn't want anyone to be able to look up my name and find out who my father was. I've kept it quiet. I didn't want anyone to judge me for his actions. It's why I can't be in a federal agency or major city for work. There's too many chances that someone could figure it out."

"What happened after he was arrested?"

"A shitshow. My mother kept hoping that it was all some big misunderstanding. As if the photos and locks of hair were placed in a secret room in our home by a complete stranger. After my father was convicted to multiple life sentences, she started to spiral. They were never loving parents. They didn't want to be parents, but they had me. It was as if I was a cat that they had to adopt and just live with. I took care of myself and I made sure the bills were paid. I managed the money when my mother couldn't. She started to use heroin and when the mortgage got to be too much, she sold the house and moved into an apartment before I went to the police academy. When she used all of her money, she moved into an apartment that was disgusting and barely standing. She does heroin all day long and prostitutes to cover her usage and rent."

I hated that my own mother was a prostituting heroin addict. I hated that she paid her rent with her body and that she used so much heroin that she couldn't even keep up with the cash to pay for the drugs. That she would be beat up and have her life on the line, all for some brown powder. It never made sense to me and it never would.

"I'm sorry you had to go through that. She doesn't want to get clean?"

"No. I've tried. Three times I've put her through rehab, but she always relapses within thirty days. A few years ago, she was in the hole ten grand with her dealers. She was almost beaten to death, so I paid 'em off. She just kept using after that. She doesn't want to be sober. And I can't make her be sober. Eventually, the drugs will kill her or a John will, but there's nothing I can do about that. I have to focus on the people that I can save, the ones that want to be saved."

"Unfortunately, that's all you can do. She has to want to be sober, otherwise it won't work. But you already know that. I'm sorry you've had to go through that. But I want you to know that it doesn't change what I think of you. I'm never going to judge you based on your parents' actions. It's your own actions that dictate your character and you have shown me that you are a good man who wants to make the world a better place," Mason said with a warm smile and it instantly hit me right in my own heart.

This man couldn't get any more perfect.

It was too bad he was only interested in sex, because I would have definitely been interested in more. From the very little I knew about him, I wanted to know more. I wanted to know everything about him, the good and the bad.

"You're a good man, too, Mason. Your PTSD doesn't make you weak and it doesn't change that you are still putting yourself through the trauma of this job to help people. To save more children. You're a good man and I am lucky to have met you," I said, flashing him a warm smile.

He gave me one in return and I could see that bit of darkness and pain in his eyes starting to dissipate. It made me feel good to know that I had been able to help him through this bout of darkness, but I also knew it was only a drop in the bucket for him. He had a long road to go if he ever wanted to be fully recovered, but I was hoping I would be around to see some of it. That after Monroe was caught whatever was going on between us wouldn't be over. Even if it was just sex whenever he could be in town, it was better than nothing.

"We need sleep. We have a long couple of days ahead of us," he said after a moment.

I gave a nod. He was right, we had to get some sleep with what we had ahead of us. If Monroe was located in a dangerous area of the city, we couldn't risk being too tired or rundown. I went to get up, but Mason's hand on mine stopped me.

"Sleep with me?" he asked, and I could hear the uncertainty in his voice. I hated hearing the vulnerability. It didn't belong on a man that had faced hell itself and survived.

MASON

"Absolutely," I said back.

He moved over and I got under the covers with him. I curled up against his chest and Koda lay down on the other side of him. I couldn't ignore how good it felt to have his arms around me. To hear his heartbeat thrumming under my ear as it soothed me to sleep. I never wanted to forget about this moment and I hoped, prayed, that it would happen again.

CHAPTER TWENTY-THREE

Mason

EVERYONE ON THE team was currently in my hotel room.

I didn't want to risk going into any field office where this cartel was concerned. I didn't want to risk being in any office where someone could be on the payroll. This cartel had a great deal of connections in order for them to evade arrests and be able to move their products over the border.

I wasn't taking any chances.

I didn't care about the cartel.

I cared about Monroe.

There was no point in trying to shut down the cartel. Whenever you take out one of the major players, someone else takes their place. It was an endless game of whack-a-mole and I had no interest in playing it. Unlike other criminal organizations that just run drugs or guns, the cartel wouldn't care that we only wanted Monroe.

I had reached out in previous cases to major drug runners and even weapon traffickers to try and find someone that was selling children. They all were helpful, especially when I told them I wasn't looking for them, nor cared what they were doing. They all provided me with information on my suspect because they hated anyone who hurt children. Cartels were different, though. Money was money to them.

"Any luck on the mass grave?" Rafe asked as he sat back with his coffee.

"Damien and Sebastian were able to locate a mass grave within an hour of town. I have a forensic team going down to handle it. It looks like a hundred bodies," I answered.

"A hundred? How the hell did he kill that many and it didn't get noticed?"

Hollingsworth instantly asked.

"Roland is looking into it. But there was a Social Worker in a nearby town, Burn, that was helping Monroe with covering it up and giving him the kids that no one would miss. Roland is going to have to run a full investigation into the foster systems in town and in the surrounding ones. It's going to be a lot of work, but each foster parent and Social Worker will have to be investigated and cleared."

"That is a massive undertaking. It's going to take months before that can be completed," Rafe commented.

"I know. Roland is going to pull in everyone he can. Damien and Sebastian are going to help, as well. It's a process, but it has to happen. There's a bigger operation going on than just Monroe and it all needs to be stopped before more children are hurt or sold."

"It has to be done. We can help once we get back to the station," Jarod said as he indicated between him and Hollingsworth, who gave a nod in agreement.

"Shit," Cooper said from his spot behind his computer.

"Do I want to know?" I couldn't help but ask.

Cooper didn't say much when he was busy trying to track someone or something down, but when he did, it was either worth it or something I wasn't going to be happy about.

"I found Monroe," Cooper started.

"Great. Where is he?" Rafe asked, not sure what the big deal was.

"He's in a Sinaloa's stronghold where the head of the cartel lives, with about a hundred armed guards."

"Shit," Ryzen agreed.

"Are you sure he's there and it's not just his cell phone?" I asked.

"I found his cell phone there so I used satellite images to confirm his presence. He is there, hiding out like a little bitch in a whore house," Cooper confirmed.

"What is he doing there, though? I know he's got a connection to the cartel, but why would they risk everything to hide him. They have to know he's wanted by now," Jarod asked.

That was what didn't make sense to me. Even Vilenti had said that Monroe was small-time. That he provided some drugs to him when his supplier was running low or it was easier to get them from Monroe than transporting drugs across the country. Cartel would use him to help fund their pockets, but if he was small-time, he wouldn't be worth having him in the stronghold. Cartel leaders keep their family in strongholds and their highest-ranking men.

Monroe shouldn't be there.

Not with the intel that we had.

"He's right. Cartel leaders don't let just anyone into their stronghold, especially outsiders," Rafe said.

"Unless he's not small-time. Maybe Monroe has been downplaying his connection to the cartel, or his role in it. We don't know how many kids have been sold over the past thirty years. We don't know if other Social Workers had a hand in it. Maybe Monroe has been supplying the cartel with kids," I said.

"Okay, but why? Why American kids?" Hollingsworth asked.

"They make more money," Ryzen answered.

"That's exactly it. Clients will pay far more for a white American child, especially ones with blond hair and blue eyes. And this cartel has ties to Brazil and

Colombia, they could be sending the children all over the world to be traded and sold. The cartel can also use them to help manufacture and package the drugs. It's cheap labor and a huge profit for them. If Monroe is their connection to children that can go missing and no one reports, he's their connection to billions of dollars," I explained.

"But that connection is burnt now, though. It's not like Monroe can wait it out and go start over in another city. Not to mention, he's almost sixty, now. He won't be able to foster any more children soon. What worth is he to the cartel?" Hollingsworth asked.

"He's gotta be worth something for them to want him alive. As a rule, when someone has lost their worth to a cartel they kill 'em to ensure they don't talk. They don't hide him away," Cooper commented.

"Unless he is still worth something," Rafe stated.

"But what?" Jarod asked.

"What if Monroe isn't a player, but the head?" I said as my mind tried to work it out.

"Head of what?" Jarod asked,

confused.

"Supply chain," Ryzen stated, but failed to explain. He really was a man of few words.

"Monroe had connections from being a cop for thirty years. He also had connections from being a foster parent and working within the drug trade. Foster parents and law enforcement go to conventions all over the country. Monroe could have been going to them and connecting with less than desirable foster parents to bring into the organization. He could be running a child trafficking ring and supplying the cartel with them. That would explain why the cartel is protecting him. He has all of those connections and without him communicating with those connections, the supply chain falls apart. Monroe doesn't have to take on any more children to still make money for the cartel. He just needs to be alive and not in jail," I explained.

"So he's a major player and the cartel wants to protect their future profits," Jarod stated, now fully understanding what was going on.

"He's going to be a real bitch to get out," Hollingsworth stated what we were all thinking.

"We gotta get him out, anyway. Coop, I want satellite images of the area and a schematic to the stronghold. We go in tonight to grab him," I stated.

"Alone?" Hollingsworth asked, shocked.

"We can't go in alone. There's too many of 'em," Rafe instantly said.

"Well, unless the three of you know any of the Feds in the field offices here that you can trust, we have no choice. We have no idea who is in this cartel's back pocket and we can't risk Monroe getting out of the country."

I knew it wasn't going to be that easy. I knew it wasn't the smartest thing in the world to be going in with just us, but we also didn't have many options here. We couldn't use local law enforcement because we couldn't trust them. We had to go at it alone, which meant we needed a plan. A solid plan that would keep us all safe and alive while we went in and grabbed Monroe. The cartel wasn't going to hand him over to us, so we were going to have to take him.

"We're gonna need more weapons," Rafe stated.

"I'll get to work on getting the images," Cooper said, before he went back to his laptop.

I could tell none of them were happy about the situation or the proposed plan, and we were going to need more weapons and gear. That, at least, I could get for us without raising any red flags within the agencies.

We had to do this smart and we needed a solid attack plan.

Tonight, we were raiding the cartel's stronghold and I was going to be ready for any possible outcome. I wanted Monroe alive, but if we had to, then we'd kill him and end this, once and for all. The investigation into the child trafficking ring he was a part of, or running, would just be started, but that was something we could handle on our own if Monroe died here. The first step to ending all of this, though, was to get inside that stronghold, no matter what.

CHAPTER TWENTY-FOUR

Jarod

I COULDN'T STOP the trembling in my hands, no matter how hard I tried. This day had not been going the way I expected it would. I didn't expect much, but this wasn't exactly it. Walking under the cover of darkness to creep through a forest that led to a cartel's stronghold wasn't exactly on my life's bingo card. I had done raids, but nothing like this. When I had done raids, it was with an extreme amount of cops against a small number. This was six guys going against an army of one hundred, all so we could capture Monroe.

It was the next level and intense, and I had no idea if I would ever be good enough for something like this. I didn't have the training that these guys had. I was very much a rookie, here, and I hated that I didn't have anything helpful to offer the team.

I felt a hand on my forearm and I turned to see Mason. We were both partnered up for our takedown position and having him here with me was the only thing keeping me together.

"Relax, it's going to be okay."

He was trying to comfort me and make me feel better, and I appreciated the effort. But I doubted there was anything he could possibly say to me, right now, that would make me feel better.

"This is insane. I'm not good enough for this."

I didn't belong in this situation.

I wasn't trained enough.

I was a liability by being here.

I could get one of them killed because I wasn't good enough.

I had no business being here.

I could feel the panic starting to rise and I knew I had to stop it or I would be having a full blown panic attack in the one place I couldn't have one.

Mason pulled the com off of his ear and did the same to mine before he placed his hands on my biceps as he spoke.

"Listen to me, you *are* good enough for this. I know you don't have many years on the job, and nothing like this, but you can do this. I wouldn't have you here if I thought otherwise. Baby, I promise you, I'm not going to let anything happen to you. You can do this. I believe in you."

And just like that, the panic was subsiding.

It was ridiculous and it made no sense, but Mason had a way of calming me. Of making me feel like I could do anything. We barely knew each other, but that didn't matter to my body, to my heart. I was still nervous. I still felt like I wouldn't be able to do this, but I did feel better. I did feel like I would be okay, that we would be okay as long as we were together.

"Sorry," I instantly said.

It was not professional for me to be acting this way. To be reacting to the situation in this manner. My mind knew that. I just needed my body to know it as well.

"Don't be. You have nothing to be sorry for. Everyone gets scared. Everyone gets nervous when doing something like this for the first dozen times. There's even some situations that I go into that I get scared of, and I've been doing this for seven years. It's a perfectly natural reaction. You got nothing to be sorry for."

As if Mason's words weren't calming me down enough, he moved and pressed his lips against mine. It was brief, but it was more than enough for my body to stop trembling.

For my mind to stop racing.

I was ready now.

Mason pulled back and flashed me a warm smile.

"We gotta get moving," he said.

"I know. I'm ready," I said, with as much confidence that I could muster up.

He gave me a nod and we both put our earpieces back in. We moved as silently as possible toward our designated entry position.

We had to be careful.

Mason had planned for us to breach at different angles so we could get into the stronghold and, hopefully, go as unnoticed as possible. The one thing working in our favor was that Monroe was positioned in the Southern end of the stronghold and he was alone. He had a couple of guards around his room, but that was it. If we could get in as quietly as possible, we had a real chance of getting to Monroe without getting caught.

"Bravo and Charlie, you in position?" Mason asked, referring to the other two teams. Hollingsworth and Cooper were together and Rafe was on his own. Ryzen had been positioned in an Overwatch post further back up on a hill so he could see everything going on.

"Bravo is in position," Hollingsworth said.

"Charlie, in position," Rafe answered.

"Echo, you good?" Mason asked, referring to Ryzen.

"All good, Boss. Clear to breach," Ryzen answered.

"All teams, breach," Mason said, before we both started to move forward.

I followed right behind Mason, keeping close to him to ensure that we wouldn't get separated. I also wanted to make sure I had his back. I wasn't going to allow anything to happen to him.

As we approached our entrance point, he stopped to look at me to make sure I was ready. I gave him a nod and he pulled the door open and we were moving.

We walked into a hallway with our guns raised. I followed right next to Mason as he guided us through the different hallways to reach Monroe's room. We had to duck behind different walls to avoid people, but it was better to avoid them than to have to fire our weapons. That would cause a great deal of noise and everyone would know we were there if they heard gunshots ring out. The last thing we needed was every guard in this stronghold to know that they had company.

"Alpha, target is still in the room with two tangos out front," Ryzen said as we got closer.

"Copy, Echo," Mason whispered.

"We're in position," Rafe said on the other's behalf.

"On my mark," Mason said.

We were both on each side of the hallway by Monroe's room. There were two guards and Mason had decided that him and Rafe would take them out quietly. They had the most training, so it made sense for them to take out the guards. I knew they would be able to do it at the same time and without firing a single shot.

"One, two, three." Mason said, before he was on the move.

I saw him and Rafe come around the corner and grab a guy each in a choke hold. To my amazement, they both snapped their necks, as if they were breaking a paint stir stick.

For some reason, it made Mason look even sexier.

That probably shouldn't be sexy, but I was past the point of caring.

With the guards taken out, we moved onto the room that Monroe was hiding out in. I put my hand on the handle and with a nod from Mason, I pulled the door open and they were storming in with their guns up.

I came up behind them and started to clear the large room. It was bigger than we had expected. Larger than what the blueprints to the stronghold had indicated. The blueprints were out of date and that could become a problem for us.

I had moved to start clearing the area around the window. There was a set up living room and I wanted to make sure he wasn't hiding behind any of the furniture. Though, why he would be, I had no idea, but it had to be cleared.

I had just turned my back from the living area when an arm wrapped around my neck and pulled me back against a hard body. A cold metal against my temple told me that it was a gun.

A gun being held to my head.

A tsunami of fear crashed into me and instantly I felt like I couldn't breathe. I had never had a gun pulled on me, much less held to my head. I must have made a sound, I don't know, because I can't remember, but I must have because instantly, everyone in the room had turned and faced us.

"Put the gun down, Monroe, it's over," Mason barked the order.

Monroe was not going to put the gun down.

We all knew it.

He wasn't the type of man who was going to toss his hands up in the air and walk away. He was going to shoot his way out of here. And considering I was his shield, I was going to be the last one he killed. I would have to watch Mason get killed and that wasn't something I could handle.

I couldn't lose him, not like this.

"You're gonna let me walk out of here or I'll shoot the piece of shit rookie," Monroe seethed.

"It's over, Monroe. We know what you did. We have witnesses that are going to testify against you. We know you were working with Burn to hide the kids you sold and killed. We found your mass grave. We know everything. Put the gun down," Mason tried.

"You're bluffing. You have no idea what I have done. You have nothing but some hearsay and it means shit here in Mexico. One shot, that's all it will take to alert everyone that you're here. The guards will come storming in here and kill you all."

"He's not bluffing, Monroe. Put the gun down and come in peacefully," I tried, but it only resulted in Monroe tightening his arm around my neck.

"Shut up, you shit. You haven't earned the right to speak," Monroe snarled into my ear.

Before another word could be said, the sound of glass shattering followed by the echo of a gunshot rang out. The pressure around my neck slowly released and Monroe hit the ground with a clear hole in the middle of his head.

I couldn't take my eyes off of him.

I knew I should be moving.

I knew I should be saying something.

That shot didn't come from anyone in the room, so Ryzen had taken the shot.

Ryzen had saved my life, saved all of our lives.

I needed to move, but I couldn't take my eyes off of the freshly dead body at my feet. I had never seen a dead body before. I had never been in a gunfight. I had never gone through anything like this and I had no idea how to process what I was seeing. A hand on my arm snapped my gaze off of Monroe and onto Mason.

"We have to go, now," he said urgently.

I knew the gunshot would be heard. We had to go, or we still risked being killed. Without giving Monroe another look, I ran out of the room after the others and we didn't stop running until we reached the vehicles.

CHAPTER TWENTY-FIVE

Jarod

WALKING INTO OUR hotel room, I could feel my whole body trembling. Now that we were finally safe, my mind was kicking back in. The memories of what just happened were kicking in.

Koda instantly came running at me. We had left him here because we had to be quiet and we didn't want to risk Koda being caught in any of the gunfire, should it go that way.

I moved slowly into the room. I had to get my mind to focus on what was going on, but I just couldn't.

"It's okay," Mason said gently as he came over to me.

He removed my gun and placed it down on the table, along with his. He then turned his attention to the vest I was wearing and pulled it off of me. I knew I should be doing it for myself, but my whole body was shaking. I couldn't control it and there didn't seem to be any way to stop it. I was going into shock or something, I don't know, but I had never felt this way before.

I never wanted to feel this way ever again.

"It's okay. You're okay, Baby," Mason said, as he pressed a kiss on my cheek.

"I can't stop shaking. What's wrong with me?"

"Nothing is wrong. Your body is reacting to the trauma of what just happened. You've never had a gun pulled on you, much less pointed at your head. You've never seen a person killed before, a dead body. It's a lot and your mind is trying to process it all. You're okay, Baby."

Mason guided me over to the bed and he encouraged me to sit down on it. He quickly helped me to get my boots off before he removed his own. He lifted my legs up onto the bed and coaxed me to lie down before he wrapped his arms around me and I turned into his chest.

"Just breathe. Nice deep and slow breaths. This will pass, I promise."

I knew it would pass, but it felt like it never would, honestly. I had no idea how this could ever be okay again. I trusted Mason, though, and I took some slow and deep breaths to try and calm myself down. I listened to his heartbeat thrumming under my ear and focused on his warm, strong hands moving over my body.

"It's all good. You're safe now, Baby," he said as he placed a kiss on the top of my head, his fingers trailing up and down my back.

I couldn't believe that this whole mess was over.

Monroe was dead.

The kids that we recovered from his house would be safe.

Tyler would be safe.

The operation was done.

I should be happy, but instead I was sad, because that meant that Mason would be leaving soon for another operation. I would have to say goodbye to him. If this was going to be my last time being held by him, I was going to enjoy it.

I closed my eyes and allowed my body and mind to soak up as much of Mason as I could. If this was the last time I was going to be able to feel him, I wanted to remember even the smallest details.

EPILOGUE

Mason

THIS HAD BEEN a very long case.

It wasn't long compared to some of the cases that I'd had to work. I'd had to chase after a criminal organization for months. I'd had to follow the trail of dead children in their wake to find them and yet, that somehow didn't feel as long as this case had. Maybe it was because of my new PTSD diagnosis, I don't know. I was just glad that this case was finally done.

With Monroe dead, we never had to deal with him again. Tyler was safe and so were Monroe's foster children. Dana had taken a plea deal when the reality kicked in that Monroe wasn't coming back for her. She would be spending the rest of her life in a minimum-security prison. It wasn't what she deserved, but it did end the case, so none of the children or Tyler would have to testify in open court. They could all start to move on and live their lives free from both Monroe and Dana.

The takedown for Monroe was intense, to say the least. I was relieved that all of my guys didn't get hurt. I almost had a heart attack when Monroe put his gun to Jarod's head. I hadn't been certain if leaving Ryzen outside of the compound with his rifle had been the best idea, but I had never been more relieved that I had left him out there. To see the gun held to Jarod's head, to see the fear in his eyes, it ate at my very soul. My whole body had gone cold and I could feel my life being sucked out of me.

I had never felt like that before.

I had never felt anything close to it.

All I wanted was for Jarod to be safe.

It didn't matter what I had to do, I would have given my own life to save him.

Thankfully, Ryzen had been on

Overwatch and he was able to make a clean shot. Even still, hearing that shot ring out, I thought my heart was going to stop. I had instantly wrapped my arms around him and pulled him to me. I didn't care what any of the guys thought at that moment.

I had to make sure Jarod was safe.

It was at that moment that I realized how much I had fallen for him.

It made no sense, we hadn't known each other long enough for me to love him, but that was the only emotion I could think of to express the depth of what I felt for him.

It made no sense, but I stopped caring about that a long time ago.

I had learned that what the world dictated as logical could all be forgotten when money was on the table. I had lost count how many times it made sense *not* to sell a child. How many times it made sense *not* to use children to traffic guns or make drugs. But when large sums of money were on the table, all of that logic went right out the window.

So why would my love life be any different?

I was in love with Jarod.

For the first time in my life, I was in love with someone and it terrified the hell out of me. I had no way of knowing what Jarod felt. I had no idea if he even wanted anything to do with me outside of great sex. There were a lot of unknowns, right then, and it was only adding to my stress for the day.

I had a plan for later on today. I was hoping that Jarod would be willing to go with me and that it turned out well. I had no idea what he felt, but I was going to find out today. I couldn't let my uncertainty or fear keep me from not going after what I wanted. Just like I couldn't keep putting my head in the sand and pretending like something wasn't wrong with me.

I had PTSD.

It was time I accepted it so I could do something about it. I was never going to get better, if I didn't start to be honest with myself. I had a lot of work I needed to do, but I was determined to do it. I was being given a second chance with this task force, and I was not about to ruin it.

Walking into the police station back in Gaithersburg had a feel of home to it. I knew it wasn't about the physical station, but rather what the future held. I would be working out of the station with the task force until we were able to secure some funds to have our own station built.

I had to prove to the Governor that the task force was going to work and be highly successful. If I could do that, then we would be able to get a lot more funding and could grow our operation.

First things first, though.

I had to see if I had a team.

The others didn't know that this task force could potentially be a long-term gig, and I was hoping they would be willing to stick around when I asked. We all worked well together and it would be nice to be able to hit the ground running with a team I could trust. If they didn't want to be on the task force permanently, I would have to find more federal agents and start from the beginning again. I really didn't want to go that route.

I wanted *this* team.

The one person that mattered the most to me, though, was Jarod. I was really hoping he would say yes to this. He was a good cop and I knew he had what it took to be a federal agent. The only thing holding him back was his connection to his father, but none of that mattered. He wasn't his father and he didn't deserve to be treated like crap or have to settle because he was afraid of the news getting out.

Working the task force, he wouldn't have to worry about any of that. He would be able to grow his skills and help a lot of children at the same time. It would be great for his career, but it would also be great for me. I would be able to spend a lot more time with him, and that was something I desperately wanted.

The energy in the station was as good as I could expect. They'd had one of their own killed. News of Monroe's death would have spread quickly throughout the station once Captain Perry marked the case as closed.

The atmosphere was tense, but I expected as much.

They had worked beside this man for the length of their careers. He had thirty years on the job. He had touched a lot of lives and most of them only ever saw the good man he portrayed himself to be. It had been bad enough that we had arrested him, but to hear that he had been killed by one of my guys, it wasn't an easy pill to swallow. It wouldn't matter that he held a gun to Jarod's head, fully prepared to kill him to secure his escape. To most of the cops in this station, losing Jarod to keep Monroe alive would have been the better trade.

To me, though, no one was worth Jarod's life and I would never allow any criminal to take one of my guys. It was just that simple to me.

I headed into the conference room to see my team was already here. Based on the uncomfortable looks and body language, both Jarod and Hollingsworth were not looking forward to being back out in the bullpen. I couldn't blame them. As far as they knew, the Feds were leaving and they would be the ones trapped here to deal with the fallout.

It was just another reason why I was happy to be heading the task force; they would have a different option and they would have backup for when shit got too intense with the local police.

"Thanks for coming in. I know we're all tired and looking to get back home," I started.

"You said it was important," Hollingsworth commented.

"It is important. First, the Governor is very pleased with our work on this case and how quickly we were able to get it resolved. He would have preferred to take Monroe alive to try and get the location of the kids he sold, however, he knows we were not given a suitable situation for that outcome. He wants you all to know that he is impressed by your work and is proud to have you serving this country."

"I'm just glad we were able to find Monroe and stop him before he could get to any more kids," Cooper said with a soft smile.

"There has been something that I've been keeping from you. I didn't want to bring it up until I knew it would be official. The Governor wants to keep the task force. He's placed me in charge and has given the task force full immunity, with the obvious exceptions. The task force is to go after criminals and criminal organizations that commit crimes against children *Nationwide*. You all have the option of staying with the task force or going back to your original positions. Ideally, I would like for you all to stay. We have something that is working, and I would like to continue working with all of you and grow together. The choice is yours, though."

I was relieved to see the interest in all of their eyes. None of them had a family. They didn't have spouses or a long-time boyfriends or girlfriends. They were all single, and didn't have children. They could easily make a career pivot if it was something that interested them.

I couldn't help but look at Jarod and I was filled with warmth to see the excitement in his eyes. This was something he was very interested in and that meant there was a high chance he was going to say yes. I would be able to spend a lot more time with him and that was something I desperately wanted.

"What exactly would we be doing?" Hollingsworth asked.

"We would be finding cases to take over the investigation for. Then, we would do what we just did. We would find the head of the snake and take them out. We would be going after large organizations like human traffickers, but we would also be going after solo offenders. Anyone that local police haven't been able to find or investigate properly. We could be all over the country at any given day. There would be a lot of traveling and we would have to work with local police, at times, as well as other federal agents. The goal is to save as many children as possible, no matter what we have to do."

"And the immunity, that covers what specifically?" Rafe asked.

"Everything but murder, sexual assaults, and crimes against children. We have a green light for everything else and that does include rough interrogations, should we find it necessary," I answered.

"I'm in," Ryzen simply said.

"Was it the rough interrogation part?" Rafe asked with a smirk.

Ryzen was dangerous, this case had taught us all that. He was a man of few words and he was deadly. He oozed lethal vibes just sitting there. We were lucky to have him on our side, because this man could have easily been on the bad guy's team and that would have resulted in a lot of deaths. Thankfully, he was playing for the good guys' team and he was going to help us save a lot of children while keeping a watchful eye over us.

"Children deserve to be safe," Ryzen simply said, and it was all that he needed to say.

"Well, I'm in. This is important work and I'm not about to pass this opportunity up," Cooper said.

"I'm in as well. Children deserve to have people like us looking for them, fighting for them. I don't got anyone at home waiting for me to get back," Rafe said with a shrug.

"What about you two?" I asked our two detectives.

"Shit, I'm in," Hollingsworth instantly said.

"One hundred percent," Jarod easily agreed.

I couldn't help but be proud of each and every single one of them. They all knew that this was going to be hard, but they were willing to go through any obstacle they had to in order to ensure that children in this country were safer. They were all good men and I couldn't wait until we would be able to take on our next case. We were going to do a lot of good for this country and I was looking forward to it.

It had been a good couple of years since I had felt excited for my job, and it was a feeling I welcomed back into my life.

"Take the week and get yourselves

situated down here. There's not much in terms of housing, just yet. My brother has offered his spare bedroom for anyone that needs it. There's also the motel in town."

That was going to be the tricky part, because in this area, there wasn't much in terms of apartments or houses that went up on the market. I had already decided I would be building my own home. It was going to take some time, but I was fine with that. Roland had told me to live with him, but I wanted my own space, even on the short-term until my house was built. I liked the motel room. It worked for Koda and me. Plus, we traveled so much for work, we didn't need anything more than a motel room, right now.

"I also have a spare bedroom," Jarod offered.

"So do I," Hollingsworth added as well.

"We'll make it work until we can find our own places. If all goes right, we won't be here very long, anyway, with all the traveling. Will we be taking on more people?" Rafe asked.

"When we need them. They don't have to be law enforcement, either. As long as they have the proven skills and take the oath, they'll be fine. We will also be working with two social workers, for now. Isaiah and Travis. We will also need to find a federal prosecutor that we can call up when we need warrants, no matter what city we are in. Roland will be joining the task force as well. Coop, I know you prefer to be in a tech position rather than as a field agent, so with Roland being here, you will be free to stay back in an Overwatch position."

Cooper was an analyst and hacker. He had no interest in being in the field, even though he was trained for it. I knew that, and I appreciated him making an exception with this case. Moving forward, though, I wanted all of my guys to be in their desired position and not to be placed in a situation they weren't comfortable with.

"Thank you," Cooper said with a huge sigh of relief.

"Moving forward, Rafe and Hollingsworth will be partners and Roland will be with Ryzen. Jarod, you will, obviously, be with me."

I knew I could have put Roland with Hollingsworth, but I wanted to try and keep a Fed with a local cop. It would even out the tactical experience throughout the team. Plus, Roland was really good with everybody, so it wouldn't matter if Ryzen said five words a day or not. Roland wouldn't care and he wouldn't feel awkward if there was nothing but silence between them.

"Sounds good. If there's nothing else, I now need to get home and get my house packed up," Rafe said as he stood.

"That's it. I'll see you all in a week," I said flashing them all a warm smile.

Everyone started to gather their things and make their way out of the station. I followed Jarod out, and once we said goodbye to the others, I turned to give him my full attention.

"Wanna go for a drive?" I asked.

"Lead the way," he said with grin.

We made our way over to my truck. Koda jumped into the backseat without any complaints this time. Once we were in, I started to head for the highway. I wanted to take him to the waterfront where we could have a private conversation. I was hoping the sunset background would persuade Jarod to give us a real chance.

I didn't want just a sexual relationship

with him.

I wanted a real relationship.

I wanted to go out on dates and learn everything there was about him. I wanted something real. For the first time in my life, I wanted more than just meaningless sex.

I could hear Roland's voice in my head now telling me "I told you so," but I was choosing to ignore it.

I was going to allow myself to be happy.

To have more than just my career in my life.

"How are you feeling about the task force?" I asked as we hit the road.

"I'm excited for it. It sounds like it's going to be a really good thing. I know it will be hard plenty of times, and I'll see things that will make me wish I could bleach my brain, but saving kids, that's something I am willing to risk everything for. What about you, though? It'll make your PTSD worse, won't it?" Jarod asked, concern flooding his voice.

I had been worried that he would look at me differently when I had confided in Jarod about my PTSD diagnosis. I wasn't really sure what he saw in me to begin with. We hadn't known each other that long, still didn't, really, but I didn't want him to see me as weak. I couldn't even begin to explain the relief I felt when that look in his eyes never changed. Still, doing this job would keep aggravating my PTSD and there would be many nights ahead of me that would be hard, but I also knew that by pushing through, I would be saving a lot of innocent children and that would be worth the sleepless nights.

I would have to find a way to balance it all out.

I would need to find a way to cope and live with my PTSD, but I would figure it out.

I was not about to let my PTSD ruin me.

Not now, not ever.

"I'll manage it. I'll start taking it seriously and speak with someone and I'll manage the triggers and stress. It is possible to do this job with PTSD. Plenty of federal agents do it all the time. I will figure it out."

Jarod reached over and placed his hand in mine as he spoke.

"We will. You're not alone in this

battle, Mason."

I turned my hand so ours could intertwine as I spoke.

"I know. What about you? Are you okay with the possibility of your father's identity coming out?"

"If it does, then it does. I'm not going to hide who I am anymore."

"Good. The guys won't care, either. You don't have to worry about that. Just be yourself. That's the best thing you can do."

He gave me a rich smile before he spoke again.

"So where are you kidnapping me to?"

I gave a soft chuckle before I spoke.

"I'll never tell."

"All right, but don't expect me to fight if your cuffs come out."

I couldn't help the groan that escaped me as the memory came flooding into my mind.

That was a good night, a very good night.

It was a night I was looking forward to experiencing many times over.

****

It was close to an hour later when I

parked my truck at the beach. The sun was just starting to set and I knew it couldn't get any more romantic if I tried. Romance was something I was new at and I was going to make a real effort with Jarod. I wanted him to know how special he was. How much I cared about him.
We got out of my truck but I left Koda in the backseat. He wasn't too happy, but I would let him out soon so he could run around and play.

"Wow, this is very romantic," Jarod said as I took his hand and walked him toward the water.

"You deserve romance," I countered.

"You deserve more than sex, even great sex. You deserve dinners, and breakfast in the morning. I know we said this would just be sex and I know what I'm about to say sounds insane. We've barely been around each other and we don't really know each other, but Jarod, I love you. And I don't want just sex with you. I want to build something real with you."

I had no idea what he was going to think or feel about anything I just said. I knew, typically, there would be more time before saying those three little words. We should have spent months having casual sex before admitting that we were in a relationship and then the I love you's would come out. However, in our line of work you weren't guaranteed a tomorrow. You weren't even guaranteed the next hour. I didn't want to waste what precious time we had, not for a single second. I had to make sure he knew how I felt, even if that meant he didn't want the same.

Jarod stopped and turned toward me. I could see the emotion brimming in his eyes and could swear they almost sparkled.

"When I first met you, I felt like I had already known you. It was as if we had met before, but I know we hadn't, because I would have remembered a man like you. It feels as if we knew each other in another life. It makes no sense, but there's a connection there. I feel it every time I'm around you; have from the very first moment I saw you. There's no logical reason for me to feel this way, because it is too soon, but I love you, too, Mason. And I can't think of anything that I want more than to spend as much time with you as possible," Jarod said with his emotions echoing in his voice.

Hearing those words, hearing that it

wasn't just me, that he loved me, too, I felt like a little kid on Christmas morning. The pure joy that flooded my entire body, I couldn't even begin to explain it. Words had escaped me, so I did the only thing I could do that would convey the love that I felt for him.

I pulled Jarod in for a passionate kiss, one he instantly responded to and wrapped his arms around my neck.

He loved me, we were in love, and that was all that I needed.

We would face the horrors of this world together and we would free as many children as we could. That was our mission, and we were going to do it together.

I would face it all with the man that I loved by my side until my last dying breath.

Thank you for reading!

Turn the page for Rafe, Book 2 in the Federal Protection Agency series.

RAFE

FEDERAL PROTECTION AGENCY

BOOK TWO

BY EVIE RILEY

RAFE

A chance to find real love...

Ex-SEAL, Special Agent Rafe Dallas spent years working for the DOJ after his medical discharge. Now, he's joined a special Task Force fighting crimes against children. After successfully completing his first operation, Rafe is determined to give everything he has to save as many children as he can.

After learning about the tragic death of his Navy SEAL buddy, John, he promises to look after the man's younger brother and do what he can to help find his daughter.

Finley Quinn is working undercover at a human trafficking ring trying to find his niece. He was set to join the SEALS eighteen months ago, following in his older brother's footsteps, when John was killed in a home invasion and his six-year-old daughter was kidnapped. He has been looking for her ever since. The local police believe she's dead but Finley won't consider that possibility and refuses to give up.

EVIE RILEY

When Rafe joins him undercover, Finley is
hard pressed not to remember the huge crush
he had on the sexy older man.

Will they save Finley's niece before it's too
late? Will Rafe ever see Finley as more than
his best friend's kid brother?

PROLOGUE

Finley

THE WHOLE PLANE was filled with music as we all celebrated another successful mission. I had been in the Navy for six years now, and I had loved every minute of it. Yes, there had been missions that left me feeling hurt on every level, but this right here was what made it all better. Being around my brothers, feeling their love and our family, this is what made everything worth it. All of the hard hours, the hard labor, the horrible things we had seen, it was all worth it to be able to be a part of this family.

"Excuse me, gentlemen, I have an announcement," our Commander said as he joined us.

The music was turned down and we all gave him our attention. I was hoping that we wouldn't have another operation. I had been looking forward to sleeping in my bed after being out for two months. This operation really had taken a lot longer than we ever expected.

"It is my pleasure and honor to inform all of you that Petty Officer Finley Quinn has just been accepted into BUDS."

I was instantly up on my feet cheering along with the rest of my brothers. I hated that I would have to leave them to become a Navy SEAL, but I would be able to follow in my brother's footsteps and I was beyond excited. I couldn't wait until I could start.

I was instantly attacked by a group hug by my brothers and it was only another reason to celebrate on our way home. As beers were given out, I took mine and headed over to a quieter place on the plane so I could video call John. I had to tell him what happened. After three rings, his face appeared on my phone.

"Hey, Baby Brother, you finally on your way back?"

"About halfway there, now. I just got word... I made it into BUDS. I'm going to be a SEAL, Big Brother," I said, with the biggest smile on my face.

I couldn't believe I had made it. My dreams were coming true and I couldn't contain the excitement that was flowing through my veins. I could tell John was feeling the same when a huge smile split his face.

"Yay! That's my boy. I knew you would. My team is all set for you. The guys can't wait to have you join us."

I couldn't wait to be there.

When I had joined the Navy, John was already a SEAL and had been working with his team for a while at that point. I had been around his team plenty of times when I was younger, and the second I graduated Boot Camp, they were all set for me to come and join them once I had enough experience to qualify for BUDS. I had even joined them on training days and completed different training courses with them to help me get ready for what BUDS would have in store for me. It was going to be insanely hard, but I knew it would be worth it in the end. I would finally get to operate with my big brother and there was nothing I wanted more in this world than that.

"I can't wait, man. Where's my little princess?"

"She's right here. She just finished brushing her teeth for bed."

John moved the phone over and handed it over to the best thing in my entire world. My beautiful niece, Lilly, was just five years old and she was my everything.

I had known I was gay when I was ten years old. I had told John about it when I was twelve and he didn't even bat an eye. He just asked me if there was a boy I liked. Whenever I had a question, he answered. He had done his own research on homosexual relationships and how to give me the 'sex talk.' It never once bothered him and that only made me love him even more. When he told me that him and his wife, Darla, were expecting, I was over the moon. I knew that little baby would be the closest thing I had to a child and I was going to love them with my whole being.

"Uncle Finnie!" Lilly said with the

biggest smile her face could make.

"Hello, my Princess. How are you?"

"Good. You come see me?"

"I am. I'm heading back home, right now. Once I get there, I'm going to shower, pack, and then head out to you guys. I'll be there in the morning and I can't wait to see you."

"Tea party?"

"Absolutely. I am packing my best tea party outfit. And do you know who else is excited to see you?"

"Mizzie?" she asked with a bright smile.

I reached over and picked up Mizzie.

Mizzie was Lilly's favorite doll. She was a twelve-inch long mermaid that had long, shiny pink hair and she was well loved. She had given her to me when I went away on this operation for good luck and I knew how much the doll meant to her. She wanted me to have her so I wouldn't get lonely and she would be able to keep me company.

Me and the guys had taken photos with Mizzie while on our operation. She had been all over the base and in the humvees. I had sent all of the photos to John to show Lilly and she loved it. She had made John print them out so she could hang them up on her wall to show off Mizzie's adventure.

"She is very excited to see you," I said as I showed Mizzie to Lilly.

"I miss her. She come tomorrow?"

"She will be with me and she can't wait to see you and tell you all about her adventure."

"Morning?"

"That's right. We're going to be there right after breakfast, my Little Princess, and I don't have to leave for a whole week. We're gonna have lots of fun together."

I was getting the week off and I couldn't wait to spend every second of it with Lilly. I already had plans to take her to a water park and a petting zoo. I was also going to spoil her with a mini shopping spree at her favorite toy store. It would drive John insane, but I didn't care. She was mine to spoil and I had every intention of doing just that for the next week.

"Okay, Uncle Finnie. Daddy says it's bedtime. I love you."

"I love you, too, my sweet Little Princess, and I will see you in the morning."

RAFE

She waved goodbye and I said a quick goodbye to John before he ended the call. Tomorrow morning, I would get to hold her and see my brother and sister-in-law. I couldn't wait to be back home with them.

***

It was just before ten in the morning when my cab turned onto John's block. I was a ball of excitement to finally be able to get to hold the two most important people in my life once again. The second we arrived on the block, though, we were at a dead stop.

I looked out of the front windshield and to my horror the street was flooded with cop cars. My blood ran cold and I did the only thing I could do. I handed over some cash for the ride and grabbed my bag. I was out of the cab and running toward my brother's house. The whole time, I kept telling myself they had to be there for another person. They couldn't be here for my brother's house. The closer I got to it, though, the more my dread increased.

The second I saw the yellow crime scene tape, I dropped my duffle bag and ran at top speed toward my brother's house. I ducked under the crime scene tape and ran inside. I didn't care about the cops that were calling out to me or chasing after me.

I had to find my brother.

I had to find Lilly and Darla.

I don't know what I was expecting as I ran into the house, but it looked like it always did. There was no sign of a struggle, no blood. At least, not on the first floor.

I ran up the stairs and headed for my Lilly's room. I had to make sure she was okay. A detective grabbed me right at her door, but it was too late, I had already seen what was waiting for me.

My brother, my hero, my protector, my idol, was there on the floor. Dead. He died right there in that room, multiple gunshot wounds to his back, and I knew without a doubt, he died protecting Lilly. I felt my legs give out, but the arms that were wrapped around me, kept me up.

"No, no, no," I said as I took in the sight of my dead brother.

"Sir, I need to know who you are," the detective said.

I needed to talk. I needed to identify

myself so they wouldn't arrest me for trespassing, but I couldn't stop looking at John.

This wasn't supposed to happen.

I was coming home for the week.

We were going to celebrate me getting into BUDS.

I was supposed to be on his SEAL Team and working with him.

We had plans and now all of that went up in flames and for what?

They didn't have much money, the place didn't look ransacked, so what was the point in any of this?

"Sir, I need your name," the detective demanded as he started to pull me away.

"Finley Quinn. That's my brother," I managed to say as I forced my body to work and take my own weight.

"Mr. Quinn, this is a crime scene. I need you to come outside with me."

"Lilly, where's Lilly?" I asked, urgently, as I pulled away so I could start looking for her.

"Mr. Quinn, you are going to potentially destroy evidence. I need you outside, now. I promise, I'll answer your questions."

The very last thing I wanted to do was

ruin any evidence that could put the son of a bitch who killed my brother behind bars. I knew I wasn't going to win an argument with the local cop, either. He could have already arrested me, but he hadn't. I followed him outside and spoke again.

"Where is my niece? Where's his wife, Darla?"

"I'm sorry to be the one to tell you this, but Darla was found dead in the home as well. Your niece isn't here. It looks like she missed out on all of this. Do you know where she was staying last night?"

"No, she was here. I spoke to them around eight on video call. She was just getting ready for bed. They were all home last night."

If Lilly wasn't in the house, that meant whoever broke into their house took her and there was no telling what was happening with her, right now.

"Are you sure she didn't go to a friend's place this morning?" the detective asked, now worried as well.

"No. I was coming down on leave for a week. They all knew I was going to be here this morning. Lilly was going to make a tea party. She wouldn't be anywhere but the house."

"Okay, I'm going to put out a BOLO. Do you have a recent photo you could send me?"

I just gave a nod and pulled out my phone, doing my best not to let my hands shake. I sent him a few photos that I had gotten just last night from John as I spoke.

"John, he's a Navy SEAL. You need to call NCIS. This could be connected to something he was doing for the Navy."

"I'll reach out to them once I get the BOLO up. Did either your brother or his wife tell you anything recently about any threats? Anyone that maybe had been causing them problems?"

"No, nothing like that. Darla, she's a stay-at-home mom. John, he works for SEAL Team Eight. I can send you his teammates names and contact information, they might know more."

"I would appreciate that. What about Lilly? Have they mentioned any new friends, anyone that maybe had been around a lot, an adult at the park without kids?"

"No, no, if someone was hanging around John would have handled it. They don't have any hired help. The front door is always locked and the alarm is set. Lilly doesn't go over to anyone's house, not even for play dates, they all happen out in public. Even at birthday parties, either Darla or John attends with her. John was paranoid with Lilly. We both were from our job. She was always protected. Her window even has a security bar on it so it can't be open more than five inches."

I wished I had someone I could point the finger at. I would have gone over to their place and beat the truth out of them. My niece, my world, she was out there somewhere and I had to find her. I wasn't going to stop until I did.

"Okay, please, don't go anywhere. I'm going to need to talk to you more. I'm going to get the BOLO out, now."

I just gave a nod and looked toward the house as the Coroner went inside.

This wasn't supposed to happen.

This was something that only happened to other people, this didn't happen to us.

They were good people, they were safe and now they were both dead and Lilly was out there somewhere.

She had to be terrified.

RAFE

I had to find her.

I turned my attention to my phone and started to call the guys on John's team. I was going to have an army out on these streets looking for Lilly and none of us were going to rest until we found her.

CHAPTER ONE

Rafe

I COULD NEVER have imagined my life would have changed this much in such a short amount of time. When Mason had called me to ask if I would join a task force to help track down Jasper Monroe, I figured it would be a nice change of pace.

Working in the Department of Justice, things were pretty routine. I was going after Federal Agents that were dirty. The crimes they were committing changed from agent to agent, but the process of it was all the same. There was nothing exciting about it anymore. There was nothing in my job that made me want to be there every day. It was getting boring and, honestly, hard to keep arresting men and women that were supposed to protect people. They were supposed to help keep people safe and put criminals away, but they were using their power to make some extra money.

And it was always about the money.

I had never arrested anyone who didn't do it for the money. Whether it was looking the other way on crimes, helping traffickers, or even murder, it always came down to the amount of money they were making off of it.

Getting that call from Mason was like getting a breath of fresh air. The chance to do something different. The chance to find another law enforcement officer, yes, but someone that had been hurting children for close to thirty years. Someone who had brought a great deal of darkness to this world.

I had to help get him.

I had to help stop him.

And when Mason told us that the task force could continue, that we would be going after anyone who harms a child, I couldn't say yes fast enough. I didn't even think about having to leave my job, leave my home, and start over again. None of that mattered, because I would be getting to use my skills to save children and that was all that mattered.

I still didn't have my own place. There wasn't much available in this town, but I was crashing with Roland, Mason's older brother. Everything had been going well, so far.

The issue, though, lay with the task force. It had been two weeks since Monroe had been killed. We all thought we would have no problem getting our next case, but we were wrong. As it turned out, Federal Agents really didn't like to share their cases, even the ones that they weren't actively working on. Not to mention, they didn't like that we were a new task force and didn't have any type of a reputation, yet. We'd had one case, which ended up with our suspect dead. It was getting hard to have cases given over to us, because no one had confidence in our skills at solving them. It was something we would have to earn. We just needed someone to give us the chance to earn it.

I was on my way into the Station when

my phone rang. "Hey, Sticks, what's happening?"

Sticks was an old Air Force buddy of mine. We both worked with a SEAL Team to help with air support and flying them into war zones. I also had my helicopter license, so I would often go into a hot zone to provide air support to the teams. Sticks and I were good friends and all that was left of our unit.

We had been flying out of a hot zone when the Chopper was hit by a missile. I had done my best to control the chopper on the way down, but we crashed all the same. It killed everyone in the Chopper other than Sticks and I. We were both almost killed, though. I spent three weeks in a coma in Germany before I finally came to.

Sticks and I were both medically discharged and where I was able to recover, Sticks never would. The crash had left him paralyzed from the waist down. He also suffered from PTSD and had a slight pain pill addiction. I had tried to be there for him as often as I could. We both were all we had.

"I gotta talk to you. Can you come by? It's urgent."

"Yeah, of course. I'm on my way, man."

I had gotten a call like this from him before. Normally, he was having a hard time with the memories. I didn't remember the crash, but Sticks hadn't been so lucky. Those memories still haunted him to this day, whereas I had been lucky enough to walk away from it without a single memory for the three days leading up to the crash. I had physical scars from it, but without the memories, I was able to overcome the pain from that day.

I sent a quick text to Mason to let him know that I would be coming in a bit late, that something personal came up. I wasn't sure about working for Mason in the beginning. He was younger than me and sometimes that led to an Agent being hot headed or arrogant. But Mason was an easy going guy who seemed down to earth. He knew how to lead a team, even if he didn't have as much experience as other team leaders. He was a good guy and I knew he would be great one day.

After a thirty minute drive, I pulled into Sticks' driveway. He had moved to live out in the country and when he had told me he would be living out this way, my initial reaction was *why*.

Now, here I was living in a small town in the country, essentially.

I was a city boy through and through. I could rough it and camp from the Air Force, but that didn't mean I wanted to do it for fun. I liked the noise from a big city. I like being able to walk to everything I wanted within a city block. In Gaithersburg, there weren't even main food chains here. It was all mom and pop shops, and it was different for me. There was certainly an adjustment period.

I headed inside and made my way over to where Sticks usually was. He tended to spend his days on the couch watching mindless TV shows. Walking into the living room, I saw that it looked identical to what it always did. The coffee table had empty beer and whiskey bottles on it. Empty and half-eaten take out containers. Small baggies with pills and a white powder in them. Sticks was hitting a rough patch again, and I was worried that one of these days I would have to bury him.

"What's going on, Sticks?" I asked as I went and sat down in a chair.

"I don't know if you heard or not, but

John Quinn died," Sticks started.

"Wait, what? When?"

John had been my best friend when we were in the Military. He was a Navy SEAL and I was their pilot. I spent a lot of time with him overseas and stateside. After the Chopper crash, I was medically discharged and joined the DOJ after I was healed up. John stayed in and had been doing a lot to help make the world a better place. We often talked, but over time we drifted apart. It wasn't uncommon with team guys that get out and their friends stay in. I got busy with my own cases and John was active and consumed with being overseas. Plus, when he was stateside, he had a daughter. Six year old Lilly Rose, and she was a sweetheart. He spent every minute that he could with her, and now, that little girl was going to grow up without a father.

"Eighteen months ago."

Eighteen fucking months ago?

The shock hit me like a ton of bricks and my mind started to spiral with should haves and would haves.

I missed his funeral.

I should have been told.

His wife, Darla, should have called me.

I would have been there for her and Lilly. I could have made sure they were well taken care of and looked after. I would have moved closer so I could be there for her. Damn it, he was my best friend, we had gone through literal war together, I would have been there.

I should have been told.

"Why didn't anyone tell me? Why didn't *you* tell me?" I demanded.

"I just found out. I figured someone would have told you," Sticks said with a small shrug, as if we were talking about the weather.

"What about Darla and Lilly? How did he die?"

"Eighteen months ago, he was stateside. One night, someone stormed into his home and killed both John and Darla. They took Lilly."

"They what?"

I was trying not to panic. I knew panicking wasn't going to help the situation and it wasn't going to make Sticks feel anything. The drugs kept him numb so he wouldn't have to feel anything ever again. I couldn't believe this, though. Both John and Darla were dead and their sweet baby girl had been kidnapped.

She could be dead.

This couldn't be happening right now.

"She was grabbed by the killers, who the Douglas police department believe to be human traffickers. They haven't been able to find her, yet, and they suspect she is dead."

No. No, no, no.

This was all a horrible dream and I was going to wake up any minute.

When I did, the first thing I would do would be to call John and hear his voice. I would hear him tell me that him, his wife, and their sweet daughter were all okay.

"This is a nightmare," I said as I stood and started to pace around.

"I know, it's a shock. I thought someone would have told you before me. I heard about it through the grapevine."

"And they don't know who did it?" I asked as I tried to get my mind to work.

"Naw. Local police looked into and so did NCIS, but nothing. Local police have it now, and it's sitting as a cold case."

Fuck.

A cold case?

What the hell!

"Okay, I'm going to look into it. I'll have the task force take it over." I didn't care what I had to do, I was getting this case. I didn't care what strings I had to pull, who I had to threaten, I would make it happen, one way or another.

"There's something else you need to know."

"Fucking great, what?" I couldn't handle any more surprises.

"You remember Finley?"

Finley Quinn, how could I forget about him?

Finley was John's younger brother. I had met him when he was a young teenager when I was hanging around with John before I changed over to the DOJ five years ago. He was a sweet kid, a bit shy, but I could see how much he loved John and how much John loved him.

I had lost contact with Finley for a long while, but then he called me completely out of the blue and I had spoken to him just a month ago. He'd sounded exhausted, in more ways than just one. Something had been going on with him, but when I tried to get it out of him, he changed the subject and turned things around on me. All I could do was talk to him about my past cases to try and help him get through whatever he was going through. What I couldn't understand, though, is why it had taken him almost eighteen months to call me. He would have been told about John, Darla, and Lilly, obviously.

I should have been the first person he called when it happened, so why didn't he?

And why did he call me a month ago?

"Of course I do. Why?"

"He went into the SEALs. He enlisted on his eighteenth birthday. He left with an honorable discharge eighteen months ago when all this shit went down. Now, I don't know if this part is one hundred percent true or not, but my source told me he's been going after the human trafficking ring. He's been working undercover for them, Rafe."

"Undercover how?"

My blood was turning cold. Working undercover for a human trafficking ring, one that targeted children, was not a place any good man should be.

Especially one who was only twenty-five.

Finley shouldn't be looking into that

alone. If he was working for the police or an agency, that would be different. He would be going in with a handler and a team there to make sure he was safe and could get out, should he need to. It was too dangerous for him to be going in alone.

"He went in on his own. He's not connected to any law enforcement or agency. He did his own investigation and worked his way in. He's been in for eighteen months almost, now. He's trying to find Lilly before he shuts anything down."

Fuck.

He might never be able to find Lilly, and while I understood his need to look for her, I would be doing the exact same thing, he might never find her. She could be long dead or sold somewhere overseas. Even if he did find her, after eighteen months there's no telling what she had been through or what she would be like.

She might not remember him.

Kids who get taken at a young age, their mind can shut off everything they knew before they were taken as a way to protect itself. She might have no idea who he was or who her parents were.

It all made sense now, though. Why Finley had called me and sounded destroyed. He was getting a front row seat to the worst this world had to offer. He was a good man sentenced to a lifetime in hell and he had no way of getting out. He wasn't going to leave without his niece, and even once he found her, it was going to be almost impossible to get her out with them both living. Even if by some miracle he did get Lilly out alive, they would have to live in hiding for the rest of their lives from this human trafficking ring. They didn't take too kindly to having their product walking off. They would hunt them down and they wouldn't stop until they were both dead.

Only, they wouldn't just kill them.

They would both be tortured until they were, finally, brutally murdered.

Finley needed help, and I was going to make sure he got it.

"How do you know? You just found out about John, and if Finley is undercover, how the hell did you hear about it?"

"I just heard about John, but you weren't the first call I made after finding out. I only met that kid once, but I knew for a fact there was no way Finley was going to let his niece be out there on her own. He's gay and he looked on that little girl like she was his own daughter. I called an old buddy of mine who's a hacker. He found out that Finley was honorably discharged within days of John's death. He cleaned out his bank account, got rid of his apartment, and then he went completely off the grid. Finley Quinn hasn't been spotted or made any transactions in eighteen months, now. Only logical explanation, is that he's working undercover to find Lilly."

That didn't ease my fears, though. If Sticks' friend was able to get this information, there was no telling what this human trafficking organization would be able to find on him. The trick was, as long as they didn't believe they needed to look he should be okay. But that was a big *if.* One I wasn't happy about.

"I'll handle it. I'll get the task force working on it and I'll get a meeting with Finley. I'll get them both out of there," I promised.

I didn't care what I had to do. I was getting both Lilly and Finley out of that hell. I didn't care if I had to go down to hell itself to make it happen, I would. I was not going to allow John's memory, his death, to be in vain. I would save his little girl and his brother, and then maybe John and Darla would be able to rest in peace.

CHAPTER TWO

Finley

FIFTY-ONE...

Fifty-one graves I'd now dug in my life. That wouldn't be too bad if I was a gravedigger. If I worked for a cemetery and my whole job was to dig graves for a living.

Only, that wasn't what I was doing.

And these weren't people who died of old age surrounded by loved ones.

No, these were innocent children.

Children that should have had the chance to grow up and pursue their dreams.

Children that should have been able to believe in magic and know that monsters didn't exist.

I should be fighting to end this. I should be going in guns blazing and killing every single one of these motherfuckers for ever even daring to think about harming a child.

I shouldn't be here burying another child that I failed to protect.

At twenty-four, I was set to be going into BUDS to become a Navy SEAL. I had my whole future and career ahead of me. I was going to be a Navy SEAL just like my big brother. John had been my idol, my hero, and I wanted nothing more than to protect him. To fight alongside him, to protect him and pay him back for all of the love and support he had given me.

Our parents were good people, but affection wasn't something they were used to giving. John, though, he had no problem hugging me twelve times a day. Telling me he loved me every chance he got. It was those moments of affection that made me feel loved. Those moments that helped me to get through some of the hardest moments of my childhood.

My whole life, my whole world, came

crashing down all around me eighteen months ago. I'd left the Navy and was now working for a human trafficking organization. I went from helping to protect innocent people, to standing around and guarding the men that brought nothing but pure evil to this world.

This was never supposed to be my life.

I still can't believe it is my life, but this was the position that I was in and I had put myself in this position. I just hoped that John wasn't rolling in his grave for my actions. I was doing this for him. I was doing this to find Lilly and I *would* find her. I didn't care what I had to do, I was not going to leave until I had her with me.

The problem was, though, I didn't know how much longer I could do this. I had seen horrors from war. I had seen people killed, blown up. I had seen the result of a suicide bomber in a well-populated area. I was no stranger to the horrors that were out there.

This, though, this was on a whole other level.

A level I wasn't truly prepared for.

When I had decided to leave the Navy and become a member of a human trafficking organization, I wasn't thinking perfectly clear. I had been devastated to get the news of my brother's death and my niece's kidnapping, and everything within my body told me to find her. That it didn't matter what I had to do or see, all that mattered was finding her.

And that was still true.

I would keep going until I had nothing left of my soul if it meant I could find her and save her. I just wasn't expecting for it to be this hard to keep it together. To stop myself from jumping in to protect the children as I searched for her.

It wasn't lost on me that I was allowing these horrors to continue to happen to hundreds of other children. I was putting her life, her welfare, over the welfare of these other children. I knew that, I did. And I knew that made me a terrible man, a terrible human being, because I should be saving all of these children's lives. I should be killing as many of these fuckers that I could and rescuing them. But if I did that, I might never find Lilly and I couldn't stomach the thought that she would be all alone and growing up in this kind of world.

Once I found her, then I could shut

this organization down. I would kill every last one of these fuckers and I wouldn't stop until I got every last member and every last man that paid to have sex with these children. I would kill them all, and then, she would finally be safe.

These children would finally be safe.

I sat down on a boulder as I fought to catch my breath. I was covered in dirt and blood, once again, and once again, it was from a child that was far too young to know this level of pain.

It was going to be another long day. Another day that I would spend in the shower trying to wash the invisible blood off my skin. I was starting to drown and it was getting very hard to keep my head above the water. Eighteen months of this hell, and I was reaching a breaking point. I could feel it coming on and there was nothing I could do to stop it.

I needed to stop it, though, because I couldn't lose it. I couldn't break down and walk away. Doing that would leave her out there on her own and I couldn't do that. She knew I would be looking for her and I was not going to let her down.

I let out a sigh and tried to get my shaking to subside. The tremors were getting worse and happening more frequently. If I wasn't careful, the others would start to suspect that I wasn't as hard as I had led them to believe. If they thought I had feelings, they would kill me, and I was not about to let that happen.

I had to get her safe first.

Her safety was the only thing that mattered to me. If I died afterward, then so be it. I didn't expect it to take this long when I went in. I thought it would be a few weeks and then we both would be out. I didn't expect for it to be eighteen months later. I didn't expect I would be still trying to find her. Something had to happen, soon, or I didn't know what I would do.

It was why I made the mistake of calling Rafe a month ago. I didn't tell him about what I was doing. I wasn't going to risk him finding me and pulling me out, or worse, jumping in and working undercover himself. I wasn't going to have him in this life. I should never have called him, but I didn't know what else to do that night.

The nightmare, the horror of this life, had been too much for me a month ago and I'd felt like I was going to break. He was my lifeline. The one person I knew that I could reach out to and, at just the sound of his voice, would take me off that cliff.

And it did.

We spoke for hours. Well, he spoke and I listened to his voice. I knew he wanted to know what was going on with me. I imagine he figured I had been on a bad operation or a shitty tour. I should have told him about John and Lilly. There was no way he shouldn't know, but I couldn't do that to him. Maybe, it was selfish that I kept it quiet. Maybe, I shouldn't have kept that information from him.

Especially, when I was able to confirm that he had no idea his best friend was dead.

It had been wrong for me to keep it from him, but at the time, I needed to hear his voice not filled with pain. I needed him to talk to me about something that wasn't connected to this trafficking organization. It was selfish, but I needed it too desperately.

Letting out a sigh, I pushed off of the boulder and started to head for my truck. It was going to be a long day and it was just getting started.

***

Freshly showered, I sat there looking down at Mizzie. I had made sure to take her with me whenever I had to go somewhere new for the organization. Sometimes, they would send me to pick up weapons or to threaten someone that could potentially screw the organization over. I kept Mizzie in my bag, buried so none of the guys would find her, because that was the last thing I needed to try and explain away. It wasn't like I could tell them I liked playing with dolls. I wasn't going to risk getting her taken from me, either. When I found Lilly, I was going to make sure she had Mizzie.

I wasn't sure what Lilly would remember after eighteen months. If her mind had blocked out her life before this to protect itself. If that did happen, I was hoping that Mizzie would be what triggered her mind back. Not because I wanted to cause her pain, but because she wouldn't be afraid of me. She deserved to remember her mom and dad. She deserved to remember the love they had for her and how hard they fought to protect her that night.

From what the detectives could piece together, John was down in his office on the first floor, while Darla and Lilly were upstairs. Lilly was asleep in her bed and Darla was reading in her bed. The intruders had cut the lines to the security system before they picked the lock. They had moved quietly, not expecting John to be out of bed. They killed Darla before she even had much of a chance to scream. The sound of gunshots alerted John and he ran up the stairs and immediately went into Lilly's room to grab her and run. He was shot in the back before he reached her bed. All of the blood in the house came back as Darla's and John's, so Lilly hadn't been hurt, at least, not enough to bleed. According to the detectives, there had been a spike in child kidnappings in the state that were connected to a human trafficking organization. They suspected this organization had grabbed Lilly. It was the same M.O.

I'd been working undercover for them ever since.

At the sound of footsteps, I quickly hid Mizzie back in my bag just as the door opened.

"What?" I asked in a hard voice.

"You're getting moody there, Chris. The Boss needs us to do a money run," Donald said.

Donald was the guy I spent most of my time with. He was my trainer, I guess you could call it. It was his job to make sure I was getting all situated with every aspect that came up. I had been in for eighteen months, so my initial training was long done. However, as I slowly moved up in the organization, I had other shit I needed to learn. The money run was a new one I was doing, and I was hoping that would lead me to something I could use later on to shut them all down.

"Let's go," I said as I climbed to my feet.

Eighteen months in, but I had never given up hope that I would find Lilly. She would get to have Mizzie back one day, even if it took my dying breath.

CHAPTER THREE

Rafe

AS I MADE my way toward the station, I pulled out my phone and called Finley. I wasn't sure if it was a number he would still have or not. It could have been a phone booth number, for all I knew. I needed him to answer, though. I had to talk to him. I had to see him and figure out what he knew and what our next move was going to be.

I was pissed beyond belief that he had been going through this alone for the past eighteen months. I knew we hadn't spoken in almost ten years, but that didn't mean he couldn't reach out to me. That I wouldn't be there for him when things got bad. I thought he would have known that, but apparently not.

After calling him for the tenth time in a row, I was finally rewarded with an actual person.

"Why are you blowing up my phone?" Fin demanded and I knew he might not be alone.

"I just heard about what happened. I didn't know about any of it, no one called to tell me. I'm heading your way. I'll be there in six hours. We need to meet. Tell me where and when."

I knew I was being demanding, but in my defense, I'd just discovered that my best friend and his wife had been murdered eighteen months ago, and their six year old daughter was trapped in hell. I should have been told. I could have helped to investigate. I could have still been investigating. I might have found her by now.

"If you want to renegotiate the price it's going to cost you. Rest Stop on 191 Highway, just past Exit 230. I'll meet you there for three. This better be worth it, Asshole."

"I'll be there," I simply said, and then, Finley ended the call.

I didn't expect a warm welcome. I suspected that he could be around others. I hadn't worked undercover on a long-term assignment, but I had worked undercover before. I knew you had to be careful every second to not let anything slip.

One single slip up and you could be killed.

I had to get in with him.

I had to make sure he was safe and his ass was covered.

I pulled into the station and immediately climbed from the car, not even taking the time to lock the doors behind me. I jogged inside the diminutive building and made my way to the conference room where I knew the others would be.

"We got a case," I said as I strolled to the front of the very small room.

"What's going on?" Mason asked, picking up on my urgency.

"Douglas, Arizona has a cold case that we need to take over. I don't care how we do it, but it needs to be ours," I blurted.

"Rafe, slow down. What is going on?"

Mason asked, his voice calm and controlled.

I knew I had to get my thoughts and emotions back under lock and key. I wasn't going to be of any use to them in a state of panic. I sucked in a deep breath, forcing myself to calm down and regain control of my emotions.

"John Quinn, he was a SEAL and my best friend. I just heard that eighteen months ago him and his wife were murdered in their home. Their five-year-old daughter at the time was kidnapped by the killers. Local police and NCIS investigated; they suspect that she was grabbed by human traffickers. They haven't found her and they suspect that she is dead. It's a cold case right now. But roughly eighteen months ago, John's younger brother, Finley, who was set to become a SEAL, was honorably discharged and he has been working solo undercover for the human trafficking organization to try and find his niece, Lilly."

"He went in without being connected to an agency?" Cooper asked, clearly shocked.

"Is that bad?" Jarod asked.

"It means he doesn't have a handler. There's no one he can call if he needs to get out. No one to offer any backup or help. He's taking on a massive risk," Mason explained.

"He's also putting himself in a dangerous position in terms of what he does. There's no agency to cover his ass should he have to help in any illegal activities. He might get his niece, but he could be arrested for any number of crimes. Not to mention, if he doesn't get the full organization, they will hunt them both down and kill 'em," Cooper added.

"Have you heard from him at all in the past eighteen months?" Mason asked me.

"I heard from him once, a month ago. He never told me what happened or what he was doing. He sounded exhausted and just dead. He didn't tell me about anything that was going on. He refused to talk about anything when I pressed to know more. I don't know why he didn't tell me what happened or what he was doing. I don't know why he called me just to hear me talk about nothing."

That was what I couldn't understand, because there was no reason for him to call me and not talk to me. He could have told me. I would have helped, but instead, he didn't talk about any of it. I literally spent three hours just talking about my life, about nothing important. I don't understand why that was what he needed.

"Because you were the closest he could get to his brother," Ryzen answered, as if it was the most obvious thing in the world.

"In that moment, it sounds like he needed to hear someone's voice that didn't bring horrible memories with it. Someone who was as close as he could get to his brother. You were his best friend and there is a chance he figured you knew what had happened to him. Maybe that was his way of asking for help without having to say the words," Hollingsworth added.

I wasn't sure if that was what Finley's plan had been, but if it was, I wished I had pressed for more information. The problem was, I couldn't have offered my help because I hadn't known John was dead or that Lilly was kidnapped. But I did now, and he was getting my help, whether he liked it or not.

"Who has the rights to the case?"

Mason asked.

"I don't know. My friend didn't know much. On my way here, I called the number that Finley had called me from. He finally answered, though he couldn't say much. I suspect he wasn't alone. He did agree to meet with me at a rest stop in Douglas at three pm today."

"All right, everyone grab your go-bags. We're wheels up in thirty minutes," Mason said as he stood.

The others all gave a nod and Mason turned to look at me. I could tell he was worried about me, but he didn't need to be. I wasn't about to let this case go.

Not now and not ever.

I would bring Lilly and Finley home.

I didn't care what I had to do.

"I'm fine," I instantly said.

"I'm sure you are, but you know how badly this could turn out. Lilly could be dead, she could be on the other side of the world. We might not be able to get her. You might have to pull Finley out."

I knew all of that, I did, but I also knew, like Finley, I wasn't going to stop until I found Lilly, alive or dead. I was bringing my best friend's daughter home, no matter how long it took.

"I'm going in with him," I stated.

Mason let out a soft sigh before he spoke. "I know. It's what I would do. It's what any of us would do. The first step, though, is making sure you come back alive with Finley and, hopefully, Lilly. Grab your stuff, let's get in the air and we can figure out our next move.

I gave a nod. Mason was right, we had to get to Douglas and we needed to get there earlier than the three pm meet. The sooner we got there and settled into a conference room, the better off we'd be.

***

Once we were in the air and leveled out, Mason rose and it was game time.

"All right, we need to know who has the rights to this case. Is it the local PD or NCIS? We need to know so we can speak with the person in charge to get the case from them. Now, it's a cold case, so we might not have much push back. We need to know everything both the local PD and NCIS know. NCIS will have a more advanced investigation as they handled the murders. We need both."

"I was in the SEALs so I'll handle NCIS," Hollingsworth stated.

"You were in the SEALs?" Jarod said, surprised.

"As of five years ago. I'll give a buddy of mine a call who is with NCIS."

"I'll handle local PD. The rest of you, let's look for chatter about any human trafficking ring that is operating in and around Arizona. They have been known to travel within a state if it allows them to grab a child. Check for anyone that has a beef with either John or his wife. Maybe this was personal and the traffickers took the opportunity to grab Lilly," Mason continued.

"Rafe, what did Darla do?" Jarod asked.

"She was a stay at home mom. Before they had Lilly, she worked as a nurse for the military hospital."

"What team was he on?" Ryzen asked.

"He was in SEAL Team Eight."

"Any past that could have come up?" Mason asked.

"Nothing that I can think of. He wouldn't have been able to tell me much, but SEALs' identities are classified," I answered.

"It takes a lot to get the identities of SEALs. Each one is labeled as a code name and a number in the records. Everything is redacted. Plus, if they did target John, they would have targeted the other members of his team. That, we would have heard about on the news. Not to mention, if this was connected to an operation overseas, they could have easily waited to get the whole team over there," Hollingsworth said.

"All right, look into it, as well, and see if something pops. We need to know everything we can about their movements. I also want the area where the meet will happen scooped out. Coop, get us some satellite images of the area. I don't want any surprises for this meet."

"Got it, Boss," Coop said.

"When you have that, I also need you to focus on getting a solid backstop started. Leave the name blank for now, we'll need more intel from Finley before you can finish it," Mason added.

"Backstop for who?" Coop asked, confused.

"For me. I'm going in undercover with Finley," I stated.

"Wait, what? How is that safe?" Jarod asked, shocked.

"Finley called Rafe for a reason. He's

been in this organization for eighteen months, seeing the worst that humanity has to offer. He's burnt out and on the edge. The only way to keep Finley in play long enough for us to shut this organization down and free all of the children, is to put someone in play to give him some support and back up. Rafe knows him the best and they have already established a level of trust. Putting him in play makes the most sense," Mason explained.

"It's dangerous," Ryzen warned.

"I know it is, but I'm not about to leave Finley on his own, there. Lilly is his niece, but she's mine, too. John and I were brothers. I was there the day Lilly was born. These animals took her and I'm going to find her. My connection to Lilly and John will bring comfort and a sense of trust to Finley about how important this is to him. I can handle dangerous."

I had survived going to war, I could handle this. I knew it wasn't going to be easy, I wasn't fooling myself. I was going to have to see things I would wish I could forget. I would have to do things I would hate myself for, but if I could save Lilly, save those children, and avenge John's death, it would all be worth it.

"You have your assignments, let's get moving," Mason commanded.

I was instantly in action, getting my laptop up and running. I needed to know everything I could about the last few weeks of John's life.

I'm coming, Finley, and together we will bring Lilly home.

I just hoped that the both of them would be able to hold on long enough for me to get there.

CHAPTER FOUR

Finley

SITTING IN THE truck outside of a stash house was not how I liked to enjoy my time. However, I didn't have to guard one of the brothel houses, so I was happy to be sitting here wasting time.

I felt my phone vibrate again and I knew who was calling me. When it first rang, I checked to see if it was one of my many bosses, but it was Rafe's number. I had been trying to ignore it, not really in the position to talk to him openly. Donald was in the stash house, but he could come out at any moment. After repeated back to back calls, I finally gave in and answered the phone.

"Why are you blowing up my phone?" I kept my voice hard so I wouldn't lose my edge when Donald came back to the truck. This was definitely not the time for me to break down. It was too dangerous here.

"I just heard about what happened. I didn't know about any of it, no one called to tell me. I'm heading your way. I'll be there in six hours. We need to meet. Tell me where and when."

So, my theory that Rafe didn't know about John and Lilly was correct. Now, he did know and I had no idea who had informed him. He'd also discovered that I was working undercover. That concerned me, because if he heard about it through some grapevine, who else could know about what I was doing?

More importantly, who I truly am.

This wasn't good. If word got out that I was working undercover to essentially go after this organization, they could figure out that I wasn't who I said I was. If they discovered that I'd been lying to them, that I was connected to Lilly, they would kill us both. Donald got into the truck as I spoke.

"If you want to renegotiate the price it's going to cost you. Rest Stop on 191 Highway, just past Exit 230. I'll meet you there for three. This better be worth it, Asshole."

"I'll be there," Rafe said, before he ended the call.

I knew I would now need to come up with some type of explanation as to why I would be meeting someone. The organization didn't like it when you disappeared or met with random people. I would have to make it work somehow. Donald looked over at me and I could see the uncertainty in his eyes.

"Who the fuck was that?" he demanded.

"My cousin."

I knew without even having to talk to Rafe that he would be joining me undercover. There would be nothing I could say to him that would change his mind. It didn't matter that I was already in and there was no need for the both of us to experience this level of horror. It didn't matter how dangerous it would be, especially with him being a Federal Agent. None of it would matter, because just like me, all he would need to know was that Lilly was trapped in this world and she needed to be freed.

"You call your cousin an asshole?" Donald asked, with a raised eyebrow.

"Yeah, he's an asshole. He's finally back in town, though."

I had to set the groundwork for Rafe joining me. I had to be careful with what I said and how I played him off. At the same time, I had to make it seem like he would be good for the organization. They didn't exactly just let anyone in. This wasn't like a gang that ran drugs or guns, this was child sex workers. It took a sick type of man who would work for an organization like this.

"Where has he been?"

"Laying low. He's a contract worker and his recent contract was a Fed. Now that they have convicted someone for it, he's free to come back to life."

I couldn't make it anything overtly public. It couldn't be anything that they could Google and find a million articles on. At the same time, I had to make it good enough for the organization to be interested in him. I wouldn't give specifics on the Fed who died, that could be something Rafe did. I knew that Federal Agents were killed all the time, but there were a few that had been killed within the past two years that were hits and not in the line of duty or an accident. With being in the DOJ, Rafe would have a better idea of who he could use to work with his cover story.

"He's hardcore."

"He's always been like that. He goes where the money is," I said with a shrug.

"And you're buying something from him?"

"Looking to purchase an old classic car he has. Why all the fucking questions?" I asked, annoyed.

"It's not like you to get phone calls outside of the guys. You've never mentioned a cousin before, either."

He was dubious, not that I could blame him. It wasn't like I had told them all my life story. In a situation like this, it was better to keep things simple and not give many details unless asked for them. I didn't go into this thinking I would have a make believe family. I wasn't planning on having a cousin, but now, I didn't have much of a choice. Rafe was going to infiltrate the organization no matter what

I said, so at least this way, I would be able to help make it a smoother transition.

"Because he needed to lay low. I didn't even know where he was. He called me last month out of the blue. He doesn't know who I'm working for, but he knows I'm working for someone."

"He know what you do?"

"Naw, we never talk about work over a phone line. We keep that shit for in person. I ain't gonna tell him about this organization."

Donald was quiet for a good ten minutes and I had no idea what to make of it. Donald wasn't high up in the business, but he had been with the organization for a good twenty years. He liked being a middle of the row man. He didn't have too many responsibilities and as long as he didn't fuck up, he didn't have to worry about being killed. If you did your job, you didn't have anything to worry over.

A lot of the guys that I'd come across had been middlemen. They didn't know much, other than what they have been trained to do. It's why I was at a stand still. I couldn't seem to figure out how to get past the middlemen and get to some of the more higher-ups. I needed the lieutenants around me so I could get to the head of the organization. I didn't even know who he was. I didn't even have a name. The weird thing was, though, Donald didn't have one, either. Whoever was in charge was smart enough to not release their name.

I also suspected that there would be a front man. Someone that everyone thought was in charge, but was really just the face of the group. Whoever was in charge was smart and I suspected they had been doing this for a very long time, quite possibly for generations within their family.

"He the type to get squeamish?" Donald asked after ten minutes.

"He's a hitman," I simply stated.

"Some hitmen kill men, some kill women, others will only kill cheating spouses. They all have their own preferences."

"He don't care who you are if the price is right. He's always been about making money. He likes living a good life with fast cars, fancy homes, and an endless supply of bitches. The price tag is all he cares about. He's done it all from guns to drugs, bringing over Asian slave workers. He doesn't care as long as the money is green."

I knew I was painting Rafe in a very dark image, but that image might be what we needed to get further in the organization. I had been doing this for too long and the longer this went on, the higher the chances were that Lilly would be killed. I knew Rafe would understand and he would handle whatever came his way. He knew how special and important Lilly was and he wouldn't put anything above her.

"You can tell him about it and see how he reacts. If you think he won't have an issue, then we could do a meet with Jaks."

"Who's Jaks?"

This was the first time I had heard that name and it got me excited. If Jaks was a higher ranking man than Donald, this might be what I finally needed to move up within the organization.

"Regional leader for the organization. You've never met him because you don't need to. But Jaks is always looking for enforcers and we're down a couple."

"I thought our numbers were good."

"We lost two a few days ago. They got too hands on with the product and we're not running a charity. If you want to sample the product, you gotta pay every time. Now, we're down two and need replacements."

That was a rule that the organization had. They didn't believe in freebies. I didn't know what to suspect in the guards and runners in this type of organization. I figured it would be men that only cared about money and didn't have any morals at all.

What I didn't expect, was how many men liked the paycheck, but also enjoyed having sex with children. I had met a couple of the "trainers" as they were called. The ones who would torture and condition the new children into this life. I had met a couple, but I had never seen it, nor did I know just what they did to the children. I was too afraid to ask. What I could tell, though, they got off on it. They loved to cause pain, but they also loved to have sex with children. There had been plenty of guards within the organization that were the exact same. If you were muscular and a pedophile, you could live out your dreams in this place. It was disgusting and there was no other word for it. I couldn't wait until I could kill every last one of these fuckers.

"I'll let him know. He doesn't tend to care about what is going on as long as it pays well. He's got no problem keeping people in line and he won't think twice about the product being children."

"What's his name?"

"Don't know," I simply said.

"What the fuck do you mean you don't know your own cousin's name?" Donald asked with a deadly edge.

"He changes it all the time. He has multiple aliases that he uses and when he has to, he kills them off. I don't know what he's going by, right now," I said with a shrug.

I couldn't give a name, because I had no idea what Rafe would be going under with. I also couldn't afford for anyone to run the name and discover that they either didn't exist or they weren't connected to me at all. I had to play it off and just hope that Donald believed it.

He just gave a nod and that didn't do anything to ease my nerves. I hoped that meant he was satisfied, but I wouldn't know until later. For now, I would have to play it off like this was completely normal. I would be meeting with Rafe in the next few hours and, hopefully, he would be able to get us moved up in the organization to their enforcer positions. Then, we could start looking at some of the lieutenants and finally get this organization shut down, once and for all.

I wasn't happy that Rafe would be mixed up in this, but I had to admit, I did feel better knowing that I wouldn't be doing this alone anymore. I had a partner and, hopefully, that would help me to hold on long enough to find Lilly.

CHAPTER FIVE

Rafe

I DRUMMED MY finger against the steering wheel as I made the short journey to the designated meeting spot for Finley. I hadn't seen this man in eight years and I had no idea what he looked like or what he had been through. I knew the past eighteen months had been horrible for him, I couldn't imagine they were anything else, but I had no idea what he was like before all of this.

He had been in the Navy and I knew that was a hard life. I had seen it firsthand. Even with being in the Air

Force, I had a front row seat to what SEALs went through and the horrors that they saw. There was no telling what Finley could have seen while he was in the Navy and what it had done to him.

I was hoping that he had something that we could use to push this case along. Something that we could use to find Lilly. There truly was no telling where she could be at this point. The sooner we could find her, the better off she and the other children would be.

I also had to be honest with myself. I wasn't sure how long I would be able to be undercover with these people, these monsters. I was programmed to protect people, especially children. Anyone that was in the military and law enforcement was. It was our sole purpose to keep the innocent safe and innocent. These children would be getting abused and raped, and I wouldn't be able to save them. At least, not right now. I already hated it, but I also knew there was nothing else I could do.

I owed it to John to find his little girl, no matter what. Once I had Lilly, then I would make sure everyone paid for what they had done. I would shut that organization down and save those kids.

The file that the local PD had was a joke. They had the rights to the case with John being dead. It was easy to get them to give it up. It was complete crap, though. They had basically washed their hands of the investigation once NCIS showed up, figuring they would take it over completely and search for Lilly.

Only NCIS didn't find their killer or Lilly.

They didn't find any leads outside of this possible human trafficking angle. They had other cases to work on so NCIS handed it back over to the local PD. It happened more times than people realized. A federal agency could do a lot, but if they didn't have anything and they had more pressing cases, the case would get pushed back down to a local level.

This was a case that never should have been handed back down.

They should have done everything they could to find Lilly.

The five-year-old daughter of a Navy SEAL had been kidnapped. That should have been all the motivation they needed to work this case into the ground. They might have been able to find Lilly before she had been put through hell.

It pissed me off that neither side seemed to be taking this seriously. I knew in Arizona that human trafficking was bad. We were close to Mexico and this State often held a great deal of cartel members and gangs. Still, we weren't talking about drugs or guns. This was *children* being taken and sold for sex slave labor. That should never be something that became common. That should never be something that local PD accepted and moved on from. They should have only worked Lilly's case, just like they should have only worked any other case where a child had been kidnapped.

It was bullshit that eighteen months later they had nothing.

Letting out a sigh as I pulled off to the rest stop, I couldn't help but scan the area to see if there was anyone else around. This was a pretty deserted area of the State and would be perfect for a meeting.

I saw a pickup truck parked at the other end of the rest stop. I drove over to it and turned off my truck. I instantly spied a man sitting on the top of a picnic table roughly fifteen yards from me. I knew this man would be Finley, but the sight of him still took me back.

He wore black straight cut jeans that went over his black combat style boots. He had a black t-shirt underneath his black leather jacket. He wasn't small, but he wasn't overly muscular, either. I could tell he had some muscles from the way his jacket fit, but I'd bet they weren't from working out, but rather manual labor. His hair was kept short and he had a five o'clock shadow that I could see from here. I couldn't make out his eyes and I knew they would tell me what I needed to know about his mental health.

Climbing out of my truck, I made my way over toward him. At the sound of my footsteps, Finley glanced over at me and my heart stopped. It had been eight years since I had laid eyes on him, but could I still remember his face as if it was yesterday. He'd had sparkling blue eyes that pulled you in, and his skin had been flawlessly smooth. Now, those same sparking blue eyes were dull and dead looking. And a long scar that went from his left eyebrow through his eye and stopped at the top of his cheekbone marked his flawlessly smooth skin. It wasn't that old, maybe six months. Someone had sliced him with a very sharp knife and he was lucky he hadn't lost his sight in that eye. Seeing it only fueled my anger.

Someone had dared to mark him.

To mark his flawless skin.

It made me want blood. It made me want to hunt down this son of a bitch and make sure he paid for that huge mistake.

I strolled over to him and Finley gave me a smirk as he held his fist up and spoke.

"You're my cousin. Sit down and act like everything is normal, I don't know if we're being watched."

I hit my fist against his as I went and sat down next to him on the picnic table. I scanned the area, but I didn't see another person or vehicle.

"Who did that to you?" I asked with a deadly edge to my voice. I couldn't help it. Seeing that scar pissed me off. I wanted blood and I would be getting it.

"He's dead. I can take care of myself, Rafe."

"Never said you couldn't, but that doesn't mean you have to do it on your own. What happened?"

I knew he was a military trained professional. I knew John made sure he could fight and hold his own, but that didn't change that he didn't have to go through this world all on his own. He had brothers that would stand behind him and fight with him.

"The organization likes to take the lower-ranking men and have them fight to the death. The others take bets on who is going to win."

Jesus, fuck.

I had done research on different human trafficking organizations from my time with the DOJ. I'd had a few cases come across my desk, but I'd never gone face to face with any of them. Most of them fit in one of two categories. Either they treated it like a business and it was very professional—no fighting, no sampling the products, it was treated just as any successful business, or it was rough and violent, the organization loved to shed blood internally and externally. It seemed like this organization was going to fall within that second category.

"How did you hear about John?" Finley asked, getting down to business.

"I found out this morning from Sticks.

I don't know if you remember him, but he was a pilot who had been on John's SEAL Team. He told me this morning. He heard it through the grapevine, finally. Why didn't you tell me, though? You had my number. I would have come down to help."

"I figured you would have heard, eventually. I wasn't thinking about making phone calls to everyone that John knew. I was focused on finding Lilly. I figured you would have known, by now. Besides, I knew you would come down and I knew you would risk everything to find her. I wasn't going to put you in the organization. I was already going in, we both didn't need to be there."

"I could have investigated. I would have helped. You didn't need to go undercover alone for these types of people. It's too dangerous."

"I'm not a kid, Rafe. I'm not that fifteen year old who you first met. I've been to war. I know what horrors there are in this world. I don't need your protection," he said with an edge to his voice.

I knew he wasn't a kid anymore. I knew he had been to war and had survived operations that were very dangerous. I knew he was good enough to be accepted into BUDS. I knew all of that, but I couldn't help but think of him as John's kid brother.

Someone that I was supposed to protect.

Someone that I had promised John I would look out for should he die in the line of duty.

I knew I didn't have to keep that promise anymore. Finley was twenty-five. He was more than capable of looking out for himself.

Still, I wanted to protect him.

"You've been undercover for eighteen months. How far have you gotten?"

We weren't going to agree on this and we didn't have the time to waste arguing about it. I needed to know what the situation was so I could prepare my backstop properly and get into the organization to start helping Finley shut it down and find Lilly.

"Not as far as I would like. It's not that easy to move up. The head of the organization is very smart. He doesn't show his face and if you aren't higher up within the organization, you won't even know his name. I suspect that the face of the organization that those higher up see, is just a front. The true leader is completely hidden."

"Shit, that's smart. Nothing probably connects back to him. He's completely in the clear unless you can get him on tape or in the middle of an illegal act. Who do you work with?"

This guy not showing his face was going to make it a hundred times harder to get everyone in the organization. If we didn't, we risked putting Finley and Lilly in jeopardy for the rest of their lives.

"I work under a guy named Donald. He was with me when you called. I told him you were my cousin and I was looking to purchase a classic car from you. He wanted to know about you. I had never mentioned any family before."

"What did you tell him about me?"

"He asked what your name was, but I told him I didn't know. Said you were muscle for hire and a hitman. That you often used aliases and killed them off when you needed to, so even I didn't know what you were going by, right now. The story is this: you accepted a contract to take out an FBI Agent. After you killed him, you went into hiding for a while. Now that the wrong man has been convicted for the Fed's death, you are free to move around again. That all you care about is making money and nothing else matters."

"Someone that would fit perfectly within the organization. He take the bait?"

"I told him I wouldn't mention anything about the organization to you, but he said I could float it and see how you reacted. I was just told that Jaks, a regional leader for the organization, is looking for two new enforcers. Apparently, the previous enforcers were taken out because they weren't paying to sample the products. That's what they call the kids. Now, they need two new enforcers."

"Which is where I could come in," I said with understanding.

It wasn't going to be easy. I was going to have to see things I wished I never did and I would be around the children and not able to help them, but if it got us closer to finding Lilly, then I would do what I had to. I'd do whatever it took and then deal with it when all of this was said and done.

"If you can get in as an enforcer, then you might be able to convince Jaks that I would be a good second choice. If we both can move up to enforcers, it would get us the names of the regional leaders and the lieutenants in the organization. We might be able to find out what region Lilly is in. I know from one of the other runners that all of the children and their transactions are kept in the books that each regional leader has. Every child is rotated all around the country. Usually, every three months they are moved to a new location."

"The book might not tell us where Lilly is right now, but it could tell us all of the other regional locations. We need to get our hands on that book. All right, I am here with my team. I work for a task force now, one that focuses on crimes against children. They are going to work the case from their end and we will work our way through the organization and report what we can back to them. We have different tech, too, that we can use for evidence collection. I promise you, Fin, we'll find Lilly."

There was no other option. I was going to find Lilly. I was not going to have my best friend's daughter trapped in this world. She was coming home, where she could heal and go back to being a child.

RAFE

Finley spoke as he handed me a folded up piece of paper. "That's where the meet is where you'll be introduced to Donald and Jaks. They're gonna wanna test you. I don't know what it will be."

"It's fine, I can handle myself. Will you be there?" I asked as I took the offered paper.

"Yeah, I'll be there," he said as he pushed off the picnic table and stood.

"I know it's hard, but you have to remember, I'm here now. You don't have to go through this alone anymore, Fin."

I wanted him to count on me. To feel like he could tell me anything and that I would be there for him. He had been doing this for so long. Too long. He wasn't alone anymore and I wasn't going to let him keep operating like he was.

"I'm fine. I'll see you tomorrow."

I watched as he headed out and I hated how different he was, now. He was tortured and it pissed me off to see it. He used to be this sweet and innocent kid, and now, he was a hard twenty-five year old who was fighting in this world all alone. I had so many more questions to ask him, but they were going to have to wait. I had to re-earn his trust, but I would re-earn it. We would get through this together and then we would get Lilly healthy and healed from this trauma. Finley wasn't alone anymore and he would come to discover that soon enough.

CHAPTER SIX

Finley

I SHOULDN'T BE this nervous, but I couldn't help it. I wasn't sure how well today would go. I didn't trust Donald, for obvious reasons, and I had never met or heard of Jaks. I had no idea what was going to happen today.

The warehouse that Donald had told us to meet at wasn't one I had been to. I was prepared for anything that could happen there today. I was hoping nothing went down, that we wouldn't be fighting for our lives by the end of the meeting.

I pulled up to the warehouse and saw

that Rafe was already there. He was still sitting in his truck, presumably waiting for me. If he was nervous, he wasn't showing it. I had to admire him for that.

I had to admit, though, even to just myself, seeing Rafe yesterday was like getting a breath of fresh air. I'd had a huge crush on him when I was a teenager. He would show up all the time in my wet dreams and fantasies. I used to fantasize about him holding me down and having his wicked way with me. There was nothing I wouldn't let him do to me. Literally nothing. Even now, I wouldn't think twice about dropping to my knees and putting his dick in my mouth if he asked me to.

I had been with other guys. Hell, I'd been having sex since I was sixteen. It was nothing new to me. I did learn pretty early on that I liked bigger guys. That I liked guys that only topped. I had tried being a top, but it didn't feel as good to me. Nowhere near as good. I was a bottom and I was proud of it.

When I got into the military, I discovered that I preferred older men. They were more experienced, but they also knew what they wanted. In my second week into Boot Camp, I ended up hooking up with one of the Captains on base. He was forty-eight and into BDSM. We spent three years together before he went and cheated on me with an eighteen-year-old in a new Boot Camp class.

I didn't mind the BDSM stuff, but it wasn't what turned me on. Though, the hand around my neck did do something to me. That was more about feeling possessed and feeling the passion from the other person.

Ever since the Captain, I'd been keeping it to one night stands or friends with benefits. I hadn't dated anyone, officially, in years. Even with the Captain, it had to stay a huge secret. Not only was he a Captain and I was a Private, but he was in the closet.

Wife and kids closet.

I was his dirty secret and I thought he cared about me. I thought he loved me. Turned out, he loved that I was young and easy to manipulate.

I guess if I'm honest, I had always been a more submissive person. John had all of the fire and strength. Whenever I got bullied in school, John kicked their ass. I didn't have to stand up for myself in school. Then, when I graduated Boot Camp and got placed on a team, the guys protected me. We all protected each other, in and out of the field. If someone hit me, before I could even swing at them one of the guys was already hitting them. Protective brothers constantly surrounded me all the time.

It wasn't until I started to work undercover did I realize how alone I was. How I had never been left to fight for myself. I could fight, but I discovered I didn't like fighting. It was one thing to fight for your life on the battlefield, but what I was doing in this organization wasn't that. I was being forced to fight to the death a couple times a month. I was being given the worst jobs and pushed around. I had no idea how I ended up the easy prey, but I suspected it had something to do with my lack of confidence and skill in standing up for myself. I had to show Rafe, though, that I could handle whatever came my way. I wasn't going to be some delicate flower he needed to protect. I wasn't a kid anymore. We were equals and I refused to be seen or treated as anything less. With that new resolve, I climbed out of my truck.

"Cuz," I said with a nod as Rafe got out of his.

"Chris," he said with a nod back.

It was weird hearing a different name coming out of his mouth for me, but we had to be careful. We had talked last night for a good hour to make sure we had our stories straight. He knew everything about Chris and I knew everything about Mark. We weren't going to get another chance with this.

We both made our way inside the warehouse and I wasn't surprised to see Donald there along with three other guys. I knew two of them, Henry and Malcolm. I figured the third man was Jaks.

It was time to get serious, time to go to work.

We both made our way toward the three of them and I could see out of the corner of my eye that Rafe was tense. He was ready for a strike and I couldn't blame him. There was no telling what would happen here. All we could do was take it play by play and hope we both were able to walk out of here alive.

"On time. I appreciate a worker that can show up when they are told," Jaks said once we were close enough.

"You don't make money by showing up late," Rafe countered.

"No, you don't. I know Chris, but I don't know your name," Jaks said.

"Mark. You must be Jaks. I heard you were looking for men."

I wasn't sure if this was how we should be playing it, but Rafe had more experience than me in this area so I was going to follow his lead. Jaks looked at both of us and I could tell he was judging us. He was evaluating us. Up until now, I was a bottom feeder and I didn't have any reason to be here outside of bringing Rafe to them.

"Chris, what are you still doing here?" Jaks said with an edge to his voice.

"Donald told me to bring my cousin by," I said.

I wasn't sure what I should be doing. If Jaks wanted me to leave, I couldn't exactly go against him. I risked being kicked out if I went against him. At the same time, though, I didn't want to leave Rafe here all on his own where anything could happen to him.

"And now you have. Get the fuck out," Jaks said with a deadly edge.

"He goes, I go," Rafe said with a simple shrug.

My gaze shot over to him. He needed to be in to help us get closer to the book that Jaks had. We needed him in and now, he was risking us both being killed. I didn't like having to leave, but I would if that got us closer to Lilly.

"What?" Jaks asked.

"I don't know any of you from shit. That's my cousin. I only work with him. I've been told you need two enforcers for your business to guard the products. I got no problem with that, but my cousin is the only partner I need in the field. He goes with me or I walk."

I did my best to not throw up, because everything in me was screaming to. I was a nervous wreck, because I had no idea how any of them were going to handle being spoken to like that. I didn't know Malcolm and Henry very well, but I knew they could be very violent when they wanted to be.

Just like I knew Donald had no problem with blood.

I had to assume that as a regional leader, Jaks was good with a slow death. They weren't the type of men that tolerate being spoken to like this. Jaks gave a dark chuckle before he spoke.

"You got balls. All right, if you both pass the test and you can both be enforcers."

That was surprising.

I felt like Jaks was up to something, but I couldn't be sure until he told us exactly what the test was. I didn't even have a clue as to what the test could be. I didn't even know where to start to guess. I was hoping it wasn't going to be anything involving a child. I knew we both wouldn't have been able to handle it.

"What's the test? I didn't exactly bring my number two pencil," Rafe said back.

Jaks just smirked as he went and gave a nod to both Henry and Malcolm. They both headed off as Jaks spoke.

"I like you. Is it true that you killed a cop?"

"No, I killed a Fed. That time, anyway," Rafe answered with a smirk.

"I've never heard of you," Donald stated.

"I'd be a shitty contract killer if you did," Rafe countered.

"That you would. Still, in this world you would think someone would have heard of you," Donald pressed, but Rafe was expecting it.

"I change up my name and look to keep my identity hidden. The underworld is filled with snitches, which is exactly why I don't trust anyone outside of my cousin."

The answers all sounded good, but I wasn't certain that Donald believed them. I wasn't sure why Donald seemed more skeptical than Jaks. Jaks outranked him in the organization. It was his call to make. Maybe Donald was trying to move up within the group, but he had never given me any indication that he wanted to move up. He seemed happy to be in the middle of the road.

At the sound of the door opening, we both turned to see Malcolm and Henry pulling two guys with them. The guys were beaten up and barely able to walk. I didn't recognize them, but I knew they had to be from the business. They were muscular and built for a fight. I suspected they were the two enforcers that were enjoying the product for free. Malcolm and Henry forced them both down onto the knees as Jaks spoke.

"These men thought they could steal

from me. They thought they could enjoy my product as much as they wanted without having to pay me a cent. For months, they have been stealing money from me. You say you are a contract killer, then prove it. You both want the new position, then kill them. Snap their necks and take their place."

Yup, that sounded about right.

At least this test involved killing two men that liked to have sex with children. As far as killing goes, this one would be easy. We had both killed bad men before while in the military. This wasn't anything new. Plus, we both knew how to snap someone's neck. I wasn't certain about Rafe, but I had done it before when we needed to breach a compound without making a sound.

"Do you want the one on the right or the left?" Rafe asked, looking at me.

"Dealer's choice," I said with a shrug.

Rafe looked at them both, playing up like he was trying to decide who he felt like killing today. He was playing this perfectly and I never should have doubted him. He was always badass, that was part of what made him so fucking sexy, especially to my younger self.

"Left. The right looks like a squirmer and I like when they struggle," he said with a playful smile to the man he had picked to kill.

We both moved over to our guy and, with practiced ease, we grabbed them in a choke hold. Sure enough Rafe's guy did squirm and try to get free, but with their hands tied behind their backs, there wasn't much the guy could do.

We both made it quick as we snapped their necks. They were pedophiles, but that didn't change that we were both honorable men and saw no need to draw out someone's death, even if they deserved it. The second their bodies hit the ground, Jaks gave us both a pleased smile before he spoke.

"You're in. Now, go bury the bodies. Chris knows where. Then meet back at the clubhouse. Malcolm and Henry will give you the lowdown on your new positions."

"Copy, Boss," I said.

The three of them started to head out and once we were alone, Rafe turned to look at me.

"What did he mean you knew where?"

"Whenever they need a grave dug, they

have me do it. Grab his feet," I said as I bent down to grab my guy underneath his arms. I was not about to drag this much dead weight to my truck.

"So you know where the kids are?" he asked as he picked up my guy's feet.

"I know where the dead ones are located in this area. But like I said, there's different regions, I've only been here."

Rafe just gave a nod and we started to carry dead man number one out to my truck. I already had a couple of shovels in my truck so we could just go and bury them and call it a day.

We got both of the guys dumped into the bed of my truck and I covered them with a tarp so they would, hopefully, go unnoticed. I had yet to be pulled over, so I was hoping that would stay true. I would hate to have to try and talk my way out of the two dead bodies in my truck bed. I doubted that an officer would care too much about them being dead pedophiles.

"You can follow me or just get in my truck, choice is yours," I said.

"I'll follow. We don't know when I'll need my truck."

I just gave a nod and climbed into my

truck. I hated that I would have to be digging yet another grave, but at least this time, it wasn't for a child that died far too young. It was for two assholes that had caused any number of children added pain. They deserved death and burying them was going to be the easiest thing I had ever done for this association. I hoped tonight went well and we would finally be able to start getting them shut down.

CHAPTER SEVEN

Rafe

I MADE SURE to pay very careful attention to where we were going on the drive to the clubhouse. I needed to know how to describe where we were, should we be in trouble and needed the guys to come and get us out. There weren't many street signs out this way, and if we needed an extract, it would be based on the places we had passed.

The clubhouse itself was a large warehouse that had been transformed to have different rooms. Fin had explained to me that everyone in the region would stay either here, or at one of three other locations. He stayed here and I would be here with him as well.

Each room had two beds and Fin didn't have a roommate, so I would be his roommate, now. I wasn't sure what would be happening once we arrived back at the clubhouse. I didn't know if there would be more tests or if there would be questions. We had passed the first test, but I wasn't foolish enough to believe that it would be the only test that we would be given. We were the new guys, at least I was, and those in a new position were often tested until they had proven their loyalty. I was ready for it, but I wasn't certain if Fin would be.

Walking into the clubhouse, I immediately saw a large open area with couches, a bar, and a flat screen tv mounted on the wall. It didn't look like a warehouse and, clearly, it had been renovated to accommodate people living here. I had to admit, though, I was surprised that the organization's leader had decided to make it so livable. That would have taken money out of his pocket, but at the same time, I guess it made sense. He needed workers, and he needed to make sure they were happy so they would stay with his organization. Having guys quitting or leaving wasn't good for him and only increased the odds of them talking. If you gave them a nice place to live and a decent pay, they stuck around.

"Bout time you got back," Malcolm said as he held two bottles of whiskey in each hand.

"I had to show him where it was," Fin stated as Malcolm handed him a bottle of whiskey before giving one to me.

"What's this for?" I asked as Malcolm handed another bottle to Henry before sitting down with the last bottle.

"To celebrate. You're now part of the family, we gotta celebrate that shit," Henry stated as he opened his bottle. Apparently, we were getting drunk tonight.

Fin and I both opened our bottles and when Malcolm held his up, we all did the same as he spoke.

"To the newest member and to the little bitch moving up in life. Here's hoping we don't have to cut off your dicks."

Charming.

We all clicked our bottles together before we took a swing.

"Fuck, we should have cut their dicks off," Henry said to Malcolm, referring to our predecessors.

"Couldn't. Boss said not to kill 'em."

"A guy doesn't die from getting his dick cut off. The artery in your junk naturally shrinks up to stop the bleeding. Makes having to take a leak pretty painful," I stated, and everyone gave me a confused look.

In my defense, the only reason I knew that was because it happened to a guy in one of the SEAL teams I was flying for. It wasn't a knife, but an explosion. Still, the premise was the same.

"How the fuck do you know that?" Henry couldn't help but ask.

"I don't appreciate someone fucking someone that belongs to me," I said with a deadly edge.

Malcolm gave a dark laugh as he sat back with a huge smile on his face. He raised his bottle as he spoke. "Well, cheers to fucking that."

We raised our bottles once again and took a drink. These guys were either psychopaths or wannabe psychopaths.

RAFE

Either way, it was easy to impress them. All you had to be was dark and dangerous and they would eat every word up. I hoped soon enough we would be able to slip away and hide out for the rest of the night. It had already been a long day and I wanted nothing more than some time away from these people.

***

We stumbled into Fin's room, or technically, *our* room, now. We would be sharing and that was perfectly fine with me. This way, I could keep an eye on him and we could have a place to chat about the investigation. Tonight was not our finest hour. We shouldn't have drank anywhere near the amount we did. Normally, I never would, but we had to blend in. We had to play the role and when they kept pouring shots, we weren't in the position to turn them down. Now, we were both drunk and barely able to walk. I knew come morning we would be hating ourselves for it with the massive hangovers we were going to have.

Fin closed the door once we were in his room and, to my surprise, there was a lock on it. He flipped it before he stumbled over to one of the two beds in the room. I assumed that one was his.

"We are so fucked for tomorrow," he said with a goofy smile, and I couldn't help but laugh as I sat next to him.

"You normally drink like this?"

"Nope, bottom feeders don't really drink with the important guys. Not that enforcers are all that important in the grand scheme of things, but they don't hang out with the low hanging fruit," he rambled slightly, and it only made my smile bigger. He was so cute. He used to ramble about nothing when he was younger. That's how you knew he was nervous.

Apparently, that applied to him being drunk as well.

I knew I shouldn't be thinking about Fin in that way. I shouldn't be thinking about him as cute or notice how hot his ass looked in his tight jeans. He was just John's cute little brother back then, and now, he was this muscular, sexy war veteran that had the most kissable lips I had ever seen. I was hard just thinking about how good he would feel against my skin. How good he would feel underneath me writhing and moaning like a bitch in heat.

"What? You're staring," Fin said, flashing me a small smile as he looked right at me.

I should tell him we needed to go to bed, that we needed sleep, but the whiskey flooding my body had a mind of its own.

Fuck it.

I closed the small gap between us and crushed my mouth against his. He was instantly moaning and it unleashed the monster within me. I deepened the kiss, sliding my tongue into his mouth and he immediately submitted to me.

I needed more.

I needed a lot more.

I moved away from his mouth and started to rip at his clothing, I needed to feel his skin against mine. We both worked quickly on removing the other's clothes and once we were both naked, I pushed him down onto his bed and flipped him over. I wanted his ass, and I was going to get it. Fin was instantly up on his knees and resting on his elbows, presenting his perfect ass to me.

"Lube?" I managed to ask as I kept my gaze on his smooth ass.

"Drawer," he said with a small nod to the shitty bedside table next to the bed.

I reached over and grabbed it and I couldn't help but smirk. He was undercover, but he still made sure to bring lube for when he needed to jerk off.

"Don't moan too loud. We can't have someone hear us."

That was all the warning I gave him before I was spreading his cheeks and running my tongue over his hole. Fin turned his head into the pillows and gave a deep moan at the pleasure.

"You taste so sweet," I moaned as I continued to lick his hole, pushing the tip of my tongue inside.

The needy moans of appreciation that I was rewarded with were almost enough to make me come. It had clearly been a long time since he had been touched by another man and all of that time was obviously making his body extra sensitive. I enjoyed eating his ass for a good five minutes before I got the lube open and quickly added two fingers inside of him. Fin gave a whimper as he pushed his hips toward me, trying to get my fingers even deeper inside of him.

"Someone is needy. Has it been a while

since you've had a dick in your ass?" I asked as I kissed along his spine.

"Oh fuck, please," he begged as he started to fuck my fingers.

I lightly bit him on the back of his neck before I spoke. "I asked you a question."

"Yes," he answered with a breathy voice.

"Yes, what?"

"Yes, it's been a while since I've had a dick in my ass."

I hit his sweet spot and the moan that he gave me, fuck, I could have come from it alone.

"Shit, please. I need you in me."

The fact that I could make him beg for my dick, it only fueled me on. I never wanted to stop hearing his moans. To stop listening to his needy begging.

"You want me to fuck you hard?"

"Yes."

"You want me to fill your hungry hole with my dick?"

"Yes, please," he whimpered.

"Beg for it," I said into his ear and he whined.

I removed my fingers from him and watched his hole clench on air as he waited for me to return. I slicked up my dick and ran it between his cheeks, lightly passing my tip over his hole. As badly as I wanted to push inside of him, I wanted to hear him beg more.

"Please, I need your dick. Fuck, please, Rafe put your big dick inside my needy hole. Fuck me hard and deep. Own my ass."

"You want me to own your needy hole?" I asked with a smirk as I circled his pucker with my tip.

"Yes, please," he whined, bucking his hips as he tried to push back on my crown.

As much as I would have loved to drag this out more, I felt like I was going to explode with just the sounds coming from him. If I didn't fuck him soon, this was going to be over before we even got started.

I placed my hands on his hips and slammed into him, pushing my entire dick inside of him. The shockwave of pleasure hit the both of us and we both let out deep moans at the sensation. I couldn't believe how tight and hot he was. I could have stayed inside of him forever. This was going to be hard and fast, there was no avoiding it, not when he felt this amazing around me.

I reached around and grabbed him by the front of his neck and pulled him back so he was up on his knees with his back arched. He let out a whimper and his hands went to my hips to help hold himself up. I started to thrust hard and deep inside of him and with the new position, my dick hit his prostate dead on with every thrust.

"You feel so fucking good," I said as I bit the bottom of his ear, causing yet another whimper to escape his lips.

I kept my grip on his neck tight, but not too tight. He would still be able to breathe and I knew he was loving the grip. His whole body was trembling with pleasure and I knew he would already be close to the edge just as I was.

"Your dick is dripping with pre-cum. I'm going to make you come without touching your cock. I'm going to milk you and watch as you come a river."

I picked up my pace even more and Fin could not stop moaning and writhing within my grasp. Thankfully, his moans were muffled with my hand around his neck.

I could feel his ass tightening around

me. He was going to explode and it was going to feel glorious. I tightened my grip on his neck just slightly as I hit his sweet spot once more with a hard thrust.

Fin's hands tightened around my hips and I knew I would have fingernail impressions in my skin for the next couple of days. He gave a deep and long moan as his ass clamped down around me as he came hard and long.

"That's it, come for me," I growled as I watched rope after rope of seed shoot out of him.

His whole entire body was shaking from the force of his pleasure. It was delicious and I never wanted this to end. But I could no longer hold on and with a final hard thrust, I buried myself deep inside of him and let go. Quite possibly the hardest I had ever come before in my life. I shot pulse after pulse of cum into his ass and I never thought it would end. The pleasure was earth shattering. It was a pleasure that consumed you and nothing but you and the person you were with existed. I had never felt this amazing before and I doubted I ever would again.

I loosened my grip on his neck as we both fought to catch our breaths. I moved us down onto the bed so we were on our right side. I had every intention of saying something, of moving, but all I could manage to do was try and catch my breath and then the need for sleep became too great and I gave into it.

CHAPTER EIGHT

Finley

OH FUCK, MY head hurt.

Why, just why, did I drink that much?

I knew better than to drink that much when I was supposed to be undercover. I knew I wouldn't have said anything I wasn't supposed to, but that didn't change that I was supposed to be able to defend myself should something pop off. And based on the headache that I was feeling right now, I wouldn't have been much help in the fighting department last night.

The sound of a groan from behind me

and then an arm being draped across my stomach had me instantly snapping my eyes open. I looked down at the hand and I would know that watch anywhere.

I was naked in bed with Rafe.

I'd had sex with Rafe.

Last night came flooding back to me. I had sex with *Rafe,* that man that I had been fantasizing about since I was fifteen. The man that I had wondered for much of my teenaged years what he looked like naked, or how amazing it would feel to have him inside of me. The man I had literally drooled over and jacked off to thoughts of *for years.*

I had sex with him.

Drunk sex.

And holy fuck, it was good.

Thankfully, I wasn't blacked out drunk so I wouldn't forget it. It was good, so very good, and it was worth the very long wait. I knew, though, without a doubt this was going to be an issue for Rafe. To him, I was still John's little brother. He was not going to be happy that we'd had sex. In my own defense, though, he kissed me.

I didn't climb his tree.

He climbed mine.

It was completely fair game after that.

RAFE

Oh fuck, it was good.

Last night was a dream, minus the whiskey. It was a dream come true for me and if I died, I could now die with a fulfilled life. It sounded stupid, I knew, but I had been waiting ten years to feel him inside of me and it was glorious.

Rafe moved again behind me, but this time his hips, and it was that moment that I realized, he was still inside of me, and his dick was hard. It took all of my strength and concentration not to squeeze his dick or move my hips. I knew he would wake up soon and he would end it, but for right now, I wanted to soak up as much of the moment that I could. In that moment, I could imagine that we were just waking up at the other's home and none of the human trafficking business was going on around us. We were just two guys attracted to each other, enjoying the other's body.

Rafe thrust his hips again as he gave a soft moan and moved his hand to my dick. Instantly, I was hard and couldn't stop the soft moan that escaped my lips. The sound stirred Rafe awake and I knew he was aware of the situation when his hand snapped away from my dick.

"Fuck," Rafe said as his mind caught up with him.

"Technically," I said with a small smirk.

Rafe groaned and went to pull out, but I quickly spoke to stop him.

"Wait, don't move."

I knew, logically, this was ridiculous, because he should be moving. He should be pulling out and we should be writing this off as a drunken mistake. I knew that was what he wanted to do and it would suck and hurt, but I would go with it.

At the same time, though, he was already in me, could one more time really hurt?

"Why?" Rafe asked, confused.

"I know there is going to be a whole speech about how it was a drunken one-night stand and it can't happen again. That we're supposed to be undercover and it's all very dangerous, blah, blah, blah... I get it."

"If you understand, then why can't I move?"

"Because, technically, you're already in me so this would count as a second round. And if it already counts as us having sex twice, why not finish?"

I knew it was insane, I didn't need him to tell me that. But in my defense, the sex was earth shattering last night.

Every man I was with after him was going to pale in comparison, so why not have one more round?

If there was a chance I could have mind-blowing sex again, why not fight for it?

I squeezed my walls around his dick and Rafe groaned deep in his throat at the pleasure, the sound vibrating through his chest at my back.

"I know you want to. How much could one more time really hurt?" I asked with a smirk as I glanced back at him.

I could see the conflict in Rafe's eyes, but I could also see the deep desire and heat within the orbs. He wanted me, whether he liked it or not. Whether he wanted to admit it or not, he wanted me.

And he could have all of me.

Rafe pulled his right hand from underneath my pillow and wrapped it over my mouth. He took his other hand and placed it on my thigh, lifting my leg up to give him more room and better access. He slowly pulled out before he slammed right back in, causing me to let out an appreciative hum into his hand at the burn that flooded my ass. Rafe bent down and spoke into my ear as he thrust hard and fast in and out of me.

"I'm going to make you mine. You are going to feel my dick inside of you for the rest of the day."

I gave a long whimper and my need skyrocketed. I wanted to feel him in me all day. I wanted to be owned by him. I loved the idea of him owning my body, belonging to him. I never wanted something more in my life.

"So needy. I'm going to fill your tight hole with my come. Touch your dick, I want to watch as you play with it as I fuck you," Rafe said as he picked up his pace.

I couldn't stop moaning as I moved my hand down and started to jerk off in time with his thrusts. He felt amazing. This was even better than last night and I had no idea how that was even possible.

"Don't come, not until I give you permission to," Rafe ordered, and it had my whole body trembling in pleasure.

Rafe's pace was brutal and I knew I would be feeling him for the next couple of days. That only fueled my arousal. He was just as much in need as I was. I wasn't sure how long it had been since he had sex, with the exception of last night, but based on his raw need, I suspected it had been a while. I could feel myself getting closer, my orgasm was reaching the cliff and I was about to fall off.

"I didn't say you could come, yet," Rafe said as he lightly bit my neck.

I gave another whimper at being denied my release, but I stopped moving my hand and focused on Rafe's dick hitting my sweet spot at a rapid pace. It was a good thing Rafe's hand was pressed tightly against my mouth, because otherwise I would be screaming by now. When I felt myself calmed down enough, I started to jerk off again. Rafe's pace became frantically erratic and I knew he was rocking the edge.

"Come for me, Baby. Milk the cum out of me with your tight, hot ass," Rafe ordered and that was all I needed to free fall off the edge.

I gave a muffled scream as I came hard and long. Pulse after pulse of cum shot out of me and it was enough to push Rafe over the edge. He bit down on the back of my shoulder and let out a deep growl as he came hard and deep buried inside of me. The feel of the added pain from the bite and the hot cum scorching my walls rocketed through me. I was shooting even more cum out from the pleasure of it all. My whole body was flying and I never wanted to come back down. I wanted to live in this euphoric bubble for the rest of my life. This bubble where Rafe's dick stayed inside of me and we spent the rest of our lives having sex. It was going to burst, I knew that, but right now, I was going to enjoy every last second of it before it did.

Rafe kissed the back of my shoulder where I knew his teeth marks would be. The thought of it almost made me hard again. I liked knowing that I would have an imprint of his teeth in my skin for the rest of the day. It made me feel like I had been marked by him and I really liked that. But I knew the bubble was about to burst so I steeled myself for it.

Rafe moved his hand and slowly pulled out of me. He got off the bed and I slowly moved to lie on my back as Rafe got up and went and grabbed his boxers.

Poof, just like that, we were back in reality.

Reality was a bitch.

"We can't do this again. Not only are we in a dangerous position with this organization. If they caught us together, there's no telling what they would do. But you're also John's kid brother."

"Fuck off with that, Rafe. I'm not fifteen. I've been to war a handful of times. I've been doing this for eighteen months on my own. I'm twenty-five, for fuck's sake. It's been eight years since I've seen you. You don't get to stand there and use my dead brother as an excuse," I growled out as I got up and grabbed my boxers.

"You're attracted to me, if you don't want to admit it to yourself, fine, whatever, but you don't get to use *him* as your reason to lie to the both of us."

I wasn't going to let him use John as his scapegoat.

That was not going to happen.

Not now, not ever.

I knew he was attracted to me. You couldn't fake that level of heat, of chemistry with someone that you weren't attracted to. He wanted me, I wanted him, but unlike him I didn't need some excuse to try and cover up my attraction. I was being honest with myself and with him. If he couldn't offer me the same, the least he could do was be honest with himself and leave my dead brother out of it.

"You're right, I'm sorry. Yes, I am attracted to you. Yes, the sex was possibly the best I've ever had. But that doesn't change the position we are in. It's too dangerous and we need to keep our focus on what matters the most. We need to get that book. If I can take pictures of the pages, I can send them to my team and they can run the names down."

"How many of you are here?" I asked as we got dressed. Rafe was right, we had to find the book and get this organization finally shut down. We needed to get back into work mode.

"Got a call yesterday before I went under from my boss. He's bringing down his brother and two private detectives that we've worked with previously to help out. There's going to be a lot of guards at the ring leader's location and he wants to make sure we have enough. We can't trust local PD because we don't know who could be in this organizations' back pocket. So, excluding the two of us, there's seven and a computer tech that is trained for the field, should they need him.”

"Okay, where do we go from here? How do we get access to the book?”

I wasn't sure what to do at this point. We had proven ourselves yesterday and were now enforcers, but I didn't know where that put us, now.

How were we going to be able to get access to the book without Jaks or anyone else seeing us do it?

"I don't know yet. We have to play the part for right now. Do as we are told and watch. We don't know where Jaks keeps the book. We don't even know what the book looks like. We have to bide our time and watch him without making it seem like we are watching him. For now, we do what we're told and play along.”

I didn't like it, but I knew Rafe was right. We couldn't push things too fast, otherwise, people would start to suspect that something more was going on and that would get us both killed. We just had to wait it out and wait for our opportunity to strike. Once we had it, then we could send the photos of the book off to his team and they would be able to start figuring out all of the stash houses for the kids and, hopefully, that could lead us to the head of the snake's location. I had to be patient, and I would be. I wasn't going through this alone, anymore. I had Rafe here as back up, and together we would make it happen.

CHAPTER NINE

Rafe

I STOOD THERE allowing the hot water to sluice down my skin. I needed to get a grip on myself. I shouldn't have had sex with Fin last night and I really shouldn't have had sex with him again this morning. I knew it was wrong, it would be a mistake, but I couldn't seem to help myself.

I could still vividly remember last night. I was trapped between wishing I did and wishing I didn't. If I didn't remember it, then I wouldn't know how unbelievable it was.

How perfect it felt.

I knew not every guy appreciated a rougher touch, but call it my kink or whatever. Some guys wanted it to be slow and sweet and that was fine when the mood called for it. For the most part, though, I liked to be a bit rough with biting and choking. The fact that Fin loved it that way, it only made the sex even better. Sex with Fin was off the chain good. It was the best sex I had ever had, last night and this morning.

Guilt plagued me, though, leaving a knot in my gut I wasn't sure would ever go away. He was John's kid brother. Fin was the kid that my best friend and I used to take out for pizza at the arcade. John would be rolling in his grave right now, knowing what I had just done to his little brother. It couldn't happen again, no matter how badly my body was screaming for it to continue. Begging for it to happen a hundred times more. Despite what Fin said, he was John's younger brother and I couldn't cross that line with him again.

I climbed out of the shower and quickly got dressed before I strolled out of the bathroom trying to pretend I hadn't a care in the world. Fin wasn't there and though I breathed a sigh of relief, I also knew I needed to find him and get caught up on what the plan was for today.

It only took me a few minutes to find him in the kitchen. There were other guys there that I didn't know. I expected there were going to be a lot of guys here that I didn't know, nor did I care to get to know.

I watched as Fin moved to grab some coffee, but one of the other guys pushed him back from the coffeemaker and grabbed the pot to pour the rest of the coffee into his mug. He then turned to look at Fin as he spoke.

"This better not taste like shit like last time, little bitch."

He walked past Fin, making sure to hit his shoulder against Fin and it sent Fin into the counter. I wanted to grab this asshole and lay him into the ground for pushing Fin around. I couldn't, though, because despite playing cousin, this wasn't the place for Fin to have his cousin fighting for him. The guys wouldn't respect him for that. In fact, the opposite would happen and they would go harder on him. They would just wait until I wasn't around. I was going to have to talk to him later about his attitude and how to handle these fuckers. Before I could get any coffee, Donald strolled into the room and spoke, nodding to both me and Fin.

"Let's go, you two. I gotta get you situated in your new positions."

Neither Fin nor I said anything. We just followed the other man out. I had no idea what either of our positions would be like, but I was hoping I would be able to keep an eye on Fin. I didn't like the idea of us not working beside each other.

***

Donald led me into an old looking mansion. Fin had been dropped off at his own location, an old looking house. It was smaller than this one, though, and I couldn't help but wonder if maybe they didn't trust him as much as he thought they did. If he was going to be responsible for less children, that told me they either didn't trust him, or they didn't respect him, at all. As if they were expecting for him to screw up so they were giving him a small job that wouldn't destroy them when he did screw up.

I knew from growing up that Fin was not a confrontational person. He was an easy going guy that went with the crowd. And that was great when you were working in a team environment, but it was not a good quality to have when you were working undercover for people this dangerous. Fin needed to have some attitude. He needed to show that he had a backbone and he was not going to take their shit lying down. The problem was, he was eighteen months in and now, there was nothing he could do about it. That was his alias' personality and there was no fixing it, now. I would be keeping a very close eye on him when I could to make sure I was there should something happen.

"This is where we keep the product that has been here long enough to know their place. They tend to be well behaved and for their good behavior we let them live here. They know their job and they do it, but at times you get the odd one that wants to take advantage of the system and try to break out. It's on you to make sure that doesn't happen. Your shift starts at nine in the morning, normally, and it goes until nine at night. You do rounds throughout the house and make sure that everything is locked up. All of the windows are locked and armed. The code is 8965. There are nine other guards in the house and on the grounds. There is one more that works the front door and deals with the clients. Now, none of the clients are allowed to be rough with the product here. If that is what they are looking for, they can go to Chris' house. Questions?"

"Naw, straight forward."

It was straight forward and there was really no need to ask any questions. I would be able to look around the house and try to see what I could use to our advantage. I also had the camera in my belt that would be able to take a photo of every client that came to the house. Fin had one, too, so the guys back in the task force would be able to run the photos and find out who they were. They'd keep track and then we could use it to arrest them later on once we get the leader. Donald headed out and left me alone to do my rounds. This was going to be a long day, but hopefully, it would lead us to what we needed to bring this organization down and find Lilly.

***

It was just after ten at night when I walked into the room I was sharing with

RAFE

Fin. It had been a long day.

I knew it was going to be hard, but it was really difficult for me to hear the moans coming from the rooms from the men. But also the fake moans that the children were making to please their forced customers.

It was hard to listen to what some of the other guards had to say about their time with the kids and not lose my cool. They acted as if we were all in a brothel with grown ass adults who were consenting to everything that was being done to them. That wasn't the reality, though. These were children.

Children that had been kidnapped and forced into this life.

Children that might have had their parents killed right in front of them before they were grabbed. Like Lilly. Everything about this was wrong and it was almost impossible not to kill every last one of these sick motherfuckers.

I walked into the room and saw Fin sitting on his bed. He looked just as exhausted as I felt and I knew it would have been harder on him today. I had the nice clients. He had the clients that got off on pain. He would have had the children that didn't want to be there, that still fought against what was happening to them. It wouldn't have been moans coming from the rooms, but screams of pain. It would have taken a toll on anyone, but especially someone with a good heart like Fin had. I went and sat down next to him on the bed before I spoke.

"Scale of one to ten?"

"I didn't have to see anything so, a seven, I guess. You?"

I had a feeling it was higher than a seven, but he wasn't about to admit it. "A five. The place Donald took me to, the kids had already been broken. They were the kids whose minds had already rewired themselves to protect them from the harsh reality of what was happening to them. They didn't fight, they did what they were told and they were rewarded for it by getting to have nicer clients and a nicer place to live. Donald said the guys that liked to be rough were to be at the house you were at today."

"Yeah. There were some pretty sick fucks that came in there today. I was on guard duty, but I heard some of their requests when they came in. Some people are sick, and I do mean *people*. There were some women there today, even. I don't know why, but I didn't even think a woman would be involved in this world."

"It's not common. Normally, a woman that likes younger men tends to target them elsewhere. Through school, community centers, at-risk shelters, they don't tend to pay for it in the underworld. They either must not be able to interact with their desired age group or they aren't confident enough that their victim won't talk. I'm sorry you had to go through that today."

I hated that he had to deal with that today. That he would need to go through it tomorrow, and every day after until we were able to shut this down. It was going to take a huge toll on him, mentally and emotionally. I was going to be here for him, but I couldn't be there when he needed it the most.

"It's fine. It takes us a step closer to finding Lilly and shutting them down."

"There is something I want to talk to you about. The guys, how they treat you, why don't you stand up for yourself with them?" I asked, gently.

Fin let out a sigh before he spoke. "I'm

not really good at that part. I've never been a confrontational person. I've always been easy going and I've never really had to stand up for myself. In school, whenever I had a problem with someone, I would tell John and we would talk it out. But before I could even do anything, John had already handled it. Then, when I was placed on my Navy team, I was eighteen and everyone was in their late twenties, early thirties. I quickly became the kid brother and whenever things got tense or when someone hit me, I didn't even get the chance to defend myself because there was already someone else handling it. I haven't really learned how to be confrontational, yet."

That made a lot of sense to me. I remembered when the SEAL team I was working with had a new rookie. They always protected him. They treated the guy like a kid brother and it was on them to protect.

It would be hard for Fin to have the strength to stand up for himself when he was used to someone else jumping in before he had the chance to even figure it out. And now that was a piece of his personality and it wasn't about to change any time soon.

"I get that. Not the best quality to have in a place like this, though. I know you can't go toe to toe with every guy that gives you shit, but you gotta start showing some attitude toward them. They won't respect you until you do. Right now, you're their punching bag. You're their bitch that they can make do whatever they want. You gotta start to squash that before it gets worse."

"I know. I'll figure it out."

We sat there in silence for a good twenty minutes before I decided to break it. We both needed a break from the operation. We needed time to unwind and try to forget about what was going on around us. I knew little moments like this would be what got us through all the dark times we were going to experience working undercover with these monsters.

"So, have you had any serious boyfriends before all of this?"

If Fin was surprised by the question, he didn't show it. It wasn't any of my business who he had dated or if he was madly in love with someone. We were just friends, and it wasn't any of my business, really.

Still, I had to know.

There was this uncontrollable desire to know.

"One, but that was back when I was eighteen. I was with him for three years. I thought it was serious, but turned out it wasn't at all. At least, not to him."

"You dated for three years, how is that not serious?"

"I've never actually told anyone this," Fin admitted.

"Well, now you have to tell me," I said with a playful smirk.

Fin rolled his eyes, but he did talk. "When I was in Boot Camp, I started to see someone. Captain Harris."

"Wait, *the* Captain Harris? The man who's a poster child for a traditional family with a wife and three kids. A house with a white picket fence and a dog? That Captain Harris?"

Holy shit.

There was no way. That man was homophobic and made a point of trying to keep homosexuals out of the military. The guy was a complete jerk and I knew he had given plenty of men a hard time for them being openly gay. Not only that, the guy was old. He would have been thirty years older than Fin at the time.

"Yes, that Captain Harris. I was training late one night and getting cleaned up in the showers when he came in. He said he heard someone in here and he wanted to make sure everyone was okay. He stood in the shower watching me and I wasn't sure what was going on, but then he kissed me and things went from there. I was young, and didn't think of what the repercussions could be. He was a Captain, for starters, but he made me feel special. He told me he was going to leave his wife and I foolishly believed him. We spent three years together. He was really into the BDSM world. I wasn't sure about it, but I wanted to make him happy. Some things he did I liked, but most of the time, I was just going along with it. He told me he loved me and soon we would have our own place together. But when I turned twenty-one, I went to the secret apartment he had for us and he was there with some other eighteen-year-old cadet he found in Boot Camp. He told me how I was too old and used up for him. That we were done and if I ever thought about telling someone what had happened, he would ruin my reputation and my career.

That was my last relationship."

It was unbelievable, but unfortunately it happened. It happened more times than people realized. Predators were everywhere, especially in an alpha male position. The military was rife with them.

At the age of eighteen or even twenty-one, Fin wouldn't have been able to see the signs. He wouldn't have any reason to believe that Captain Harris was a liar and just looking for someone to control and dominate. If I ever saw him again, I was going to be knocking his teeth out. Fin belonged to me and I was not going to tolerate anyone treating him like that, past and present.

I had to mentally slap myself for what I just thought.

Fin didn't belong to me.

He couldn't belong to me.

Even if my body wanted to own him.

We couldn't be together again. I had to keep that wall up between us, because I couldn't let myself fall for him.

"I'm sorry. He's an asshole and he doesn't deserve you. He'll get what's coming to him one day. You haven't been with anyone since?"

"I've had one-night stands or friends

with benefits over the years. No boyfriends, though. What about you?"

"A few boyfriends, but none that were serious. My job requires a lot of my time and I could be called at a moment's notice and have to travel. A lot of people don't like that aspect of my job and often don't last long," I said with a shrug.

It didn't bother me that I hadn't had a real serious boyfriend in my life. I wasn't looking for a husband to build a home and family with. My job was important and I was good with being married to it.

"I get that. Maybe one day, you'll find the right guy that won't care about all of that."

"Maybe."

I wasn't holding my breath, though. Not because I didn't believe that guy was out there, but because I didn't really want him to show up. I was good with casual sex and focusing all of my energy in my work, especially now, with the task force. It was important work and it deserved all of my attention.

That was what I had to keep reminding myself so I wouldn't get lost in the feelings and memories of Fin. Once this case was over, we would go our separate ways and chances were, I wouldn't see him again. What we had was fun, but that's all it would ever be. That's all I could ever let it be and that was fine.

So why did that thought hurt so much?

CHAPTER TEN

Finley

IT HAD BEEN two weeks since Rafe had joined me undercover.

For the past two weeks, we had been trying to get access to the book that Jaks allegedly had. We needed it, if we were ever going to be able to move forward with making arrests and finding Lilly.

Over the past two weeks, Rafe and I had been keeping things professional. I understood, but I couldn't ignore the slight hurt that went through me. It was no surprise that I was still attracted to him. I had been attracted to him for ten years. Getting the chance to have sex with him, even though it was a drunken one-night stand, it was still a dream come true. It had only fueled my attraction to him and now, more than ever, I couldn't stop thinking about him. He was invading my dreams every night. Every morning, I was waking up rock hard and more needy than ever. It was insane how much power he had over me like this and, even still, it didn't bother me.

Sex with Rafe was like heroin to me.

I was addicted and I needed more.

Unfortunately, I wasn't going to be getting any more so my body would just have to accept the detox I was going through.

Today was, hopefully, going to be a good day for us. Rafe had been able to discover that Jaks kept the book in his room at the clubhouse. His door was kept locked so no one could go in without a key, but Rafe knew how to pick a lock. The plan was for me to distract everyone so Rafe could go into Jaks' room, find the book, take photos, and then get back out to the main area of the clubhouse before anyone knew he was missing.

What I wasn't looking forward to was

the distraction part.

The only thing I could think of to distract everyone in the house would be to challenge someone. That would most definitely bring everyone to the fighting pit, just off of the main area of the clubhouse, to watch the fight. I would have to pick someone that had been a pain in my ass the whole time. I would have to make it like I was exploding from all of the shit I had taken from him. The risk was, though, there was no guarantee I would win. The fights there were always to the death, and if I didn't win, I was dead. It was just that simple. I knew Rafe wasn't happy about it, but it was the only way we could get access to the book. I just had to hold on long enough for Rafe to get in and get out.

"This is a bad idea," Rafe said once more as we stood in the bedroom.

"It's the only plan we have. I'll challenge Roth and I'll drag the fight out as long as we need for you to get into the office and get back. Once I see that you're back, I'll end it. I will handle the distraction. You focus on getting that book without getting caught."

Rafe couldn't be the distraction,

because I didn't know how to pick a lock. We had no choice but for him to go after the book.

He needed to remember that I *did* know how to fight. I was a military trained fighter. I could handle my own, even against someone the size of Roth.

Rafe let out a sigh and I could tell he desperately wanted to have another plan, but this was the best we could do. He gave a small nod and we both headed out.

We made our way to the main area of the clubhouse where the others would be hanging out. Normally, the guys all sat around there, drinking and sharing different stories of what they had seen from their shift. It was a weird group of guys, but they all seemed to enjoy hearing the gory details of their shifts.

I stood off to the side and waited for my moment to make a move. That came ten minutes later when Roth climbed out of his chair to go and grab another beer.

I calmly strolled over and plopped down in his spot. It might seem like a small thing to fight over and if it happened anywhere else, it would have been overlooked. However, the guys there all believed that everything belonged to them. By me sitting in a chair that Roth just got out of, he would take that as the same as if I was stealing his property. And by doing it in a room full of men, he wouldn't be able to let that go.

The second Roth turned around to go back to his seat, he stopped dead in his tracks at the sight of me in it. I didn't take my gaze off of him as he stalked over to me, waiting until he stood directly over top of me before he spoke.

"Get the fuck out of my spot, bitch."

"I don't have to leave shit. You weren't in it," I said, sounding a lot more confident than I was feeling. I couldn't just walk into the room and demand to fight Roth, that wouldn't work. I had to make it seem like it was Roth's idea for us to fight.

"I won't tell you again, bitch. Learn your place and get the hell out of my seat and go take a spot on the floor where you belong."

"Why don't you take a seat on the floor? You're the one running errands all day long. Seems to me like you're the bitch in this group," I said with a smirk.

If it had been possible, steam would have come out of his ears. Roth didn't like it when you talked back to him. None of the guys did, but especially Roth. He always had the need to prove that he was the top dog. I suspected he had an abusive father and that resulted in him having to prove that he was the strongest man in the room. Normally, I wouldn't give two thoughts about it, but it was working to my advantage, right now.

"Get the fuck up. It's time you learn your place," he seethed to me before he spoke loud enough for everyone to hear. "What do you say, boys? I think it's high time this bitch got what he deserves."

The guys started to cheer and whistle. They knew what Roth was saying. He had just challenged me and I could only do one of two things. I could agree and fight to the death, or I could back down and then everyone would do whatever they wanted with me, and in this crowd, that wouldn't be a good thing.

What Roth didn't know, though, was that I'd wanted him to challenge me so Rafe could get to Jaks' book. He had given us the perfect distraction that would, hopefully, shut this organization down.

I stood and I could hear snickers. They didn't think I would agree. I looked Roth right in the eyes and made sure my back was straight, my chin tilted up.

"Let's go."

He was shocked that I had said yes. I knew he wasn't expecting it and it showed on his face. His eyes widened and a reddish flush began to creep up his neck as his anger rose.

What was interesting, though, was I was treated like a piece of shit, and yet, I was the one who had the most fights under my belt. I had never lost a fight, obviously, since I was still alive, but in the past almost nineteen months, I had been in a fight nineteen times. I had killed nineteen other guys in a hand-to-hand combat fight.

The guys there didn't like me, but they knew I could fight and challenging me meant you could very well die. It was why most stopped challenging me anymore. My personality, though, made them assume I would be submissive and turn down an opportunity to fight when I didn't have to.

I turned on my heel and started out the door, walking toward the fighting area, and called back to him over my shoulder. "You coming or are you going to grab me a beer, bitch?"

The guys snickered and guffawed loud enough that I heard the sounds through the door, but this time it was directed at Roth and not me. That sealed the deal. There was no way Roth was going to lose face. He would die to keep it and that was exactly what was going to happen.

I wasn't cocky or arrogant when it came to my skills, but I had a lot more to live for than Roth. I was fighting for so much more than what Roth was and because of that, I would win.

We all filed into the fighting area and a quick scan of the faces told me that Jaks was here and Rafe wasn't. I just needed to draw this out until Rafe was able to get back here. I didn't know how well Roth could fight. I hadn't seen him fight in the time I'd been here, and I suspected he didn't fight unless he had to, but I was hoping that meant he wasn't very good.

Roth made the first move with a swing of his right arm and it was on.

***

The trick with fighting is it's hard to tell how long it has been since the brawl started. Even as a trained military fighter,

RAFE

I couldn't keep track of the time on the clock.

We were both getting tired. Roth wasn't a professionally trained fighter, but he was a street fighter. He was also bigger than me, so he was able to land a good number of hits, but he wasn't going to take me down. I knew I was going to be sore for a good week and the bruising was going to take time to heal, but it would all be worth it if Rafe was able to get photos of the book.

I gave Roth a strong right hook just as I saw Rafe appear out of the right corner of my eye. He gave me a very small nod and I knew that meant I could end this.

With Rafe now there, I didn't need to draw this out any longer.

It only took me a few more moments before I snapped Roth's neck and dropped his dead body to the ground. The sounds coming from the guys were a mixture of satisfaction and displeasure. It all depended on who they'd been betting on. Most of the guys knew to not bet against me, but if they did and I lost, they would get a rather large payout.

I didn't give any of it any attention. I just started to head out. I knew someone would have to bury the body, but right now, I was too sore to care. The pain was starting to come through as the adrenaline faded and the numbness started to dissipate. I vaguely heard Jaks telling one of the newer guys to clean up as I headed back to the bunkhouse and down the hallway to get back to my room. I could hear footsteps behind me, but I knew it was Rafe without having to look.

The second we were in the room, Rafe closed the door and his hands were on me. He guided me over to my bed and sat me down before he bent down in front of me and started to take inventory of my injuries.

I could feel blood trickling down my face. I knew my head was bleeding, my nose was busted up and my lip had split and was swollen to twice its original size. My whole face hurt and so did my torso. It wouldn't be surprising if I had a couple of cracked ribs and a bruised kidney. I was also starting to get dizzy, which wasn't a good sign.

"Did you get it?" I asked with a shaky voice.

"I got it. Don't worry about that, right now. We need to get you fixed up first.

How is your head? Any dizziness, headache?”

"Yeah. Feels like a concussion. I've had 'em before. I'll be fine."

I knew the signs of a concussion. This wasn't my first rodeo. Hell, I'd had two concussions since being in the organization. I could handle them. I could push through and get the job done.

"I gotta get your shirt off," Rafe said as he placed his hands on the hem of my shirt.

"Yeah," I said softly, fatigue hitting me fast.

He slowly and very carefully got my shirt up and off. It hurt having to raise my arms, but I got through it without wincing too much. There was bruising already starting to appear all over my torso. I had blocked as many hits as I could, but some did make their way through.

Rafe gently touched my ribs and it hurt, but it wasn't excruciating.

"They don't feel broken, but they are badly bruised. You need to take a shower. It'll help get the blood off, but also with your sore muscles and your concussion. Then you can sleep the rest of the day and night away.”

I gave a very miniscule nod in agreement and Rafe helped me to stand up. The second I was standing, though, the room spun, and if it hadn't been for Rafe's hands on me, I would have fallen over. I had no idea how well the shower was going to go over.

“It's okay, I got you,” Rafe said as he started to guide me over to the bathroom.

Once inside, he had me sitting on the closed toilet seat before he got the shower going. With it ready, he stripped down, to my surprise and approval, before he helped me to get out of the rest of my clothes.

Apparently, we were taking a shower together.

If I hadn't been in so much pain, this would have been very erotic and fun. As it stood, I was in pain and could barely stand up from the dizziness.

We got into the shower and the warm water hit my skin. I couldn't help but put my head down against his chest.

Rafe wrapped his arms around me and made sure he had my weight.

“I got you, Baby. I just need to get the blood off of you and then you can lay down."

I gave a soft hum as I fought to keep my eyes open. I felt Rafe's hands on me, trailing gently over my body. He tenderly washed my hair to get the blood out and then he picked up a cloth to get the blood off of my face.

The whole time, he made sure to keep a hold of me so I wouldn't fall. I had never had anyone help me in the shower or show me so much care before. He was extra gentle with me and it warmed my heart.

It also hurt, because I couldn't have him.

We would never get to have a fun shower together. We would never get to spend mornings in each other's arms. We would never get to go out on a date. It was just sex those two times and that was all I would ever get. I was good with that, but feeling how gentle he was with me right now, it was making me wish we could have had more.

I must have fallen asleep for a moment because when I opened my eyes the water was off and Rafe was moving me out of the shower and wrapping a towel around me. He sat me down on the closed toilet seat once again as he quickly dried off and dressed. He then disappeared and I figured he was getting me something to wear. A moment later, he came in with some boxers, but that was it. Working together, we got the boxers on me, and then I tumbled into bed. I wasn't even sure how I got into the bedroom from the bathroom, but I suppose it didn't really matter in the long run.

"I saw Mizzie," Rafe said after a moment.

I opened my eyes, but just barely, as I spoke. "Lilly sent her with me so I wasn't alone on my assignment. I wanted to make sure she got her back. I don't know what she's going to be like, so I thought maybe it would help her calm down and not feel so scared. I don't know if she'll remember who I am. She's so young," I softly explained.

"It's good that you brought it. She's going to feel really happy that you brought her. I was able to take photos of the book. I'm going to send them off to the guys."

"Did you read any of it?"

I knew he didn't have long, but I was hoping he might have skimmed through it while he took the photos.

"I didn't read it fully, but I did keep an eye out for the name Lilly. She was in it. She was here for the first six months after John's death. But she was moved to another brothel within the State."

I had expected as much. What hurt, though, was knowing she had been in the same city as me for six months and I hadn't found her. For close to a year, I hadn't been allowed to be around anyone that could have had contact with the children. Not even Donald had contact with the children. So, it made it hard to know where they were. Even knowing that, though, didn't make it any easier. It didn't make it hurt any less. If I had just been able to get a hold of Jaks' book back then, I would have known where Lilly was and I would have been able to get her out. The problem with that, though, was the fact that I didn't even know Jaks existed until close to a month ago when Rafe was brought in. I knew I couldn't have done anything differently, but that didn't make it any easier.

"She was so close and I didn't even know it."

"You couldn't have known where she

was. You know that. Organizations like this are not designed for every person working for them to know what is going on. You had no way of knowing where Lilly was. Now, we have a place to start and the team will be able to find the other locations. You just gotta be patient a bit longer. We took a huge step in the right direction."

Part of me couldn't help but wonder if he truly believed that or, if he *had* to believe it. We both knew that there was a good chance Lilly and any number of the children had been shipped off all over the world, by now. Thinking about it wasn't going to help, though. I knew that. All I could do, was take things one step at a time and just hope that by the end of this ridiculously long tunnel there was a bright light at the end that would lead me to Lilly.

"Get some sleep, Baby. I'm going to send the photos off. I'll keep an eye out in case someone decides to come in here."

Maybe it was the concussion that had me not questioning Rafe on the new term of endearment he had called me a few times today. Maybe it was my fear that he would stop calling me it. Either way, I just closed my eyes and let the darkness swallow me whole.

CHAPTER ELEVEN

Rafe

IT HAD BEEN three weeks since I started working undercover with Fin, a week since he had been in a fight to the death with Roth.

For the past week, I had been very worried about him. I knew his ribs weren't broken, but they were bruised all to hell and it was very painful for him to move and breathe. He was still having a hard time with moving around and bending down. Thankfully, when we were on guard duty we just walked around. He didn't have to be doing any manual labor. When we weren't working, he was resting and recovering.

His concussion was all but gone, but I knew he was still getting headaches and the lights could bother him at times. I had been feeding him proper food to help his body fight off the concussion a bit easier. Foods that helped to reduce headaches. I learned pretty quickly that Fin did not like taking pain meds, even the over the counter stuff. They made him tired and he didn't want to be tired or have a foggy mind while working undercover. I could understand, but that didn't make it any easier to see him in pain and not be able to do anything about it.

Tonight, we were at another brothel location. This one was bigger and had a variety of clients. We were set to patrol the outside of it, something we were both thankful for. Still, even on the outside we could still hear what was going on inside. Unlike the house I'd previously guarded, this one was more geared toward fetishes and it was more than moans from the men that I could hear. I don't know what was happening to some of the children, but they were in pain and begging for it to end. It was very hard to listen to and I wanted nothing more than to storm in there and kill every last one of these fuckers for putting their hands on a child.

"You need to try and block it out," Fin said from where he was leaning against the back wall.

To me it was all new, but to Fin, this was just another night to him. He had been going through this for a couple of weeks, now. He had been forced to listen to the screams and begging for twelve hours a day, seven days a week for weeks. It made sense that he had figured out how to block the noise out. How to stop it from hitting his mind. It was the only way he had been able to do this job and not kill everyone.

I knew we had to play the part. I knew there was a lot on the line and we couldn't act until we knew where Lilly was. I understood that, I did, but it didn't make this any easier.

"I know, I'm trying, it's just... it's hard. It's a lot more difficult than I thought it would be," I admitted as I leaned against the building by him.

"You have to force your mind to think about something else."

"I'm trying. It's not that simple."

"I create a whole world in my mind. A world where John and Darla are still alive. It's what would have happened when I arrived at their house eighteen months ago, roughly. I had a whole week off and I was planning on spending it with them. We were going to take Lilly to a water park. I was going to take her to play glow in the dark mini putt. She hadn't been before, but she was finally old enough to enjoy it. We were going to get dressed up and have tea parties and I was going to take her on a mini shopping spree. John would lecture me about spoiling her and I would tell him it was my job to spoil her. It was supposed to be a perfect week before I started BUDS."

The pain in his voice told me how hurt he still felt at the loss of his brother. Not that I could blame him, I was grieving him, too. He was such a good man and I could picture him lecturing Fin about spoiling Lilly while trying to fight a smile on his face. He knew how much Fin loved Lilly. How he viewed her as his own daughter. There was nothing that Fin could do that would ever make Darla or John feel like he was in the wrong. They wanted Lilly happy and full of life, and I knew from the few conversations I'd had with John, that Fin's presence brought so much to life in her.

So much happiness.

"I'm nowhere near as creative as you are," I said. I knew it was a sore subject for Fin and I didn't want to upset him. Especially, not while we were trapped here with these sounds.

Fin let out a soft sigh before he pushed off of the wall and stood in front of him. He then, to my shock, kissed me. I was instantly pulling back. This was neither the time nor the place to be doing this. Not to mention, I had told him this couldn't happen again.

"What are you doing?" I asked.

"You need a distraction before you blow our cover. Stop thinking about it and just feel."

This was a terrible idea.

I couldn't be with Fin.

We couldn't do this again.

It didn't matter what I was feeling toward him. It didn't matter that I had wanted to kiss him for weeks, now. He was in a vulnerable spot with everything going on around him. He was my best friend's brother. We shouldn't be doing any of this. I knew that, and yet, my body was screaming for him. Every time I closed my eyes, I was right back there with him. I was inside of him, listening to his moans and his throaty voice begging me for more. I had lost count how many times I had woken up in the middle of the night and gone into the bathroom to jerk off just so I could get back to sleep.

The attraction I felt for him was all consuming and I shouldn't feel this way for him. I hadn't felt like this with him when we were younger, and I didn't get why I was feeling it now. The sex was amazing, yes, but I'd had amazing sex before and never grown feelings for the other person.

Yet, with Fin, I couldn't stop thinking about him. I couldn't stop looking at him and wishing he was underneath me again.

Fuck.

I wanted him so bad it felt like my skin was on fire.

Fin placed his hand on my clothed groin and I knew he felt that I was already hard just thinking about his body. He rubbed my dick through my jeans as he spoke.

"Stop thinking and just feel."

There were a hundred reasons why we couldn't, but all of them flew out the window the second his hand touched my dick.

I pulled him in for a rough kiss, one he quickly submitted to and allowed my tongue to storm his mouth. His hands quickly worked at my belt and freed my hard dick. He broke the kiss before he dropped to his knees. He looked up at me as he ran his tongue along my tip, moaning as the taste of my precum hit his tongue.

I threaded my hand through his hair and I guided his mouth down onto my dick. I gave a light groan as the heat of his mouth engulfed my dick.

Suddenly, everything disappeared.

We were no longer in some deserted area at a brothel with kids inside. We were at the back of a club in some alley and Fin was sucking me off.

I scanned the area before my gaze landed right back on Fin. He looked right at me as he moaned and took me all the way down to my base. I could feel his throat working my dick and it was beyond glorious. I was a large size and most couldn't take me all the way in their mouth. The fact that Fin could deep throat me almost had me coming right then and there.

Fin moved his mouth up and down all along the length of my shaft. He didn't take it slow, either. He had no problem deep throating me at a rapid pace.

I couldn't help but thrust my hips slightly at the sensation. Me taking control caused Fin to give a hum of appreciation that sent vibrations of pleasure all up my spine.

"You like that, Baby? You like when I fuck your throat?" I softly whispered.

Fin let out a whimper and I knew he was loving this.

I picked up my pace just slightly as I continued to thrust into his mouth. I had never been with a guy that loved to have his mouth fucked. The fact that Fin was writhing and whimpering on his knees for me was only driving my pleasure sky high. I wanted this to last forever, but I knew I wouldn't.

I had been too worked up over the past couple of weeks. My body had wanted to feel Fin's for too long and now that I was getting what I wanted, I wasn't going to last very long.

With a snap of my hips, I pushed myself all the way into Fin's mouth and I gave a soft growl as I came hard down his throat. Fin moaned as he swallowed every last drop of essence that I had for him. The feel of his throat constricting around my dick only caused me to pulse more.

He felt so good.

When I had stopped pulsing, I expected Fin to pull his mouth off of me. Instead, though, he continued to work my semi-hard dick within his mouth. My eyes rolled back for a moment with how sensitive I was. Apparently, Fin wasn't ready to stop playing, and I was not about to stop him.

"You want more, Baby?"

Fin moaned as he worked my dick even harder to get it fully hard once again. I watched as he moved his free hand to his pants and started to undo them. He pulled out his hard shaft, the slit weeping with precum, and started to tug at it.

"No coming until I say you can," I ordered, and I saw a shiver of pleasure go through Fin's body.

This man was going to break me.

I wasn't supposed to be with him, but fuck it. I knew John wouldn't be happy but, as bad as it sounds, he was dead and he didn't get an opinion any longer. I liked Fin. My body wanted Fin and I was done trying to convince myself otherwise. Fin was an adult, we both were, and that meant we were capable of making our own decisions. If we wanted to have sex and build a friends with benefits relationship, then we should get to. Even if it only lasted while we were undercover. It would help relieve stress and give us something to distract ourselves with. Feeling pleasure in a world that was so dark only made sense.

I was going to enjoy Fin's body. I was going to enjoy feeling his mouth around my cock. I was going to enjoy being inside of his tight, hot ass. And later on tonight, when we got back to the room, I was going to enjoy the feeling of Fin's dick in my mouth. I was going to finally taste him and I knew he was going to be sweet. We wouldn't be able to have sex tonight with his ribs, but once they were healed up a bit, I would be having my way with him once again.

From now on, I was just going to allow

myself to feel the pleasure and joy that I got from being with Fin. I was going to block out the voices and just allow myself to be selfish for a little while. After all, Fin clearly wanted me and there was no point in denying what our bodies were desperately craving.

CHAPTER TWELVE

Finley

WE WERE A month into working this undercover operation together. It had been a very long month.

I had been in for nineteen months now, and I wanted to run screaming from this place. I was trying to hold out hope that we would be able to find Lilly's location. That she was alive. But as each day ticked by, I was getting more and more terrified that we would never find her, or worse, she would be dead when we did.

I just needed to find her.

I needed to see her again.

I needed to know she was alive.

I knew she wouldn't be okay, but I didn't need her to be okay, I just needed her to be *alive*. Anything else could be worked out. Anything could be healed and fixed. All that mattered was that she was alive so I could heal her.

For the past week, Rafe and I had been holding on and trying to keep it together. It was getting harder with the more we saw, with the more we heard coming from the children. It was taking a toll on the both of us, but I felt like I was drowning a lot faster than Rafe was. Maybe that was because I had been in longer than him—a lot longer—or maybe it was the strength of his mind compared to mine. I couldn't help but feel like I wasn't strong enough for this anymore. The world was getting darker and darker and it was getting very difficult to see the light at the end of the tunnel.

It was so dim now, I could barely make it out.

I needed this to end soon.

I knew it was eating away at my soul, but I also knew Lilly was out there somewhere, and if I gave in, there was a strong possibility that she would never be found.

That she would never be free from this nightmare.

Lilly's name had been in Jaks' books, so we knew without a doubt that she had been picked up by this organization. She had been moved to another location in the State six months after John and Darla had been killed. I was praying she would still be in the State and not out in the world somewhere. I was trying my best to hold on, I really was, but this shit was getting hard.

"Hey, I got a message from Ryzen," Rafe said, snapping me out of my darkening thoughts.

"Who?"

"Our sniper. He says we need to meet. He's meeting us at the same spot you met me. We don't have anything going on, so we should be fine to sneak out."

I just gave a nod and grabbed my coat. We made our way out and I didn't say anything until we were in his truck where we wouldn't have to worry about someone overhearing our conversation.

"Did he mention what this was about?" I asked.

"No. He kept it short just in case someone was listening. We'll know soon enough. Chances are, they discovered something that we can use."

I was hoping that was the case. We needed something to finally point us in the right direction to shut this organization down. It had been going on far too long as it was, we couldn't waste any more time working our way through the rankings. We needed something that skyrocketed us ahead and we needed it now. With a bit of luck, hopefully, Ryzen had something that we would be able to use to find Lilly and shut it all down. I needed to find her before my mind broke and she was lost forever.

"We need to find her," I said with a great deal of pain in my voice. I was trying to be strong, but it was getting so hard.

So fucking hard.

Rafe reached over and placed his hand on my thigh as he spoke. "We will find her, I promise you. I know this is hard for you, and it has been since you started this nineteen months ago, but you can't give up. She's fighting. I know she is. She is waiting for you to find her and she is not going to give up hope. She knows you'll find her. You just need to hold on a bit longer, Baby."

I knew that I needed to hold on, but some days, some nights, it was so unbelievably tough to keep going. To not give up and just wait for death to finally take hold of me. I knew going into this that I would go through dark days. That I would go through moments where I wanted to give up. Knowing that, though, and actually going through it were two very different things. It was getting hard to keep fighting. In the beginning, I could fool myself into believing that it would get easier. That I wouldn't be here that long, that I could handle it. Nineteen months later, I was about to hit a wall if something didn't change soon. If we didn't get some indication that we were reaching the end. I needed that light at the end of the tunnel to start shining again, otherwise, I wasn't certain I would even make it to the end of it.

We drove the rest of the way just listening to the music. We both liked Country so we didn't have to fight over the station, which was nice. It was a bit stereotypical of us, but we both liked American muscle cars, trucks, and country music. We were military and that went hand in hand most times. That, and a love for dogs and guns. The guys in my unit used to say all the time, "you can fuck with anything in my life, but if you fuck with my truck, dog or gun, you fuck with your life." So many people never understood why those three things mattered so much, but to us it was our way of life. We'd had a K9 in our unit, just like every unit did. And that dog was our brother or sister. It wasn't just the K9 handler that took care of the dog, we all took care of them. We all owned the dog and when we were down range and bullets were flying, we all made sure our K9 was with us and safe. If you pulled a knife on him, you pulled a knife on one of us. It was just that simple.

You don't mess with our guns, because they save not just our lives, but the lives of our brothers. As for the truck, for most guys all they had to show pride in was their truck. A lot of them went through girlfriends and wives like you wouldn't believe. The job ate away everything good in your life at times. It was a hard life to expect a significant other or kids to understand. Some guys didn't have much in terms of possessions, but they had their truck and they took great pride in it. It might sound sad, but that was the life they knew they were signing up for, and they still signed on that dotted line.

I still signed on it.

Everyone always says, "thanks for your service," but it's not because we fight an endless war. It's because we agreed to go into a place where we could not only be killed, but lose a body part or forever be mentally scarred all to keep this country safe.

That was something that I had missed over the past nineteen months. My brothers. I hated that I hadn't been able to contact them. Before I went undercover, I stopped at the base just briefly to sign my honorable discharge papers. Everyone knew what had happened to John and they knew Lilly was missing. They didn't have to ask, they knew what I was going to do. They knew I would be looking for Lilly, but they didn't know to what extent I would be doing it. I hadn't told them, because I didn't want them to worry about me. I also wasn't certain they would let me go in alone and I didn't want them giving up their careers for me. They all needed each other and I was supposed to be set to go into BUDs. I wouldn't be around them as it was, so me going undercover into this organization wasn't important for them to know. It wasn't worth them risking their lives and throwing their career away. I knew they would feel differently once I did reach out to them, but that was a bridge I would cross later.

Rafe pulled off into the rest stop area and once again, there was no one there but a single car. Rafe parked off to the side and we climbed out. We both checked around the area to make sure there was no one watching us. It was pretty deserted here, making anyone within the area stand out.

The beauty of the desert.

We headed over to the building for the washrooms and walked around the back. There, leaning against the wall was a guy. Ryzen, I suspected. He was dressed all in black and he had black hair. He wasn't too tall, about average height for a guy. He was wearing black sunglasses that seemed to have a bit of a thicker lens and I couldn't help but wonder why.

"Hey, man, what do you got?" Rafe

asked.

"The book was written in a code for the locations. It took Coop some time to figure it out, but now we got it. We know every location there's a brothel or a stash house for where the kids get moved around."

"That's great. When can we move in on them?" I asked.

If they had all of the locations, that meant we could get the kids. We would still need to find the organization's leader, but we could at least rescue the kids."

"The Boss is working on getting some help from different agencies to move in on the locations in a coordinated attack. That way no one squeals to anyone," Ryzen answered.

"What about the leader? Do we have anything on him?" Rafe asked.

"We know who he is. It took some digging, but the money led to a variety of shell corporations that all go back to an LLC that goes to only one person. *Harold Arthur.* A CEO of an accounting firm. He has multiple bank accounts in the Cayman Islands and he makes too much for an accountant."

"That's our leader. Where does he live?" I asked.

This was exactly what I needed to hear today. They'd not only found where all of the children were being kept, but they had identified the leader. We could now shut this organization down once and for all. We were reaching the finish line and, after nineteen months, it felt so unbelievably amazing.

"About thirty minutes from here. The team will move on his house. You both need to move on another location," Ryzen answered.

"What location?" Rafe asked.

"The last few pages of the book were heavily coded. The further into the book we went, the more the code became extravagant. Almost as if they suspected someone could be working undercover."

"They might have suspected someone. Or the leader was feeling anxious. I know there was that big bust a few months back by the FBI. They took out three human trafficking rings from an informant that worked as a guard in all three organizations. This Harold Arthur could have told the regional leaders to change the code up to protect his investment if they ever got into the wrong hands," Rafe stated.

"It's possible. Cooper was able to break it. We found Lilly. She's here in town," Ryzen said as he looked right at me.

Everything went silent the second those words hit my ears. The world around me disappeared and all there was were Ryzen's words floating around within my mind.

Lilly was not only alive still, but she was here.

She was in town.

I finally knew where she was and now I could save her. We could save her. She was going to get to come home. She was finally going to be safe and be able to heal from all of this trauma and darkness. She was going to get to be saved. I would get to see her again. To wrap my arms around her and know she was safe. It was finally going to happen and I wanted to rush to her address, right now. I wanted to go and save her right this second. To not leave her with these monsters a moment longer.

"Where?" I managed to ask.

"In a house roughly fifteen minutes from the clubhouse. We did some recon. There are ten guards in and around the house. There are only a handful of kids there. There are no clients, though. We think it's a stash house for the kids they are getting ready to sell to another human trafficking cell or to a private buyer from overseas."

That made my blood run cold.

To hear that they were looking to sell her.

That I had come extremely close to losing her for good.

If she had been sold, it would be virtually impossible to track her down. We had to move quickly. We needed to get her out of there before someone bought her.

I was this close to her.

I couldn't lose her now.

"When's the raid happening?" Rafe asked.

"Twenty-two hundred hours, tonight. You need to hit the house at the same time. Here's the location, read it, then give it back to me," Ryzen said as he handed a folded up piece of paper to Rafe.

Rafe took it and read it real quick before handing it back to Ryzen, who pulled out a lighter and set it on fire. Ten o'clock tonight, we would be able to move in and get Lilly. It was only one in the afternoon, which meant I had close to nine hours to wait and I wasn't certain I would be able to.

I wanted to get to Lilly and do it now.

"We'll see you tonight at the hospital," Ryzen said as he pushed off of the wall and jogged off.

"They found her," I said, completely in shock as Ryzen left.

Rafe gave me the warmest smile I had ever seen on his face as he spoke. "They found her, Baby. Our girl is coming home."

For the first time in nineteen months, a true smile overtook my face. It wasn't just that we had finally found Lilly. That she was going to get to come home. It was hearing Rafe refer to Lilly as *our girl*. I knew I would be raising her, but maybe, I wouldn't be doing it alone. Perhaps, Rafe would stick around after all of this was over with. We could possibly have a shot at being something more than just friends with benefits.

Maybe.

Right now, though, that didn't matter. All that mattered was Lilly was going to be coming home. I didn't have a home for her, technically, but I would find one for us. Me and her could find one together.

That didn't matter. All that mattered was that we would be together.

John and Darla would finally be able to rest in peace knowing their little girl was safe.

CHAPTER THIRTEEN

Rafe

IT WAS FINALLY nearing ten o'clock and Fin and I were able to sneak out of the clubhouse and make our way to Lilly's location.

Keeping Fin distracted for the past almost nine hours had not been easy. It did involve a great deal of sex to make the time go by. Otherwise, he was pacing around the small room, and after a hundred laps, I was getting dizzy watching him.

He had every right to be anxious over this. After a long and hard nineteen months, he was finally going to get to lay eyes on Lilly. He was finally going to be able to save her. That would make anyone anxious. I was anxious and I had only known about this whole situation for thirty days.

I was worried about the team. I knew they were all capable of handling themselves, but this was still going to be a major bust. I knew Sebastian, Damien, and Roland had come down to help out, but that was just three more guys and not an army.

At the other locations they were going to have full teams going in to arrest as many guards and Johns as they could while freeing the children. They would have more than enough guys doing the raid.

The Task Force guys were the ones that were taking all of the risks, myself and Fin included. We were going in with just the two of us to take out ten guards and free whatever children were in the house. We had minimal intel and no way of knowing if there were more guards in there than we all expected. It could be considered suicide, but it was a risk I knew without a doubt we were both willing to take.

"What's Ryzen's story?" Fin asked, completely out of the blue.

"Um... I don't know. We'd only been around each other for two weeks before this operation started. He doesn't talk much. Keeps to himself."

"Who does he work for?"

That was the million-dollar question. On the first operation, I had tried to get him to talk a bit when we were grabbing something to eat or at the end of the day back at the hotel. He didn't really talk. I couldn't tell if it was because he was used to not talking so social situations are confusing for him, or if he just didn't have any interest in conversation. He was a sniper and from the whispers I'd heard about him through the grapevine, he was a very good sniper. One of the best in the country. That could be why he was so quiet. Snipers, they tend to always be alone because they are alone up on whatever perch they have made for themselves. When everyone is storming into a raid with a group of brothers, snipers are left alone to be their eyes and protector. If Ryzen had always been a lone wolf, it would make sense why he didn't have much conversation in him. Still, though, I had no idea what agency was claiming him, because every agency was using him when they needed an impossible shot.

"Honestly, I have no idea. He's never said. He doesn't tend to talk much. He's done work for various agencies and local law enforcement. If I was a betting man, and I had to pick, I'm betting on the CIA. I could be wrong, though. He's a man of few words with a twelve foot, bulletproof steel wall up around him."

"Makes it hard to get to know someone that way. If he does work for the CIA, how would he be allowed to be in the Task Force?"

"CIA loans people out all the time. It happens more than people realize. DEVGRU Teams, they all have a CIA handler for their operations to gather intel and build go-packages for them. CIA isn't just spies invading a country."

The mention of DEVGRU cut a bit. John had wanted to apply for Green Team at one point to become a Tier One SEAL. For most SEALs, being in DEVGRU that was like their Disneyland. It was a place that would make memories, but a place where your name could become a legend and your legacy would live forever throughout the generations. It was a huge deal to even be accepted into Green Team and if you could make it through and get picked by a team, you were given a family that would never leave you. There was a deeper and richer brotherhood within DEVGRU and for those that didn't have much in terms of family, it was one they risked dying to have.

"I guess only time will tell," Fin said as he kept his gaze on the window, watching the scenery passing by.

I reached over and took his hand in mine as I spoke. "We'll be there soon and then, we will get her. We have to be smart and clear the house as we go. It's all one level and a basement, so the kids could be in the basement or kept in one of the rooms. We'll clear the top floor then go into the basement."

There was no telling where the kids would be kept, not until we got in there. We had to clear the whole place, though, otherwise we risked missing any children that could be hidden away. My gut was telling me the kids would be in the basement and only taken into a room when a buyer wanted to test out the product. They were most likely restrained, somehow, in the basement. I had my lock picking set on me, so I would be able to get any restraints off of them if they were shackled.

"We breaching together or one at the front door and one at the backdoor?"

That was the question because, normally, you would breach from both sides to ensure no one ran out the back and escaped. The problem with that currently, though, was we had two people and an unknown number of guards on the inside. We each had a gun, but we only had one clip apiece.

Jaks didn't let any of his enforcers or lower ranking men have guns outside of their working shift, and when you did work, you only got a single clip. The organization had to make sure that no one on the inside could eliminate main players in terms of clients and men within the organization.

So, it was just the two of us against ten guards that could have a full clip each if they hadn't needed to fire at anyone. We were outnumbered in bodies and in bullets. And to make it even more fun, we had no vests.

So, if we got hit by a bullet, we could die.

"We breach together through the front. It's safer that way."

We might lose some guys out the backdoor, but at least we would both have a better chance of not being killed in the fight.

I pulled up behind the house, staying within the trees. Once we had the kids, we would run out the backdoor and get them into the truck. I was hoping by keeping the truck behind the trees, it would blend in a bit better and the guards wouldn't spot it before we had a chance to get inside.

I turned my attention to Fin and I saw his warm eyes looking back at me. There was a light in them that I hadn't seen in the past month. He was excited to see Lilly, to finally end this. This was the last step and then, they would both be free from this organization. I placed my free hand on the side of his face as I spoke.

"We go in together, we come out together."

"Promise," Fin easily agreed.

We both knew that could be a lie, but

it was one we weren't going to question, right now. I moved in and pressed my lips against his. If I was going to die tonight, I wanted to have the feel of his lips against my own as I did. I kept the kiss short. We weren't exactly in a place to make out.

With a final nod to each other, we climbed out of the truck, closing the doors quietly, and made our way to the front of the house. We stayed low by the windows so we wouldn't alert any of the guards that we were here. We had never been to this house before, so it wasn't like we could knock on the door and pretend we were here for a shift change that no one knew about.

Once we arrived at the front door, I tested the doorknob and was not surprised to find it locked. They wouldn't risk leaving it unlocked in case someone tried to rob them, which wouldn't be the first time someone in a competing organization tried to steal money and the children for their own.

I looked over at Fin and with an encouraging nod, we both pulled our guns and then I kicked the door down. It made a loud bang and instantly alerted everyone within the house that someone was breaking in.

We both made our way inside shooting. We each took out two guards before the others had their guns out and started to fire back. We both quickly slid across the floor and took cover behind a wall.

"I counted ten," Fin said.

"That's what I got. Six, now."

Six against two wasn't great, but we had something these guys didn't. We were military trained shooters. We weren't wasting bullets like they were, shooting at the wall hoping the bullets would hit us. We stayed low to the ground and underneath the spray of bullets they were firing at us.

I belly crawled to the edge of the wall, poked my gun out, and fired, hitting one of the guards in the chest before I quickly took cover. I saw that Fin had done the same.

Four now.

"You cover, I'll aim," Fin said.

I gave a short nod and got up on my knees. I poked around the wall once again and started to fire rapidly at them. I heard Fin's aimed shots and together we quickly took the remaining four guys down. We both stood and kicked their guns away from them. Chances were they were all dead, but we didn't need one half-dead man reaching for a gun while our backs were turned.

"Let's start clearing," Fin said as he moved toward the rest of the house.

We needed to clear it to make sure there were no other guards, but also so we didn't risk leaving behind any children.

When the gunshots started, I didn't hear any screams, confirming what I suspected, that the children were in the basement. Had they been in one of the rooms, we would have heard them scream.

We quickly cleared the main level of the house and just as we were about to leave the last room to get to the basement, we heard a shit load of cars pulling up. I took a quick peek out the window through the slats in the boards and saw there were at least fifteen cars and a van.

"Fuck," I said.

"How many?" Fin asked.

"There's at least thirty guys, including Donald. They must have gotten wind of the other houses being hit. They got a van to move the kids. We gotta hurry. We sure as shit don't have enough bullets to fight all of them."

We were never going to survive a gunfight against that many guys, there was just no way. Even if we could get into the basement, there was no way we would be able to get the kids out of there before they all stormed into the house. The second they walked inside they would see the dead guards and that would bring them directly into the basement. We didn't have very long.

Fin went over to the window and started to pull one of the boards down.

"What are you doing?" I asked.

"We need a distraction. Go get the kids and get them out of here. I'll hold them off as long as I can."

"No, not happening. We will both go and get the kids out of here."

There was no way I was going to leave Fin in here all alone. Once his bullets ran out, they would be storming into the house and coming into this room first. There was simply no way in hell I was going to allow Fin to do this.

"We don't have time. You're the only

one of us who knows how to pick a lock fast. You have to go and get them. I will hold these guys off for as long as I can. You have to focus on the kids, Rafe. Get them to the truck and get them safe."

"I'm not leaving you."

I couldn't leave him.

Even if a bullet didn't kill him, they would capture him and torture him until they got what they wanted from him. They would know he was a mole and they would want to know who he was working for and where the kids were. I wasn't going to leave him.

Fin grabbed me by the side of my face and pulled me in for a deep and passionate kiss that left me feeling lightheaded and weak in the knees all at the same time. I could feel the love he had for me. The intense feelings he had for me were expressed all in one single kiss and I couldn't help but feel like he was saying goodbye. All too soon he was pulling back and speaking.

"Tell Lilly I love her. I know you'll take good care of her."

"I'm not leaving you," I said around the lump that had formed in my throat.

"You have to. You have to save her,

save the other kids. You have to go and hurry. I'll be okay. No matter what, I'll be okay. Lilly will be safe. She will be loved and I can die in peace knowing that she'll always have you to look out for her. Go now, hurry."

Fin pointed his gun at the window and started to fire. I didn't want to leave him, but my body was moving, running toward the basement door and then down the stairs.

The second I got down there, I saw five children all with shackles attached to their left ankle. I quickly scanned the room and saw Lilly sitting against the wall. I ran over to her, pulling out my lock pick and spoke in as calm of a voice that I could manage. She pulled back a bit, her fear evident, but I didn't stop from bending down and getting at her shackle.

"It's okay, Lilly. Do you remember me? I used to work with your Daddy."

She looked at me for a moment before she spoke in the softest and tiniest voice she could manage. "Uncle Rafe?"

"That's right, Sweetheart. I'm gonna get you guys out of here, okay?" I said, flashing her a warm smile. She gave me a teary nod and once her ankle was free, I worked quickly on the others. I then scooped up Lilly in my arms as I spoke to everyone.

"Listen, I know you're scared but we have to move very fast. I need you all to run with me. We're going to go out the back door and into the trees where my truck is. We're gonna get you all home, I promise. I just need you all to be brave for a little while longer, can you do that? Can you guys run as fast as you can for me?"

They all gave me small nods and I was more than happy with it. They were all between the ages of four and twelve. I saw the older boys taking the hands of the younger children to help them.

We all went up the stairs and I couldn't hear any more gunshots. The kids started to run toward the back door and I turned around to see Fin fighting with the guards as they started to enter the house. I wanted to go over there to help him, but I knew we would both be taken. I had no choice but to turn and run out the back door with the rest of the children. Turning my back on Fin when he needed help sent a knife through my heart.

I hated this, but I had to focus on the

children.

Fin was right.

We had to save them.

Arriving at the truck, I quickly shuffled them into the back seat. They huddled together to make it work and I was grateful for the couple of older boys helping the younger kids. I climbed into my truck and started to back out. Once I cleared the trees, I had a full view of the front driveway. I saw them dragging an unconscious Fin to the van before they tossed him in and closed the doors.

I hated that he was on his own, right now, but he wouldn't be for long. I was going to find him and I was going to rescue him. I was not going to leave Fin to die a slow and painful death. I had to get the kids to the hospital, but then I would be calling Mason and telling him what happened. We would find Fin and we would get him back.

I turned my truck around and started to drive to the hospital. I had to get the kids someplace safe first and then I was rescuing Fin. I would rescue the man that I was quickly falling in love with.

This was not how our story was going to end.

This was not how *his* story was going to end.

He was going to get to see Lilly again. He was going to get to raise her and maybe, just maybe, the three of us would get to be a family.

CHAPTER FOURTEEN

Finley

MY MIND SLOWLY floated back to consciousness. I wasn't sure what was going on, though. Everything was fuzzy. I knew I was supposed to remember something, something important, but I couldn't put my finger on it. Maybe if the pounding in my head would stop, I would be able to think clearly.

My head was killing me, but so was my right eye. It was pulsing with pain, but that was a familiar pain. It was from being hit, from a fight. I immediately figured I had been chosen to fight again and for some reason my opponent didn't kill me. I had just been in a fight a week prior so Rafe could get a hold of the transaction book.

Wait, the transaction book.

Lilly, that was it.

We'd found Lilly!

Or Rafe did.

We went to the house that was holding her and Rafe found her, but the guards stormed the place. They grabbed me.

Fuck.

I forced my mind to stop thinking about the pain throbbing throughout parts of my body, and to focus on everything else that was going on around me. I was sitting up. Sitting on something hard, but it felt rough against my skin.

Wood.

A wooden chair.

My wrists were wet, but the metallic smell and the pain told me it wasn't water. Whatever was being used to keep me in the chair was sharp and cutting into them.

Wire, maybe.

I didn't feel anything against the skin of my ankles, but I did feel my jeans were still on. I could feel my boots, as well, so I could have some type of restraint against my ankles and just not feel it. I felt the cold air against my chest and I knew my shirt was no longer covering me.

I didn't feel anything over my face or anything around my mouth. So, if I opened my eyes, I would be able to see where I was. The trick was, I wasn't sure I should be opening my eyes at that moment.

I couldn't hear anyone, so I might be alone, but I also knew I wouldn't be alone for long. If they all thought I was still passed out, I might be able to figure out a way to escape.

I couldn't wait for someone to come and rescue me.

I'd told Rafe to get Lilly out and I meant every word of it. I knew he would take care of her. I knew he would love her like his own daughter and give her a great life. Lilly was the only thing that mattered. Giving her the chance to have a proper life was the only thing that mattered. If I died here today, I would do it happily knowing that my niece was finally safe.

I finally decided that I couldn't sit here with my eyes closed forever. I needed to find out what my situation was and how to escape. I couldn't do that if I never opened my fucking eyes.

Slowly, I opened my eyes just a bit, but all I could make out with my head down was my lap. I was in a wooden chair and my legs were restrained to the chair legs with what looked like barbed wire. I didn't need to look to know that was what they restrained my wrists with.

I would need to be careful. If I struggled too much, the wire would cut down to my bone. Letting out a faint sigh, I knew I had to lift my head if I was ever going to get any answers about my location.

I raised my head and I could instantly see Donald, Malcolm, and Henry standing across from me. None of them looked happy and I knew this was going to hurt. It was going to be a slow and painful death, but I was okay with that, because Lilly would get to live a happy life far away from these assholes.

They were never going to get near her again.

The guys from Rafe's task force were able to locate the main house for the leader of the organization. The head of the snake was cut off and all of the children in the organization would be rescued. I had done my part and I could die in peace knowing they were all safe.

"You know, Chris, you really had me fooled. I have to give it to you, I didn't see this coming. I've dealt with plenty of undercovers from various agencies and police forces that have tried to shut my organization down, but none ever made it past the first month," Donald said as he moved closer to me.

Wait, did he just say *his* organization?

"Yours?" I asked, confused.

"The house your friends raided was where I kept my front man. Harold is my true front man and not Michael. Michael is Harold's front man. It keeps all of the attention off of me and allows me to keep an eye on my profits from within the organization. I knew Feds would be trying to shut me down when I hit the half a billion dollar mark. There's only so big an organization can get before all eyes are turned onto you."

"You hide in plain sight, but as a mid-level man. You wouldn't be important enough for a federal agency to pick you up to try and flip. It's ingenious."

I had to give it to him, it was a genius move. He could hide completely in plain sight and have a front row seat to any of the new guys that joined. If you slipped up, he ordered your death and moved on to the next guy. He would also get to be there for the killing and the kidnapping.

He got his violence with his safety net.

Fuck.

The man that I had been looking to take out for eighteen months had been sitting right beside me the whole fucking time.

I was an idiot.

I should have seen it.

I should have known something more was going on. I could have ended this organization months ago. A year ago. All of those children who were killed, that I had to bury, they could have been saved. I could have saved them if I had been smart enough to see what was literally right under my damn nose.

"It's kept me in business, but now, because of you, I have to start all over again in a new State. I'm going to be out millions because of your ass. Now, you are going to tell me everyone that helped you get into my organization. You're going to tell me your name and what agency you work for. Make things easier on yourself and just tell me. Then, I'll give you a quick death."

I wasn't going to be giving him anything. I wasn't about to give him my name or let him know that he killed my brother and sister in-law, and then abducted my niece.

Lilly was going to stay free from him no matter what.

"Go fuck yourself," I said with a smirk. If I was going to die, I was going to die fighting. They weren't getting shit from me.

"Fine, have it your way," Donald said as he waved Malcolm and Henry over.

I was fully prepared for what was about to happen. I could take a beating. I wasn't going to give them shit. I would die with my honor, just like John and every fellow Sailor I had the pleasure and honor to fight beside did.

There was nothing they could do to break me.

***

I coughed up the water that I had managed to inhale. I was trying to not breathe as they waterboarded me, but the longer they kept the hose going over my face, the harder it was to not breathe in, searching for the air my lungs were desperate for.

I wasn't sure how long we had been doing this. My whole entire body was sore. They had beaten me for a long time with their fists first and then a crowbar when their hands got too banged up. I knew I had at least three broken ribs, my right eye was completely swollen shut, and my left was not far behind. I was dizzy and I knew that meant I had a concussion. What hurt the most, though, was the electrical burns from the cattle prods. The burns were all over my torso and they were still burning. I knew my body could hold out longer, but I also knew that more pain was going to come my way before Donald gave up and killed me.

"How much longer do we really need to keep doing this, Chris? Just tell me what I want to know and I will end your pain and suffering," Donald said as he bent down in front of me.

I spat right in his face before I spoke.

"Fuck you."

RAFE

A cold hatred washed over Donald's face and flooded his eyes. Before I even knew what was happening, there was a knife sticking out of my lower abdomen before he pulled it out. The pain was intense and instant. I couldn't help the small scream that escaped my lips. Blood started to pour out of the wound and I knew the wound itself wouldn't kill me, it hadn't hit anything major from what I could tell, but if left untreated to bleed, I would definitely bleed out.

"You will tell me what I want to know. I can do this for years with you before your body gives in. I'll keep you locked away to be tortured and passed around to the highest bidder. I will make you my prized whore and start earning some of the money back that you stole from me," Donald growled through clenched teeth.

Apparently, he was pissed and didn't appreciate being spat at.

He had more of a temper than I thought he had. He'd never showed any anger issues during the year and a half that I spent with him. He was able to keep it all hidden. It was impressive, but it only showed how much of a psychopath that he truly was.

Before I could even respond, a hole appeared between Donald's eyes and he was falling down to my feet. Before any of us had a chance to process what just happened, the door to the room was being kicked open and shots were fired. Malcolm and Henry were killed instantly with multiple bullets to their chests and they collapsed down to the ground.

My gaze instantly flashed to the one person I wanted to see more than anything at this very moment.

Rafe.

He had his gun in his hands and he was running to me. He put it away and bent down in front of me. I was still trying to get my mind to process what just happened.

"Rafe?" I asked, softly.

"It's okay, Baby, hang on," Rafe said to me, before he spoke to the other three men in the room. "We need something to cut the wires."

"I got cutters," a man said as he ran over to us with a red bag in his hand.

"Who?" I only managed to get out.

"That's Sebastian. He's one of the private detectives I told you about. That's Damien and my boss, Mason," Rafe answered as he pointed to each man.

Sebastian cut the wire off of my wrists while Damien put some gloves on and I could see the red bag was open. It was a medical bag. With my wrists free, Rafe grabbed me and carefully laid me down onto the ground. I couldn't help the small scream that escaped from the movement.

"I know, I'm sorry, Baby," Rafe instantly said as he cradled my head in his lap.

Sebastian and Damien both started to try and stop my stab wound from bleeding. The added pressure on my stomach was doing nothing for the pain that was surging through my body.

"This is Supervisory Special Agent Mason Wright, I need an ambulance to 1033 Palace Rd., ASAP," Mason barked into his cell phone as he moved back slightly.

"Lilly?" I asked as I stared up at Rafe.

"She's safe at the hospital. The rest of the team is there to keep her and the other children safe."

"Good," I slurred as I was losing the fight to keep my eyes open.

My whole body felt like I was sinking. Every ounce of strength that I had when this had started was slipping away at a rapid pace.

"Baby, Fin, stay with me. Keep your eyes open, Baby."

Rafe's voice was faint and sounded further and further away. I knew I needed to keep my eyes open. I knew I needed to fight the darkness that was threatening to swallow me whole, but I just couldn't do it.

The darkness pulled me under and everything went silent.

***

A constant beeping sound pulled me out of the darkness.

The second my mind surfaced, all I could feel was numb. I was expecting pain, but I didn't feel anything. The beeping and the smell of antibacterial cleaners told me I was in the hospital and I must have been on some type of drugs for me to not be in any pain. I felt terrible, though. I was dizzy and I just felt exhausted and like total shit.

I forced my eyes to open and had to squint at the brightness in the room. I must have made a noise because suddenly there was movement beside me.

RAFE

"Hang on, Baby," Rafe said softly and I watched through slitted lids as he moved around the bed and closed the blinds.

Once it was darker in the room I opened my eyes fully and Rafe immediately moved back toward me.

"H..." I tried to speak but my throat was so raw I instantly started to cough.

Fuck, did that hurt.

"Hang on, take small sips, Baby," Rafe said as he held a plastic cup with a straw in it for me.

I took a couple of small sips and the cold water felt amazing against the sandpaper that was my throat. I wanted to drink the whole thing, but Rafe pulled it back after only a few sips.

"You gotta go easy, still. You had surgery to repair the knife wound."

"Lilly?" I asked with a very hoarse voice.

"She's okay. She's in the bed right next to you."

I slowly turned my head to the right and saw the second hospital bed in the room. There, curled up with Mizzie in her arms, was my beautiful Little Princess. I was finally getting to lay eyes on her after eighteen months and it instantly brought tears to my eyes.

"Is she okay?" I asked as the tears flowed down my cheeks.

"She's going to be okay. She's got some bruising and cuts. She's also dehydrated, malnourished, and exhausted. The doctor said she will be fine, though. She just needs rest and some love. I gave her Mizzie. I hope that's okay. She was really upset and scared. I thought it might help calm her down."

"Yeah, of course. Does she remember?"

"She remembers what happened. She remembers Darla, John, and you. She even remembered me from the video calls. She didn't know they were dead. I had to tell her. She's been really worried about you. We moved her in here to try and calm her down."

It broke my heart to know that Lilly went through all of that hell and pain only to be rescued and then, told that her parents were dead. I hated that she had to go through that and I would have given anything to take it all away from her.

To give her John and Darla back.

But I couldn't.

All I could do was be there for her and give her the best life that I could.

"Thank you for getting her out. For coming back for me."

"I will always come back for you, Baby. I will always protect you both. You don't ever have to worry about that. You both belong to me and nothing is ever going to change that."

My heart filled with heat at hearing his words. That I belonged to him. I knew some would take it a completely different way, but to me, it was the most romantic thing he could ever say to me. I was his and I didn't want to belong to anyone else. I wanted my body to belong to him. I wanted my heart to belong to him. Just like I knew his body and heart belonged to me. At least, I hoped they both did. That didn't need to be figured out right now, though, because I was safe and so was Lilly. That was more than I could ever ask for at this moment.

"Can she be moved? Can she come over here with me?" I asked, not sure what Lilly's injuries fully were.

"Yeah, I can move her," Rafe easily said.

He went over to Lilly's bed and very carefully picked her up bridal style. Lilly squirmed slightly and I saw her open her eyes. She settled pretty quickly when Rafe gave her a warm smile right before he placed her down.

"Someone wants to say hello," Rafe cooed, as he placed Lilly down on my bed right next to me.

"Hello, my beautiful Little Princess," I said with all the love I could manage.

"Uncle Finnie, you're awake," Lilly said as she was instantly curling up into my side.

I wrapped my right arm around her as I heard her start to cry. I wished I could take the pain away from her. I would have gladly traded places with her in a single heartbeat. All I could do, though, was hold on to her and promise her that she would have an amazing life from this point forward. I wasn't going to let John or Darla down. I was going to make sure their little girl, *our little girl*, had the most amazing life she could possibly have.

"It's okay, my Little Princess. Everything will be okay, now. I promise," I said, and placed a kiss to the top of her head. Based on the heat and strength within Rafe's eyes, I knew we would both be keeping that promise and that was more than perfect to me.

EPILOGUE

Rafe

IT HAD BEEN two months since we were able to find Lilly and get her free. Two months since we made the arrests to shut down the human trafficking ring that Fin had spent almost nineteen months undercover for.

It went fast once I was undercover with him and the team was looking for the ringleader. We never expected for the ringleader in all of this to be Donald. Fin had been working beside him the whole time and he had never given any indication that he was more than just a mid-level guy. I knew Fin was still kicking himself over it, and it didn't matter how many times I'd told him it wasn't his fault, he didn't believe it. We'd all told him he couldn't have known.

Donald was smart.

He made someone else the face of the organization while he hid in plain sight. He would be able to see everything that was going on within the lower levels. He knew that if an agency was able to get someone into the organization undercover that it would be within the lower levels. He just didn't know that person was the same man he had worked beside.

The past two months had been good and bad. The good news was that both Lilly and Fin were fully recovered from their physical injuries. They were both staying with Roland in his spare bedroom and I knew Roland and Tyler had been a huge help with Lilly while Fin was recovering from his injuries.

I knew they weren't ready yet, but I could tell they were going to make amazing parents one day. There was going to be a child in need of a home and that child was going to have won the lottery with them.

RAFE

With our second case under our belt, and a major bust to go with it, the task force was no longer having a hard time getting cases. In fact, it was just the opposite. We had an endless amount of calls coming in for cases that we couldn't even keep up with answering. Mason was getting close to five hundred emails a day from local law enforcement and agencies begging him to take their cases. They were all of crimes against children. Some were missing kids, others were of criminal organizations using the children as runners. We were going to be very busy. So busy that I knew Mason was looking to expand our numbers and bring on more people. The trick with that would be where to put them. This town wasn't exactly equipped to handle all of us.

The bad news, though, was both Lilly and Fin were suffering mentally and emotionally. Lilly did remember John and Darla and she did remember what life was supposed to be like. She had broken down and told us that she often thought of them when she was in captivity. That she would dream of her Daddy and Uncle Finnie storming into the place and rescuing her. Even though she had seen

John being shot trying to protect her, she thought he was still alive. She didn't know Darla had been killed, either. Her captors had told her her parents were dead, but she'd always refused to believe it. It was hard having to watch as she realized that they really were dead and she would never get to see them again.

Even after two months, she was still crying and begging to go and see them.

It was taking a huge toll on Fin and I knew it was going to be a long road before they were both healed from these events. I would be there for them, though, every step of the way.

"I want to thank everyone for coming by this afternoon. I know we've been busy the last couple of months with cases, and more are coming in every day. The Governor wanted a report of where most of these incidents are taking place. After reviewing all of the locations, Louisiana had the most cases. I have reached out to a Director with Family Services and he has informed me that the human trafficking in the State is atrocious. They have been trying to control it and shut them down, but the legislation has it set that Family Services are responsible for chasing down leads that are reported by witnesses or victims," Mason started, as we all sat around the backyard.

"That's the dumbest thing I've ever heard," I said.

Social Workers were great for after the fact, but they weren't that great for talking to victims and getting them to open up. Gathering evidence to shut down an organization that is as intricate as a human trafficking ring, that should be handled by local police or Federal Agents.

It still blew my mind that there wasn't a set agency for human trafficking. It was a multi-billion dollar global enterprise. They should be more focused on it than the drug organizations.

"I agree, and so does the Governor. The Task Force is being relocated and given a name. From this point forward, the Task Force will be known as the Federal Protection Agency and we will be operating out of Baton Rouge, Louisiana. We will continue to go after those who commit crimes against children and we will help clean up Louisiana's crime rate against children," Mason stated.

"Wait, we're being relocated?" Roland

asked, shocked.

I couldn't blame him. This was shocking. We had all been led to believe that we would stay in Gaithersburg and work here as the main hub. It was a small city, though, so I could fully understand why the Governor wanted us to move. A major city like Baton Rouge would give us plenty of room to expand in numbers. It gave us all housing, an airport in the city, and an actual building we could work out of. If we wanted this Task Force to grow, we had to relocate.

And now, we had a special name.

We were official within the country.

We had proven ourselves and this was our reward. It wasn't something we should be turning down or seeing in a negative light.

"We are. Now, I can't order anyone to relocate, it's up to you if you wish to make the move with the Task Force, or technically, with the Agency, now. The choice is up to you," Mason said.

"I'm in," I easily stated.

"Me too," Ryzen said, but I knew he would agree. I also knew Jarod was obviously going, with him and Mason being together.

"I got nothing keeping me here," Hollingsworth said with a shrug.

"I'll go wherever you need me. I don't have any family. All I have is you guys," Cooper said next.

And then, all eyes turned to Roland.

I knew Mason would be fine if his brother wanted to stay here. He was still a detective and the man that he loved was here. We could continue on without him.

"You should go," Tyler said to Roland.

"It's not that simple," Roland started, but Tyler cut him off.

"Yes, it is. Those children need you and you need this task force. You've come alive in the past two months that you have been working with them. You were born for something so much greater than just being a cop in this town. I'm not ready for a big city like that, not yet, but you were made for it. We can figure out long-distance and we can visit each other. I promise, I'm not going anywhere, and one day, I will be ready to join you. You need to go, Babe. You need to help those kids."

Tyler was a very special man. It took a lot to say goodbye to the man that you loved. To know that he is out there getting shot at and putting his life on the line in very dangerous situations every day and still be okay with it. He could have told Roland not to go and Roland would have agreed to stay. But he wasn't. He knew that Roland was too good for this small town cop life and he wasn't holding him back.

It was at that moment, I knew those two were meant for each other and I would make sure to protect Roland whenever I could so they could have their life together when Tyler was ready for the move.

"Okay, I'm in, but expect vacation days," Roland said, flashing a pointed look at Mason.

"With us being an official Agency, everyone will be entitled to vacation days, sick days, and even a pay raise. I got all the paperwork at the office that everyone will need to sign. We will also be getting official badges," Mason said.

"Wow, we're badge official," I said with a teasing grin that caused the guys to laugh.

"We are. Finley, I would like to offer you a position within the Agency, as well, should that be something you are interested in. You have more than proven yourself of being capable in the field and with investigative work," Mason continued after the chuckles died down.

My heart was instantly filled with warmth and dread at the same time. Warmth, because Mason had seen what I had already seen. Fin was an amazing operator and he would be a great addition to the team. Dread, though, because I knew that meant he would be getting shot at and could die on me. I didn't think I would be able to handle that.

The past couple of months had been amazing with him. We had gotten to talk and get to know each other on a more personal level. The chemistry was off the charts between us, but we needed to know who the other was still. Even though I didn't know everything about him, I was madly in love with the man. And that love only grew stronger every day as I watched him with Lilly. He was an amazing man and I couldn't wait to see how much more he blossomed over the years.

I wanted to be there for it all, the good and the bad.

"I appreciate that. I'll get back to you

on that," Finley said.

I was surprised that he didn't say yes right away. It was something that we would need to talk about later, when we could have a moment alone. I wanted to make sure he wasn't still blaming himself for Donald.

Mason gave a nod and the guys started to ask questions about where the building and housing would be. I was happy to hear that the Governor had set us up with a real estate agent who would help us all find homes. We would be moving within two weeks, so we had a lot we needed to get sorted. It would be nice, though, to have my own place again instead of a motel room or crashing at someone's house. I needed to have a home again. A place where I could go to unwind after a bad case. We all needed that.

***

It was a couple of hours later when Fin made his way inside.

I followed behind him a few moments later. I was hoping to speak with him while we had a minute alone. I found him in the kitchen grabbing a bottle of water. Fin leaned against the counter top as I went over and placed my hands on either side of the counter, trapping him where he stood.

"Careful, the guys might see," he said.

"So what? I don't care if they see us together. I don't care if they see me kissing you. Do you care?"

We had never discussed public displays of affection. It wasn't something I thought we had to talk about. I knew he wasn't in the closet and he knew I wasn't. I figured we would be good on the PDAs.

"I don't care, but I figured maybe you wouldn't want the guys you work with to see you kissing a guy," he said, slightly unsure of himself.

I swear, if I ever found Captain Harris, assuming he was still alive, I was going to kill him myself for putting that self-doubt on Fin.

I leaned in and pressed my lips against his. I moved my hand and brought it up to cup the side of his face as I closed the distance between our bodies. Fin hungrily kissed me back and gave a soft moan when our crotches touched. I was going to make sure he knew exactly what I felt for him. He was never going to have any self-doubt about us ever again. I deepened the kiss even more and we were both so lost in the other that we missed someone coming in.

"I'm just gonna sneak around you, there," Cooper said.

I knew he was trying to get to the fridge, but I didn't care. I didn't stop kissing Fin. I didn't care who saw us and I was going to make sure Fin knew that one hundred percent.

I didn't pull back until the need for air became too much for the both of us. By the time we did pull apart, Cooper was back outside and Fin's lips looked properly ravaged.

"That was... wow," Fin said as he tried to get his mind to work again.

"I never want to stop kissing you. And I will kiss you, whenever I want. I don't care who is around. I don't care who has a problem with it. You are my man and I'm going to make sure everyone knows it."

Fin shivered at the possessive tone to my voice. I loved that he liked feeling possessed. I would never take it to an extreme level, but I did like it when the guy I was with knew he was mine. When everyone around us knew he was mine and they couldn't have him.

Fin was mine to protect, mine to care for, mine to love.

It was just that simple.

"Move in with me," I said.

"What?" Fin asked as he got his mind back in working condition.

"Move in with me. You and Lilly."

"You can't be serious," Fin said, completely shocked.

I knew this would be shocking for him. His past relationships, or *relationship*, I should say, didn't go well. It would be shocking for him to have someone who wanted to live with him. Someone who wanted to shout it from the rooftops that they were together. But that was exactly what I wanted to do.

"I have never been more serious about something in my life. Fin, I love you. I want to spend whatever time I have on this earth with you and Lilly. You are both my family and I couldn't imagine not having you both in my life every single day. I want to wake up next to you. I want to make waffles and drop Lilly off at school. I want family dinners and game nights. I want bedtime stories and checking for monsters under her bed. I want it all with you. With you *both*. Say you want that, too."

I had no idea what Fin wanted. I had no idea if he felt the same about me, but I knew I would have to be the one to make that step. He wouldn't be able to do it himself. He needed me to do it and I was perfectly fine with it. I loved him, I loved Lilly, and I wanted us three to be a proper family.

I couldn't leave them behind.

There was no way in hell that I could do that.

"I love you, too, Rafe. And I want that. I want to live with you and have a family. But you just heard what Mason said. Louisiana is a violent State, especially against children. I don't want Lilly hurt," Fin said, fear flooding his voice.

"I know and I don't, either. But I have more than enough money saved up between the military and my DOJ position. I can put a huge chunk down on a house in a gated community. We can send Lilly to a private school when she is ready to go to school again. We can live in the safest area within Baton Rouge. She can be safe. We will make sure of it."

That was my main priority. If I didn't think Lilly or Fin would be safe in Baton

Rouge, I wouldn't be going. I would be staying here or any other city that Fin wanted to be in. They were all that mattered to me and I would do anything that Fin wanted to do.

I saw Fin thinking about it for a moment and I felt like I couldn't breathe. No matter what, we would be together, but I would prefer to not have to leave the Agency. Leave the guys. They were becoming my family, too, and I didn't want to leave my brothers behind.

"If it's safe for her, then okay," Fin finally said.

"Are you sure?"

"Yes. If we're in the safest part of the city and she's protected by gates or rolling security guards, then I'm okay with it. I just want her to feel safe, and you belong with the Agency, with the guys. You were born to do this job and I want you to keep doing it. Children all over need a man like you looking for them."

"You can be one of the men looking for them, too."

I wasn't too sure how Fin felt about Mason's offer. I knew he might want some time off to stay with Lilly and make sure she was healing and getting back into a normal living routine for a six year old girl. Afterward, though, it would be good for Fin to get to use his skills and keep helping people.

"And I appreciate his offer, but it's not for me. If working undercover has taught me anything, it's that I don't want to see the violence in the world anymore. I don't want to be there for the aftermath. Not when I could possibly try and prevent it. I'm not ready yet. Not until Lilly is better adjusted and back in school. But I would like to work with at risk kids and maybe open my own self-defense school to help children be better prepared in case they do get grabbed."

"I think that's a great idea, Babe. You need to do what you feel is best for you and for Lilly, and I will one hundred percent support you. I also won't lie, it makes me feel better and breathe easier knowing that you'll be safe and won't be getting shot at."

It was a huge relief to hear that Fin didn't want to join the Agency. He wouldn't be putting his life on the line to stop these criminals. I knew he was more than capable of handling himself alone in the field, but that didn't mean I wanted him to be dodging bullets. It was good that he wanted something different and a self-defense school would be perfect for kids and survivors. He would be able to help them in a different way, and that was an honorable thing.

"I know I should be in the field, using my skills to help save children. But I take one look at Lilly and all I can see is this little girl who has lost both of her parents. I can't be the reason she has to go through losing another. It's better for her if I'm not in the field. I'll help anywhere I can with the kids after they are rescued."

"There's going to be a lot that has to get worked out as we rescue different children. I am sure Family Services will love all the volunteers they can get," I said, flashing him a warm smile.

Fin gave me a rich smile in return before he leaned in and pressed his lips against mine.

I knew without a doubt that there was nothing we wouldn't be able to accomplish together. We had a huge adventure ahead of us, but it was one we would conquer. The criminals who liked to hurt children had better be on alert, because our Agency was coming for them, and we weren't going to stop until every last child was free.

Thank you for reading!

Turn the page for Ryzen, Book 3 in the Federal Protection Agency series.

RYZEN

FEDERAL PROTECTION AGENCY

BOOK THREE

BY EVIE RILEY

RYZEN

True evil lurks in the darkness...

Recruited at eighteen by the CIA, Ryzen is one of the best snipers in the world. Now, he's working with the Federal Protection Agency to aid them in their fight to track down the vile people who perpetuate crimes against children. Always hidden behind his dark sunglasses, Ry is a mystery to everyone and he prefers it that way.

Ry remembers Knox from when he had his psych evaluation, and that the profiler's report was what resulted in his discharge from the CIA. He's not impressed with the man, and even more disturbed by the way he makes Ry feel.

A profiler with the FBI, Knox Hunter is investigating a series of murders. The victims are all male, between twelve and fourteen, and all have the same MO. With the Mayor pushing for re-election, a report of a serial killer could jeopardize the campaign's success, so Knox is sent in to work with the FPA to try and close the case, fast and by any means necessary. The only problem is, Knox is an office man, not a field man, and this new path could be the most dangerous one of his entire career.

Will Ry be able to keep Knox safe while they track down and put away this serial killer, or is he destined to be the biggest threat—to Knox's heart?

CHAPTER ONE

Knox

"WE FOUND HIM. He was dumped in a dumpster along Plank Road in between the twelve hundred and thirteen hundred blocks. A shop owner found him roughly an hour ago. I got a crime scene heading there now, and local PD has the scene blocked off."

That would be my boss, Special Agent in Charge Greg Mathers. He was a short and stocky man, but that was only to fool you. The man looked like a short Santa Claus, making you believe he would be jolly and a fun elf. In reality, he was a mean son of a bitch that ran his unit with an iron fist. If you got on his bad side, well, let's just say you better start praying, whether you believe in a God or not.

I, thankfully, had never been on his bad side. I did my job and I did it to the best of my ability. As a FBI Profiler, my whole job was to analyze people, criminals mostly, and study their behavior. It was on me to find killers, sex offenders, arsonists, and any number of other dangerous felons to get them off of the street and into prison where they belonged. I loved my job and I was one of the best profilers in the country. I knew that fact was the only thing saving my ass from getting tossed overboard by my boss.

For the past three months, I had been working on the same case. Three months of me trying to find one single person in a city of just over two hundred thousand. It sounds insane, but when you are used to finding one single person in an entire country, it really should be nothing. I was one of the best profilers, I had all of the accommodations and solve rate to prove it.

So why the hell couldn't I find this son

of a bitch?

I was working on a series of murders with the victims between the ages of twelve and fourteen. All were male. All had been kidnapped and tortured. No signs of sexual assault, so it wasn't a pedophile kidnapping and killing young teenage boys. They were all grabbed and killed within seventy-two hours before being dumped. There were now twelve victims. My killer had a one week timeframe, so not much of a cooling off period. We had a serial killer in Baton Rouge, and it was one targeting young teenage males, putting close to fifteen thousand kids at risk of being kidnapped.

I was spinning my wheels with this case. There didn't appear to be anything connecting the twelve victims. They didn't go to the same school. They didn't go to the same church. They were all with different religions and extracurricular activities. Some came from a perfect, two parent household, and others were in foster care. Different dentists, different doctors, different areas of the city. They didn't look the same. Nothing was the same. It was as if the killer was going out of his way to pick the most random kids possible. And even then, it wasn't random. He wasn't grabbing the kids at the first available opportunity. He was watching them and learning their patterns. He knew when to strike and grab them so he wouldn't be seen. He wasn't caught on camera at the abduction site or the dumping site. The dumping was always in a dumpster, but in a city this size, it wasn't like we could stake out each dumpster.

My boss was frustrated, but so was I.

"I don't want to admit this, but I have nothing. I have no idea who he is or how he is connected to them. I'm spinning my wheels on this one, Boss. We really need to tell the public. These kids need to be warned. Their parents need to be warned."

You would think with now twelve murdered boys that it would be all over the media. It wasn't. The Mayor had issued a gag order to all media outlets to not report what had been happening. Nowhere in the press would you be able to hear or read about these boys.

At least, not yet.

I had done that before in other cities when I traveled to help local law enforcement with solving their cases. Sometimes it was better to not report the crimes. For two reasons, the first, it makes the unknown subject, or UnSub as we call them, think they are safe and no one is looking for them. With that perception of safety, they keep making mistakes, and they don't run, so we can grab them. The second, a lot of the time these UnSubs like the attention they get from the media. They want to be known, they want to go down in history. By stopping that from happening, they get angry and they make a mistake.

That's wasn't the case here, though.

Nope, the Mayor was up for re-election and what does not get you re-elected is broadcasting about a serial killer that targets young males and had been killing and torturing them for three months, now. That didn't look good on a campaign poster, and like a true politician, she was opting for saving her own ass and not the people she is supposed to serve.

"You know that won't happen. The Mayor is not going to lift the gag order, so I suggest you find out who this son of a bitch is. This is the only case you are going to be working and you won't be working it alone."

"I appreciate the offer of help, Boss, but too many profilers in one kitchen is not a good idea."

It wasn't that I was against working a case with someone. The opposite in fact, I loved working with different law enforcement. What I did not love was working with other profilers. As a profiler, your job is to analyze everything, it's programmed into your mind. We all tend to have a degree in Behavioral Science, putting us within the psychologist category. We examine every word, movement, or look that someone gives, and we evaluate them based on that.

And I do mean everyone.

I did it just this morning with my Barista who kept eyeing her co-worker when he wasn't looking. She liked him and he had no clue.

A typical man in that sense.

But everywhere I go, my brain is always on, just like most profilers. Which is exactly the problem with working with them. They analyze your every movement, look, and word spoken. They over-analyze every tiny detail and when you get more than one in a room, it becomes a debate on everything. They always think they are right and everyone else is wrong. I don't have that issue. I have no problem with brainstorming and seeing what puzzle pieces we can put together, but it's exhausting having to play referee in a room full of grown ass adults.

"I didn't say you were working with other profilers on this. There's a new Agency in town. They got here about a month ago. They have made a name for themselves within the community already. The Federal Protection Agency, they focus on crimes against children. They have put an end to an enormous human trafficking ring, have cleaned up the foster care system in parts of Maryland, and they have been working closely with DCFS to help clean up the foster care system here and try and locate kids that have been scooped up by the human traffickers. They have already started to generate reputation in the community for being able to stop criminals that go after children. The team has been given immunity by the Governor of Maryland, who then, had it transferred over here in an agreement with our Governor. If there's anyone that can get this case solved, and quietly, it's them."

I had heard about the small waves the FPA had been making since they got into town. It never bothered me that they were here, but I knew some of the other Feds had an issue with it. They didn't like that the Agency was made up of Feds and local police from out of state. From what I had heard, they also had a couple private detectives that worked with them as well. It was random people put together, but it was somehow working. They had been able to do some good since getting here.

Still, I wasn't certain on the keeping it quiet part.

They had immunity, which meant they didn't have to answer to the Mayor. They could do whatever they wanted, scream about the murders from a rooftop, should they think it was best. Their immunity protected them from a gag order.

But then, maybe that was Mathers' point.

Take the case to someone that didn't have to play politics. Someone that could blow it wide open to the public and maybe force my UnSub to be smarter. Either way, I was good with the offered help.

"I'll head over there with my case files.

I want to go to the scene first and make sure it is secured."

"Make sure you stay within the perimeter and if you need to leave it, you have an officer with you."

"Copy, Boss," I easily agreed.

He headed out and I quickly grabbed all of my case files for all twelve victims. I would need to add to this victim's file, but I could do that in the car once I visited the dump site. With everything set, I headed out for my car. With being a profiler my job was mostly in the office. It wasn't very often I would go to a crime scene or chase after a suspect. Sometimes, I would go to the scene to get my own view of it, but most of the time I could go off of the photos and videos taken by the lead detective.

Whenever a victim or a loved one of the victim needed to be spoken to, they mostly came into the station where I was working at the time. It wasn't often I had to go out to them. I wasn't a field agent. I didn't have a gun. I didn't have any formal combat training. I was the brains of the operation and not the muscle, and that was perfectly fine with me.

I worked out to stay in shape. Working

out was my stress relief. It helped to go the gym and clear my mind when I was stuck on a case. So, physically it looked like I could fight, but honestly, I had never thrown a single punch before in my life. That wasn't the life that I had, even when I was younger.

My parents were great people. It was just the three of us so I didn't have any older brothers I had to fight against. We lived in a good area. I went to a private school and played on the chess team. I went to Harvard with a full scholarship for my Behavioral Science Degree.

I had a really good life growing up.

A life that didn't involve violence or pain.

I knew I was one of the lucky ones and I never took it for granted, especially since I had been working as a profiler for the past fourteen years. The greatest weapon I had was my mind and I didn't see the need to end a situation with more violence, not if I could talk the UnSub down.

Once I arrived at the scene, I parked my vehicle in the area of the other patrol cars and climbed out. I could already see the locals gathering around to watch the scene unfold. It was a common occurrence with crime scenes.

The human mind always wants to learn and know information. When someone is killed or even when the police show up, everyone is always looking out their windows to see what is going on. Part of human nature was being nosy and gossiping. Something like this would be talked about for a couple of weeks, at least.

The area itself was a mixture of old businesses and rundown homes that had been converted into one or two apartments. The area was in the higher crime rate within the city. They weren't strangers to police cars in the streets and I knew the prostitutes and drug dealers would be laying low for the next couple of days until the police presence disappeared. Then they could go back to making money.

What I also knew, though, was no one would talk. There would be no witnesses, not even when you told them it was a young teenage boy. They didn't talk in this area, too controlled and afraid of the gangs that would kill anyone who dared to speak to a cop or a Fed.

"Special Agent Hunter," I said, holding up my badge as I walked onto the crime scene. "Who is in charge of the scene?" I glanced around at the local PD officers standing around the area.

"That would be me, Detective Jonah West with Homicide. What can I do for you, Special Agent?"

"The FBI have been working a case and your victim is connected to an ongoing investigation that I have been running. The FBI will take over the case. I would appreciate it if you could send me your notes and any of the crime scene photos."

"Look, I got no problem sharing, but I'm not about to hand over this case fully to you. That's a twelve year old boy in that dumpster. Someone left him there like trash after torturing him. I'm not going to hand it over to anyone, Fed or not."

It was always hard to convince local law enforcement to give up a case, especially when it involved children. I could tell he had a child, probably a boy around the same age. The passion within him was not going to go away overnight. This would be a case he was going to keep a close eye on and make sure it got solved. I understood that and I completely respected it.

"I understand you don't want to give this case up. However, I have jurisdiction over you. If necessary, I can very simply call your boss and order it be handed over. I can't tell you about an ongoing investigation, however, I can tell you that I will be working with the Federal Protection Agency to get this case solved. We will get who did this and they will go to jail for the rest of their natural life. And I promise you, I will keep you updated and informed throughout."

I didn't want to have to pull rank. Pulling rank always left a bad taste in my mouth and it did nothing to help improve working relations with local police. However, I also couldn't allow him to work this case and potentially release information that was under the gag order. I also wasn't convinced it would be ideal to broadcast that we had a serial killer. I wasn't certain which direction this UnSub would go if he was dragged out into the light. I needed to figure him out more first.

"I'll make sure everything gets sent your way," he said in a tight voice.

"Thank you, Detective West. I truly

appreciate it," I offered, flashing him a warm smile.

The Detective ignored me and turned on his heel, walking away.

Well, I wasn't making a new friend out of him, but at least I had control of the case. Once I finished up here, I would make my way to the new Agency's field office and, hopefully, we would finally be able to get something on this case to bring us closer to our UnSub.

The clock was already ticking on the next victim. If we didn't want another kid to die, we had seven days to stop this killer.

I just hoped we would make it in time.

CHAPTER TWO

Ryzen

"MORNING," ROLAND SAID as he walked into the conference room.

I just gave him a nod. We were going to be going over potential cases to work this morning and I was hoping for a good one. Not that there could really be a *good one* when you were dealing with crimes against children, but to me, if we could shut down another organization that was hurting a great deal of children, that was a good one. I was all for saving as many children at one time as possible.

"Are you ever going to talk to me?"

Roland asked with a teasing smile.

I was quiet, everyone knew that. What they didn't know, was that it was programmed into me. Growing up, if they couldn't hear you, you couldn't be hurt. It was all about survival and it stuck with me. Besides, I didn't have anything interesting to say most of the time. I didn't have many social skills, even at the age of thirty.

I had never been to school, not grade school or high school. But that's what happens when you grow up in war torn areas of Africa following a mission around. There was never a time for me to be able to go to school. I learned from the people in the mission and that translated to taking care of various injuries and shooting. There wasn't any need to learn history, science, geography, or English literature. The one thing I could do better than your average person was math, but that went into my trade craft. If you want to be one of the best snipers within the world, you better be able to do advanced math in your head at a moment's notice.

"Hi," I said back.

"There we go, progress," Roland said, and flashed me a warm smile.

"Tyler?"

I knew Roland and Tyler were having a bit of a harder time adjusting to the long-distance relationship they found themselves in. Over the past two months, we could tell that Roland was missing him. Their relationship hadn't grown in a typical sense. More often than not people had a grace period of six months or even years before they moved in with someone. Roland and Tyler were practically living together almost right away. They had to learn how to live apart now, and not just in the same town, but a four hour plane ride or seventeen hour car ride away from each other. They had to go from seeing one another 24/7 to only video calls and text messages.

Tyler had said he wasn't ready for a move like the rest of us had made, and that made sense. He had a whole life he was still trying to piece together. He was young, he had a lot left to learn about himself, and for the first time, he had a stable job and a home, plus friends in Gaithersburg. I knew, eventually, he would move down here to Baton Rouge to be with Roland, though. You could tell they deeply loved the other. Still, it was likely the waiting was going to take a toll on both of them, especially Roland.

"He's doing good. He's decided to get his GED. He's thinking about the future and maybe even going to college one day. He's been working with the occupational therapist to help him with his reading. He's doing really well and building up some confidence in himself," Roland said with a proud smile.

Tyler has dyslexia, just like Mason. Though unlike Mason, Tyler didn't have anyone growing up to diagnose him or to help him rewire his brain so he could read. Roland had helped Mason with it growing up and I knew he had been helping Tyler as well. The only time you could tell that Mason even had a learning disability was when he had been up for too many days straight. That's when his ability to read went to shit. It never bothered us, though. There were plenty of us that could read a report for him. And wasn't exactly like he needed to be able to read to shoot straight.

"Here before the Boss, must have a new case," Cooper said as he strolled in with his extra large coffee. The man was going to have a heart attack one day from all the caffeine he drank.

"I wonder what it is," Hollingsworth said as he sat down beside Rafe.

Jarod strode into the room.

"He got a call early this morning from someone in the FBI. Whatever is going on has to be big enough that the FBI is looking for our help," Jarod informed us as he slid into his usual seat.

Mason and Jarod were still going strong. They had their own place together and you would often see them and Koda everywhere. Where one went, the other two generally did. I was happy for them, even if I didn't show it. I was happy for all of the guys. They had started to become my brothers and I wanted them to be happy and in great relationships.

And speaking of relationships.

"How's Lilly and Fin?" I asked Rafe. The two newest members of our misfit family. Fin was the younger brother of Rafe's best friend, John, who had been murdered in a home invasion. Lilly, John's daughter, who is six now, had been kidnapped when she was five by a human trafficking organization. The same organization who had killed Fin's brother. Fin had gone undercover to find her.

When Rafe got word about the whole situation, he decided he was going undercover with Fin to shut them down and find Lilly. We all went down to help and brought everyone home successfully.

When we were all relocated to Baton Rouge with the Federal Protection Agency task force, Fin and Lilly made the move with Rafe and they had been living together for the past two months. They lived in a house in a gated community with rolling guards 24/7. It might sound extreme, but it made Fin and Lilly feel safer and that was all that Rafe cared about.

"They are doing really well. They are both going through therapy and Lilly is doing well with the support group she is in. She has a hard time being around men still, and she's plagued with nightmares almost every night, but she is able to play during the day and be a normal six year old, for the most part. We're thinking about getting her a service dog. Her therapist recommended it and Mason said it could really help her."

"I know a lot of Veterans who have PTSD dogs that have helped them a great deal, especially with being around people," Roland said.

"Same, that's what I told him. We're gonna look around and see what puppies are available from the local service dog breeders. See which one she would like and what breed would be easier. Thankfully, they didn't use dogs in the trafficking organization so she's not scared of them," Rafe commented.

"When we've gone around with Koda, she lights up when he's there. I think it'll be good for her," Jarod added.

I wasn't a huge fan of dogs. I could handle being around them, but I wasn't a dog person. I had been bit by a dog a few times growing up, from either one of the wild dogs in Africa or by one of the guard dogs that the Rebels had. I was fine around Koda, though. He was a good dog and he listened to whatever command you gave him. But that didn't mean I wanted to hang out with Koda all day long, or any other dog for that matter.

The clicking on the floor told us that Koda was coming down the hallway and that meant Mason would be as well. Hopefully, this case wouldn't be too hard to shut down. Koda came into the room first followed by Mason, but then everything went to shit when *he* walked into the room.

Fucking Special Agent Knox Hunter.

The man responsible for the end of my career. He was a Profiler, supposedly one of the best within the Country. Before being let go, I had worked for the CIA since I was eighteen. They had scooped me up right out of Africa for my shooting ability. There wasn't anything I couldn't hit, from any distance. I was gifted where a gun was concerned. Five years ago, the CIA decided they needed to make sure I was mentally sound after killing people over half of my life. Knox was the Profiler that was picked to evaluate me. According to him, I was too mentally unstable, due to a personality disorder, to be capable of making a right and wrong decision. That it would be best for the Agency and the Country for me to no longer be working as a sniper. According to Knox, I wasn't able to see the difference between right and wrong and it was only a matter of time before I became a black hat sniper and started to go against the Agency.

And just like that, the CIA kicked me to the curb.

Sure, I could have taken on contracts

and become a black hat sniper. Gone after anybody and everybody that had a high price tag on their head. Instead, though, I continued to be a white hat sniper and take out targets that other Federal Agencies all over the world didn't have the skills to do. I had done freelance work. *Legal* freelance work.

Knox had a firm belief in good and evil, black and white, but the world didn't work that way and that was what he failed to see. The world was made up of millions of shades of grey and what works in one situation doesn't always work in the next. Sometimes, you have to do something questionable and not fully legal in order to take a dangerous threat out of the world.

Knox had no idea what true horrors there were out in the world. Even working as a Profiler and handling murder cases, he still didn't get it. I'd bet my ass he grew up in a perfect house with perfect parents and had the perfect childhood and adulthood. He'd never had to fight for his life. He'd never had to feel his stomach eating itself for weeks because there wasn't even a scrap of food to eat. He'd never had to eat literal garbage to survive.

He had no idea just how fucked up this world really was.

All *I* knew was how horrible the world was.

I knew all about the evil that lived in plain sight. Some of the worst criminals there were lived right out in the open for the whole world to see, but no one ever did. Everyone was just happy to live with blinders on and pretend like the world wasn't going to complete shit.

Guys like Knox.

"All right, listen up. This is Special Agent Knox Hunter. He is a Profiler with the local FBI Field Office. He has been working a case for three months now, and we are being asked to assist," Mason started.

"What's the case?" Roland immediately piped up.

Knox's gaze had fixated on me the moment he walked into the room and was still on me. I could tell he was trying to figure out how the hell I was here. I guess he assumed that after being kicked out of the CIA, I would go and crawl into some hole. Or maybe, he expected to be chasing me down one day. Joke was on him, I was still a Fed. I was still doing what I was born to do.

"Agent Hunter," Mason said, and that seemed to snap Knox out of it.

I couldn't help but smirk at his clear discomfort.

"Right, um... I have been chasing a serial killer for the past three months," Knox started, but Rafe cut him off.

"Wait, we haven't heard anything about a serial killer in the press."

"It's a re-election year. Part of the Mayor's campaign is the crime rate going down. This would prove otherwise," Knox stated.

"But the crime rate isn't going down," Hollingsworth pointed out.

"It is in certain areas. Areas in the city that cater to middle and upper classes of society. Those numbers have gone down, while other crimes are either not being reported, or they are being swept under the rug to pad the crime rates. People will believe the numbers and not realize that violent crimes have, in fact, been going up in certain areas of the city. The Mayor has placed a gag order on the press, so they can't report anything until it's been lifted."

That was the problem with politicians.

They only cared about being elected. They didn't care about the people they were supposed to be serving. They didn't care about protecting people. If there was a serial killer for the past three months, then the city should've be made aware of it so the potential victims would be on alert, know that they were potentially at risk. It was bullshit.

"Why are we getting brought in?" Jarod asked.

"The UnSub, the killer, he's killed twelve people so far, one a week for the past three months. He is targeting males between the ages of twelve and fourteen. The twelfth victim was just found a couple of hours ago. All were kidnapped and then dead within seventy-two hours. They were all tortured before death, but no signs of sexual assault."

And that is why he was coming to us. We focused on crimes against children and a serial killer was a major crime against children. This UnSub wouldn't stop until he was caught or killed. My vote was to be killed. A man like that deserved to die and not get to live the rest of his life in a jail cell.

"Any connections between the

victims?" Mason asked.

"Nothing. I have gone through their entire lives, and the parents, there is no nexus. They appear to be chosen completely at random. I have all of the case files with me. I haven't spoken to the latest victim's parents just yet."

"All right, everyone, divide and conquer. I want the names divided up and let's dig into their lives, into their friends' lives, both kids and parents. Coop, see if you can find the same MO in the database, maybe he was in another State before moving here. Serial killers don't pop up overnight. He had to have other victims from when he first started," Mason instructed.

"Based on my profile, he is a single male, most likely white, and appears non-threatening. He's getting the kids to go with him somehow, and my best guess is without force. No one heard any screams or cries for help from his victims when they were grabbed. Serial killers are born or made, and we need to know which one he is to better understand him. There will be signs in his childhood and early adult life, whether that is animal cruelty, setting fires, or assault. His first victim would've been someone close to him and it would have been unorganized and messy. If we can figure out who his first victim was, there might be evidence that was collected from the body or the crime scene that could connect us to him," Knox added.

"Coop, do your thing. Ry, you go with Knox to the latest victim's house," Mason ordered.

"I'll stay," I said, hopefully making it clear to everyone that I wanted nothing to do with Knox. I'd never defied an order before so they had to know something was up.

"Okay, I don't know what happened between the two of you and I don't care. Knox is not cleared to be in the field alone, he has no combat training or a weapon. Until this UnSub is caught, Ryzen, he's your new partner and it's on you to keep him alive. You're the best shooter and field agent we have. So grab your gear and head out."

The very last thing I wanted to do was go anywhere with this asshole, but Mason wasn't going to let me get out of it. Knox couldn't be in the field alone, and with my skills, I was the best person to make sure he didn't get himself killed. What Mason failed to realize, was that I didn't give two flying shits if Knox got himself killed.

And I sure as shit wasn't taking a bullet for his ass.

I got up and headed out of the room at a brisk walk. If Knox wanted to follow me that was his choice, I didn't care. The sooner this case was wrapped up, the better, and not just for the young males in town. The sooner I got Knox the fuck out of my life, the better off I would be.

CHAPTER THREE

Knox

I COULDN'T BELIEVE my luck. Out of all the people they could have in their agency, they picked Ryzen. How the hell he even wormed his way onto the Federal Protection Agency was beyond me. Clearly, there hadn't been an interview or screening process, because otherwise they never would have picked him.

Agent Wright didn't appear to be that incompetent that he would allow a man like Ryzen to be in an agency dedicated to protecting children. The man saw no line in the sand. To him, everyone deserved to be killed. The world was nothing but darkness and there were no good people left in it. The man had no morals or any beliefs. Nothing that would keep a man from doing harm to the innocent people in the world. On top of that, he had one of the highest kill rates I had ever seen. If he hadn't been working for the CIA, he would be considered a mass murderer and being hunted himself to be put down.

This was ridiculous.

He had been fired from the CIA after I filed my evaluation on him. I was thrilled to hear that he had been let go. He needed to be kept away from guns for the rest of his life. However, I knew he was angry about it and it wouldn't surprise me at all if he pulled a gun and shot me in the back of the head the first chance he got.

And don't even get me started on his personality, or the lack of one. The man barely spoke to me while I was doing his evaluation. He just sat there with the same stupid sunglasses on.

Who the hell wears sunglasses inside?

Even today he had them on, it was ridiculous and completely rude. A person deserved the respect of being able to look you in the eyes. It was common courtesy to offer that respect to everyone we spoke to, inside or outside. It was as if basic social manners had never been taught to him and he never bothered to learn them. I had no idea what his childhood was like, but I had arrested men with his psychopathy for arson and serial killings.

Ryzen was a ticking time bomb just waiting to explode.

And now, I was truly expected to have him around me. I didn't need a babysitter. No, I wasn't a field agent, but I didn't need anyone to go with me to talk to the parents of a victim. I didn't need someone slowing me down.

I didn't know what Agent Wright was thinking partnering us up. He clearly knew there was a problem between us, and that right there should have been a red flag for him. He should have placed me with someone else and kept Ryzen far away from this case and from me.

I spoke, breaking the silence between us, as we pulled up to the latest victim's house. "Don't mention the gag order or the fact that it's a serial killer. It would be best for you to not speak at all. Which shouldn't be an issue for you."

As I got out, I just faintly heard Ryzen's voice. "You talk enough for the both of us."

He actually said it faintly, under his breath, so there was an actual chance I wouldn't hear him. Like we were twelve and trying to pass insults to each other without the other hearing it. It was only further proof how unprofessional and childish he was. Hopefully, this would be the only time I had to deal with him.

I made my way to the front door and rang the doorbell. I was pleased to see that there weren't any reporters out front. I knew local PD had notified the parents already. I had hoped they would already have had a chance to get over the initial shock and pain and be calm enough for us to talk. It wasn't that I had a hard time with grieving loved ones, it was that we were on a clock this time, and if the clock ran out another child could die.

The door opened a minute later to reveal Mr. Burnsworth. His eyes were red and his clothes were disheveled. He had allegedly been worrying about his son for seventy-two hours, give or take, ever since they had discovered the boy had been kidnapped.

Standard practice is for the parents to wait by the phone and be there for a ransom demand. What most didn't understand was three quarters of the time a ransom call never came. When a child is grabbed, it's more often than not for a sexual reason and it often results in the child being kept or killed. It all depended on the UnSub and what they were looking for and if the child could provide it for them.

"Mr. Burnsworth, I'm Special Agent Hunter and this is my associate, Ryzen. I hoped to speak with you and your wife about your son, Kevin."

That was another thing that drove me absolutely insane. It was always just *Ryzen*. There was never a last name attached to it, not even in the CIA file that I was given. Now yes, the file was heavily redacted, but his name was clear as day. There was no last name on file. As if he decided to wake up one day and be like Cher. It was infuriating.

"Of course. Please, come in," Mr. Burnsworth said as he moved back to allow us to enter his home.

The house itself was very nice. We were in one of the suburbs that catered to higher income families. I knew from the quick research that I did, that Mr. Burnsworth was a doctor and his wife was a stay at home mom. They lived within their means and they didn't have any criminal background or debt. There were no signs of marital problems online, but I knew online and in real life were often two very different things. They appeared to be loving and doting parents to Kevin. They'd reported him missing within an hour of him failing to show up when he said he would. He had been at a friend's house and had left at seven at night three nights ago. He was to be home by eight and it was only a twenty-minute walk. The area was a nice area so they felt like it was safe enough for their twelve year old to walk home alone. Not that I could blame them, he should have been more than safe.

We were guided to the living room where Mrs. Burnsworth was sitting on the couch. Ryzen didn't remove his sunglasses and I swear it took everything in me to not rip them right off from his face. I swore I was going to do it one day.

I sat down on the chair across from the grieving couple as Ryzen started to wander around the living room. I didn't care what he was doing, it was no business of mine as long as he stayed quiet and didn't break anything.

"Mr. and Mrs. Burnsworth, I'm sorry to have to put you through this, but there's some questions I need to ask you about your son," I started.

"We understand. We just want whoever is responsible to pay. You go ahead and ask your questions," Mr. Burnsworth said with as much strength as he could manage.

"Have either of you received any threats within the past few months?" I started.

"No," Mr. Burnsworth answered, and looked at me quizzically, furrowing his brow.

"What about Kevin? Anyone at school bullying him or was there someone you noticed had been hanging around him?"

"No, nothing like that. The school doesn't tolerate bullies and we're all a close-knit neighborhood. We look out for each other's children. No one has even moved in within the past two years," Mr. Burnsworth answered again.

"Have you had any work done recently

on your home?"

The UnSub had to have gotten to the children somehow. I just couldn't figure out how. I needed that nexus to be able to pinpoint who this UnSub could be. I needed the nexus to start to form a list of suspects. Until I had it, I had nothing to go off of and I hated feeling like a failure or useless, especially when children's lives were on the line.

"No, the house was built brand new when we purchased the land five years ago. We haven't had anyone do any repairs or inspections. Nothing new has been installed since we moved in," Mr. Burnsworth answered.

"He's not yours," Ryzen said, before I could get a chance to ask another question.

I snapped my head around at his words just as the Burnsworths snapped their heads up at him. I didn't know if I was more horrified or pissed by what he just said. Of all the things to say to grieving parents, he had the audacity to state that their child wasn't theirs. We needed the parents to work with us. We needed them on our side, and attacking them like this, making that kind of statement, was only going to do the opposite. I could see the anger swirling within both the Burnsworths' eyes. They wanted to rip Ryzen a new one and I was inclined to allow it to happen.

"Excuse me? What right do you have to come into my home and say that to me?" Mrs. Burnsworth asked with tears building up in her eyes.

"I'm sorry for what my associate has said. He's still trying to learn decent human behavior," I said with a pointed look at Ryzen, hoping he would get the message and shut the hell up.

"I meant no disrespect, ma'am. Your whole family took a picture, uncles, aunts, grandparents, but all of them have brown hair and brown eyes. Kevin has blond hair and blue eyes. Biologically, he can't be yours."

Holy shit.

If Kevin was adopted, then maybe that was the nexus. Maybe the other kids were adopted as well. That opened up a lot of possibilities that I could work with. There were social workers, therapists, and people working in family court that would have access to those records. The UnSub could be targeting them for one reason or another.

If that was true, then the UnSub might be adopted.

"Yes, he's adopted. Kevin has known since he was five when he asked why he was different to everyone else. He's been fine with it, though," Mrs. Burnsworth stated.

"The adoption, was it open or closed?" I asked.

Now this was exciting. This was something new. Not all adoptions were available to be viewed, even by law enforcement. You had to petition a judge to unlock the records. We would need to run the kid's names with a family court judge to see if they popped in their system. Then petition the court to get the records unsealed.

"Closed. We met Kevin's biological mother when she was seven months pregnant. She was fifteen and wasn't ready to be a mother. We offered to have it set as open, but she felt it would be easier for her to let him go if she couldn't see him. It would be easier for her to heal and we've always respected her wishes," Mr. Burnsworth answered.

"Do you know her name?" I asked.

"No, she only told us to call her Amanda. She wanted to remain as anonymous as possible. I always got the feeling that she was worried about her parents. She carried a rosary and a Bible all the time. I got the impression that it would be best for her and her family to act as if it never even happened," Mrs. Burnsworth stated.

That wasn't uncommon. The biological parents didn't have to give their full name to the adopting parents if they didn't wish to. They could remain completely anonymous, should they choose. The system never cared because they were focused on the child and not the biological parents.

I pulled out the line up of the previous eleven victims. I had carried the string of photos around with me as each new victim presented themselves. These were their school photos and not their death photos. I placed the strip of eleven photographs down on the coffee table in front of the couple as I spoke.

"Do either of you recognize any of these boys?"

They both looked at the photos, but I could tell they had no idea who they were.

I had hoped that maybe one set of victim's parents would recognize someone in the line up. Someone that could give us a place to search. Knowing that Kevin was adopted was a huge win today.

"No, I'm sorry, we don't. Who are they?" Mr. Burnsworth asked.

"I'm not at liberty to speak about an on-going investigation. I was just curious if maybe you recognized any of them."

"Why adoption?" Ryzen asked as he came and stood next to the chair I was currently sitting in. There was a free chair; he should have sat. It was like wolves raised him.

"I wasn't able to conceive a baby. My doctor had said my egg count was too low and it would be basically impossible to get pregnant. We wanted to have a family and it didn't matter to us if the child was biologically ours," Mrs. Burnsworth answered.

I pulled out a pad of paper and handed it over to them along with a pen as I spoke, "Could you write down the name of the adoption agency, who you spoke with there, and anyone that you can remember who was involved in the adoption process. I'll also need the name of your physician, at the time, who recommended you try adoption, please.”

“If you think it’ll help,” Mrs. Bursnworth said as she took the offered items.

“Why the interest?” Mr. Burnsworth asked.

“In a case like this, it’s better to have too much information rather than not enough. We know someone you all know didn’t take your son. And we know there was no ransom demand, so it wasn’t about money. Money that you both clearly have. Kevin was taken for another reason, and now that we know he was adopted, he could have been targeted for that very reason. It would be helpful to have the information so we can verify the alibis of everyone that knew he was adopted outside of your circle of family and friends,” I explained.

I knew it would have been simpler to just tell them it was because we were chasing a serial killer, but I couldn’t break the gag order. And in this situation, I wasn’t certain it would bring any comfort to them to know that he had been killed so horribly. As it stood, they just knew he was killed. They didn’t know about the torture and it should stay that way for as long as possible.

Once the list was completed, I pulled out my card and handed it to them as I spoke, "We won't take up anymore of your time. I am truly sorry for your loss. If you have any questions or if you remember something, please don't hesitate to call me."

"Thank you," Mr. Burnsworth said.

I stood and we both headed out, leaving the parents to grieve in privacy. This was going to be something that affected them for the rest of their lives. I knew I had to find their son's killer or they would never be able to properly move on from this. There was no chance of moving on if there was never justice.

We climbed into Ryzen's car and drove back to the station. This time around, I didn't care that the car ride was completely silent, not even the radio played, further proof that something was seriously wrong with this man.

My mind was too busy asking questions that I knew were going to take time to answer. I was okay with that, though, because now, I had questions that could receive answers. I had a chance of being able to discover answers that could lead us to the UnSub.

This case had finally hit its first serious lead and it was one that I was hoping would pay off. Yes, if they were all adopted there would be a lot of suspects, both old and new, working within the adoption circuit, but having too many suspects was a hell of a lot better than the zero we were currently facing. I pulled out my phone and called Mason. He answered after two rings.

"You're on speaker."

"We just discovered that Kevin Burnsworth was adopted as an infant. It was a closed adoption. We need to run the other victims' names to see if any of them were adopted as well."

"Coop, pause what you are doing and start running the names. We need to see how many pop," Mason said before he spoke to me again. "It could be a one-off, but we might get lucky and find a soft connection."

"I'm hoping the majority were adopted and that could point us in some direction that we could use to generate suspects. With every new piece of information that we get, it makes it easier for me to build a realistic profile of our UnSub and we can then cross reference the profile with potential suspects. He's killing one a week, so we only have seven days to stop him before he grabs someone else."

"We'll have the names run before you get back. We'll keep working the cases and re-examining all of the evidence. Nice find, guys."

"Thanks."

I ended the call and I couldn't help but be slightly annoyed. The *nice find* was from Ryzen and it hurt a great deal for me to admit it. He had noticed the difference when my mind didn't even register that Kevin's parents had brown eyes and hair. Of course they wouldn't be able to have a blond hair, blue-eyed baby. Genetically, it wasn't possible.

This was the one time I was glad that Ryzen didn't have any desire to talk, the very last thing I wanted to hear out of his mouth was I told you so.

"Nice work, Profiler," he commented, disgust lacing his voice at the mention of my title.

Asshole.

CHAPTER FOUR

Ryzen

OF COURSE KNOX wasn't going to give me any credit for giving us the first real lead he'd had in a case he'd been working for three months. I still couldn't believe it. Three months he'd been working this serial killer case, twelve victims, child victims, and he had jack shit. He was supposed to be one of the best profilers in the country and he couldn't even find one serial killer in his own town.

It was ridiculous, and it only further fueled my anger toward him.

This was the guy that had cost me my

position in the CIA. He was a hack and it was just that simple. The sooner I got him out of my life, the better off I would be.

I forced my thoughts to go back to this case. I could tell right away that Kevin was adopted by looking at his parents. I wanted to scan the photos, though, to confirm there wasn't anyone else in the family with blond hair and blue eyes. Families could have a mixture of hair and eye color, but when it was a dominant gene that every family member had on both sides, there was no way Kevin wouldn't have inherited it. The only way for him to have blond hair and blue eyes was for him to be adopted. I wasn't a geneticist, but I knew quite a bit about genetics.

I always wore my sunglasses because the lights hurt my eyes. It was a side effect from having grey eyes. It was one of the rarest eye colors there was and it was from a hereditary gene mutation. The lack of melanin in my eyes meant my eyes were unprotected from the harsh UV rays from the sun. The sunglasses helped protect my eyes from potentially developing eye cancer. Plus, any bright light hurt them.

It was a real bitch when I lived in Africa.

When I arrived back in the States when I was eighteen, I had gone to see an eye doctor. He advised me of the specialty sunglasses that I should wear to help protect my eyes. There were no cancer signs back then and the glasses would help to, hopefully, prevent eye cancer from developing. Other than the light sensitivity, my eyesight was perfect.

I knew people had questions about why I always wore the sunglasses, even indoors or on a rainy day. It wasn't any of their business, though. Even the lights at my house were all low wattages, including the fridge light. I also had headaches from too many concussions and a couple of skull fractures, so the low light helped to prevent any headaches or migraines from glares on reflective surfaces.

The Burnsworths, their reactions looked genuine. They were genuinely grieving their son, which made me believe they weren't involved, and if they suspected anyone, they would have given them up. They weren't looking to protect anyone that could have done this to their son. They seemed like nice people.

And that was the shitty part in all of this.

They had done something nice, adopted a child that could have been abused through the foster system. They provided a loving home with toys, books, food, clothing, everything a child needed to survive and feel loved. They had endless family photos of trips, holidays, and sporting events that Kevin clearly participated in. They had his report cards framed, for fuck's sake. They were good people that provided a loving and safe home for a child. And here they were mourning the loss of their son who had been kidnapped and brutally murdered.

It wasn't fair, but that was life and I learned that a long time ago.

The second we arrived back at the Agency, Knox jumped out of my car before I even shifted to park, and all but sprinted for the door.

I followed behind him and made my way up to the conference room. We had turned an old office building into our own agency field office. We each had our own offices, we had a couple of conference rooms, interview rooms, there was a kitchen, a lounge area with a TV, and even a ping-pong table. We also had a holding area built with cells to keep any suspects on site. There was plenty of room left to expand, and I knew Mason hoped to grow with more techs and Agents so we could work multiple cases at one time. I was all for expanding if that meant we could help more people.

"Good, you're back. So far, Cooper has been able to confirm five of the other children were put up for adoption. The records are sealed, though," Mason stated.

"And the others weren't?" Knox asked.

"Don't know. I can't find them, but that doesn't mean they weren't adopted. Not everyone is placed on the adoption registry. You'd have to call a family court judge or a federal prosecutor with enough pull to run their names," Cooper answered.

"I got a guy," I said as I pulled out my phone.

"What guy?" Rafe asked, clearly shocked.

These guys always seemed to forget that I had a life before them. I had plenty of different contacts that I could reach out to for information or help, should I need it. I'd worked for every agency in this world and that brought a lot of connections in both the legal and illegal worlds.

"Federal prosecutor," I said as I headed for the door to make the call in private.

"Of course you have a lawyer," Knox said, and I knew he wasn't impressed. Though, he probably figured I needed a lawyer so often I had one on speed dial.

I headed down the hallway a short distance to reach my office. I closed the door as I hit Noah's name on my phone.

Noah Riley was a Federal Prosecutor with clearance to work in any State. He was thirty-eight and already making one hell of a name for himself in getting convictions on some of the most high-profile cases of the decade. That's who everyone saw him as, but to me, he was just *Noah*.

My big brother.

No one knew that I had any family and I kept it that way on purpose. I didn't want anyone targeting him to try and get to me. I had enemies; it was common practice when you killed as many high value targets as I had. When you had eliminated cartel leaders, mafia leaders, terrorists, and dirty politicians, the hard earned reputation was bound to rack up some enemies. It was why I didn't use a last name; it was why I didn't go by my legal name at all. The only one who knew my actual name was Noah and he never even called me it. He knew how dangerous my job was and the best thing about him, he never tried to pressure me into doing something different. He never tried to pressure me, period. He knew something horrible had happened to me growing up, something that permanently changed who I am, but he never pushed for answers. He allowed me to go at my own pace and I couldn't possibly love him more for it.

We were technically half-brothers. We had different mothers. Our father was a sorry excuse of a human being. Noah's mother refused to allow him in his life, whereas mine had hoped he would be this amazing man. In fairness to her, though, she was addicted to heroin so she could make herself believe she was a unicorn some days.

I had met Noah for the first time when I was nineteen and he was twenty-seven, at our father's funeral. Neither of us wanted to be there, but it was the only form of closure we were going to get. I was shocked to discover I had a brother, even a half-brother, and so was Noah. He instantly wanted to know me and he picked up that I was uncertain, too. We took it slow and now, eleven years later, I couldn't imagine going through life without talking to him at least once a week. He was the only person I had ever been able to open up to and talk for hours with.

"Hey, Brother. How are ya?" Noah asked the second he answered the phone.

"Good. Working a case I'm hoping you'll be able to help me out with."

"I'll do what I can. What do you need?"

"I'm working a serial killer case with the victims all male between twelve and fourteen. We have six confirmed to have been adopted. I'm hoping you could find out if the other six were as well. And maybe help with unsealing the adoption files."

"You think they might have been targeted for being adopted. That would mean someone that handled the adoption paperwork or has access to it, now, could be the killer. Yeah, that works for a warrant. Shoot me off all of the names and I'll pull what I can. I'll get my hands on the adoption records and send them over to you. You should have them tomorrow morning."

"Thanks, that's going to be a huge help. Everything okay with you?"

I knew he had been working some pretty challenging cases in the past few months. He was burning the midnight oil, and for a man who enjoyed sleeping, I knew it was taking a toll on him.

"I'm good. I just wrapped up a case in court this morning. I will get what you need and then I am off for a week. So, let me know if you need any other warrants or anything to help with your case."

"Appreciate it. Next time I get some vacation days, I'll come up your way. You can introduce me to this new man of yours."

Noah had started to see someone new a few months back. They weren't anything serious, but I still liked to make sure they were good enough for him. He hadn't been very lucky in love.

"Sounds good. I guess we'll see, if he's still sticking around by then. And hey, maybe you'll have a boyfriend as well."

That was highly unlikely. I didn't trust anyone enough to date someone. I didn't even have sex. But that was a whole other nightmare. One I wasn't looking to get into, right now.

I had to focus on these kids.

"Maybe. I gotta get back. Thanks, Noah."

"Anytime, Brother. Be safe. I love you."

"Love you, too."

I ended the call and then made the trip back into the conference room. I could see everyone's eyes on me and they were all clearly very interested in how I was connected to a federal prosecutor. I wasn't about to tell them.

"My guy is on it. He'll have the adoption files over for the morning."

"Perfect. Then we will be able to confirm if all twelve were adopted and who could be connected to them. Knox, the Governor has informed me that in the next hour there is going to be a press conference held out front of the Agency. You are going to address the press about the serial killer. The Governor is pulling rank, he wants everyone to know about the killings and he wants everyone keeping their eyes on the kids in every neighborhood," Mason said.

"The Mayor isn't going to like that," Knox instantly said, and I had to fight not to roll my eyes.

He was always so straight laced and afraid to do anything that might piss someone in the chain of command off.

Who cares what the Mayor wanted?

These were kids we were talking about. Parents deserved to know what was going on out there. Not to mention the kids deserved to know to be vigilant and not trust a stranger.

"Governor outranks the Mayor. I want the age mentioned to be between ten and sixteen. I know he's only killed between twelve and fourteen, but we don't know what he will do if he can't get the age that he wants. He might be willing to go lower or higher to satisfy his need. While you are working on a speech, the rest of us will be going through the files. Let's get everything up on the board. I want to know what their injuries were, let's see if there's a pattern. Coop, you trace the injuries and see if anyone else that was killed or kidnapped within our age parameters had that injury. He didn't just develop his method overnight. He had to have practiced and perfected it. Ry, check into what he might need to torture and hold his victims. Let's get a list going so we can start cross referencing names," Mason ordered.

I gave Mason a nod and then went and sat down with my laptop. We needed as many lists as we could get so we could start cross-referencing and circling any that kept popping up. It wasn't solid evidence, but if there was a name or two on multiple lists, they were someone we wanted to look into more and interrogate. Sometimes, in an investigation like this, all you had to go off of in the beginning were lists.

***

It was roughly an hour later when I stood off to the side downstairs. Knox was starting his press conference and my job was to make sure no one looked suspicious. So far, all I could see were reporters far too eager to hear what had been going on. They had all been under a gag order for so long they were practically drooling to get some intel.

They were vultures, every last one of them.

From my position, I could see everything and hear what Knox was saying. I didn't really pay attention to him, though. I had heard all about the case and I didn't need to actively listen to it again.

What I could tell, though, was he enjoyed being up there. He enjoyed talking into the cameras and answering all of the questions. It made him feel special and that was the dumbest thing I had ever heard of.

Who the hell cared what a bunch of strangers thought of you?

Press conferences and high profile cases were what Knox was all about. Anything he could use to push his career forward. It wouldn't surprise me, at all, if he was planning on writing a book about the cases he'd worked on.

Don't get me wrong, I had nothing against ambition or making money, but to gloat about your accomplishments was petty to me. Cops and the like should show up and do their job because they believed the world was going to be a safer place if they did. They shouldn't be doing their job in the hope of getting a gold star and a promotion out of it. That didn't make a good person, and I doubted that Knox truly was a good person deep down. As far as I was concerned, it was all a show, just an act he put on to make himself feel better.

God, I couldn't stand him and I hoped I would be able to leave soon and get the hell away from him. He didn't belong there, and after three months of having no suspects or leads, he didn't belong on the case. Clearly, he wasn't capable of solving this one and it would have been better to have another profiler on the case.

My opinion wasn't going to matter, though.

So, all I could do was what was in my capabilities and solve this case. Then, Knox would be out of my life for good and that would be the sweetest reward I had ever received.

CHAPTER FIVE

Knox

THE PRESS CONFERENCE had gone as well as could be expected. The reporters were starving for more information. They had been sitting on these homicides for months now, completely unable to report on them. It also didn't take them very long to start asking about why the Mayor had issued gag orders on these murders.

I'd tiptoed around those questions to the best of my ability and instead, had them focus on the children. They were what mattered the most in this situation. I also knew we would be getting a flood of calls from the victims' loved ones very soon. All of them would be demanding to know why they hadn't been informed of this earlier. Why we had stayed quiet, even with the gag orders.

They would be furious, but I couldn't blame them for that. There was a very real possibility that some of their children might still be alive had the Mayor not issued the gag order and had reported this serial killer to the press. It was also possible it wouldn't have changed anything, but the unknown of the 'what ifs' the parents were going to put themselves through would be devastating.

I hated that I hadn't been able to be honest with the victims' loved ones from the very beginning. I didn't like to lie and I hated not being able to give a parent all of the information they needed to understand what happened to their child.

Why their child had been killed.

It didn't matter how old a child was, they were always going to be their parents' baby. They were always going to be that sweet little child they brought home from the hospital, even if they were fifty at the time of their death. It was even hard to lie to the parents when it was something like this. When their child had been killed only because a serial killer had decided to make them his next victim.

There wasn't anything I could say to them to help them understand why this man was killing children. I could give them the profile and explain that, psychologically, he was born broken, but that wouldn't help them understand.

Because there simply was no understanding something like this.

Not when it was your child you had to bury.

I did mean every single word that I said about finding this sick bastard and putting him right where he belonged. An eight by ten hole in the ground where he would never see the light of day again.

We had been working away for a few hours, trying to combine lists and compare them. We had a lot of potential suspects, too many at this point. In a town like this, there were too many criminals; too many whack jobs that lived off the grid in a place where no one would hear someone scream.

I couldn't even be certain that our UnSub would even have a criminal record. Yes, he would likely have past offenses with either killing animals, or assaults, or starting fires, but it all depended on his family life growing up. Most parents didn't report their own children to the police. And if he came from a wealthy family, they could have easily paid the victims to cover it all up. He might not be in the system, which made everything we were doing even harder.

"Why no rape?" Ryzen asked, snapping the silence out of the room.

"What?" Rafe asked, obviously as confused as the rest of us.

I had to give it to Ryzen. When he decided to talk, he usually got everyone's attention. Though, that was mostly because he said something that confused everyone in the room as to what the hell he was even talking about. It would help if the man could speak full sentences.

"The UnSub. He goes through the trouble of kidnapping, torturing, and then killing, all without leaving a trace of himself on the bodies or at the kidnapping or dumping site. Why no sex?" Ryzen expanded.

I had to admit that was close to the

most words I had ever heard him speak before.

"That *is* weird. He holds them for seventy-two hours and there's no indication that he touched them sexually, either with himself or an object," Mason said, understanding where Ryzen was going with this.

"Not every serial killer is a sexual sadist. A good number of serial killers torture and kill because it makes them feel good. Torture is foreplay to them, something they do that gets them off. They then fantasize about it later when they are masturbating. Now, if there had been signs of sexual trauma from an object, that would have meant that our UnSub isn't able to physically perform. But that's not the case here. Sex isn't something our UnSub wants with his victims. It's more about him satisfying his urge, his craving, to hurt and kill. He's a sadist. He gets off on the pain his victims are going through, but he's using that to pleasure himself afterward. He might even masturbate in the room with the boys just to see the fear in their eyes," I explained.

"All of the boys were naked for their captivity, based on the injuries not having any clothing fibers in them. If he gets off on fear, there's nothing that scares a young teenage boy more than the fear of being raped," Ryzen said.

It wasn't necessarily the words that he used, but the tiniest hint of emotion that laced his voice that had me wondering. It almost sounded like he was speaking from experience and that piqued my interest.

When I had been evaluating Ryzen, it wasn't my original intention to have him fired. All I had was a file and most of it was redacted. My job was to make sure he could handle killing, essentially. He was a Government trained assassin and that took a mental toll on a person, especially when said person had been doing it for their entire adult life. At the age of eighteen, your mind is still developing, you are still learning not only who you are, but right and wrong. Physically, your mind isn't capable of processing killing other people in a healthy manner. Medically, it's not possible. That was why so many young adults had a hard time when they were in the military. They go off to war at the young age of eighteen or nineteen and see the horrors that war has to offer. They then can't deal with what they have seen or done, so they turn to drinking and drugs. They develop PTSD, and then it's a straight shot down from there.

For Ryzen, I wanted to make sure he was handling the killing. I wanted to make sure it would be safe for him to keep killing. However, his attitude and his lack of words at the time told me he couldn't be killing. It told me that his view of the world had become too dark for him to know the difference between right and wrong. But I had wondered if that view had been skewed before he even arrived at the CIA.

Hearing him speaking like this, it only made me wonder if my initial thoughts were correct. That the world had been dark for him long before he even stepped foot in the CIA. If that was true, though, that opened my mind up to all sorts of questions, and especially, one of the more pressing questions.

Was he picked up by the CIA for another reason?

"This UnSub would probably get off on seeing the fear. He might have even given his victims the choice of being hurt or raped. It's quite possible they picked being tortured over being raped. Unfortunately, unless we can get the UnSub to talk, we might never know exactly what he has done to them," I stated.

"There doesn't seem to be a pattern in the torture. One victim he electrocutes, another he burns, another he cuts. It's all random and each one has some that are similar, but they also have something new each time," Roland said as he flipped through the photos.

"He could still be perfecting his method," Jarod supplied.

"Most likely, he hasn't discovered what will bring him the greatest pleasure, yet. Serial killers are just like heroin addicts. The first time they kill, it's messy and unorganized but it feels amazing. Most have been dreaming, fantasizing about killing someone for years. It's built up inside of them and when they get to experience it the first time, it's orgasmic to them. However, just like a heroin addict, they have to keep chasing that first time experience. Each kill doesn't give them the same high that their first kill did. So, they have to do it more often and they have to do more to their victims to get that same first time feeling. It's why each victim has more torture done to them. He's trying to figure out what will give him that level of satisfaction that his first kill did," I explained.

"Does it work in our favor that he is still learning?" Rafe asked.

"It could. He's still learning what works for him, so he's inexperienced and that can lead to him making a mistake. I suspect that he's younger as well. In his mid-twenties to mid-thirties. He's not impulsive, because he can wait a week in between victims. He has to be relatively physically fit to be able to carry dead weight of up to eighty pounds, too," I answered.

"He's not leaving behind any fingerprints or hair, so either he's bald and wearing gloves, or he's covered when he tortures and dumps them," Cooper said.

"That seems smart for a newbie," Ryzen commented.

"That's the thing, there's no short supply of serial killer books. During his fantasy stages, he could have easily been doing research on best practices. On how to kidnap and dump a body. Studying how law enforcement caught other serial killers and learning from their mistakes. The Internet and science helps us catch them, but it also helps them evade capture. It's a double-edged sword," I stated.

"He hasn't perfected his method yet, so he has to be new. Coop, did you get anything from past police reports on animal cruelty?" Mason asked.

"A very long list. Even after I eliminated any females and recent reports."

"Any name pop up more than once?" Hollingsworth asked.

"A bunch. People are really screwed up in this town."

"There's more black magic and witchcraft in this state than anywhere else in the country. A lot of those animal cruelty charges will be connected to black magic, sometimes they sacrifice an animal for their rituals, or rooster fighting. There's a large underground cock fighting group here. In the reports, though, it will specify what they were for. If you add black magic and rooster fighting to the filters, it will eliminate them and give us a better picture of what we're dealing with."

"I'll do that now," Cooper said as he turned his attention to his computer.

"Well, given the black magic angle, could this be ritual?" Roland asked.

I had wondered that myself when the first victim appeared. It wouldn't be the first time someone was killing a person and offering them up as a human sacrifice. However, the second victim told me that wasn't what was going on.

"Human sacrifices are usually drained of their blood as part of the offering. They also have symbols painted or carved into their body. They don't get tortured, because it can ruin the offering. They all die from exsanguination. They are placed within a pentagram and they are bled until they stop breathing. It's a long death, but a relatively painless one," I explained.

"Definitely not what this guy is doing," Hollingsworth said.

Mason's phone rang and he pulled it out to answer. He moved outside to speak with whoever was on the other end. I hoped it was some good news for us. That whoever was calling would be able to give us a clue as to who this UnSub was. The call didn't last very long, and Mason strolled back into the room. Based on the look on his face, he wasn't happy with whatever intel he just received.

"Calls are coming in on the tip line. Most of them are people asking for more information. However, there was a series of calls that had been placed using a burner phone and a voice modulator. The man claimed to be the UnSub and he has been calling threatening to kill Special Agent Knox Hunter."

"He's just posturing. I don't fit his victimology. Assuming he even is our UnSub."

I knew that some serial killers would reach out to the media. I had gone through this before when they weren't happy that the Feds were investigating them. They wanted fame and glory and killing was how they were going about getting it. But this time around, we had no reason to believe it was the UnSub and even if it was, I wasn't a twelve to fourteen year old boy. He wasn't going to come after me. He didn't have the courage to.

"Regardless, your boss is not looking to take any chances. He is ordering you to be placed in protective custody until this

UnSub has been caught. And I agree. There's no point in taking the risk of you being grabbed. When killers have been backed into a corner, they lash out at anyone. If he believes the investigation into him dies with you, he won't think twice about killing you," Mason stated.

I knew there was no way I was going to get out of this.

I didn't need to be in protective custody. I highly doubted this UnSub would come for me. Even if he thought he could keep killing by killing me. I was a lot bigger than he was used to grabbing. Plus, I was a high profile Profiler. Grabbing me would mean the full force of the FBI would come down on him. It was essentially suicide. He had been smart this whole time. He wasn't going to make that fatal mistake.

"Fine, I will go to a safe house every night," I conceded.

"And that would usually be perfectly acceptable. However, your boss also informed me that you don't always do as you are told when you get a lead on a case. That you have gone out into the field before without backup because you figured something out. Because of that, you are going to be staying with one of us to ensure you don't leave on your own."

This was ridiculous.

The few times I had gone out on my own it was perfectly safe. I didn't go to a killer's house or some deserted area of the city. I went to populated areas to chase down a lead. Nothing ever happened to me. Now, I was being stuck with a babysitter again and I didn't appreciate it.

"Who gets him?" Rafe asked.

"Well, only two of you have the safest homes on the team. But I am not going to place him with you, Rafe, because I'm not going to put Lilly at risk. Not with a serial killer targeting children," Mason started, but Ryzen cut him off.

"No."

"You have the safest house," Mason started.

Oh hell, no.

I was with Ryzen on this one. I would rather be captured by this UnSub then trapped in a house with Rumpelstiltskin. It also didn't surprise me that his house would be one of the safest. He probably had ten guns in each room and a bomb that would go off if you stepped on the welcome mat the wrong way.

"He's not living with me," Ryzen pressed.

"He is, because I'm ordering it. We have to keep him alive. The safest place for him to be is your house. If you don't want your house being used as a safe house, don't turn the thing into Fort Knox. It's been a long day. I suggest everyone go home, get some sleep, and then we can start fresh tomorrow morning. We will have the court files by then and, hopefully, that will shed some light for us," Mason said, his tone firm and final.

I knew there was no arguing against him on this. I was rooming with Ryzen, whether I liked it or not.

He would probably murder me in my sleep.

CHAPTER SIX

Ryzen

THIS FUCKING SUCKED.

The very last person I wanted anywhere near my home was Knox. I didn't make my home secure so it could be used as a safe house for any stray that came along. It was designed this way to ensure I would be safe while inside. To ensure that none of my enemies would be able to get to me as long as I was in my home. So I could sleep at night and not have to be on edge waiting for an attack.

There were people out there that would love to get their hands on me. Either to kill me or to try and get me to turn against my country and be a sniper for them. I didn't survive the shit I did growing up just to be captured as an adult. Not while I was old enough and strong enough to defend myself. The reality that I lived in was the fact that I would always have enemies. It was part of the reason why I never dated anyone. They didn't need a target on their back.

Besides, dating was overrated.

There was no point to it. It was just another social convention that made no sense and was completely useless. If the world needed to increase in population, which it didn't, people could just have sex and make a baby. They didn't need to date to have sex.

Sex was also overrated.

Everything involving sex was overrated. From kissing to the actual deed. There was no point in any of it, at least not to me. It also hurt and anyone that said sex didn't hurt had clearly never been a bottom. There was nothing pleasant about the experience and it only left me feeling empty. I never got off on it. I'd never had a guy make me come. Fuck, I almost never got hard when someone touched me. Sex was animalistic and should only be done when the need to increase the population called for it.

If that meant you never had sex because you were gay, then so what?

It wasn't like a person needed sex to survive. You didn't need an orgasm to keep living and even if you did, that's what your hand was for. I was done with sex. I was done with all of it a long time ago.

There was nothing I could do or say to make Mason change his mind about Knox coming to stay with me. As much as I would have liked for him to stay with Rafe, I also understood why that was a terrible idea. There was no way any of us were going to risk Lilly. We knew Fin would be fine to take care of himself, but Lilly had already been through so much, we weren't going to risk putting her through anything else.

I didn't say anything. I just got up and strolled out the door. If Knox was going to be staying with me, then he could follow or not, the choice was up to him. Personally, I didn't give two shits if the UnSub grabbed him or not. I could hear him following me, though, so apparently, he cared. We got into my car once again and he spoke.

"I need to pick up some clothes at my place."

"Address?"

"1033 Parkview Ave."

I started my car and headed for his address. The sooner we solved this case, the better off I was going to be. We drove in silence for a good ten minutes before he felt the need to break it. I don't know why.

"Who is Lilly?"

"What?"

"Lilly. Mason said I couldn't be with Rafe because of Lilly. I was just curious who she was."

It wasn't any of his business who Lilly was or anything about our personal lives. At the same time, though, it wasn't like Rafe or any of the other guys wouldn't share the information with him. I could refuse to answer the question, tell him to mind his own business, but that was going to put him in a sour mood and I was going to be stuck in my house for the next twelve hours with him.

"It's a bit of a story. Basically, Rafe went undercover with his boyfriend,

Finley, into a human trafficking ring. Lilly is Fin's six year old niece, almost seven, now. Fin's older brother and his wife were killed so the trafficking ring could take Lilly. Fin worked undercover for nineteen months, eighteen alone and one with Rafe, before we found Lilly and shut it down. They all live together, now."

"My God. That poor girl. Is she healing okay?"

There was genuine concern to his voice and that surprised me. I didn't think he was capable of caring about anyone. He always seemed to be more interested in reading the paperwork than actually getting to know someone without judgment first.

"She has her dads, she'll be fine. She's in personal therapy and group therapy. She stays home from school, for now, but they live in a gated community with good security. She's safe. They've been thinking about a service dog for her. I guess the nightmares are bad."

I knew what it felt like to have night terrors. I knew what it felt like to be scared to close your eyes, to dread what you'd see. I still had that issue. All too often, I'd stay awake for a few days before going to sleep. My insomnia was always on, no matter what I did. It wasn't easy for me to just fall asleep. Not after all of the horrors I had lived through. The horrors I had seen. Despite what everyone chose to believe, despite what Knox thought he knew about me, the killing did bother me. I was taking a life and it didn't matter if the person was a criminal or not, I was still collecting souls and I had a lot of them. Close to a thousand now, between growing up and the CIA. It was a lot of souls to carry around and they did get very heavy.

I kept doing it, though, and not because I was gifted with a gun, but because these people needed to be taken out. They were too dangerous to keep alive. Not killing them meant thousands more would die and that wasn't something I could live with. It was just better to kill them and carry around their soul, compared to thousands of other innocent people that I refused to protect because I refused to pull the trigger.

It was a lot to try and live with and I wasn't certain I had figured out the balance for it, yet. I was trying. I was trying to sleep and have more of a normal life, but it wasn't working so far.

When Mason had reached out looking for help on the Task Force, I had thought about saying no. I had never worked within a team before. The CIA always worked alone, and even if they didn't, as a sniper, I sure as shit did. Growing up, I was always on my own so there was no team playing there. I wasn't really sure how to operate on a team or if I even wanted to be on one. Still, I didn't have anything else going on and it was a chance to take down a corrupt cop. When it was over, I was ready to leave, but then Mason had said we could stay and keep working the Task Force. It seemed like the right thing to do.

I had never wanted siblings. I had never wanted brothers. I never felt like I needed anyone in my life, but working alongside the guys, it was different. It made me feel different. The hole that had always been inside of me wasn't so big anymore. It was still there, but it wasn't as big and I didn't feel so empty. Working for the Agency, with the guys, it all felt right and I was glad that I had taken Mason up on his offer. I was glad that Mason had called me when most probably wouldn't have.

"A service dog will help with the nightmares. And a weighted blanket can do wonders for insomnia and anxiety. That might be something they consider as well. Unfortunately, all they can really do is keep her in therapy and wait it out. The good news is that she is young enough her mind will bounce back. She'll be able to have a normal life without the trauma destroying her."

Hopefully, that was true, but I knew from personal experience the things you saw at Lilly's age could haunt you for the rest of your life. As for the weighted blanket, I knew they worked. I had one permanently on my bed to try and help me at night. On the nights I could bring myself to close my eyes, it helped with the nightmares and anxiety about sleeping. I was hoping that Lilly would recover better than I did and she would be able to be happy and healthy. She had two great dads in her life, though, so I was sure she would.

After a quick stop at Knox's place and a pizza joint, we arrived at my house. The house wasn't in the outskirts, but I wasn't right in the middle of town, either. There was a metal, electrified fence all around my property. My closest neighbor was half a block away. I had an alarm on both the front and back doors, along with every window in the house. It was a two-story house with a fully completed basement. I had that set up as a gym with my treadmill and my weight set. It was a nice house. It was small and that was how I liked it. I didn't want too big of a house, there were too many spaces someone could hide and it would be too much work to clean.

We climbed out of my car and I strode over to unlock my door with my keycode. I didn't do keys, too easy to copy, but having a lock with a passcode meant someone would need my fourteen digit code to unlock the door. And then, they would need my iris scan to shut my alarm off. I knew Knox was going to have some comment about the high level of security, but if it helped me to sleep, if it helped me to feel safe in my own home, it was worth it to me.

"I guess Mason wasn't kidding with the Fort Knox joke," Knox commented as he stepped inside behind me and closed the door.

"When you've made a living taking out some of the worst criminals in this world, it's vital to have a strong security system," I said as I brought the pizza into the kitchen and slid it onto the counter.

"Fair enough," Knox said, and I could tell he was already looking around and trying to analyze everything. It was just another reason why I didn't want him in my home. I didn't need a Profiler psychoanalyzing me.

I turned the lights on in the kitchen and spoke.

"I don't have a spare room, so you'll have to sleep on the couch. I'll bring you down a pillow and blanket."

I didn't wait to hear any comments from him. I went upstairs and quickly grabbed him a pillow and spare blanket before I went back down and dropped them on the couch.

Knox was still standing in the kitchen and I could tell he wanted to go and explore the house. I just grabbed a plate with some pizza and a water bottle from the fridge before I headed back upstairs, leaving him to do whatever he wanted to do. I wasn't dealing with him tonight. I had done my job. I got him here and he was still alive. It was on him to entertain himself. I was certain he would be able to do that easily enough with profiling my home. I was sure, come morning, I would hear all about how my home told him I was a whack job who needed to find a different career. That would only give him more ammo, only give him more confidence in his decision to end my career with the CIA.

Well, he could entertain himself in his perfect black and white world. I would be too busy trying to fall asleep tonight. I hadn't gotten any sleep in the past two days and I really needed to try and catch a few hours tonight. Though, with having someone in my home, chances were I would be spending the night staring up at the ceiling and waiting for the sun to rise.

CHAPTER SEVEN

Knox

THE SECOND I heard Ryzen's bedroom door close, I couldn't help but look around. I couldn't believe the security he had for his house. At first, I thought he was being paranoid. That wouldn't really be too uncommon with snipers. They were always hyper-vigilant and believed that someone was always watching them. But hearing that he had dangerous enemies out there, that did make a lot more sense. It made sense that he would have this level of security on his home.

I didn't know what type of targets he

had killed, but I did know that the CIA took out major terrorists, cartels, the mafia, and high-powered weapon traffickers. There were an endless number of criminals out there who would want to take revenge on someone like Ryzen. I wasn't going to hold the security measures against him.

I moved into the living room and turned on the lights. I noticed right away that the lights weren't very bright. Even in the kitchen they were dim. I'd thought at first that maybe the bulbs were starting to burn out, but when the living room was just the same it just made me more curious. Plus, the curtains were blackout curtains and they were pulled closed. It was definitely weird. But maybe with being a sniper, he was worried about someone looking in. That hyper-vigilance again, I guess. Shrugging, I continued my perusal.

The furniture in the room was basic and looked either secondhand or like he'd had them for a good five or so years. There was a black suede couch, a black leather chair, and a matching recliner. Other than the furniture, there was a coffee table and two end tables that were brown, and a flat screen TV that sat perched on a brown entertainment stand on the opposite wall from the furniture, and that was it. There was nothing else in the room at all.

Hell, there was nothing else on this whole floor.

Not even a kitchen table.

There was nothing personal in the whole main level of the house. Nothing on the walls, not even any of those scenescape type photos that you could pick up in a store. The walls were completely bare. No family photos, though that could be blamed on him not wanting any enemies to know anything personal about him. But he could at least have a photo of a sunset or something. It didn't have to be anything with family in it, but something that reflected who he was. Something, *anything* that made the place feel like a home and not just a rest stop.

I shook my head and then made my way into the kitchen and opened the cupboards to see what he had. There were only a handful of plates and bowls, and two mugs. That was it for dishes. In the other cupboard, there was instant powdered coffee—*nasty*—and a stockpile of military MRE food. Why the hell he wanted to eat that crap I had no idea. I could understand the need while he was working in a remote area for the CIA, but he wasn't a sniper anymore. He could cook food while working for the Agency.

I moved over to the fridge and saw that he only had milk in the whole thing. Checking the freezer next showed me the single portion, microwavable meals. For a man who was highly trained in hand to hand combat and shooting, I would've thought he'd eat better. Though, now that I thought about it, maybe with him working for the CIA since he was eighteen, he didn't actually know how to cook. If he had been working a lot of hours and always traveling, learning how to cook wouldn't be high on his priority list.

I was going to assume that if I gave him a cookbook, he wouldn't take too kindly to it.

I closed the freezer and grabbed a plate, sliding a couple slices of pizza on it and balancing it in one hand before I grabbed my laptop with the other and strolled over to the couch. I had some work I could do on this case and, eventually, I would get some sleep. Hopefully, tomorrow we would be able to find our connection through the adoption files and stop this UnSub before they grabbed another kid.

CHAPTER EIGHT

Knox

IT WAS JUST after seven in the morning when I finally woke up. I had drifted off to sleep around midnight, give or take, so I had a good seven hours under my belt.

I stretched and then sat up. The couch was surprisingly comfortable and I could understand why Ryzen would have kept it around. I was a man who loved function, so if the couch was comfortable, I was all for it. Same as a bed. There were two things that I needed to be comfortable in my life, my couch and my bed.

I climbed to my feet and decided it

would be safe to open the curtains and let some of the sunlight shine in. The sun was already coming up and it instantly brightened up the room. I was about to make my way into the kitchen when I heard Ryzen coming down the stairs. Apparently, he was an early riser as well.

He let out a groan as he covered his eyes and spoke. "Fuck, close the curtains."

I had no idea what was going on, but I instantly yanked them shut, blocking out the bright rays that had been beaming into the room moments before. He wasn't wearing his sunglasses. I spoke as I walked over to him.

"Sorry, I didn't think it would be a problem to open the curtains."

"It's fine," he said, and for the first time I could see his actual eyes.

They were grey.

They were beautiful.

That thought surprised me, because I had never found another man's eyes to be beautiful before. I was straight, always had been, but *beautiful* was the only word I could think of to describe them.

"You have grey eyes. That's why you have the blackout curtains and always wear sunglasses, why the lights are so dim," I said with complete understanding.

"And you figured it was because I was paranoid and an asshole," he said as he went to grab the instant coffee.

His statement was fair, because that was exactly what I thought. I might be overanalyzing him and that wasn't fair to him.

"I'm sorry. I get too comfortable with being a Profiler that sometimes I forget that not everyone fits into a box perfectly. Look, to clear the air between us, I didn't know the CIA would fire you. I thought they would put you into a different position. You'd been a sniper for them for close to ten years. That's a very long time with a very large kill count. Psychologically, it's not good for you to keep being a sniper that long."

I knew there was a massive elephant in the room between us and it would be better to clear the air so we could work with each other without all of this hostility between us. It was great to hope that we would catch this UnSub within the next forty-eight hours, but the odds weren't in our favor. It would be nice to be able to work beside him without feeling like nails were going through my skin.

"I know how to handle my job. It wasn't your place to tell me or anyone when to stop. I didn't become a black hat sniper like you claimed I would. I still work for the good guys."

"Part of my job as a Profiler is to give those evaluations and decide if someone is mentally able to handle the work, still. I honestly thought it would be better for you, Ry, to not be a sniper with the CIA. But like I said, I thought they would put you in a different position. I'm sorry if you felt like I made the wrong call or like my decision was an attack against you. I was just doing my job, that was all."

"Sure. We should head out soon. If you want to shower, bathroom is the door on the left."

He wasn't going to talk to me about it, that much was clear. The situation and my responsibility in it, wasn't something we were going to see eye to eye on. There wasn't a point in me trying to get him to understand, we were too different, but hopefully now, we could at least get along a bit better if he were willing to consider that I didn't have it out for him.

Maybe.

I went and grabbed my bag so I could take a shower and get changed. I decided I would wear jeans today. Everyone else in the Agency wore jeans and not dress clothes, so I figured it would be better to blend in with them.

I jogged up the stairs and the first room I walked by was his bedroom. The door was open and I couldn't help but to go inside. The same type of blackout curtains covered the windows, leaving the room dark. I now knew it wasn't paranoia. I flipped on the light and moved further inside. The black blanket on his bed had me going over to it. I picked it up and confirmed exactly what I thought.

It was a weighted blanket.

The most common reason someone used a weighted blanket was anxiety. I had suspected that the killing didn't bother Ryzen, and that was one of my main concerns and why I suggested he stop being a sniper, but maybe I was wrong about that. Maybe Ryzen had just gotten very good at hiding his anxiety and emotions. This room also had nothing personal in it. I couldn't help but wonder if maybe Ryzen didn't know how to have a home, so he didn't know how to make it into one, either.

Crap, now I had even more questions about him and I'd thought I was done with questions for him. I thought I had already figured him out and now, it looked like I truly didn't know anything about the man, after all.

CHAPTER NINE

Knox

"WHAT ABOUT A woman UnSub?" Ryzen asked, breaking the silence.

For the past few hours, we had all been combing through the adoption files that Ryzen's friend had managed to get for us. As it turned out, all twelve victims had been adopted, and most of them were closed adoptions. It gave us a huge suspect pool, but it was a start and it was something we were diving headfirst into.

"Out of all serial killers in the United States, only approximately eleven percent are females. Female serial killers are very rarely sadistic. They tend to kidnap children because they feel like they need to be rescued. They take care of them and they die because they failed to properly feed or give them water. It's not because they physically killed them. Any female serial killers who were sadistic, they targeted males or females who they felt did them wrong in some way. It could be as simple as a woman accidentally bumping into her man. The killer will kidnap that woman and torture her to death while justifying her actions because that victim must have been trying to steal her man. They never go for children to hurt," I explained.

If the victims hadn't been tortured, I would be thinking our perp was a female as well. It would explain how the victims were lured, since most children will trust a female over a male. When a child is abducted, people are looking at the men in the area as potential suspects and they ignore the women. But with the psychopathy of this UnSub, it just wasn't possible.

"So we can eliminate the women on the lists," Cooper said, nodding as he got to work on eliminating potential suspects.

"Anyone over the age of forty, to be safe, and younger than twenty," I added.

"I would imagine they can't be well known, either. If a judge was walking down the street and grabbed a kid, someone would notice," Mason pointed out.

"Correct. Anyone who had been in the news as often as judges are would have been noticed. We can also eliminate anyone who has been out of the state during the past three months, and anyone who has been arrested or in the hospital. Our UnSub was able to stalk all of his victims for at least a week. That takes time and dedication," I said.

"Anyone check parking tickets?" Ryzen asked.

"From the courthouse?" Jarod asked, confused.

"Outside of the victim's home, and at the kidnapping or dumping site. The UnSub stalked them, so maybe he got a ticket while he was following them on foot," Ryzen explained.

"That's smart. He might not have paid attention to the parking bylaws if he was fixated on his victim. Each parking ticket is recorded into the system with the license plate and location. Can you run them?" I asked Cooper.

I hadn't even thought about looking for parking tickets. I was so focused on finding our UnSub that I didn't think to try and find his car. If we could find the car, we might be able to track it back to an address or a neighborhood, at least.

"I can run them. It'll be a lot, though, but I can cross reference them with the locations and record the path the victims took around their kidnapping," Cooper said.

I knew it wasn't going to be that simple for him. It wasn't like we had a make or a model for the car. We didn't have anything he could truly use to do a targeted search, but he might be able to narrow it down enough that we could compare it to our long list of suspects. We didn't have much, but I felt like we were at least getting somewhere.

For the first time in three months, I was getting somewhere.

CHAPTER TEN

Knox

AT TWO IN the morning, you would think I would be asleep. Instead, I couldn't get my mind off of the case. I couldn't stop thinking about it. We had been able to accomplish a lot and still nothing all at the same time today. We had a very long list of suspects, even after all of the refining we had managed to do. We had a lot that we could be looking at and yet, at the same time, we had nothing more than we did yesterday. It was frustrating, but at least there hadn't been another child taken, yet. Not that I expected there to be.

We still had five days before he would strike out again.

I noticed a shadow coming down the stairs and glanced over to see that Ryzen was still awake, too. He walked into the kitchen and I figured he was grabbing a glass of water.

I pushed the blanket off of me and made my way into the kitchen. Ryzen had no shirt on and was just wearing sleep pants. Even in the dimly lit room, from the light that I had left on, I could see the scars covering his back.

I can't even explain what happened at that moment, what made me respond the way I did. It was like a magnet had been attached to the both of us and I was suddenly being pulled to him. Before I could even register what I was doing, my hand lightly ghosted along the one scar on his back. The whisper of the touch had him tensing, but he didn't pull away.

I knew what this scar was.

It was long, but not jagged. I had seen these type of scars from photos during my training days at Quantico.

Ryzen had been whipped.

Someone had actually taken a whip to his back; not once, but fifteen times. His back was covered in them, along with other smaller scars.

Someone had done this to him.

Someone had tortured him.

I felt my breath hitch and my fingers tingled as I traced each scar. My heart ached for what the man must have gone through, how this torture must have felt.

The scars were old. This horrible torment had to be done to him close to a dozen years ago.

All before he was eighteen.

Christ, he'd been just a child.

My mind played his words over again in my head. The words he spoke about the fear of being raped to keep a child in line. My stomach turned at knowing that he must have been speaking from personal experience. Anger grew in the pit of my stomach and bile rose up my throat. I had never truly felt this angry before, but I wanted nothing more than to go and find the person responsible for these scars and kill the fucker with my own bare hands. To do this to someone, to do this to a child, it was disgusting, and it only painted a clearer picture as to why Ryzen was the way he was.

He wasn't a killer.

He was a fucking warrior and I had completely misjudged him.

"Who did this to you?" I growled out as I fought to control my rage.

CHAPTER ELEVEN

Ryzen

I HADN'T REALIZED Knox was awake. I had been in my room, laying in my bed and trying to get myself to close my eyes, but no matter what I did, I just couldn't do it. I was so tired, completely drained, mentally and physically, but I couldn't sleep.

Insomnia was a cruel bitch.

I figured I would come down and grab a glass of water and maybe go for a run on my treadmill to try and wear myself out even more. I was so used to being alone in my house that, in my exhausted state, I didn't even remember Knox was down here until I saw him lying on the couch.

I heard him coming over to me and I was hoping he was just going to comment that he couldn't sleep, either. I wasn't expecting him to touch me. I wasn't expecting the anger in his voice at the sight of my scars.

I had made peace with my scars a long time ago. They weren't something I felt I needed to hide away from the world. I had, in the beginning, tried to ignore them, pretended like they weren't there. But every time I removed my shirt, I was reminded of them. It was unavoidable. There was nothing I could do to cover them up. I had even entertained the idea of getting tattoos to cover them, but there were far too many to cover and I really didn't like needles, which would be a hiccup for getting a tattoo.

In the handful of times, I had been with someone sexually since I was eighteen, the person was always freaked out by them. They didn't like touching them, they didn't like seeing them and always had me hide them while we were having sex. For a long time, they made me feel like I was worthless and disgusting.

Disfigured.

Noah was the one to help me understand and see that they weren't a sign of weakness. They weren't something that I should have to hide away like a dirty secret. They were proof of how strong I was. They were proof that I was a fighter and any guy that didn't understand that could go fuck themselves.

I was comfortable with them being seen, but that didn't mean I wanted to openly talk about them. Especially with a man like Knox. I couldn't tell if he was asking me about them because he genuinely wanted to know, or because his Profiler's mind was working overtime at seeing them. I could hear the anger in his voice, but that didn't mean he wasn't examining me in a Profiler way. There were plenty of Profilers that I'd come across in my time with the CIA that could get angry and upset at the sight of a hurt victim, but that didn't change that they were still analyzing their every move. I wasn't looking to be analyzed or dissected.

"I don't need an e-val," I stated.

"No, that's not why I was asking. I was asking because I would like to get my hands on the asshole who did this to you. Put him in a dark hole for the rest of his fucking life," Knox said as his voice shook with anger.

His fury truly did surprise me, because I wasn't expecting it. It was no secret that we didn't start off on the best foot. We didn't like each other. We were polar opposites. I doubted he had experienced anything horrible in his life. I doubted he had ever gotten his heart broken. I knew his parents raised him right and he went to Harvard for his degree. A degree he proudly framed and hung in his office for everyone to see.

I had never even been to high school. I hadn't even been to grade school. I spoke English, not always that well, and a few African dialects that I'd picked up in order to survive. I had never been referred to as the brains. I was always the muscle, always the shooter, and that was perfectly fine with me. I was damn good at shooting. I had been taught from a very young age how to do it. Knox barely knew how to hold a gun.

He didn't care about me, so why the

hell would he care about getting his hands on the person who did this to me?

"Why do you care?"

The question probably didn't matter and I doubted I could believe what he said, but I still found myself needing to ask it. I needed to know why he would care so much about who had hurt me.

"Because you didn't deserve to have any of this done to you. Because I can tell they are from your childhood. Whoever did this to you is a monster and they deserve to be punished. Mostly, though, because I judged you when I shouldn't have. I don't tend to get my perspective on people wrong, but with you, Ry, I admit, I got it very wrong. I thought the killing didn't bother you. That you had shut down emotionally and socially. That was why you didn't talk and why you acted as if you didn't care. But you *do* care. You haven't slept in days. I can see it in the way your movements are getting a bit slower. I saw the weighted blanket on your bed, telling me you have anxiety. You don't have it during the day, though, I haven't seen any signs, so it's just around sleeping. Nightmares, would be my guess. These scars, they tell me that you are a survivor. They tell me that you are a warrior and you became a sniper not just because you were good at it, but because you wanted to protect people. You wanted to make the world safer for children. And you quietly pay the price for it without complaint."

Fuck.

I wasn't really sure what to do with that. It would have been a lot easier if Knox had just stayed the cold-hearted, single-minded asshole that he was that day five years ago in his office. It would have made things a lot easier to handle, to deal with, if he had. This wasn't something that I talked about, because the scars didn't come from a single person. There wasn't one person who could take the blame for every mark on me. There was one person who started the chain of events, but he was already dead. There was no one to go and arrest. There was no one to put into the ground. They were already dead and not by my own hands. It should have brought me some semblance of peace knowing that they were dead and they couldn't hurt me or another child ever again, but it didn't. I knew there was someone else taking their place and keeping the practice going. There would always be someone else to take up the mantle and keep hurting children. It was an endless merry-go-round and it wasn't going to stop. At least, not in my lifetime.

"The people responsible are already dead and no, it wasn't by me."

"Good. They're in Hell where they belong. Can you tell me who they were?" he asked, cautiously.

Clearly, he didn't want to cross the line or push when he shouldn't. I could tell he wasn't too sure where the line was, though, and he was trying to see if it was okay for him to know more or if I needed him to stop. He was leaving the ball in my court and I greatly appreciated it.

I turned to face him as I spoke. "They weren't anyone special. My father wasn't a good man and my mother was a heroin addict. She overdosed when I was five and my father's idea of parenting was to send me to Africa to live within a missionary. They traveled around the war torn villages trying to help where they could."

"Did your father know that?" he asked, as his hand lightly traced a scar that went over my heart and down my left side.

"I don't think he cared enough to find out. I was nine when the rebels attacked the camp the missionary was living in. They grabbed me and I was turned into a child soldier for them. I was with them until I was rescued roughly three years later by a mercenary who was a sniper. He taught me everything I know. For five years, we traveled all over the country taking out major threats against innocent people. CIA caught wind of me and the rest is history."

Being a child soldier hadn't been easy. There were plenty of moments in my life back then that made me want to give up. That made me want to conform to what they were demanding of me. Maybe it would have been easier to give in, to let my mind be conditioned into doing what they wanted. However, I didn't want to be a murderer. I didn't want to kill innocent people, other children, all because they didn't want to join an army. I knew I was a murderer, it was a fact that I'd had to deal with and I would have to continue to live with it for the rest of my life. I had killed innocent people, all before the age of puberty. I wasn't trying to focus on that. I was trying to focus on all of the lives I had saved by taking out dangerous targets. Maybe then, I could tip the scale in my favor.

"I'm so sorry. You should never have been put into that position. Your father never should have sent you there. That mercenary never should have turned you into a weapon and the CIA should never have recruited you. They should have freed you, not used you, too."

"I chose it. The CIA gave me a choice and I don't regret it. I've saved thousands of lives by the kills I've made. I'm well aware that, under different circumstances, I would be a serial killer, a mass murderer for all of the souls I've collected in my life. But every time I killed a target, I was saving thousands of innocent lives and that is always worth the price to my own soul."

I'm not sure when it happened, but the distance between us had become considerably smaller and not just in a physical sense. I shouldn't have told him any of this, but I wanted him to know. I wanted him to understand why I am the way that I am. That it wasn't for the reasons he'd suspected. That it wasn't for the reasons that he'd put in his report to the CIA. Yes, I was mad about losing my position in the Agency. However, if I had still been working for the CIA, I never would have been able to take Mason up on his offer to join his new Agency. As much as I wasn't certain at first, I didn't want to work for anyone else. I wanted to work for the Federal Protection Agency and keep helping children who believed no one was coming for them. Losing my position at the CIA might actually have been the best thing to ever happen to me, and I couldn't hate Knox for that.

Knox was so close to me, now, that I had to tilt my head back to be able to look him in the eyes. He was taller than me by six inches and, more often than not, I hated it when a man was this close to me, looking down at me. However, with Knox, I didn't feel like he was trying to intimidate me. There was an emotion in his eyes that I couldn't pinpoint. I had never seen it before, in anyone's eyes. It wasn't pity, hate, or disgust. It wasn't even sadness. I didn't know what it was, but it made me feel weird. Having him this close to me, his hand on my chest over my heart, it was all making me feel weird.

"You're a good man, Ry. You are sacrificing so much of yourself for people you don't even know. Not many men would be able to do that. You don't have to carry it alone, though. I'll always be there for you, should you need to talk or just don't want to be alone."

What was happening?

Why was he making me feel this way?

What the hell was this feeling, anyway?

I had been with a handful of guys since I was eighteen and I had never felt like this toward them. They had never made me feel like this. I didn't even know how to describe it. There was just this *warmth*. It was weird and I wasn't certain I liked it. He shouldn't be this close to me.

So why didn't I want him to move back?

Why couldn't I stop looking at his lips?

This was insane. I wasn't attracted to him. I *couldn't be* attracted to him. We were too different and one of those major differences was him being straight. I knew he was straight. I had seen the photos of him and a girlfriend in his office. Everything I'd heard about him through the grapevine was that he liked women.

He had never been with a guy before.

But if he was only attracted to women, why was he standing so close to me?

Our bodies were touching, he had his hand on my chest, but his arm wasn't extended. We were touching fully. I could feel his stomach against mine. I could feel the silhouette of his dick through his sweatpants against my lower stomach and I knew he could feel mine on his upper thigh.

If he wasn't attracted to men, why could I feel him getting harder?

Why was he looking at me like this?

His hand traveled down from my chest and slowly moved down my left side and to my hip. My sweatpants sat low on my hips and his hand dipped under the elastic waistband to rest lower on my hip. I could see the heat in his eyes and it shocked me.

Knox wanted to kiss me.

I should pull away. I should push him away and put that wall back up between us.

This was so wrong.

He wasn't interested in guys. He was just caught up in the moment. He would regret this later and then things would be awkward between us and I didn't want that. We had finally made some real progress with not hating each other, I didn't want there to be this huge awkwardness between us.

Especially because he kissed a boy for the first time.

Why couldn't I bring myself to pull away?

What the hell was it about Knox that had me turning into an idiot?

He started to close the gap between our mouths and I couldn't help but hold my breath. My heart pounded in my chest. I wanted to feel his lips against mine. The need for it was almost unbearable and when his lips were just about to touch mine, the sound of our phones ringing broke the moment and we both snapped back. He was across the room and going over to the coffee table faster than I could even blink.

And just like that, the warmth I felt was gone.

I was back to feeling cold, but unlike before when it didn't bother me, I hated it. I wanted the warmth back. I couldn't even remember the last time I had felt anything other than cold and empty. Knox didn't make me feel that way and I wanted that warmth back, damn it.

"It was Mason. There's another dead body. He wants us to meet him at the crime scene."

"It's only been two days. You said this UnSub has a cooling off period of a week, though."

It had only been two days since the last victim. It didn't even fit with our UnSub's MO of torturing his victim for seventy-two hours. We shouldn't have another body, yet.

"The press conference must have forced him to move up his timeline. He now has to only grab whatever kids are available to him within his victimology. He's like a heroin addict, remember? We essentially just snatched up every drug dealer in town and now, he's craving a fix. He has to get it somewhere."

"And if he can't get the heroin, he'll get whatever he can," I said with complete understanding.

"Exactly. We gotta go, now. We have no idea how many bodies he'll drop before we stop him."

Fuck.

There was no telling what this UnSub

would do now. Or who he would go after next. We needed to stop him and I just hoped that in his haste to kill again, he made a fatal mistake that we could use to stop him once and for all.

CHAPTER TWELVE

Knox

WHAT WAS GOING on with me?

I'd almost kissed Ry.

I'd almost kissed a man.

I'd *wanted* to kiss him.

I had never felt like this before. I knew, psychologically, it would make sense that I would want to kiss him. He had been through something horrible and I felt for him. As a human being, I saw Ry in a new light and my mind was processing that. A comfort kiss when he was feeling upset and having to relive horrible moments from his childhood would be perfectly understandable.

So why did I still want to kiss him?

And why did it make me excited to feel his body against mine?

I knew it was a natural reaction to get an erection when being touched on your dick. I knew that. But I also knew that *I* had never been hard before when another guy had just casually touched me or brushed up against me. Growing up as a teenager, I'd had sleepovers and we would sleep in the same bed. I never got hard. I'd never looked at another man and thought he was beautiful or attractive. I'd never looked at a man and thought I wanted to have sex with him.

So why did I want to kiss Ry?

Why did I want to touch him and feel his skin against my own?

I was thirty-five years old. I knew I was straight. I was too old to be questioning my sexuality now, and yet, here I was, doing exactly that. I should be blowing it off as a one-time lapse in judgment. Convince myself that I had gotten caught up in the moment and leave it at that. I shook off the thoughts, pushing the issue to the back of my mind.

I didn't have time to think about it

right now, anyway. Not when there was a serial killer on the loose who was not only targeting children, but had made threats against my own life. I had to take those threats seriously, even if I didn't quite believe he would do anything.

Serial killers who went after children never went after an adult. If they were strong enough to take down an adult, they wouldn't be targeting children. Children were easier targets in the sense that they didn't fight back. They could overpower them and that was worth the higher risk of being caught.

We pulled up to the crime scene and climbed from the car. Yellow crime scene tape surrounded another dumpster that sat between two closed buildings, one was a bakery and the other was a pizza shop. Typically, an UnSub picked a location where they figured no one would find the victim until sometime in the morning when the businesses opened. And even then, depending on how full the dumpster was, they still might not have been noticed.

That was one thing that this UnSub hadn't done. He'd wanted the bodies to be found because he made sure that the dumpster had already been picked up and taken to the dump. If the UnSub wanted to keep the bodies hidden forever, they would have timed it right so the dumpster would be taken to the dump and the body would most likely be buried for the rest of time. Our UnSub wanted recognition. He wanted to be known for his kills. And now, he was getting that recognition from the press conference. Every journalist in the city and soon, the State, would be reporting on him and it wouldn't take long before someone came up with a name to call him.

"No Koda?" I asked Mason as we joined him and Jarod. I had never seen Mason without Koda. They were always together.

"He is staying with Lilly for the night to see how she does with having a dog with her," Mason answered.

"What do we have?" Ry asked, looking to get started.

"We've got two victims in the dumpster this time. A homeless man who was looking for some food found them. A patrol officer is with him down at the diner getting him some food and his statement," Jarod started as we headed into the alley.

"Two bodies? Are you sure this is our guy?" I asked.

He had never taken two victims before and it would be unusual for him to escalate like that. Before, he had no real confidence in his craft. You could tell by him changing up the torturing methods. He was still learning. Taking two victims at the same time and having to dump them, it would be a lot. He would have to control both victims and be confident enough that they couldn't escape and find help. It was twice the work and a huge risk to him.

"Both are males, between twelve and fourteen. Both are naked and tortured. Now, here's the weird part. They were tortured in the exact same way, and I mean, *exactly*," Mason stated.

I looked into the dumpster and saw what he meant. They hadn't just been tortured the same way all over their body, but rather the exact same spots. If one had a cut on his fifth rib, the other did as well. He'd made them symmetrical. This wasn't erratic, this was planned and he took his time. He was meticulous this time around.

He'd gained confidence.

"Shit, he's getting confident. He's being recognized for his work, now. He's an artist and now, he is getting attention. He wants to showcase his work more. That's why he grabbed a second victim. The fucker's showing off. *Look what I can do.* He's taunting us at the same time by grabbing a second victim and grabbing two so close to dumping the last one. He's essentially saying, *you can't stop me,*" I explained.

This was going to be bad. With that newfound confidence, his kills were going to be closer together. Chances were, he already had his next victim in his sights and he would grab him before the day was over.

"We need to know who they are. Someone must be missing them," Rafe piped up.

"The M.E. can run their prints and DNA. We might get a quicker match with a photo of them through the missing person's database. They don't appear to be homeless. They are clean and not starved. Someone loved them enough to take proper care of them. They would have been reported missing by now," I said.

"I'll take their photo and run it through the database," Hollingsworth said as he pulled out his phone.

"When's the M.E getting here?" Jarod asked.

"Thirty minutes, roughly. Coop is already going through any camera footage in the area. Both businesses have cameras on their front door, so hopefully, they caught something," Mason answered.

"What are you doing?" I asked Ryzen. He was looking all around the dumpster and on the ground, as if he'd lost something.

"Do you hear that?" he asked.

We all got quiet to try and hear what he was referring to, but I didn't pick anything up.

"No," I said, and I could tell the others were in agreement to me.

"There's a hum. I can't tell where it's coming from."

"Oh yeah, there is a soft hum. Like from a computer running or something," Jarod said as he started to look around him.

I could just faintly hear it. It was most likely nothing, but I had to agree, it was odd that something was humming. We were in the middle of an alley. There was nothing electrical around us. There weren't any machines like generators or air conditioning units that would account for the noise. They were located on the roof of the buildings and even though it was two in the morning and quiet, we still wouldn't be able to hear them. Not to mention, the machines should all be off with the businesses closed for the night. I was thinking it might be a camera. Maybe the UnSub wanted to watch our investigation and see what we knew. It wouldn't be the first time I had come across a hidden camera at a crime scene. Sometimes a reporter will leave it if they stumble onto the crime scene first. The sudden beeping sound snapped all of our heads up. Before any of us could even say anything, Ryzen had beaten us to it.

"Bomb, get down."

I saw the others running out of the alley, but Ryzen and I were on the other side of the dumpster and further away from the opening of the alley. Before I could run, Ryzen's arms were around me and he put himself in front of me just as the bomb went off. The blast was so strong we flew in the air. I could feel

Ryzen's arms still around me, but I felt weird as I flew in the air back further into the alley. It was a surreal moment that felt like it was happening in slow motion. When we hit the ground, we rolled and Ryzen ended up half on top of me. Dust and debris filtered down all around us and it was hard to see anything through the smokey air.

I knew I should be sore, but I couldn't really feel much. My ears were ringing and it felt like I was having an out of body experience. Like I couldn't connect mentally to my body. I was in shock, I knew that, but I also knew I couldn't afford to be in shock. We had just been blown up, for fuck's sake. I had to make sure we were okay.

"Jarod! Baby?" I heard Mason yell.

"Get the med bag!" Rafe yelled.

Someone was hurt.

We had to move.

I forced my mind to focus and I looked down to make sure I had both of my legs. Thank fuck, they were still there. I checked the rest of me that I could see and I was happy to report I had all of my parts. I didn't see any blood on me. It didn't hurt to breathe. I was good. Ryzen had protected me from the blast.

Ry...

Shit.

I turned to look at Ryzen, who was lying partly on me. His eyes were closed and with a shaky hand I reached over to see if he had a pulse. I almost cried when I felt it thrumming underneath my fingers. I wanted to move him off of me, but I wasn't sure what his injuries were. I didn't want to risk it.

"Paramedics are three minutes out," Hollingsworth yelled.

"Ry, Knox?" Rafe called out.

"Here! I need help with Ry."

It was only a moment later when Hollingsworth's face appeared above me. He had dirt on his face, but he wasn't bleeding. He quickly began to look Ryzen over.

"The others?" I asked.

"Mason and Rafe are good. Jarod has a piece of metal in his lower left side. AS long as we leave it in, her should be fine until he gets to surgery. Are you all right?"

"Yeah, I'm good. Ry protected me from it."

He finished looking over Ry. "There's

no shrapnel in his back. I'm going to secure his neck and then I need you to gently roll him off of you."

"Got it."

Hollingsworth went over to Ry's head and secured his neck with his hands and together, we slowly rolled him over so he was on his back. I was relieved when I didn't see too much blood on him. Nothing to indicate that shrapnel had hit him. He had some blood on him from various cuts that would need to be cleaned and most likely stitched up, but that was about all I could see at that point. I was worried that he hadn't woken up yet. He could have a brain injury.

"Ry, can you hear me? I need you to wake up for me."

I made a fist and rubbed it against his chest plate to try and garner any sort of a response from him. I was very pleased when he groaned and slowly started to regain consciousness.

"That's it, let me see those eyes of yours," I encouraged.

Ry slowly blinked open and I could tell his head was hurting him. He was squinting and trying to keep them open. I could also tell his mind was trying to catch up on what was going on.

"There was a bomb. You protected me from the blast. I need you to stay still until the paramedics come. We don't know if you injured your neck or spine," I explained calmly.

"The others?" Ry asked, and he had to cough around the heavy air that was settling around us.

"Everyone is okay, but Jarod has a piece of metal to his lower left side. He'll have to go to the hospital as well. Just relax, the ambulance is almost here," I said. I could hear the sirens getting closer.

"He set the bomb. He knew we would come. He knew *you* would come. He wants you dead. It's not just a bluff," he said with a rough voice.

"I know."

My hope that this UnSub was just bluffing when it came to me literally went up in smoke. He wanted me dead, which meant I had no idea who this guy was. He was crossing profiles all over the place. He was contradicting himself. He went after children, but he had no problem building a bomb and trying to kill not only me, but the others on the team. He had gained so much confidence in such a short amount of time. It was throwing me through a loop and I had no idea what profile to give this UnSub, now. I was going to need to figure it out, because without a proper profile, we were never going to find him.

The paramedics came running over to us and Jarod. I stayed where I was, but Hollingsworth moved back a bit to give them some room to work. I watched as they put a c-collar around Ry's neck to secure it until he could be cleared at the hospital. They checked his vitals and they were stable and nothing indicated that something was wrong. When they lifted his shirt up, I could already see the bruising all over his ribs. If they weren't broken, they were badly bruised and he was going to be very sore for the next few weeks.

The paramedics loaded him up into the ambulance closest to us and I saw Jarod being loaded into the other. Mason was instantly climbing in behind him. I climbed into the back of the rig with Ry and sat down next to him while the paramedics got ready to transport him. I took his hand in mine as he spoke.

"You need to stay."

"I'm going with you." I was not about to leave him alone and injured in a hospital.

"You have to work the scene. I'm gonna be okay, but those kids are now blown up, too. You have to be there and gather the evidence. You need to see the scene, Knox. You need to feel it. Get into his mind."

"I don't know this time around. I don't know who he is. He's jumping all over the place," I said, sounding completely lost.

"Stop trying to think of him as a box. He's not going to check one. Think chaos. Let the scene talk to you and not the textbooks. You can do this."

"Sir, are you coming with us? We need to get moving," the paramedic said.

I looked down at Ry and I saw him give me a wink. He was right and I knew it. I had to work the scene. I had to see it from the UnSub's point of view. The place was now going to be crawling with cops, he wouldn't be able to get me here.

"I'll come see you soon," I promised.

I climbed out of the ambulance and watched as they closed the doors and drove away. I hated not being there with him. I wanted to be there to make sure he was all right. But Ry was right, I had to catch this son of a bitch. He had just injured two law enforcement officers and there was no telling what else he would do.

I looked behind me and saw Rafe and Hollingsworth. They were both covered in dirt, but they were both determined. Their eyes were hard and I could see they wanted this guy's blood. They wanted to make sure he paid for hurting two of their brothers.

And he would.

He was going to pay for every life he had taken. He was going to pay for every mark on Ry's and Jarod's body. We were going to catch him and then, he was going to wish he never stepped foot in our city.

CHAPTER THIRTEEN

Ryzen

HEADING TO A crime scene for a child victim, the last thing I expected was to deal with a bomb going off. I knew serial killers could attack if they felt backed into a corner, but that wasn't what this felt like.

It felt personal, and personal toward Knox.

He had been a Profiler for close to fifteen years now, so he was bound to have enemies even without going into the field. I knew he'd had to testify against major felony criminals, all part of the job.

Any one of them could be this killer.

Maybe the killings didn't fit into a set box because they were designed to grab someone's attention.

Maybe all our UnSub wanted was attention and what better way than to brutally kill a young teenager?

We all had more questions than answers at this point and we were getting nowhere.

I hated this feeling. I hated not being able to know who the target was so I could go after them. I wanted this to end. We *needed* it to end.

I knew the guys could handle hard cases. We had dealt with our fair share before this new Agency and since being a part of it. However, I wasn't certain that Knox would be able to handle the weight of this case. It was already bad enough that this UnSub had been killing and torturing children. But now, he was targeting Knox, and he was also trying to kill anyone who was around him in the process.

If I hadn't grabbed Knox when that bomb went off, the shrapnel could have killed him. I didn't even think, I just reacted. All I knew was that I had to protect Knox from the hit. It didn't even matter if it killed me, as long as it didn't kill him.

How the hell had we gotten here?

How did I go from hating his guts and waiting for the day he finally got what he deserved, to this?

To me risking my own life just to protect him. To not caring if I died in the process. It was like he was some kind of Jedi and he'd somehow put me in this mind controlled state. I still wasn't over the fact that I wanted him to kiss me.

That I wanted to kiss him.

I was still missing the warmth I'd felt when he was that close to me. I wanted to keep feeling it. All of this was insane and it made no sense. I didn't know what the hell I was supposed to do with all of these uncertain emotions.

How the hell was I supposed to get through this case without constantly worrying about Knox's safety and state of mind?

A sigh escaped my lips before I could tell my brain not to do it. My head hurt and the bright lights in the room were not helping. I had gotten so used to having dim lighting and my sunglasses that my eyes weren't used to the brightness anymore.

It was hard to believe that I grew up in a hot and sunny country like Africa for so long. Back then, I was always in pain and just lived with the headaches. It was crazy to think of what I used to live with before I knew better. Looking back, I was such a stupid kid for putting up with so much shit. Though, it wasn't really like I had much of a choice. It wasn't like I was in a position to tell the rebels to leave me alone or to go off and make my own life. Even though it was hard growing up, even though I had been through a lot, things that still haunted me some nights, I wouldn't change any of it.

I knew, logically, I should *want* to change everything. I knew most normal people wouldn't say they would go through hell again if they had a second chance on life. But everything that I experienced led me here and I wouldn't change who I am now and my career for anything. Working for the FPA had given me a second chance at life. A chance to have brothers and a place in this world. I had been looking for a brotherhood like this my whole life and now that I had it, I wasn't going to give it up for anything.

The door to the room opened and I was hoping it was the doctor telling me I could get the hell out of here. I wanted to get changed and showered. I had a crime scene to work and an UnSub to kill, hopefully. At the sight of Knox strolling into the room, that warmth started to build back up inside of me.

What the hell was going on with me?

"Hey, how are you feeling?" Knox asked as he made his way over to where I was sitting on the bed.

"Some stitches and badly bruised ribs, killer headache. I'm good, I've had worse," I said with a small shrug.

He pulled out a pair of sunglasses and handed them over to me as he sat down on the edge of the bed facing me. "Here, I know yours got busted and they aren't as thick as your lenses, but they should help a bit."

"Thanks. Where did you find these?" I asked as I took the sunglasses and put them on. They weren't perfect, but it was better than nothing.

"My car. I wasn't sure if you had an extra pair at your home or not. Are they going to keep you for concussion watch?"

"No, I can leave once the Doc comes back with my discharge papers. They checked, I don't have a concussion and I'm not at risk of developing one. The blast just knocked me out. Jarod?"

"He's still in surgery, but the doctor did say that he was set to make it. The shard hit his liver, but they are confident they can save all of it. If it turns out that the bleeding won't stop, they'll take a piece of his liver and he'll be on desk duty for three months until it grows back to full size. Mason is in the waiting room. He wants everyone working the case who can. We all need to meet back at the Agency in the next two hours to go over everything that we know and have."

"Good. We gotta get him."

I was happy that Jarod was going to be okay. It would suck if he had to lose a part of his liver but, thankfully, it regenerated so he should be back to normal health in a few months. I knew Mason would take very good care of him. We were going to get this guy and make sure he paid for the pain that he caused both Jarod and Mason with this attack. The door to the room opened once again, but this time my doctor walked in.

"Okay, Agent Ryzen, you are all cleared. You will want to take it easy for a few days with your ribs. You're going to be very sore. I can prescribe you some pain medication, if you'd like."

"I'm good." I hated taking pain medication. Anything that wasn't over the counter always made me feel very weird. They made my mind sluggish and fuzzy and that wasn't something I could afford to have happening, right now.

"Fair enough. Over the counter pain medication will help take the edge off and then use ice packs to help with the swelling and pain. Twenty minutes at a time so you don't hurt your skin. Any questions?"

"No."

"Okay, you are cleared to head out. I wish you a speedy recovery, Agent," the doctor said, turning on his heel and heading out of the room.

I was already in motion and climbing off of the bed. I needed to get home, showered, and changed, before heading back to the Agency. We needed to figure this shit out and, hopefully, this crime scene would give us something new to work with.

"I have the car out front," Knox said as he started to walk beside me.

He stayed close and I could tell he was worried I was going to collapse. I was sore, but I was good at ignoring pain. I wasn't going to rest until we got this UnSub.

We made our way out of the hospital and I carefully worked my way into his car. I sat back into the seat and closed my eyes as he headed off for my place. Usually, I preferred to drive, but with my ribs, that wasn't happening so I'd deal. Thankfully, Knox wasn't in a chatting mood and he stayed quiet on the drive back to my place.

We got there a lot faster than I expected and I couldn't help but wonder if maybe I fell asleep for a moment. If I was honest with myself, I was tired. I hadn't slept in close to four days now, and sleep sounded really good right about then. I knew it wasn't going to happen, though. We had to meet the others back at the Agency in two hours, which gave me just enough time to shower to get the blood and dirt off of me.

Once we arrived at my place, we climbed out of the car and I went through the process of getting the door unlocked and the security system disarmed. Once inside, I spoke.

"I gotta shower."

"Are you hungry?"

"Fuck no."

The thought of food had my stomach turning. I needed the pain to calm down a bit before I could eat something. I headed upstairs and grabbed a change of clothes before I made my way into my bathroom. I just needed a quick shower, something to, hopefully, wake me up and get the crap off of me. The hot water felt good as it sluiced over my sore muscles, but it made the fresh cuts sting for a moment. I had a total of fifty stitches in various places from the cuts. They had all been cleaned and stitched up, and I knew they would be fine within the next two weeks. Stitches were nothing new to me. I knew they would be a bit sore to the touch for a few days and then, they would start to itch as they healed. Chances were they were only going to make it ten days before I took them out. Hopefully, this UnSub was in jail or in the ground by the time I did remove them.

As badly as I would have liked to stay

under the hot water longer, I knew if I did, I was going to have even more trouble keeping my eyes open.

Turning off the water, I got out and quickly dried off. I managed to get my jeans on before I walked out into the bedroom. There, sitting on the end of my bed, was Knox. I wasn't expecting to see him there and I wasn't certain why he was in my room.

"Sorry, I just know how much bruised ribs hurt when trying to get a shirt on. I thought I would see if you needed any help," Knox said as he got up and moved a bit closer to me.

He appeared to be nervous, unsure of himself, and I couldn't help but wonder if maybe there was more to him being there. We both knew I had gotten my shirt off by myself, that I was more than capable of getting dressed.

Would it hurt?

Sure, but I could handle it.

His nervousness could be connected to our almost kiss just this morning, but he should have been over that by now. We had been blown up since then, and that kinda washed the slate clean. Maybe he was feeling awkward about it all still, though. He was straight, so I would assume almost kissing a guy would make any straight man feel weird.

"That's not why you came in here, Knox. You don't have to lie to me. It's okay if you feel weird about this morning."

I didn't want him thinking that there was something wrong with him because we almost kissed. It was the heat of the moment, emotions were running on high. It wasn't either of our fault. We could just forget it and move on.

"I don't feel weird about it," Knox said as he closed the distance between us. He lightly touched the bruising that went across my left side.

The brunt of the impact from the bomb had hit me there. I had some more bruises on my right side from landing on the ground but they didn't really bother me.

"You could have been killed. Why would you do that? Why would you risk your life to protect mine?"

That was the question, but the thing was I didn't really have an answer to it. It was all instinct and typically, my instincts tell me to protect myself. This time around, all they wanted was for Knox to be safe. I couldn't explain it.

"I don't know. I didn't think. I just reacted. In that moment, all that mattered was keeping you safe. You put a spell on me, Knox. I went from wanting you dead to wanting to protect you," I softly admitted.

I wasn't sure how he was going to respond to that. I figured he would throw out some psychological reasoning and we would be able to move on from the whole experience.

What I didn't expect, was to suddenly feel his lips against my own.

The shock of it had me sucking a deep breath in that caused a sharp pain to shoot up my side. I wasn't expecting him to kiss me. I figured he would sweep that moment in my kitchen under the rug and never bring it up again.

And now, his lips were against mine.

They were soft and uncertain. He wanted to kiss me, but he was so new to this whole experience he didn't really know what to do. Before I could even truly kiss him back, he pulled away and the warmth of his lips left mine. I couldn't help but lick my lips slightly to get the taste of him on my tongue.

"Sorry, I shouldn't have done that."

I could tell he was sorry, but it wasn't because he kissed me. It was because he knew I wasn't expecting it. But he had nothing to be sorry for. I was glad that he had kissed me. I didn't want him to stop. There was literally nothing for him to be sorry for. I could have told him that.

I should use my words and tell him it was okay, but I wanted to make sure he understood fully that I was perfectly okay with him kissing me.

I grabbed the front of his shirt and pulled him back down to me. The second our lips touched, I took control of the kiss. I was a bottom, but I did enjoy being in control rather than submitting to someone. It was different, I knew that. I knew most bottoms were submissive in the bedroom, but that was never my personality.

I had been submissive before, with the first guy I had been with, and I hated every second of it. It had made me feel like throwing up and I never wanted to feel that way again. It was just another reason why I didn't tend to have sex. Most guys wanted to be dominant and that wasn't something I enjoyed, that I could handle.

The fact that Knox submitted to me, that he allowed me to have control over the kiss, only fueled me on. I was actually turned on. For the first time in, I don't even know how long, *I was turned on.*

The soft moan that escaped his lips was the sweetest sound I had ever heard and I wanted to hear more. I moved my hand to the side of his face and flicked my tongue against his lips, seeking permission. When he parted his lips and allowed my tongue to touch his, I moaned as his flavor burst across my tongue.

He tasted so sweet, like honey.

As we kissed, I felt Knox gaining confidence and he placed his hands on my hips, and then he moved them over to my ass. He gave my butt cheeks a small squeeze and that little bit of pressure forced my hips to move closer to his. If we didn't have the slight height difference, our dicks would have rubbed together.

I was shocked by how desperately I wanted to feel him against me. I placed my hand against his chest and started to push him back toward my bed as we continued to kiss. The second the back of his knees hit the bed, he was moving onto it and laying flat.

I straddled his hips and the new position put our cocks right against each other. Knox apparently needed to feel me against him just as badly, because before I could even move my hips, he was grinding his groin against mine.

We both moaned into the kiss as our arousals rubbed against each other. I couldn't even remember the last time I had been hard, but it certainly hadn't been with any of the guys I had been with.

For a straight guy, he definitely wasn't being very shy.

He ground his hips into mine and matched my pace. We were both dry humping and making out like teenagers, but the thought of stopping made my dick hurt.

"Fuck, Ry," Knox moaned as he broke the kiss.

I pressed my lips along his neck and Knox turned his head to grant me better access. He felt so fucking good against me. Knox was a moaning mess underneath me and it was only pushing me closer to the edge. We were both close and I knew soon enough, we were both going to be flying over that edge.

"Oh god," Knox moaned as he arched up slightly and I knew he was going to explode soon.

His cell phone going off in his pocket sounded like a siren echoing through the room.

Damn.

This could not be happening.

We couldn't actually be getting called right now.

"Ignore it. Don't stop, Ry. So close. Don't stop, please," he begged.

Not a chance. I was not stopping.

"You feel so good. Come for me, Baby. I'm right behind you."

I sat up a bit so I could watch him as he came apart. I wanted to remember this forever. I wanted to know what he looked like when he hit the peak of his pleasure.

Knox gave a deep moan just before he bit his bottom lip and I felt his dick pulse out cum into his pants. I watched as he panted as he came and the sight of it, the feel of his dick pulsing against mine, had me falling over the cliff.

I let out a deep groan as I came hard against him. I placed my forehead against his and we both panted as we tried to

catch our breath.
   Wow.
     That really just happened.

CHAPTER FOURTEEN

Knox

HOLY SHIT.

I didn't even know what else to say, what else to think. That was the best orgasm I'd ever had. That was even better than all of the sex I'd had in my life. He didn't even touch me, we dry humped, and it was the best orgasm of my life. It shouldn't have felt that good. It should have felt weird and awkward, but it just felt *earth shattering.*

O.M.G.

When I kissed him, I wasn't sure what would happen. I wasn't sure if I would like it or not. If I would enjoy kissing a man at all. All I knew was that my mind and body kept screaming at me to kiss him. To see what his lips felt like against mine. It was only a quick peck, because that was all the courage I had within me. I had never kissed a guy before. I had never wanted to, never felt the attraction or the urge toward a man, and yet, all I wanted was to kiss Ry and finally, I did.

It felt good.

His lips against mine had felt amazing, if I am being honest. It was different to kiss a guy, but I was surprised at how good it felt. It wasn't weird like I thought it would be. His full lips were smooth and soft and his five o'clock shadow actually felt nice as it brushed against my skin. I never thought I would enjoy kissing another man, but kissing Ry was somehow better than any woman I had ever kissed.

I'd never questioned if I was gay or not. I always knew I was straight. At least, I thought I was. The thing was, though, in the past sex was just sex for me. It wasn't earth shattering, not even the first time. Sex had felt good, being with a woman had felt good, but it was never rock my world good. It never made me all shaky and left me in desperate need for more like other guys claimed it did for them. I hadn't read too much into it, though. I just figured that was how I responded to sex. Not everyone was a sexual person. It was perfectly natural for me to not be hugely into sex.

A very short time with Ry and I was already hungry for more. I should be freaked out, I knew that. But at the same time, it just felt right. It should have felt weird, but it didn't. I could freak out and deny what I was feeling. I could try to deny that it felt good, but I was never the type of person who cared about labels, or lying to myself. I wasn't the type of person to over analyze every single aspect of my life. I was a Profiler and yes, that meant I had to over analyze everything, but that didn't extend to myself. And even if I was talking to a victim right now, I would tell them to do whatever felt good and screw the labels.

Once I got my breath back, I reached into my pocket and pulled out my cell phone. I noted that the missed call was from Roland.

"Roland called."

"We should get cleaned up and start heading in," Ry said, his voice hitching as he sat up and then groaned in pain.

In my pleasure, I had forgotten that his ribs were bruised, and apparently so had he. I placed my hands on his ass and carefully lifted him up as I got up. Preventing him from having to hurt his ribs as he twisted to stand.

"Sorry, I forgot about your ribs. Are you okay?" I inquired once I got him on his feet.

"Yeah, you're not the only one who forgot. You know, for a straight guy that just ground his cock against another man's, you are taking this surprisingly well."

I couldn't help but smirk. I guess Ry really expected me to freak out about all of it. Though, that seemed like a logical thing to do, but when it felt so right what was the point?

"I'm not going to freak out. Whenever I've been with a woman, it's always just felt okay. I've never felt insane pleasure that takes you to new heights. I just assumed I wasn't a sexual person. But it didn't feel that way with you. Maybe I'm gay, maybe I'm bi, I don't care to label it. I like you, it's just that simple to me."

"I like you, too," he whispered, his voice sounding slightly shy and uncertain, which was different for him. Ry was usually extremely confident. He didn't talk much, but when he did, he had no waiver to his voice.

I placed my hand on the side of his face, cupping his cheek as I spoke. "Come on, let's get to the meeting and then tonight, we can talk some more if you are feeling up to it."

There needed to be a conversation about what was going on between us. Even if we just decided to be friends with benefits, there needed to be a conversation about actual intercourse and expectations. I had no idea if he was a top or a bottom. I had never been with a man before, so I had no idea what to do sexually or if I would be a top or bottom. Before we could take this further, we had to talk about it.

He just gave me a nod and we quickly got cleaned up and headed out. Once again, I drove while Ry leaned back in his seat to try and ease the pressure on his ribs. I felt bad that his ribs were hurting more because of our time together. He really should be back at his home and getting some rest in his bed, but I suspected that wasn't going to be an option for him.

Ry was used to pain, his body was proof of that. He was also a mission man; he didn't stop until the mission was complete. There was nothing I could say to him that would make him stand down. He was going to see this through and the best thing I could do for him would be to accept that and help him.

When we arrived at the Agency, we both climbed out of the car, Ry a little more carefully than me, and made our way inside. As Ry strolled into the conference room, I made my way to the kitchen to grab us both some coffee, him some ice, and something for him to eat. He hadn't eaten anything since last night's pizza and that was only a couple of slices. If he was going to keep going, he needed food in his system. After making him a sandwich, I grabbed our coffees and the ice and headed into the conference room. I walked in and saw a man that I hadn't seen before looking Ry over.

"Ice, perfect," the guy nodded as he

held his hand out for the bag of frozen cubes. I passed it over and he placed it against Ry's ribs as he spoke.

"Okay, leave it on for twenty and then take it off for twenty. The swelling is starting to get bad and it will help reduce it. It should also help control the bruising. You really should be in bed resting, still."

"I'm fine," Ry insisted.

"You're not gonna get him to stand down," Rafe simply stated. "How do you know so much about medical things, anyway?"

"He was a boy scout," another man that I didn't know piped up.

"All right, Sebastian, he good?" Roland asked, and I could tell he was looking to get started.

"As good as he can be," Sebastian responded as he moved back.

I handed Ry over a coffee and a sandwich as I spoke. "You need to eat something."

"He's right, you're pale. You need food," Sebastian agreed.

"Knox, this is Sebastian, Damien, and Max. They are from Gaithersburg, where we used to be located. Sebastian and Damien have helped us in the past, and

Max joined them this time. After the bombing, I called them for some backup," Roland began.

"It's nice to meet you," I said as I sat down.

I was all for having more help with this case. We were at risk of it getting out of hand, and the sooner we could get this sorted, the better.

"First, let me start by saying that Jarod has made it out of surgery. He lost a third of his liver, but the doctor said the bleeding has stopped and he will make a full recovery. He will be in the hospital for a week before he can be released. He'll be on medical leave for six weeks before he can do light desk duty and then he's going to have to work his way back up to active duty after three months," Roland stated.

The guys all clapped and I could feel the relief in the room. They might not have all worked together for very long, but they all had a bond together. They were all happy to hear that Jarod would be okay. I couldn't blame them, I was happy about it, too. These were all good men and they were all trying to save as many children as they could.

"I have told Mason to stay with Jarod, that we would handle this. Sebastian, Damien, and Max have all been briefed on the case. Now, someone tell us something we don't know," Roland commanded.

"I ran the security feed for that area. No vehicles were caught on camera. The only thing the cameras did pick up was the UnSub dropping the two boys off, one at a time. He wore all black, had no skin showing at all. He had a full face mask, a ball cap, and a hood. There's nothing I can get on facial characteristics. All I can tell you is that he's tall. Based on the height of some of the objects in the area, he's six foot eight inches. And approximately three hundred pounds," Cooper started.

"Like fluffy or muscle?" Hollingsworth asked.

"He's not the Stay Puff Marshmallow Man. He didn't look like the Hulk, either. So, I'd have to say a bit of both."

"Crime scene has run the bodies for any DNA or fingerprints, but they came back clean. Our UnSub didn't leave anything of note behind. However, the M.E said it's possible there may have been something in the dumpsters around the bodies, or even on them, but it would've likely been destroyed in the blast. Both of the bodies were blown up pretty good," Hollingsworth said.

"We did get IDs on the two kids, thanks to crime scene photos taken before the blast. Facial recognition came back as two boys listed in the Missing Person's database. Brady and Jimmy Johnson. They were brothers and both of them were in the same foster home. Isaiah was able to pull their files and they were awarded to the state when they were surrendered at three and five. They were handed over to a Pastor at a local church. The Pastor stated he had never seen the mother before, but she'd apparently said she couldn't handle having two children any longer. According to the Pastor, she seemed high at the time. He suspected she was a drug addict and the boys would be safer in the system. They were always kept together and placed in the same foster home," Damien jumped in.

"They had only been in three foster homes in the past nine years. The first time they were relocated was because their foster parents were getting too old. They were in their seventies and their health was deteriorating. They made the decision to have all five of their foster children relocated so the kids wouldn't have to see them die. The second foster home was a resting stop of sorts. They stayed there for a couple of months until they were placed with their current foster family. They had never been abused, no files or claims of being treated unfairly. Same as the other children in the homes," Sebastian added.

"We've reached out to their current foster parents and the school. Everyone said the same thing. They were good kids. Brady looked after Jimmy and they both got straight A's. They never came to school with bruises, they always had food, their homework done. They were clean and in proper clothing. Whenever a field trip came up they got to go. Both boys played extracurricular activities. Brady was into basketball and Jimmy, baseball. Their entire foster family went to every game. Both of the foster parents were distraught when they heard the news of the boys' deaths, and they had reported them missing within forty-five minutes of them not showing up at home after school like they always did," Max concluded.

"Basically, if the foster parents are putting on a front, they deserve an Oscar. They had nothing to do with this," Damien stated.

"Were they thinking about adopting the boys?" I asked.

So far everyone had been adopted. These two boys should have been adopted as well, but it sounded like they were just foster kids. The ages lined up, but that part of our UnSub's victimology didn't.

"We asked, because the kids had their last name. However, both their foster parents explained that, for school, it was easier for the boys to have one last name. They only had two other foster kids in their home and they'd had them since they were toddlers. They thought it would make the boys feel more welcomed if they all shared a last name. When we asked if they were interested in adopting them, they stated that they had already adopted them in the only way that mattered. Those boys were their sons and they didn't need a piece of paper to confirm it," Damien answered.

"These kids actually manage to find a foster home with good and loving people in it, and they get killed," Ry declared with a small shake of his head.

"This world sucks a lot of the time," Max commented.

It was possible that our UnSub thought the boys were adopted and that was why he went after them. It looked like they had been and if he had been watching them, he would know how loving and doting the foster parents were. It could easily be a simple mistake. Still, though, to grab two boys and not just any boys, brothers who played sports was odd. They were athletic. Even at a young teenage age, they could run. They probably could have outrun him, so why didn't they?

"Anything on the bomb?" Ry asked.

"Crime lab is trying to piece Humpty Dumpty back together again. Right now, we don't know much about it other than it wasn't designed to kill a lot of people. Just whoever happened to be standing by it when it went off. The Crime lab has to put it back together to see if it was a remote trigger, a timer, or a sensor that triggered the blast. They are also going to look for a signature to see if we can trace it back somewhere," Roland answered.

"The trick is, with the Internet almost

anyone can build a bomb," Rafe stated.

"I'm stuck on the two kids. Two athletic brothers. I know they were only twelve and fourteen, but Roland, think back to when you and Mason were that age. I know you are a good number of years apart, but if you were both supposed to be walking home and a stranger came up to you, what would you do?" I started.

"I'd have put myself in front of Mason and kept walking backward to get away."

"Right, and if that didn't work, you would run," I hypothesized.

"As fast as we could. I'm older so, I would make sure Mason was ahead of me. I'd tell him not to stop, no matter what, until he gets home. Or if we're around houses, to run into the first door that opens."

"See that, that right there. Kids are programmed to run when a stranger is chasing them. When a stranger tries to grab them. And our Perp can't use the line of a lost puppy or offer candy to get them into a vehicle. Kids are too smart. They are taught from a very young age not to interact with strangers. But if they are being chased," I started, but Ry cut me off.

"They run and find the first person they can trust for help. A business, a first responder, or a woman."

"Exactly. These kids are being grabbed in populated areas. It's not late at night, so businesses are open. People are in the streets, but no one ever sees anything. So the question is, how is a guy of a very large size getting kids to willingly go with him without making a single sound. Without causing a scene and screaming for help?" I said. It was starting to click for me. Piece by piece, it was all starting to make sense.

Of course we couldn't find the UnSub, because we weren't looking in the right area. We were so focused on finding this criminal. Someone who would have abused animals in his childhood. Someone who was damaged, but trying to blend into society. That wasn't what we were looking for at all.

"Son of a bitch," Ry uttered, and I knew he was on the same wavelength as me.

"Our UnSub is a first responder," Max stated exactly what I was thinking.

"Cop or a paramedic is the most likely.

A cop would have access to the database for adoptions through the court. He would also have access to bomb making knowledge if he studied how to dismantle them in the police academy. But a paramedic would also know how to torture someone without killing them," Roland confirmed.

"All they would have had to do was put on their uniform and approach the kids. Your mom and dad are hurt. I need to bring you to the hospital. Once they are in the car, they can't open the doors. My money is on a cop. Someone who has paid attention to everything. Someone who has extensive first aid training. He would have taken it because it would have interested him in knowing what can cause the most pain. It would have excited him. He probably worked in the bomb squad or he studied it. Again, not because he was concerned with saving lives, but because it would have interested him. All of the pain and death that can come from a bomb. He would have liked it when people were maimed and not killed. To see them live with that pain. That's how he's been able to not kill until three months ago. He had his fix while on the job. It's possible he's no longer working or he's been suspended. It's also possible, that the violence within his job is no longer enough. He needs more," I concluded.

This profile was now starting to come together. We were finally getting somewhere with this case. Our UnSub had taken things too far this time around and he had made a fatal error. He'd showed us a piece of himself and now, I could use that to figure out exactly who he was.

"He could have been there today. He could have detonated the bomb. He could have been at any of the other crime scenes watching it all play out," Rafe said.

"He could have been the one to deliver the news to the parents," Hollingsworth added.

"Coop, run every police officer and detective who is connected to the crime scenes. If there's a serial killer who is a cop, there's no telling what he's done in his career," Roland stated.

"Run Detective Jonah West first. He was at the crime scene on the Burnsworth victim. He seemed very interested in being kept in the loop. Often a serial killer will reach out to law enforcement to try and get involved in the investigation as a way of keeping tabs on the evidence."

I wasn't certain that something was going on with Detective West, but it was worth a look. He had been the only Detective not willing to hand over the case so quickly. That either meant he was a good detective, or he had something to hide. We needed to know which one it was.

"The rest of us, we got a lot of evidence we need to start combing through. We got a suspect pool, but it's massive. Let's start cross referencing the lists we have and see who we can eliminate," Roland ordered.

We did have a massive suspect pool now, but we would also go through it quickly. We had a huge starting point and soon enough, we would whittle that down to a small pool and then, we would find our UnSub. I just hoped we could accomplish that before another innocent child was killed.

CHAPTER FIFTEEN

Ryzen

WALKING BACK INTO my place tonight was a relief. I was having a very hard time keeping my eyes open. I was closing in on day five of no sleep and my body and mind were hitting a wall. I needed to get some sleep.

My ribs were sore from sitting hunched over a table all day. We had gone through a crap load of police officers and detectives, but in a city this large, the number was astronomical. It was going to take a bit more time to find someone that we could use officially.

Detective West was looking like a possibility, but I wasn't too sure. He had a twelve year old son, so it seemed odd that he might be killing young teenage boys around the age of his son. It seemed unlikely that he would be killing boys that could very well *be* his son. He had a lot of experience in the police department. He had worked with SWAT, did a six month stint with the Bomb Squad, and he was even trained as an EMT in the department. He checked a lot of boxes, but I wasn't seeing any violence in his file. He didn't get into fights and everyone said he was a great cop. Even the locals in the bad areas of town had put in compliments about him. He genuinely seemed like a solid cop and not our UnSub.

I sat down at the small island in my kitchen as Knox went and slid the bags containing the few things he'd bought down on the counter. We had made a stop at the store on the way home because Knox had wanted to pick up a few things. I'd had no idea what he was looking to get, but I didn't care too much. I'd fallen asleep for a few minutes in the car while he was in the store.

I watched as he started to look

through different cupboards for a frying pan. I didn't really have much in the way of cooking gear. I had two pots and one frying pan. All of which I didn't use. I stuck with the MREs because they were easy and what I was used to. I had no idea how to cook. It wasn't like I had anyone growing up to teach me how to cook and then, once I had my own place, I was gone most days out of the year working for the CIA.

"You cook?" I asked as he crumbled the hamburger into the pan.

"I do. I love to cook. I would ask you the same thing, but I already know the answer," he said, flashing me a warm smile.

"Never really had the desire to learn. I only spent twenty days out of the year stateside. Cooking wasn't a big deal." I shrugged.

"I get that, but now that you don't have to travel all the time, it *is* okay for you to eat normal food. You don't have to keep eating MREs. You can build a life for yourself. You can have a coffee maker and food in your cupboards. You don't have to worry about going overseas at a moment's notice."

I knew that, I did, but it wasn't that simple to change my habits after all of these years. I was used to being ready to leave without any notice. I was used to getting phone calls in the middle of the night and being on a plane within thirty minutes. I was always ready to leave, even now. The concept of having a home, or making one, it was still so foreign to me. I didn't really have a desire to try and figure out how to cook, how to turn this place into a real home. I had more on my plate that I needed to work through, but maybe one day I would. Maybe one day, I would want to make dinner with someone and maybe, that someone would be Knox.

As shocking as that was.

"Maybe one day," I simply said.

Knox seemed to accept my answer as he continued to prepare what I discovered to be pasta in silence. I watched as he moved around my kitchen, grabbing whatever utensil that he needed. He seemed to fit so well in my kitchen, as if he hadn't only been in my home for a couple of nights. I couldn't believe it'd only been a couple of days.

Fuck, it really felt like he'd been there for months.

It was weird how I could go from hating the guy to wanting him around me. He wasn't who I thought he was and that was a good thing. I knew we would need to talk about earlier, but I was hoping with how well he seemed to be handling things, he would want to explore more. I had never wanted to explore something with a guy before, to take things further than a one night stand or a quick hookup. I didn't know what it was about Knox, but I wanted to be with him again more than I wanted my next breath. I wanted to take things further with him. I wanted to kiss him, to touch him, to feel him inside of me. I had never felt like that about anyone before and it felt a bit confusing why I wanted him so badly. Thankfully, it wasn't something I needed to figure out right now. I was too tired to even try and process it all. I had to get some sleep tonight and then, hopefully, tomorrow things would be clearer.

Once the food was done, Knox placed the plates down onto the table. It smelled amazing and I knew it was going to taste good as well.

"Thanks," I said.

He gave me a warm smile as we started

to eat. It did taste amazing and I knew I would need to start making a true effort to learn how to cook. Something as basic as this, I could make a pot of it and eat it over the course of a few days.

We ate in comfortable semi-silence. Mentioning bits and pieces of the case as they popped into either of our heads. It was mostly things we had already talked about today, but I could tell that Knox needed to get his thoughts in order and he was more of a talking person. He needed to talk things out to help his mind process the information. He talked a lot, but it no longer bothered me. The sound of his voice didn't make me cringe and want to hit him any longer. He actually had a very nice voice; it was warm and soothing.

After we finished eating, we worked together to get everything cleaned up. This was one of the major benefits of me not cooking; I never had to clean anything. I wasn't against doing dishes, but the dishes I had to do in my day were normally just a mug and a spoon. With everything cleaned up, we went and sat down in the living room.

I was exhausted, but I knew that we

needed to talk and I needed to give my stomach the chance to digest anyway. I knew we needed to talk about what happened and I was worried that he had changed his mind about wanting to see where this thing between us could go. I would accept it if he wanted whatever was between us to remain platonic. I would miss the warmth that I felt from him, but I wasn't going to put anyone in a position they didn't feel comfortable being in.

"I think it's important to talk about what happened between us. I know you're gay and have obviously been with men before. I, obviously, have not been. I know what we did this morning felt good. I know I like you and I feel an attraction to you. I would like to explore this with you, but I also have no idea what to do."

I didn't expect for him to know what to do sexually with a man. He had never been with a man before, so it would make sense that he didn't know what to do in the bedroom. I had enough experience for the both of us, though probably not as much as he thought. I could still walk him through it. I had never been with someone who hadn't been with a guy yet, though. A virgin of sorts. I liked the thought of teaching him.

"I can show you. I'm not that experienced, either, truth be told. I've had sex, obviously, but it's never been amazing. Foreplay has never even felt anywhere near as good as it did with you, so I can only imagine what it's going to be like if we do more. I've only been with a few guys since I was eighteen. I've never really dated anyone, or at least, not seriously. Sex just isn't all that important to me. It's been a means to scratch an itch on occasion, but usually, I am happy on my own. We can go as slow as you need to."

"I'm glad I could make you feel good. I've never felt that way before, either. Sex for me had never been earth shattering, but maybe that was because I actually might prefer men over women and didn't know that until now. The best I have ever felt was with you today and I would like to explore that. I know I have a lot I need to learn, but maybe you wouldn't mind teaching?" he said, flashing me a grin.

"I don't mind at all. Though, I should warn you, I do like to be in control. I'm a bottom, but I don't like being dominated."

I was hoping he would be okay with

that. I didn't want him to feel like I was going to dominate him and make him my bitch or anything. But I didn't want to feel like I had to submit to him, either. I didn't need to be tossed around and owned in a sense.

"I have no problem with that. I'm not a very dominating person. If it feels good, that's all I care about. I have no problem with control or giving it up. And it's good that you are a bottom, because I don't think I am, so that works out nicely," he said, flashing me a warm smile, a hint of pink coloring his cheeks.

I was glad that he was okay with me liking to be in control more in the bedroom. The guys I had been with before usually had an issue with it. Maybe that was why I couldn't get hard. Maybe that was why I didn't enjoy it.

There was never very much foreplay or kissing beforehand. There was definitely no cuddling or post-coital pillow talk. It was always just stick it in, bust a nut, and then they left afterward.

I hadn't been looking for anything serious in the past, I worked too many hours out of the country and it wasn't like I could tell people what I was doing. I always had to lie about my job or where I was. It was why I gave up on dating and had settled for friends with benefits. Technically, though, they were really just fuck buddies, because with a FWB you'd usually hang out with them afterward. They knew about your life or at the very least, they knew your real name. I no longer had to travel overseas all the time for work. I no longer worked for the CIA so I could, in theory, build something with someone. Maybe if things worked out well between Knox and I, we could work on building a real relationship. For now, we were just going to embrace this new found attraction and see where it took us.

We sat and watched a bit of television before it got too difficult for me to keep my eyes open. I could tell he was just as tired as I was, so I decided it was time to call it a night and let him have the couch to himself. After all, that was where he slept.

"I'm heading up to bed," I said as I climbed to my feet, yawning.

"Are you going to sleep tonight? You haven't in days."

I wasn't surprised that he had noticed I hadn't been sleeping. He was always observant; it came with his job. I let out a small sigh, because I truly didn't know if I would be able to sleep tonight. I was hoping. I was begging the universe to let me sleep deeply tonight.

"It's not that easy for me to sleep. Normally, I only get a few hours when I can fall asleep," I admitted.

He stood up as he spoke. "It's common for people who are snipers and have been through trauma. The act of falling asleep brings out anxiety because your mind shuts off and you can't control what you dream. I have an idea that might help."

He offered his hand to me and I easily took it. If he could get me to sleep more than a few hours, I was all for it. He pulled me upstairs and into my bedroom. He started to remove his jeans and that really caught my eye.

"No offense, but I've tried that before and it didn't work," I said with a small smirk.

"It's not sex," he said, flashing me a grin.

I started to remove my own jeans and my shirt before I closed the door and turned off the lights. We climbed into my bed and he pulled the blankets over us. Then, he was pulling me against him. I placed my head on his chest as he wrapped his arms around me.

"Feeling someone with you, hearing their heartbeat, it can be therapeutic and relaxing. It can help you fall asleep, but also put you into a deeper sleep, allowing your mind to not notice the dreams," he explained.

If it helped, I was all for it. I had never been a cuddly person before, but I did enjoy feeling the warmth that being close to Knox brought me. Being able to hear his heartbeat was actually helping me to relax.

Maybe it was a combination of things, his body heat, the hum of his voice as it reverberated through his chest, the steady, repetitive *thump thump thump* of his heartbeat under my ear, or his fingers trailing casually over my skin, but before I could even register what was happening, darkness descended.

CHAPTER SIXTEEN

Knox

WAKING UP WITH Ryzen curled up against my chest felt incredible. It felt positively right. Like he belonged right there, in my arms. We had both slept all night, he hadn't even stirred and I was very pleased about that. Ry had needed some solid sleep and I was happy that I had been able to help him get it.

Ryzen sucked in a deep breath and I knew he was waking up. I ran my hand up and down his arm as he blinked his eyes open. He looked up at me and I couldn't get over how beautiful his eyes were. The grey in them truly was breathtaking.

"Morning," I said, flashing him a warm smile.

"Morning. What time is it?"

"Six. Far too early, in my opinion."

"It's been a long time since I've slept that many hours straight."

"You obviously needed it."

Ryzen turned and started to press his lips sporadically along my neck as he spoke. "Yeah. I did. Is there something *you* need?"

I was already hard and I suspected that he could feel that against his leg. I could certainly feel his hardness pressing against mine. Waking up with his hard, warm body pressed against mine felt amazing.

I ran my hand down his back and rested it on his ass. Ryzen trailed his hand down my chest and over my still-covered dick. The feel of his hand even over my boxers instantly had me moaning and in desperate need for more. I wanted more than just his touch.

I *needed* more.

I knew we were looking to take thing slow, but I wanted to taste him. My desire and craving to taste him overpowered all logic and all thoughts of taking things slow at that moment. It was consuming me.

I had never really cared for giving oral sex to any of the females I had been with. I wanted to know what Ryzen tasted like, though. What his dick would feel like in my mouth, sliding over my tongue.

"I want to taste you. I want to feel you in my mouth," I admitted, heat building in my groin and my mouth watering as he slipped his hand underneath the elastic of my boxers. The feel of his rough palm against my sensitive skin only fueled my need for him.

"You sure?"

"Completely," I said with complete confidence in my decision. "Show me how?"

"Take your boxers off," he ordered, and I did not need to be told twice.

I tossed the covers off of us and we both slipped out of our boxers, dropping them on the floor on each side of the bed.

I wanted to see him, all of him, and the sight did not disappoint. He looked glorious naked. His dick was thick, rigid, and already dripping with precum. We were about the same size and I instinctively knew he was going to feel so good in my mouth. The thought should be freaking me out, but it was only turning me on even more. I couldn't believe I had been missing this for so long. That I hadn't realized I was attracted to men. At the same time, I was glad that my first experience with a man would be with Ryzen.

He moved, turning so he was lying on his left side and we were face to face with each other's hardness.

I licked my lips in anticipation. I couldn't help myself as I flicked out my tongue to lick over his tip, getting a taste of his precum. He tasted like a blend of sweet and salty. It wasn't anything like the musky taste of a woman and I liked that it wasn't. He tasted good and I instantly wanted more.

I felt Ry's tongue run along my shaft and I moaned deep in my throat. I followed his lead and mimicked his movements, cupping his balls in my hand and rolling them between my fingers.

At the same time, we took each other into our mouths and I couldn't help letting out a hiss around his cock as Ry took me right down to the base in one fell swoop. His mouth on me felt magnificent. His dick in my mouth felt amazing. The combination of us both sent my mind whirling and I felt my balls tingle and tighten. I sucked in a breath around his dick, trying to press off the impending orgasm a little longer.

I tried to take a bit more of him into my mouth and slowly worked my way further down his shaft bit by bit. His velvet over steel hardness felt amazing along my tongue. His mouth felt glorious wrapped around my dick. It was so warm. It was unlike anything I had experienced before and I never wanted it to stop.

I couldn't stop moaning as he worked my dick faster. I followed his lead and did the same. I could hear him moaning and the vibrations it sent along my shaft only added to my pleasure. I could feel him growing harder, his cockhead swelling even more in my mouth, and I knew he was close. Just knowing that he was close, that I would be getting a true taste of him, brought me closer to the edge.

Ryzen gave a deep groan as he came hard down my throat. I let out a whimper and then an appreciative hum as his sweet taste flooded my mouth. The feel and taste of him alone was enough to push me over the edge and I followed right behind him, erupting down his throat. The feeling of his throat closing around my dick as he swallowed only resulted in me coming more. This was even better than the dry humping.

He felt amazing.

So fucking amazing.

I knew now, just how easily this could become an addiction.

I swallowed every last drop that he had for me, hollowing my cheeks around his dick, before I allowed him to pull out. I felt his hot mouth leave my dick and I was already missing it. He moved back and kissed his way up my chest, stopping to nibble for a moment on my still hard nipple.

"Well, that was the best thing I've ever experienced," I gushed.

"Me too. You feel so good."

I pulled him in and slanted my mouth over his. The second our tongues touched, I could taste the combined flavor of both of us. I loved the mixture that slid over my tongue and danced along my tastebuds. I knew I was never going to get tired of this.

The sound of my alarm trilling out into the room had us pulling back. As much as I would have loved to spend the rest of the day in bed with Ryzen and exploring more, we had a serial killer to catch. Once we did, though, I planned on spending many hours naked in bed with him to celebrate.

CHAPTER SEVENTEEN

Knox

IT WAS A good six hours later when we had finally narrowed our list of suspects down to ten. We had all agreed that we could eliminate Detective West. Even though he had the skill set for this UnSub, his connection to the people of Baton Rouge, and with having a son, made it very unlikely that, emotionally and mentally, he would be capable of harming a child. It would also be difficult for him to go unnoticed in the kidnapping and dumping sites. He was currently being brought in so we could narrow the list down further.

With any luck, Detective West would have some insider knowledge that could help with eliminating potential suspects. If we could narrow it down to only a few, then we could bring them in and question them. We would, hopefully, be able to obtain a warrant to search their homes.

I was willing to bet that our UnSub had some type of trophy. Nothing was missing on the bodies, so he most likely took a photo of his victims and had pasted them in a creepy scrapbook or shrine of some sort that he could then look back on and enjoy again later.

There was a knock at the door and I looked up to see Detective West standing there. He didn't look uncertain at all. In fact, he looked like he belonged up here. It was always funny to me how some people were just born for their profession, that no matter where they went, they fit in instantly. Detective West looked like he had been working here for years with the ease that he had walking around and approaching a room full of federal agents and a few detectives. I also had to hand it to him. This wasn't an easy room to approach. For the most part, everyone was very muscular and looked like they could snap a grown man in half over their knee. West had no problem blending in with any of us.

"Detective West, we appreciate you coming down," Roland started.

"I'm happy to help. Though, you weren't real clear on the phone with what exactly I would be helping with."

I hadn't told him why we needed him to come down. I wasn't certain how he would take this conversation. Some cops believed in the Blue Wall and you did not go against the Blue Wall. The Blue Wall was the protection that all cops had for each other. It was ironic, because so often with a case you had to try and convince someone to snitch on another person. Cops would often try and convince a civilian that they need to give their friend up or talk when they had witnessed a crime. And yet, when one of their own was being called dirty and being investigated, they all clammed. No one would dare to speak out about another officer, even if that officer was dirty. There were a few, though, that were willing to go against the Blue Wall if it meant saving lives. I hoped Detective West would be one of those cops who would only care about stopping this UnSub from killing more kids.

"Please, come in and have a seat," I said, flashing him a friendly smile. I wasn't sure how he was going to react to the news and it would be better to get him in a position where he would be willing to listen.

"Do I need a lawyer?" he asked skeptically as he strolled over and sat down in one of the available chairs.

"No, not at all. We just need your help on this case. As you know, we are chasing after a serial killer who is targeting young teenage males. We have a list of ten potential suspects and we were hoping you will be able to help us narrow that down more," I answered.

"You think it's someone from one of the neighborhoods on the Southside?"

Detective West was very well known on the Southside. Everyone seemed to like him and trust him when he told them that he would get whoever hurt one of their own. I respected the work that he had been doing for the Southside and helping them to trust at least one cop within this city.

"We have no solid evidence. What we

have is a profile that supports the actions of the victims. None of the victims screamed or ran away from the UnSub. No one saw anyone out of place at the kidnapping or dump sites. The victims were all adopted, with the exception of the last two. However, they did go by their foster parents' last name, so it is possible he was mistaken in his rush to grab another victim," I started.

"The UnSub also tried to kill us with a bomb he planted on the back of the dumpster at the last dump site. There's no evidence on the bomb in terms of DNA or fingerprints. However, the UnSub does have knowledge of bomb making and how to build a bomb that can be used to target a small group of people. He wanted to kill Agent Hunter but not anyone around him," Rafe added.

"I'm still not sure how you think I can help," Detective West said, and I could tell he was getting nervous about why he was truly here.

"We suspect the UnSub is a cop. We have ten potential suspects that fit the UnSub's profile and we're hoping you might have some insider knowledge on them that could help us narrow that list down further," I finally said,

I could see the shock flicker through his eyes for a briefest of moments before he locked his emotions down. He was good. He had a solid poker face and I knew he had developed it with his time on the force. I couldn't tell by his facial expressions or his body language if he believed the profile pointed to a cop or not. I couldn't tell if he was going to help us or not. I was really hoping he would believe us, trust in our investigation and judgment, and help us find the UnSub.

I already knew the UnSub would be out there looking for his next victim and he could grab them at any moment. He was speeding up his timeline because we'd forced him to. He was also now getting the recognition that he had wanted and he was going to seek that attention even more now. It was why he'd grabbed two victims last time, and there was even more of a chance he could do it again the next time.

"Who do you have?" Detective West finally said, and I couldn't help but let out a small breath that I hadn't known I was holding.

"These are the ones we've narrowed

down," Roland said as he passed over the files.

Detective West took them and looked at the names real quick. I figured he was seeing if there was anyone he knew and with how quick he was looking over the names, my hopes were fading. There was a chance that Detective West didn't know these guys or hadn't heard of them. Baton Rouge was a good size town and there were plenty of cops in the city. Not every cop knew every cop. He stopped on Marcus Long's file, paused for a brief moment, and then he picked it up and tossed it down onto the table as he spoke.

"That's your guy."

"You sound confident," Ry commented, but I could hear the skepticism in his voice. He was going to need more from Detective West before he felt confident enough that we had our UnSub.

"Detective Long is forty and has been within the police department since he was eighteen. Ever since he graduated the academy, there have been problems that have come up. I've heard a lot of rumors through the grapevine, but I've also worked with him on a good chunk of cases since I've been a detective and he's not right in the head. He comes across as normal, but I've never trusted him and I would never let him around my kid. There's just this vibe from him. You could feel it whenever we went to a crime scene of a brutal murder or a horrible assault or rape. Where most people are disgusted by what they see, Long wasn't. He had no problem finishing his breakfast sandwich at a triple homicide where the walls were covered in blood. He loved watching the autopsies."

That sounded like our guy. He would be able to work in a position where he could see all of the destruction that he needed to satisfy his cravings. Long had also had experience within the Bomb Squad, so he would be able to build a simple bomb. He hadn't been on any of the scenes, though, but that might be due to his lack of control. If he saw his own artwork, he might not have been able to restrain himself from enjoying it.

"Here's what only a handful of people know about Long. I only know this because I overheard Long talking about it with one of his long-time partners at the bar one night. He was placed in foster care and had been adopted when he was eleven. Now according to Long, his adoptive parents were horribly poor and had to give him back up to the foster care system when he was thirteen," Detective West shared.

Jackpot.

He was targeting young males who were adopted right around the age of when he was given back up from his own adoptive parents. I doubted them being poor had anything to do with it. He would have started to show signs of being dangerous. They would have needed to get him help and not knowing what else to do, they put him back into the system. The system *should* have spotted his psychopathic tendencies and put him into treatment. They obviously hadn't if he was working as a police officer. Detective Marcus Long was our guy; there was no doubt about it, now.

"That's our guy," Ry stated.

"We gotta find him. Is he at work today?" I asked Detective West.

"I don't know. I haven't seen him. We're in the same station at the moment, too. He just got transferred three months ago."

"Why?" That caught my attention.

Three months ago was when the killing started.

"I don't know. No one will say why. But he had been working out of the twenty-sixth for close to ten years. He didn't submit a transfer form. Upper Brass made the decision to move him."

"I'll look into it," Cooper said, already knowing we needed that intel.

"That's gotta be the stressor. Something had to happen that initiated the move and that forced him to start killing. If we can get that intel, Coop, we might be able to better understand what happened," I stated.

"We need everything on Long. We need all the addresses that he could have. We gotta find where he is. I'll call the Station and see if he's in today or working any cases," Roland said.

"I'd be happy to help out if you need another hand," Detective West offered.

"I appreciate it, but I need you to go back to the Station and quietly ask around about him. See what you can find out. We gotta find where he could be keeping the kids. He could also have another victim," Roland said, pressing his lips together.

"I'll call if I get something." Detective West nodded as he stood.

The room was buzzing now. We had a name. We had a face. Now, we just had to find out where he was and then we would have our UnSub. We would, hopefully, be able to arrest him and be able to ask him why. I also wanted to make sure there were no other victims previously that we didn't know about. Every family, every victim deserved to have closure and only Long could give it to them. We were so close now, and hopefully, by the end of the day, we would have Long in our sights and we could finally end this once and for all.

CHAPTER EIGHTEEN

Ryzen

"THIS CASE ISN'T going the way I suspected it would three months ago when it started," Knox piped up as we got into my car.

"I can see that."

It wasn't everyday that you discovered the person killing and torturing young teenage boys was a cop. Someone who is supposed to be there for them and help protect them. Even though we would have the proof that we needed for an arrest once the warrant came in, that didn't mean everyone in the police department would believe it. I couldn't help but wonder if Detective West would receive some blow back due to his involvement in the case. We would make sure to keep his name out of it, but eventually, people would discover that he had been at the Agency right before the warrants were drafted for Long's home.

"Are you sure your guy can get the warrants?"

I hadn't told anyone that my guy was actually Noah, my brother. It wasn't that I was hiding him from the world, I just didn't like people knowing too many personal things about me. If no one knew about Noah, then my enemies couldn't track him down and try to hurt him to get to me. I suppose, though, considering how close Knox and I had started to become, and I hoped that we could continue to explore whatever this was after the case, it would be safe to tell him.

"He's not *my guy*. He's my brother."

"You have a brother?" Knox asked, surprised. I couldn't blame him. It had never come up, not even when he was evaluating me. He had asked about family, but I never spoke.

"An older half-brother. We have the

same dad, different moms. His mother, though, unlike mine, left when she was pregnant. She knew our father wasn't going to be a good dad, that he wasn't a good man. It was fine to have sex with a bad boy, but once she got pregnant, she got her life together and had Noah. My mother didn't have the same belief. We met at his funeral when I was nineteen. He didn't know about me, either. We've been talking ever since."

"I'm not going to lie and say I'm sorry your father is dead. Your brother's a lawyer?"

"Federal prosecutor. He's cleared to operate in any courtroom all across the country. He was the one who got us the adoption files."

"Your team doesn't know about him," he easily stated.

"No. It's not about trust, I just prefer for him to be hidden from my enemies. It drives him nuts that I am so protective of him. He always tells me he's the older brother and it's his job to protect me, not the other way around. I don't want anything to happen to him, though. I couldn't live with myself if he was hurt because of someone trying to get to me."

Knox reached over and placed his hand on my thigh as he spoke. "It's natural for you to want to protect him. Younger brother or not, you are the one with the training to fight. It's in your nature to protect people. One day, when you are ready, I know you'll tell your team and they'll get to meet him. And maybe one day, when you are ready, I can meet him." He flashed me a smile.

"I'd like that," I said back with a small smile as I brought my eyes up to meet his gaze.

I had never had anyone meet with Noah. I had kept him a secret, but the thought of him and Knox meeting didn't make me want to scratch my eyes out. I knew they would hit it off. Maybe one day.

Just as I turned my gaze back to the road, there was a loud crunching sound and then the car was flipping. Glass shattered all around us as we rolled not once, but twice, before coming to a stop upside down.

The world around me was swirling in and out. Whatever had hit us, hit on my side directly. I could feel the door crushed against my right side. Blood was dripping off of my face and forming a small puddle right below me.

I looked over and saw that Knox was okay, or as well as could be expected. He was awake and mostly just in shock. The brunt of the force hit my side, protecting him. The airbags had gone off and I could see there was a bit of burn specs on the side of his face from the airbag powder. Other than that, he appeared to be all right.

"Ry? Ry, are you all right?" he asked as he looked over at me.

"Yeah. Can you get out?"

"You're in pain, I can hear it in your voice. What hurts?"

I wasn't really sure exactly what hurt at that moment. My body was still in shock and running on adrenaline.

"Figure it out after we get out," I said.

Before any more could be said, though, his door was pulled open. My mind instantly went to someone helping us. It wasn't a very busy street, but a car was bound to go by at some point. To my horror, though, when the man bent down it wasn't a good Samaritan. It was Long. Before I could warn Knox, Long had pulled out a stun gun and hit Knox against his neck, effectively knocking him out cold.

"You son of a bitch, Long. I'm going to kill you for this," I growled out as I fought to get the seatbelt off of me.

Long didn't even bother with responding to me. He was fixated on getting to Knox. He had the seatbelt cut and he was pulling him out of the car.

I had to move. I had to get to Knox and end this. Finally, the seat belt buckle released and sent me crumbling onto the roof of the car. I felt the glass from the windows cutting into my arms, but I ignored it as I crawled across to the driver's side door. Just as I stood, I watched as Long drove away, with Knox unconscious inside of the truck. I quickly pulled out my phone, thankful that it was in my left pocket and not my right, and dialed Roland.

"Roland."

"Long kidnapped Knox. He smashed into our car, tased him, and drove off. Get Cooper to run this plate. JRD 382, it's a white pickup truck heading East on Boulder Ave."

"Copy. Stay where you are. We're on our way to you."

I ended the call. I didn't want to stay, I

wanted to go after Knox, but I couldn't. I had no car, and no way of knowing where they were heading. The best chance I had was waiting here for the team and letting Cooper track the truck.

One thing was for certain, Long had made a fatal mistake tonight. He should never have grabbed Knox. Now we knew without a doubt that it was him killing those kids. And we were going to stop at nothing to get Knox back. Soon enough, Cooper would have his location and then we were going to storm in there and I would kill him for taking Knox.

CHAPTER NINETEEN

Knox

THE WORLD SLOWLY came back to me. My head was killing me, but I guess that was to be expected given the crash. I did remember what happened and for that, I was thankful.

Most wouldn't be thankful for remembering getting kidnapped, but I was at least aware of the situation and could get my mind to think clearly. I had to be able to think clearly if I was going to stand any chance of surviving this.

Marcus Long was a seasoned detective and a serial killer. He was going to be intelligent and harder to manipulate. I just needed to bide my time until the team found me.

Until Ryzen found me.

I really hoped that he was going to be okay. The truck hit him dead on and I knew that could lead to serious injuries. The only comfort I had of knowing that he was still alive was hearing him call out to me just before everything went black. I distinctly remembered the feeling of the stun gun against my neck and I figured that accounted for the massive headache I had going on.

I forced my mind to feel my surroundings. I was sitting and not laying down. I had my clothes on, a fact I was eternally grateful for. My wrists were restrained to the arms of the chair, but it didn't feel sharp. It was scratchy so I suspected it was just thick rope.

I had no idea what Long wanted with me, why he was so fascinated with me. I knew serial killers could fixate on a law enforcement official, I had seen it happen before in my career, but I had never been the one fixated on. Yes, I'd had serial killers contact me through the press or their kills because they wanted to play 'catch me if you can' with me. That was normal. This, this didn't feel professional. It felt personal and I had no idea why. I decided that the only way I was going to get any answers was to actually open my eyes.

The room I was in could only be described as a basement. The walls were made from cement blocks and it looked like some had grey-white mould growing on them from the dampness. The place smelled damp and musty and I suspected that there were no windows down there. I didn't see any from where I was positioned, anyway.

I was, in fact, tied to a metal chair with rope. I looked over to my left and just saw a single wooden door. To my right, however, there was a metal table with restraints attached to each leg. And leaning against it with his arms crossed over his chest was Long.

"About time you woke up," Long said in a gruff voice.

"Long, you know this won't end well for you. You need to turn yourself in," I started in a calm voice.

He gave a dark chuckle at that and I knew he wasn't about to walk into a police station and turn himself in. He was a serial killer, but also a detective. He knew what awaited him in prison. Serial killers also didn't stop killing unless something stopped them. Most of them go down fighting and are happy to die before ever stepping foot in a prison cell. That fight was going to be even stronger with Long being a cop.

"I ain't doing that and you know it. The question is, though, did the big, smart Profiler figure out why him?" he said in a teasing, sing-song voice.

We both knew I hadn't figured it out. I had no idea why Long had it out for me. I had never crossed paths with him professionally. I would remember him. I would remember the darkness in his eyes and how he felt like death. I would have investigated him, silently at first, until I was able to uncover his state of mind. I would have made sure his badge was taken and I wouldn't have regretted it for a single moment. This man was what I'd thought Ryzen was and it sickened me that I ever thought they were the same type of person.

Ryzen was nothing like Long. He was a good man losing pieces of his soul to help keep others safe.

Long was a devil in disguise and he deserved to have his badge stripped away from him.

"Why don't you tell me, Long?" I asked, still keeping my voice completely calm.

"You were supposed to be the smart one. Not so smart now, are you Mr. Ivy League? Mom and Dad picked the wrong one to give away."

"Are you talking about your adoptive parents?" I asked, slightly confused.

The way he worded his sentence, it felt weird, it felt off. As far as we knew, Long was an only child, so who *was* he referring to?

"No, I'm talking about Mom and Dad. Keep up, little brother," he said with a smirk.

I couldn't help the confusion that overtook my face. I had no idea what he was talking about. I didn't have a brother. I was an only child. I would have known if my parents had another child. I grew up with aunts, uncles, grandparents, and cousins. Not one single person had ever let slip that there was another sibling in my household. There were no photos of another child, nothing. He had to be mistaken.

"Long, I don't have a brother. I'm an only child. You're mistaken."

"Figures they never told you about me," Long started as he moved around. I could tell he was getting aggravated. "David and Moriah Hunter, the perfect parents, the perfect couple. Of course they didn't tell you about me. They couldn't risk having their perfect image destroyed by what they had done. You might not remember me, but I remember you. I was five when they left me at that church. They didn't need me anymore, because they had you now. They loved you more, and when I accidentally killed your new kitten they went insane. Started going on and on about how dangerous I was. They never understood me. They never tried to. I was just a little boy, but to them I was disposable," Long declared, getting more aggravated by the moment.

I knew I needed to speak to calm him down, but I couldn't get my mind to process everything he was saying fast enough to form words. He was talking so confidently that his parents were mine, but that couldn't be true.

I would remember having a brother,

right?

I knew if I was two I wouldn't have any memories of him, but still, I couldn't imagine my parents would completely erase him from their lives. Not only their lives, but everyone elses. No one in my family had ever mentioned another child. I was finding it hard to believe that they would have been able to keep a secret that massive from me. I didn't have to believe it, though, because Long did. To him, it was real, and I had to play within that reality.

"I'm sorry, Long, I just don't remember. I wasn't old enough to remember having a brother. I don't remember anything from that long ago. They never spoke of you. I had no idea you were out there. If I had, I would have looked for you."

I would have looked for a brother, but he wasn't my brother. We didn't even look alike. There was just no way. He had to be confused. A secret like this wouldn't have been possible for everyone in my family to keep. Something would have slipped. It was simply human nature.

"They didn't want me. Said I was a danger. I heard them whispering to each other, they thought I was too stupid to hear them. They said I was too dangerous to have around, that I could hurt you. All they cared about was making sure their precious baby was safe. And now look at where we are. Both of us are law enforcement. You followed in my footsteps, baby brother."

"Is that why you called the tip line looking for me? You wanted to reach out and let me know you existed?"

"We have the exact same DNA, baby brother. I didn't know you lived here, but then three months ago I saw you and our parents coming out of a restaurant. The way they were smiling and hugging you. They thought they had the perfect son, but I knew I wasn't alone. That you were going to be just like me. So I did my own investigation and discovered you were an FBI Profiler. You loved death and destruction just as much as I do. Together, we could be unstoppable."

"You want to be partners. But you told the tip line you wanted me dead. You planted a bomb that could have killed me."

If he wanted us to be partners, if he believed that we were cut from the same cloth, then why try and kill me?

Why go out of his way to cause harm to me?

"I wanted you to get taken off the case so you would be free to join me. If you were off the case, it would be handed over to some hack and we would be free to do whatever we wanted. And I wasn't trying to kill you. It was that other guy I wanted dead. I saw the way he looked at you. He's been infected and I wasn't going to let him infect you with his disease," Long snarled.

"Ry. You were trying to kill Ry, because he's gay?"

I had to try and catch up with him. His thinking was bouncing all over the place. He was more unstable than I expected and that was most likely due to him having to keep it together for so long. It had to be exhausting on his mind to keep up his persona in the police department for so long.

"He's walking around with that disgusting disease. I wasn't going to let him infect you, too. Now, he's dead and we're free to be ourselves. You can finally let it out. You don't have to keep in all of that darkness anymore, baby brother. You can be free like me and together we can make every parent pay."

"You killed the children to make the parents pay?"

"They needed to be taught a lesson. They needed to know that if they hadn't given their child up, they could still be alive. Parents aren't supposed to give up on their children. They are supposed to support them and love them. Now, those parents have to live with knowing they got their child killed."

"Because our parents gave you up and then your adoptive parents did the same. It's important that they have to pay for their actions and decisions," I said with complete understanding to my voice.

I had no idea how I was going to get out of here. I was doing my best to not think about the possibility that Ryzen was dead from the crash. I had to have faith in him. I had to believe that he would be okay. That he was a warrior and he could live through this.

Before anymore could be said, the door to the basement was kicked open and there, walking through with a gun up and pointed right at Long, was Ryzen. He was dressed in his tactical gear, and my god, did he ever look good.

"It's over, Long. Get down on the

ground," Detective West ordered as he walked in behind Ryzen.

Long wasn't going to get on the ground. He wasn't going to surrender himself. There wasn't anything they could do or say, he was going to fight. I knew that. So when Long went and pulled out a gun from behind his back, I was prepared for the shots to ring out.

Neither Detective West or Ryzen were going to risk him shooting either of them or me, they had to fire. Normally, that would bother me. I would feel like I had failed in getting my UnSub to put his weapon down and turn himself in.

However, in this situation, I knew it was for the best. Long had killed too many children. Too many parents were going to have to bury their child and live the rest of their lives without them. It would be easier on all of the victims' loved ones if this could just be over. If they didn't have to go through the pain of a trial.

"Are you okay?" Ryzen asked as he quickly bent down in front of me.

"*Me*? You got hit by a truck. You should be in the hospital right now."

He looked amazing, but he also looked

like crap. He had cuts all along his face, there was bruising coming through, and I knew for a fact that his whole right side had to be killing him. On top of all of that, he still had the injuries from the bomb going off. He should be in the hospital and not here.

"I'll be fine," he ground out as he cut the ropes off of me.

"He actually isn't. He really needs to get looked at, but he's been refusing to this whole time," Roland said as he made his way into the basement.

"I'm fine," Ry insisted, and before I could even say anything to him, his hands were on the sides of my face and he pulled me in for a kiss.

I easily kissed him back, not caring that there were others in the room. The feel of his lips against mine instantly made my headache go away. Every ache in my body disappeared at the feel of his lips against my own.

"Is everyone in your agency gay?" I heard Detective West ask in a teasing tone.

"It's a hiring requirement," Roland quipped back as his voice started to drift away.

"You got an application?" Detective West said as their voices disappeared and I knew Ryzen and I were alone now. Well, aside from the dead body.

I lost myself in the feeling of his lips against mine. Nothing else in the world mattered at that very moment. We were both alive; we were okay, or going to be okay. We had the chance to explore more of the spark between us. For the first time in my life, I had the chance of having something more than just my job and dead end relationships. I had a chance at something real with Ryzen and I couldn't wait to get started.

CHAPTER TWENTY

Ryzen

IT HAD BEEN a couple of months since we had stopped Marcus Long.

For the past couple of months, I had been healing and spending time with Knox. I had a good number of broken ribs between the bombing and the truck slamming into me. For the past eight weeks, Knox and I had been working on getting to know each other better and not just each other's body. We had yet to have sex and I was good with that. I knew we both wanted to, but we also wanted to wait until we knew more about each other. Not to mention, I was still in pain from my ribs and when we did finally have sex, we both wanted to make sure I wasn't in pain during it.

Today, we had taken a trip to New Orleans where Knox had grown up. We had discovered that there might have been some truth to what Long had said. When Knox had informed the team of what Long had said about them being related, we had dug into it a bit. As it turned out, Knox's parents did give birth to another son three years before Knox was born. What happened to that son, we had no idea. There was no death on record. He simply just vanished. That child's name was Tristian Hunter. Knox had said to leave it alone, and we did.

However, now he needed to know what the true story was. He needed to know for his own closure if Marcus Long was actually Tristian Hunter. And I needed to know if I'd killed Knox's older brother.

"Are you ready?" I asked as we stood in front of his parents' front door.

"As I'll ever be for this conversation," he said, clearly slightly nervous.

I couldn't blame him for being nervous. He was about to ask his parents if they had been lying to him for practically his whole life.

He sucked in a deep breath before he used his key and unlocked the door before walking inside. I had to admit, it was a nice house and clearly his parents had put a lot of effort into keeping it well kept and to give Knox a good childhood. I followed Knox as he called out.

"Mom, Dad!"

He took us to the living room just as his mother called out.

"In the kitchen, Sweetie!"

I followed him into the kitchen, noticing the photos that were all over the walls. His parents had photos of him all over the wall from the age of infancy all the way up to his FBI academy graduation. They even had framed newspaper clippings of every arrest that Knox helped to make all over the country. These were very proud parents and it was clear they wanted everyone to know just how impressive their son was. It was very loving and I could tell that the love they had for Knox was sincere. They were good people that I suspected were dealt a hard hand thirty-five years ago.

"Hey, Sweetie, what a lovely surprise,"

his mom said as she wrapped her arms around Knox.

"Hey, Mom. Sorry for just popping by like this unexpectedly."

"Oh nonsense, this is your home," she said as she pulled back.

His father came over and gave him a quick hug next and it was all very strange to me. I didn't grow up with love and hugs. Parents showing affection to their children was still very odd to me.

"Mom, Dad, this is Ryzen. He's my, um..." He hesitated for a moment and I knew he wasn't sure what word to use for me. We hadn't talked about what we were going to call ourselves. I didn't care for labels, but I knew it was needed when making an introduction to people.

"His boyfriend. It's nice to meet you both," I finished for him.

"It's wonderful to meet you, Ryzen. I'm Moriah, and this is my husband, David," his mom said before she wrapped her arms around me.

I glanced over at Knox and could see him smirk at my obvious discomfort. I didn't even know where to put my hands. People don't hug me. I don't hug people. Outside of Knox, people generally don't touch me. They know better. Apparently, Moriah didn't know better.

"Okay, Mom, let's let Ry go. He was raised by wolves; he's not used to being touched by people," Knox said, taking pity upon me and guiding his mom away from me.

"Nice to meet you," his dad said as he held his hand out to me. I easily took it as I spoke.

"It's nice to meet you, too."

"Come, let's sit down and we can all talk," his mom prattled on about inconsequential things as she guided us all into the living room.

Ry and I sat down on one of the couches and his parents sat on the other couch across from us. I placed my arm around the back of the couch as Knox sat close to me. I knew he was going to need support to get through this conversation.

"Those are some thick sunglasses, Ryzen," his dad started.

"I have a strong sensitivity to light."

"Ry has grey eyes and that makes them vulnerable to light of any kind. He wears them everywhere that's not his home, or my home, now," Knox added.

"Oh, you live together?" his mom

asked, obviously surprised, but also sounding pleased.

"No, no, we don't live together, Mom. I changed my light bulbs to a lower wattage so he doesn't have to wear them at my place. We've only been dating a couple of months."

"And you thought now would be a good time to introduce him to your parents. It must be going well," his dad said, flashing us a smile.

"It is going well, but I actually didn't bring Ry here just to meet you. I have something I have to talk to you about," Knox started and I could tell he was very nervous already.

"Is everything okay? You're not sick are you?" his mom asked and I could hear the fear within her voice that something could seriously be wrong with Knox. Only further confirming that she loved him dearly.

"No, I'm not sick. Ry and I were working a case a couple months back. I was chasing a serial killer in Baton Rouge that was targeting young males between twelve and fourteen. He had been killing for three months and, by the time we stopped him, he'd killed fourteen boys."

"Yes, we heard about that on the news. We saw your press conference. It was terrible, absolutely terrible and it was a cop, no less," his Dad commented.

It wasn't surprising that they had heard about it down here. It was all across the country. It was major news. It was great for the Agency with being able to be connected to a high profile case. With each new case we took, the greater our reputation grew and that allowed us to take on bigger cases and help more children.

"His name was Marcus Long. His biological family had given him up when he was five after he killed a kitten. He then was dropped off at a church and eventually, was adopted by the Long family. They then handed him back over to the system when he was a very young teen. He was killing these children around the same age he was when his adoptive parents gave up on him. He stated that he was killing the kids to make their biological parents pay for giving them up."

"That's absolutely terrible," his mom said and I could tell she was disgusted by it all. I knew it was about to get worse, though.

"I had the chance to speak with Long before he was killed. He told me that he was my older brother. That when he was five, he killed my kitten that you had gotten me and you left him at a church. I didn't believe it. I figured he had gotten confused about his biological family. After all, there were no mentions by you or anyone in the family about another child. There were no photos of another child in our family. Only during and after an actual investigation, we discovered that you both did have another son. Tristian Hunter."

I could see the understanding in their eyes. They weren't shocked. In fact, they looked almost relieved. As if they had been waiting for this day to come and now they could finally get it off of their chests.

"We didn't know what happened to him. Though, I can't say I am surprised that he grew into being a serial killer. You have to understand, Sweetie, your father and I tried everything we could think of," his mom started.

"Thirty years ago there wasn't much help for kids who were showing violent tendencies, especially at the young age of three. Tristan started to become violent not long after you were born. At first, we thought maybe he was jealous of having a new baby around. There had been a moment when you were in a bassinet and he was sitting next to you. Your mother and I went into the kitchen to get dinner ready and we heard you scream. We ran out and saw that he had covered your face with the blanket and he had been pushing on your mouth."

"We thought maybe it was just a one-time thing. That he didn't know any better. We made sure you weren't alone with him again. As you started to get older, he started to show more disturbing signs. He would draw pictures of all of us dead. Of him with a knife standing over us. He had started a small fire in the basement that we caught early enough that there wasn't really any damage. When you were two, we wanted to get a pet for the house. We thought about a dog, but we figured we would start with a kitten. You loved the little guy; he slept with you all the time. One afternoon, we couldn't find the kitten. You were very upset. We looked for hours, only to eventually find it in the backyard with its belly sliced open. Tristan had said he wanted to see what was inside of it."

"We knew then that he was born broken. We took him to doctors, we tried different programs with him, but nothing worked. We were worried he would hurt you and we couldn't risk it. We didn't know what else to do. No one was taking us seriously. No one was willing to help us. We even asked our family doctor about putting him in a psychiatric facility, but he laughed it off. Said he was young and just being a curious boy. We had no choice but to leave him with the church. The Pastor said he would be able to get him the help that he needed. We trusted that he would."

I had a feeling they had given him up because he was a danger to Knox. It was the only reason a parent, a good and loving parent, would give up their child. They had to protect Knox and, unfortunately, the only way to do that was to have Long elsewhere. It was a horribly hard choice for any parent to make, but they made the right one. There was a good chance that Long would have killed Knox at the rate he was going.

I felt terrible for Knox, though. This was not how anyone wanted to discover they had an older brother. And now that brother was dead and there was nothing he could do to try and help him. It was going to take time for him to heal from the loss and from the shock that this whole situation had brought to him.

"No one said anything growing up," Knox said with a heavy voice.

"We had told the family that it would be better to keep it quiet. It wasn't that we didn't want you to know, it was that we were worried that you would try and find him. That you wouldn't understand at a young age. As you got older, it never felt like the right time to tell you about him. When you told us you wanted to become a Profiler, we suspected you might find him, eventually. And we were ready for when that day would come. I am terribly sorry, Sweetie. I never wanted you to find out the way you did. We loved him, we still do, even after all of these years, but we were just so terrified that he would hurt you," his mom said with a teary smile.

"I know. I wouldn't have been able to understand growing up, but I do now. And there wasn't anything you or anyone could have done to change him. There was no fixing him. Dad is right, he was born broken and, unfortunately, there isn't anything that can cure that. I'm sorry you had to go through that," Knox said.

The fact that he could understand and wasn't holding it against them only spoke volumes about how good of a man he was. I didn't know if I would have been able to handle it as well as he had been.

He climbed to his feet, then went over and pulled both his parents in for a hug. I knew that moment was when they were finally going to be able to start healing. His parents had been carrying that secret around for close to thirty-five years and I couldn't imagine the toll it had taken on them both. They were good people who didn't allow what happened to their oldest son to shadow how they raised and loved Knox. They'd raised an amazing man and they didn't deserve to blame themselves for how Long had turned out or the choices they'd been forced to make. Maybe they would have an even closer relationship with Knox and each other, now that this secret was finally out in the open.

EPILOGUE

Ryzen

IT WAS JUST after seven that night when we arrived at the hotel. His parents had tried to get us to stay at the house with them, but we both wanted to have our own space with each other.

The sexual tension between us had been growing over the past two months and it was all set to erupt. The second the door was closed, I couldn't hold out any longer. I pushed Knox up against the door and slanted my mouth over his, kissing him deeply, seeking entrance between his lips.

He instantly submitted to me and allowed my tongue into his mouth. Our tongues danced with each other as he trailed his warm hands down my back to my ass, pulling me to him and bringing our hips together. We both moaned as our hard dicks touched the other's body.

I grabbed a handful of his shirt and pulled him back as I walked us backward to the bed. The second the back of my knees hit the edge of the mattress, we ripped the others' clothing off as fast as we could. Fingers fumbled as buttons popped and zippers swished down.

I tossed my sunglasses down, the light in the room being kept dim for me. I wanted to be able to look him directly in the eyes, for him to see mine. With us both finally naked, Knox moved his hands to cup the bottom of my ass cheeks and easily picked me up. I wrapped my legs around his hips as he laid us on the bed, then he rolled so I was on top of him. He knew how much I liked being in control and I loved him for it.

"I have a surprise for you," I said as I guided his hand over to my hole.

He let out a whimper as his fingers ran over the end of the butt plug I had put in this morning.

"Have you had this in all day?" he asked, heat reflected in his eyes.

"Since I got up this morning. I figured today you were going to need a nice surprise."

I felt him slip the plug out of my ass, and then his fingers were inside me. I moaned at the feel of the new intrusion, the heat of his skin against mine as we pressed our bare dicks together, precum already leaking from us both.

I rocked my hips back and forth, trying to get his fingers in even deeper. We had done this before, but we had never gotten to the main event. Tonight, that was going to change.

"You're all stretched and slicked up for more. But is it my fingers that you are craving inside of you?" he asked, flashing me a playful, knowing smirk.

"No, I want your dick inside of me. And I want to feel you coming deep inside of me."

He removed his fingers from my hole and placed his hands on my hips as he spoke. "Take what you want. Use my body for your pleasure, Baby."

I moaned at his words. He had no

problem being a submissive top and I loved that he was completely open to it. It was freeing to be in charge in the bedroom and it meant a great deal to me that he was perfectly happy to allow me to be in charge.

I sat up straight and hovered over his hardness for a brief moment. Fitting his crown against my hole, I kept my eyes on him as I slowly pushed down onto his thickness. The second his tip breached my hole, we were both moaning and I didn't stop until I had taken him inside me all the way down to his base. He was so big, stretching me to my limit, but he felt perfect inside of me. We had been waiting for months to do this and it was definitely worth the wait.

I saw the pleasure flood across his face at the tightness and heat that my ass engulfed him with. This was only just the beginning, though, and I knew the first round was going to be fast. We had too much anticipation built up to last long now that we were finally together. But the rest of the rounds, they were going to be longer. I was going to draw out his pleasure until he was begging me to come many times tonight. I intended to drain him dry and leave him so sated he couldn't move.

I pulled myself up his shaft until his tip was barely left inside of me before I slammed myself down on top of him. I groaned and Knox whimpered as the pleasure within our bodies skyrocketed. I made sure to hit my sweet spot each time as I rocked my hips at a rapid pace on top of him. He kept his hands on my hips as I bounced on his dick, holding me tight in his grip as I took my pleasure. I could tell he wanted to match my movements, but he remained still and allowed me to bring us both the pleasure we sought.

"Fuck, you are so tight. So beautiful," he breathed out between pants, and I could feel his cock swell and harden even more inside of me. I could tell he was getting close to that edge.

When he moved his hand to grip me in his fist and started to jerk me off, I was in blissful heaven. I clamped my walls around him, gripping his dick inside my heat as I shunted my hips faster. It didn't take long before I was coming hard, my seed spouting out of my slit in long, thick ropes, heat and wetness trickling down my cock and all over his hand.

The tightening of my walls pushed him over the edge and we both let out a loud moan as he came. The feeling of his hot cum hitting my inner walls, searing my insides, was glorious and unlike anything I had ever felt before. I knew I was going to become addicted to this and I was never going to get enough of him.

I had thought sex was never something I would be overly interested in, never something that would possibly be able to bring me this much pleasure, but with Knox it was all I wanted to do. I had a gut feeling he felt the same and I couldn't wait to start our future together. Our bodies had woken each other up, ignited our desire for each other, and I had an inkling we weren't going to sleep again. At least, not any time soon.

"I love you," he said with complete love and devotion to his voice as he wrapped me in his arms.

"I love you, too."

I never expected to be in love in my life, but Knox was impossible not to love. He completed me and I knew he felt the same. I didn't believe in soulmates, but if they were real, Knox was mine and I was thrilled that we had been able to find each other. The future was ours to explore together and I knew it was going to be an exciting journey. Starting with a full night of sex, sex, and more sex.

Who would have thought that a serial killer case would bring me the love of my life?

I already couldn't wait to work our next case together. To be able to wake up next to him and show him off to the world as mine. Knox Hunter belonged to me and I belonged to him, and I wouldn't have it any other way.

Thank you for reading.

Turn the page for a preview of Cooper, book 4 in the Federal Protection Agency series.

PREVIEW

Jonah

MY WHOLE BODY was sore. It had been a long night at work. Hell, it had been a long week.

I hated doing shift work, it was always hard getting used to going from days to nights without much notice in between. That was the life of a detective, though. Everyone had to take turns working overnights so we could all get the chance to enjoy sleeping in our own bed at night and being outside during daylight hours. The trick was, though, when I caught a case, it wasn't like I could just go home when my shift was over.

I worked in the homicide division, so when a case came in, we only had forty-eight hours to try and solve it before our chances of finding the killer went down drastically. Which meant it was quite often a lot of long hours, working all day and night just to try to get justice for the victim. Today, I had been going for thirty-six hours straight and I was in desperate need of some sleep.

It was eight in the morning when I pulled into my driveway. It was Wednesday, though, so I couldn't just head up to bed. I had to get my twelve year old son ready for school.

Andrew, or Drew, as he preferred, was the reason I worked so hard. I wanted to make sure these streets were safer for him, because I knew all too soon he would be off on his own and carving out his own path in this world. I wanted to try and make it at least a little bit safer for him to be out on the streets at night. My greatest fear was getting a call to go out to a crime scene only to discover the victim was my son. It was something I knew I would have to face when his mother got pregnant. I wasn't really sure I was ready to be a father at that point in my life, but I knew I couldn't walk away from him.

My whole life, I had tried to fit within the right box. The box that society said I was supposed to fit into. I had always been athletic. I played on the football team, and I was on the basketball team, too. I loved playing sports, I still do. I was a guy's guy. However, I was a guy's guy who liked to look at other guys naked.

I knew I was gay from the age of twelve. I knew it wasn't normal to enjoy watching the other guys change in the locker rooms or see them showering. I was well aware that I enjoyed it too much. However, I was also well aware that the other guys would never be cool with being around a gay man. I couldn't be gay, not back then, so I did what every other guy was doing. I dated girls. I had sex with girls, even though it wasn't really who I wanted to be with, and I told myself that was going to have to be good enough. I suppressed my gay self in favor of fitting in where society expected me to.

I was eighteen when I joined the police

academy and once more, I was faced with an environment that wasn't open minded and welcoming of gay men. I continued to hide and I even got married to Melissa. When I was twenty-three, she gave birth to my son.

I was twenty-nine when I finally decided I couldn't do it anymore. I couldn't keep living the lie. I couldn't keep my desires at bay. I couldn't keep having sex with my wife and wishing it was a man underneath me. I just couldn't do it anymore.

So, one night when my son was six, I told Melissa that I was gay and wanted a divorce. She didn't handle it well. I knew she wouldn't. She tried telling me that I was just going through a phase. That I was confused. That I enjoyed having sex with her. After all, we had a son. She didn't appreciate it when I pointed out that I only got off on the friction of having sex with her and the vivid fantasies I would have while we had sex. Fantasies of a guy underneath me, whimpering and begging for more. She really didn't appreciate that part. Though, in her defense, I shouldn't have said it, but I was so sick of listening to her going on and on about how I was confused. I wasn't confused. I was just sick and tired of living in that small closet. After twenty-nine years, I had every right to live my life for myself. I wanted to explore my own sexuality, for the first time in my life.

I knew we would get divorced. It was going to be a very easy divorce, because there was no fixing us. I was into men and so was she. There was nothing either of us could do or say that would ever change that.

I had truly hoped that we would be able to co-parent and be friends. I knew it wouldn't be right away, but Melissa had always been open minded and okay with different sexual orientations. She had male and female friends who were gay. I figured once the dust settled and the hard feelings had passed, that she would be okay with me, too. I was very wrong. She was okay with other people. She was not okay with me. Not her husband. Nope. She had never been okay with me since the day I told her I was gay.

The divorce was simple. She signed it almost immediately and she wanted to avoid having to go to court. I thought it was great, that we were going to be able to get along and co-parent, that she had been taking this all so well. And then, it was time to work out the custody agreement and she ghosted us.

She had signed over full custody to me for Drew. According to the document she sent me along with the custody paperwork, she couldn't stand to look at either one of us. She felt that Drew would only remind her of the worst years of her life. Of the deception that I had put her through. She felt like I had somehow conned her into loving me and giving me a child. As if I was some sort of con man using her for her money and a kid. She wanted nothing to do with me and, even worse, she wanted nothing to do with Drew.

We hadn't seen or heard from her since that day. Six years, now. Not a single fucking word. Drew never received a phone call, no text message, no birthday card or Christmas card. Nothing. Having to explain to my son at the age of six where his mother was and why she wasn't coming back wasn't something I ever thought I would have to do.

At the age of six, he didn't understand why his own mother wasn't around. It wasn't like she hadn't been around for his whole life. When she was there, she had been a loving and doting mother. She was always helping with his playgroups and then with his school. She was on the PTA and spearheaded every fundraiser and bake sale. She was an active mom and I thought she loved being a mom.

I knew we were still young when we had him. She was twenty-two, but I figured we both had our jobs and we were responsible adults. I never missed going out to bars and clubs and partying all night. I didn't think she missed it, either. She never showed any signs of missing that life.

But at the first chance she had to leave and wipe the slate clean, she did.

For months afterward, Drew would sit in front of the windows in the living room, staring out at the driveway, waiting for her to come home. The first birthday and Christmas were hard. He was so confident that his mother would come by for them and when she didn't, there was no amount of comfort that I could give him that made him feel better.

That first Christmas was heartbreaking for me. He ran down the stairs Christmas morning and completely ignored the presents under the tree. He sat up on his knees on the couch and looked out the window and waited for Melissa to come over. When I tried to get him to open his presents from Santa, he refused and said he would do it when Mommy got there. All day, he sat there on his knees just watching the driveway, and every time a car drove by, he got his hopes up that it was Melissa. He went to bed that night crying his heart out and with not a single present opened.

I had to call my parents and they drove fourteen hours to come down to spend a few days with us. Only when his grandparents had arrived did he finally feel like opening presents.

My mom was amazing, because she had brought everything to cook for a full Christmas dinner. It had been a hard day, but we all got through it. Drew had gotten through it.

I had to hand it to my parents, they were older and they generally had traditional beliefs, but they supported me in being gay. It was a bit shaky at first, but when they discovered that Melissa had abandoned Drew, they were outraged.

My father called her a closed minded bitch for not being able to accept me as gay and raise our son together. They were old fashioned, but to them abandoning your child was a far worse crime then being gay and raising one.

We didn't talk about my sexual orientation and I hadn't really brought a guy over to their house. We kind of had a bit of a Don't Ask, Don't Tell rule, but that was okay with me. It wasn't like I wanted to talk to them about my boyfriends, anyway.

As I walked inside the house, I was fully prepared to see Drew running around and grabbing the last of his things. I didn't have a babysitter for him when I worked nights. He was twelve and I knew he was responsible enough to handle being on his own. It wasn't like I went into work at five or six o'clock at night. I went to work at ten and he was in bed for ten-thirty. When he was younger, I'd had a babysitter, but now we both felt he was old enough to sleep alone in the house with all of the windows and doors locked.

I also had a security system with an alarm on every door and window so he was perfectly safe once he was in the house. And he wasn't old enough to go sneaking out at night. That would be something I knew I was going to have to deal with when he was around sixteen. Thankfully, I had at least four years before that would happen.

Drew was also very mature and responsible for his age. I never had to worry about him doing something incredibly stupid. He made it easy to trust him alone.

What I didn't expect to see when I walked into my home was the obvious signs of a struggle. The house was a mess and the further I walked in, the more worried I became. There were lamps shattered on the floor, the coffee table was broken, furniture was turned over, the picture frames on the walls were crooked and some were on the floor, the glass broken. What had my heart stopping, though, was seeing the directional blood drops leading from the living room to the front door.

"Drew!" I screamed as I ran from room to room, trying to find my son.

The detective in me knew I was being an idiot. I was running around an obvious crime scene, potentially destroying evidence, but I had to find my son. He could be hurt somewhere in my own home and I was not about to leave him injured on his own while I waited for the crime scene techs to get there.

I searched every room in the whole house, but Drew wasn't there. My son wasn't there. I could feel panic starting to claw at my throat, but I fought through it. Me panicking was not going to find my son any faster.

I had to focus.

I had to work the scene and follow the steps.

I had to think.

I had to follow proper procedures.

I sucked in a deep breath and let it out slowly. With a shaky hand, I pulled out my cell phone and called the kidnapping in. The fact that I had to actually call my own son's kidnapping in tore at my heart.

With the crime reported, though, I then turned to calling every single one of my son's friends to see if they had heard from him since last night. I needed to know if he had been missing only an hour or two, or if he had been missing all night. Just like with murders, the first forty-eight hours in a kidnapping were the most crucial. If we didn't find him within forty-eight hours of the time of his disappearance, we might never find him. Or worse, I might find him dead.

I had to work this case, but I knew there was no way in hell my boss would let me. It was too personal. I was too close to it. I understood that, I did, but I was not going to sit on my ass and let this son of a bitch have my son.

No one knew these streets better than I did.

I had informants and contacts in the Southside. They wouldn't talk to any cop but me, and if they knew my own son was missing they would help me. But in order to get them to help, I would need access to this case so I could point them in the right direction. And the only way I was going to get access to this case was if I was working it.

The second the patrol cars pulled in, I gave them my statement before I got into my car and headed off for the one place that I knew could help.

The Federal Protection Agency.

I had helped them with one case two months ago and they all seemed like stand up guys. They were all capable of stopping a serial killer. I knew they were making a rather impressive name for themselves within their area of expertise. They focused on crimes against children and my son's case was exactly within the realm of their specialty. I needed their help and I knew I would have a better chance at convincing them to let me work the case with them then I did with my own boss.

I also knew they didn't have to follow the letter of the law. They had immunity; they could break the law and do whatever they had to do to get their cases closed. To save children. I needed that right now. I needed to know that someone would kick in the door to save my son even without a warrant. I needed to know that we wouldn't have to wait around for evidence or for a judge to issue a warrant if we didn't have anything solid.

The FPA working the case increased the odds of my son being found and that was all that mattered.

The second I pulled up to the building, I ran inside and up to their office floor. I strolled right into their conference room without stopping. I saw some new faces as I walked by, but I ignored them. I needed to speak with Mason. He was the only person who mattered right now. I knocked on his office door before I walked in without waiting to be granted entry.

Mason was in charge of the Agency and his K9 partner, Koda, was never far from his side. I didn't have the pleasure of working with him on the serial killer case. He had been in the hospital with his boyfriend, Jarod. Their serial killer, Marcus Long, who was also a detective at the time, had been killing young teenage boys and torturing them before leaving them in a dumpster.

The Agency had been brought in by a FBI Profiler, Knox Hunter, to help after he'd had nothing on the killer for three months. At the last crime scene, Long had planted a bomb designed to hurt Ryzen, a man who worked for the Agency and was ordered to protect Knox. In that blast, Ryzen had ended up with some bruised ribs, but Jarod had taken a large shard of metal to his stomach. He had to have part of his liver removed and had been placed on medical leave, followed by desk duty for three months.

"Detective West, what brings you by

unannounced?" Mason asked.

"My twelve year old son, Drew, has been kidnapped. I need your help."

I was hoping, I was praying, that he would say yes. That he would take this case over and then I could maybe take a breath, finally. I knew the guys in the Baton Rouge Kidnapping Division were good, don't get me wrong. The problem was, they had too many cases and not enough detectives. The Crime Lab was backed up, too, so any evidence that could help you find a missing child was delayed by weeks, sometimes months. They weren't fast at solving cases and that wasn't their fault, but I wasn't going to wait for months to find my son. I was going to find him before he was killed. There was simply no other option.

"Tell me everything," Mason said, and the tightness that had been wrapped around my throat started to loosen up, just a tiny bit.

Snag your copy of <u>Cooper</u> at your favorite online retailer!

OTHER BOOKS BY EVIE

Federal Protection Agency

Mason

Rafe

Ryzen

Cooper

Noah

Damien

Sebastian

Gabe

Logan

Ruthless Empire

Courting Danger

Chasing Danger

Kissing Danger

Smokejumpers

Hawke

Cyrus

Jase

Gage

Jackson

Xavier

Jasper Springs
Cade
Dawson
Drew
Grayson
Riley
Mitch

From The Edge
Shattered
Runaway
Jaded
Rescue
Hidden
Tormented

Gray Vale Pack
His Fated Mate
His Wounded Warrior
His Healing Heart

ABOUT THE AUTHOR

Evie Riley is a prolific, neurodivergent author known for her captivating MM romance novels. She has gained a significant following and topped the LGBT+ action and adventure bestseller charts with her series.

Evie's writing style often explores dark and gritty themes where her men must overcome difficult obstacles in their search for love, but she has also ventured into sweeter small-town romances, incorporating tropes like enemies-to-lovers, friends-to-lovers, age-gap, and forced proximity. She is known for crafting engaging romantic suspense novels and has a knack for creating interconnected series worlds that keep readers invested.

Interestingly, Ms. Riley has hinted at exploring new genres, such as Alien Omegaverse Romance, in the future.

Outside of writing, she enjoys spending time at the beach and has a quirky personality, described by her partner as ranging from cute to deadly, depending on her blood-chocolate levels.

Evie spends her nights writing bad boys in love, and her days wrangling the sweet boys she loves.